Alex Gray was born and educated in Glasgow and is the author of the bestselling William Lorimer series. After studying English and Philosophy at the University of Strathclyde, she worked as a visiting officer for the DHSS, a time she looks upon as postgraduate education since it proved a rich source of character studies. She then trained as a secondary school teacher of English. Alex began writing professionally in 1993 and had immediate success with short stories, articles and commissions for BBC radio programmes.

A regular on Scottish bestseller lists, she has been awarded the Scottish Association of Writers' Constable and Pitlochry trophies for her crime writing. She is also the co-founder of the international Scottish crime writing festival, Bloody Scotland, which had its inaugural year in 2012.

Alex Gray

BEFORE THE STORM

sphere

SPHERE

First published in Great Britain in 2021 by Sphere

1 3 5 7 9 10 8 6 4 2

Typeset in Caslon by M Rules
Printed and bound in Great Britain by Clays Ltd, Elcograf S.p.A.

Papers used by Sphere are from well-managed forests
and other responsible sources.

Sphere
An imprint of
Little, Brown Book Group
Carmelite House
50 Victoria Embankment
London EC4Y 0DZ

An Hachette UK Company
www.hachette.co.uk

www.littlebrown.co.uk

This book is dedicated to Donnie, with love.

With all its sham, drudgery and broken
dreams, it is still a beautiful world.

MAX EHRMANN

Out of the south comes the storm,
And out of the north the cold.

Job 37:9
New American Standard Bible

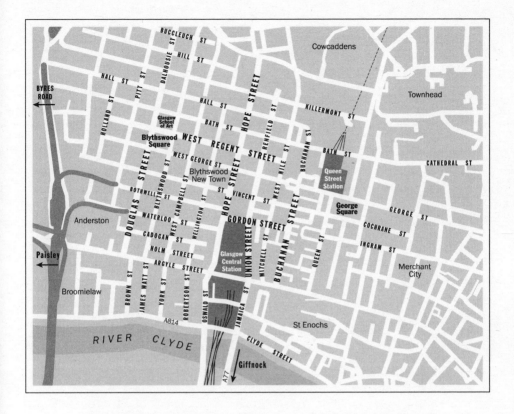

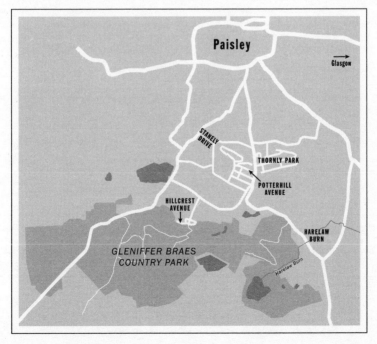

PROLOGUE

The skyline was seared with an orange glow against the inky darkness of night. That meant one thing and one thing only.

Fire.

Here in Zimbabwe the sun dropped like a stone each night, leaving no strange afterglow, and so, as he drove towards home, Daniel knew for certain what it was that he could see.

He pressed his foot to the pedal, eyes fixed on the dusty road ahead, a sudden prayer that it would not be his house lighting up the night sky.

Yet a sick feeling in his stomach told him that he had the worst to fear. After all, hadn't he been warned time and time again what would happen if he didn't do their bidding?

House after house passed him by, the suburban outskirts of Harare giving way to fewer dwellings, most of those now shuttered against the night. They'd chosen a plot close to the district of Marlborough after his last promotion, their house a loving statement of Daniel's need to provide for his little family.

Dear God, don't let it be ours, don't let it . . .

A cloud of pale smoke appeared as he rounded the final corner, blotting out his prayer.

Then he gazed into the inferno beyond.

Daniel pulled on the handbrake and leapt from the car.

'Chipo! Johannes!' he screamed, rushing up the narrow lane that separated the road from his home. The sound of the fire was like some fury from hell roaring curses, fingers of flame clawing towards the night sky.

Where were they? Not still inside . . . ?

He was vaguely aware of figures running towards him, dark shapes bent against the scorching heat, scarves across their faces.

'Chipo!' His voice faltered as he began to cough, smoke filling his nostrils, the intense heat driving him back a step, arm across his mouth, eyes blinded by flakes of ash.

Daniel stopped moving as a deep rumble roared within the heart of the fire, followed by a sudden booming noise. He watched in disbelief as the roof disappeared into the maw of this devouring beast.

Voices were shouting his name, then he felt arms pulling him back as the heat intensified, the crash of falling masonry drowning out their words.

Daniel struggled against the men holding him, sobbing. He wanted to run headlong towards the place where his front door had once stood, now a sheet of furious yellow flame barring his way.

'It's too late, Daniel,' he heard a voice say.

'No,' he cried, turning to see who had spoken and recognising for the first time Joseph, his friend and neighbour. The man's dark curls were thick with white ash, his eyes red-rimmed.

'We did everything . . . ' Joseph shook his head, the small gesture telling Daniel that the nightmare he had feared had come to pass. Then he put a protective arm around Daniel's shoulders, turning him away from the blaze and pulling him back down the lane.

'You must leave, before they come for you too,' Joseph said urgently.

'But—'

'The pastor is waiting,' Joseph told him. 'We knew this was coming, Daniel. We saw who it was that did this . . . ' The old man turned his grizzled head back towards the burning building. 'Need to get you away. Now.'

Then other hands were on his shoulders, pushing Daniel down the slope towards a jeep, its headlights facing the narrow dirt road. He was scarcely aware of the men who shoved him into the passenger seat or of the bag being pushed onto his lap.

Daniel wanted to cry out loud the questions pounding inside his head.

Why had his prayer not been answered?

Why were they gone?

And, how could he ever believe in a loving God after this night?

He twisted desperately in his seat only to see the flames reaching out, greedily licking the treetops next to his home before the jeep accelerated into the night.

It was an image that would haunt Daniel Kohi's dreams for a long time to come.

CHAPTER ONE

It was cold. The sort of cold that crept into his bones as if to remind him that this was an alien landscape more suited to the pale-faced people scurrying by. He stood for a few moments, suitcase on the shiny marble floor, blinking as if he had just awoken from a long sleep. Above him the glass roof, criss-crossed by metal beams, exposed the icy skies.

This was it, then. Glasgow. The city notorious for its knife crime in the past, but also boasting its other accolades: City of Culture, host of the Commonwealth Games and where Nelson Mandela Place nestled at its heart. Even these thoughts failed to warm him as he hesitated, looking around the station concourse. Daniel had already zipped up his fleece-lined jacket against the chill but nothing seemed to stop him shivering as he regarded the exit to a grey street with tall stone buildings. It was so different ... He bit his lip, trying to stop the perpetual thoughts of what he had left behind. Comparing the past with this present life was a useless exercise, doomed to pull him down once more into the black despair that had almost claimed him.

It will be a good place for you to settle, they'd told him, encouraging smiles meant to raise his spirits as he'd said his goodbyes at that other railway station. *Folk are known for being friendly*, one had added, and Daniel hoped that this was true. The journey itself had passed without incident, his fellow passengers all absorbed by whatever they were seeing on their phones or tablets, several of them listening to unheard melodies of their choice, none of them even giving Daniel a curious glance. Was that good? He'd thought so at the time, convincing himself that his appearance was nothing out of the ordinary. There was an Asian family along the corridor, the children noisy and clamouring for attention, parents and elderly family members indulging their every whim. Nobody stared at the solitary black man seated by the window, staring out at the landscape as the train sped north, taking him ever further from the place he had once called home.

He had gazed out of the window as the train slowed down, looking for clues that might inform him a little more about this city. At first it seemed the usual urban mish-mash of old and modern architecture, glass and steel structures jostling for space with towers and spires from the past. On the gable end of one building a giant pink poster proclaimed PEOPLE MAKE GLASGOW, a sign of pride in their city, perhaps, and something that made his lips curve into the ghost of a smile. Perhaps all he'd been told was true after all, he thought, sitting back as the carriage window was battered by a squally burst of hail.

*

The stream of passengers slowed to pass through the ticket barrier then fanned out. He saw a tall man with a shoulder bag stooping down to be met with hugs from family members, little children squealing with excitement to welcome Daddy home. Daniel swallowed down the rising pain and looked away. He stared instead at the shops curving around the station, their lights brightening the grey concourse and the ubiquitous Christmas tree, dressed exactly as the one in the station from which he had departed hours before, its conformity to a pattern of gold and silver baubles doing nothing to raise his flagging spirits.

Chilly air swept into the station as his feet took Daniel closer to the moment when he must step out at last into the city streets. For a moment he lingered, the warm familiar smell of coffee laced with the sweetness of vanilla wafting from a nearby café. But it looked too crowded and he had no wish to push and shove his way amongst strangers, burdened as he was with suitcase and rucksack, gifted by his church friends to hold the possessions he'd accepted from different charities.

Instead he took a deep breath and steeled himself to step out of the relative shelter of Glasgow Central Station into the open air.

The first thing he noticed as he emerged was a beggar sitting on the kerb, streams of people leaving or entering the concourse apparently oblivious to the man's presence. Poverty and despair existed everywhere, Daniel thought, gazing down at the bundle of rags huddled close to the station wall. Lank, greasy hair, face tilted upwards to catch the eye of anyone passing by who might fling a coin or two into the plastic cup clutched in a pair of bony hands, lips moving in a continuous mantra that always ended in *God bless, have a nice day*, words that had long since lost any meaning. What story was here? Was this a fellow sufferer escaping from his own past, reduced to becoming such a wretched specimen?

A sudden jolt from behind made Daniel start, fists clenched in automatic response.

'Awrightbigman?'

Daniel took a step back, feeling the stranger's grip on his arm. His first thought was for his wallet with all its precious papers tucked carefully inside his jacket, impossible for a random pickpocket to steal. But perhaps that hadn't stopped this person trying his luck on a traveller burdened with a suitcase and a heavy pack?

It was second nature to stare hard at the man, taking in every detail of his dishevelled appearance. He'd seen that same glazed expression and doped-up smile a thousand times in different streets, different cities. But when this guy held up his hands in a gesture of surrender, his gap-toothed grin almost comical, it was as if he could sense Daniel's latent authority.

'Naebotherson,' the junkie said, shaking his head as Daniel made to pass him by.

The body language told him more than the strange words; there was a sort of obsequious cringing as though this man expected a blow, was used to them, perhaps. But there was also an eagerness to befriend the stranger he'd bumped into by accident. He seemed harmless but whatever he'd uttered was a mystery to the man who had stepped off the train and entered a new country.

Daniel gave him a brief nod and strode out into the street, wind blowing icy arrows onto his skin, turning umbrellas inside out as pedestrians struggled against the slanting rain, scraps of litter playing chase along the gutters.

Hitching his backpack securely, he looked left and right, remembering the directions he'd read and reread. Hope Street, that was the one he must cross then follow, an irony not lost on Daniel whose own hopes had died all those long months ago.

But he would not think about that. Not now. Not when he had a difficult meeting ahead of him. The sigh that escaped him was for the weariness of it all, the perpetual journeys from one place to the next, repeating his tale to some official whose only aim seemed to be to fill in yet more forms and pass him on to another. Once upon a time Daniel had found the choices given by an automated voice so irksome whenever he tried to call someone by telephone. Now he would have gladly spent an hour pressing buttons instead of being sent day after day, week after week to different authorities that might or might not make some decision about his future.

A police car sat on the kerb, yellow, blue and white, bright colours chosen for their visual impact. He looked at the two officers in the front seats then moved on. There was no need to consult the paper he'd been given with its hand-drawn map; he could visualise it in his mind's eye right now. Out of the station, turn left then cross the road and head uphill.

A black figure loomed out of the gloom, making Daniel stop and stare. The breathing apparatus on its face reminded him of pictures from the history books, gas masks protecting humans from those poisonous onslaughts. Someone else's war, he reminded himself. Someone else's suffering. However, this was no old soldier, but the representation of a fire fighter, the statue rather squat as though the sculptor had imagined the inhabitants of this city as small men. He shuddered, pushing down the memory of fire. What this strange black memorial was doing there was one of the mysteries that Daniel might solve in the coming weeks, but for now the traffic lights had changed to green and he crossed, dodging the stream of fast-flowing water sluicing the roads.

As Daniel climbed the sloping street he remembered someone telling him that Glasgow was built on several hills and in his mind he had created a vision of tawny slopes rising above a scattering of houses. Looking ahead, all he could see was a patch of bruised sky obliterated on each side by tall office buildings, no curve of green in sight. Beneath his feet some of the paving stones were crumbling and broken, the persistent rain no doubt a contributing factor. Under the swirling streams he noticed spots of white, discarded gum that had speckled the pavement. Fluorescent orange and yellow graffiti streaked metal bins next to the stone walls of buildings he passed by, words or parts of words that made no sense to Daniel.

A brightly lit window caught his eye with a word that was only too familiar, and Daniel backtracked, staring at the line of travel brochures displayed: AFRICA. He breathed in sharply. There it was, the dusty background in shades of ochre, a leopard superimposed by some graphic artist. He'd never seen a leopard in the bush, though once he had heard a clawing noise from a compound out in Hwange and the ranger had confirmed that yes, a leopard had visited during the night. No wildlife in this city, at least none that crept on large, silent paws.

Between the buildings ran narrow cobbled lanes, mossy green in the shadows where sunlight could never penetrate, man-made yellow lines flowing from one end to the other. These lanes dissected the main streets and he caught glimpses of slow-moving traffic running downhill to his right. It was a grid system, he knew, and now he had an inkling of how this city centre might operate. In his past life Daniel had learned all about streets and alleyways, how to navigate them by car or on foot, and he was confident that it would not take long to learn the geography of this place.

It was as he paused to shift the weight of his suitcase from one hand to the other that he saw it.

There was no sound, just a movement caught in his peripheral vision, one man stepping out from behind an open door. Nothing unusual about that, except for the large knife clutched in his right fist, a wet stain at its tip that was almost certainly blood.

For a moment Daniel froze, every instinct urging him to drop his bags and rush along the lane. In another place, another time, he would never have hesitated.

Then the door swung shut with an audible clang, leaving him to stare at the empty lane, trying to make some sort of sense of what he had just seen. And, because such matters had concerned him in his past life, Daniel Kohi found him-self asking the question of what to do about it.

CHAPTER TWO

Detective Superintendent William Lorimer smiled to himself as he regarded the calendar fixed to his office wall. Not a single date was circled in red, a satisfying thing to note as it meant a month without a homicide in the whole of Scotland. Deaths had occurred, to be sure, accidents on the roads and in the mountains where there would be that extra frisson of danger for climbers now that the first snows had fallen. However, the statistics were on the side of law and order, it seemed, Police Scotland managing to shut down several organised criminal enterprises, preventing any outbreak of violence. Perhaps the bad old days were almost over at last, he pondered. The times of gang warfare suppressed by the ever-growing sophistication of technology that aided officers around the country.

He had seen so many changes in his career and, with only one more year until his thirty years' service, it was not surprising that Lorimer was feeling a tad nostalgic. The biggest change, of course, was in the creation of Police

Scotland after decades of separate constabularies throughout the country. That had been to his advantage as the head of the Major Incident Team here in Govan, free to investigate serious crimes anywhere without the worry of upsetting the local cops. Nowadays some of them were only too delighted to have the team on their patch taking over some higher profile cases. Yet there were other changes, too. Gartcosh, the Scottish Crime Campus, had been of enormous benefit with its various departments including the very best in forensics. He recalled one member of the public telling him in awestruck tones how much safer she had felt after being escorted around the Counter Terrorism unit. So many men and women worked hard to ensure the peace and stability of the populace, most of whom were blissfully unaware of those guarding them against some very real dangers. Hopefully he would be of help to prevent yet another such coming into his city, he thought, with a quiet sigh.

He swung the chair slightly to one side and gazed out of the window where the dark streets were slick with rain on this late November afternoon, traffic slowly making its way towards the M8. His vision shifted a little to see his own reflection in the glass. He blinked as if surprised to see the man staring back at him. One hand swept over his head. There was no sign of losing his hair yet, unlike several of his colleagues, not even a receding hairline, though touches of grey were frosting the dark brown hair beside his ears. If he were to compare the photograph of his twenty-year-old self in uniform with what he could see now then, yes, the years had taken their toll. Deeper lines were etched between his eyes and around his mouth, testament to the dreadful sights that he had seen, things that no single person could have endured but for the strength of will to do his duty and see justice carried out.

What would he do next? There was no need to retire if he felt capable of carrying on, although so many fellow officers quit the force, as if afraid that the extra years of service might take their toll. And yet he'd seen a few men retire only to drop dead of heart failure a couple of years later, and others take on less onerous work simply to fill their days. What did he want to do? Carry on with this job or look further afield for a new adventure? His reflection smiled back at him, shaking its head as if to mock the very idea of putting his energies into anything else as demanding as the job he had carried out for nearly three decades.

A knock at his door broke the reverie and Lorimer swung back to face the person entering his office.

One look at DCI Niall Cameron's face told him all that he needed to know.

'Body found, boss. Looks like a nasty one,' Cameron told him.

Lorimer's eyes flicked towards the wall calendar. One of these numbers would be ringed in red before the week was out, he thought, giving a sigh of regret.

CHAPTER THREE

The man was lying on his back, head to one side, arms raised in a pugilistic stance as though he had tried to fight off the encroaching flames. Any clothing had been burned away, his leather shoes practically welded to the blackened flesh.

'Going to be a difficult one,' DS Judith Morris, the crime scene manager, said, turning to the tall detective. 'Hard to identify him after what's been done.'

'Multiple stab wounds?'

'Yes, we can see that at least,' Morris confirmed, hunkering down beside Lorimer and pointing at several gashes on the burned corpse with her gloved hand. 'Someone's been busy trying to destroy their handiwork.'

'We should get something from the tissues, though. DNA to compare with our databases.'

'If he's on any of them,' Morris grumbled. 'Whoever did away with him made a right job of it.'

The scene of crime manager had opened her mouth on seeing Lorimer as if to ask what on earth the head of the

MIT was doing there but had evidently thought better of it and closed it again in a firm, if discontented, line.

Lorimer looked down at the charred and blackened remains of what had once been a living, breathing human. Someone with hopes and dreams of his own, expectations that had not included a grisly end like this. He had seen dead bodies before where the corpse had been burned and he imagined the horror of being trapped behind a sheet of flame, knowing there was no escape. It would take a post-mortem examination to determine whether the fellow had died before the fire had consumed his flesh but looking at the lacerations across his chest and neck, Lorimer hoped that, despite the raised arms, it was a dead man that had been set on fire. The alternative was too horrible to contemplate.

'Who found him?'

'Wee boys bunking off school. It might be St Andrew's Day, but that's not a school holiday locally. They're with the family liaison officer right now back at the station.' Morris pointed across the field. 'One of them was sick over there.' She shook her head. 'God knows how long this poor soul's been lying here. But the smell's pretty bad, eh?'

The woman risked a smile in Lorimer's direction but the detective superintendent merely nodded his agreement.

'At least they had the sense to dial 999,' Morris admitted. 'And they swear blind that none of them touched the body.'

'Hmm. We need to take their prints just to be on the safe side,' Lorimer said. He could imagine the lads daring each other to reach out and feel the stinking corpse. Something to boast about later to their pals.

'Scene of crime officers need to do their stuff before we

can move him,' Morris said. 'Ah, here's what I've been waiting for.' She nodded, standing up and turning as two officers arrived carrying the tent between them. Soon they had it erected over the body, protecting it from the elements as much as from further prying eyes. Though who, thought Lorimer, would be out in this lonesome part of the country apart from lads skiving off school?

There was a road about a hundred yards away where a line of official vehicles now stood, but this edge of the field was hidden from view. Anyone approaching had to climb the hilly slope then descend once more towards the line of bushes, the dried-out gully making it a perfect hiding place. Someone knew this area, Lorimer thought, someone who was familiar with the terrain in this part of the world. And that, he decided, was going to be one of the starting points of this new investigation. All sorts of actions would need to begin, his officers busy tracking down the identity of this man. Missing persons, house-to-house enquiries, sourcing whatever accelerant had been used to destroy the remains . . . The minutiae of a serious criminal investigation mattered so much, especially at the start, every tiny piece of evidence gathered with the greatest care in the search for whoever had carried out this hideous crime.

He looked up towards the grassy slope. It would have taken more than one man to carry a corpse that far, he decided. Yet there had been no attempt to bury him. And he wondered why.

DS Mairi Falconer stood up as the man opened the door. In all her years as a family liaison officer the woman had never personally encountered the tall detective who was head of the Major Investigation Team in Glasgow, though she had heard plenty of stories about him. It was said that he had an uncanny gift for making people open up to him and Mairi guessed that was the reason why he was here right now. DI Brownlee was senior investigating officer in this case and the FLO was curious to know what her boss made of this detective superintendent. Word had it that Lorimer was turning up uninvited to different crime scenes across the region but exactly why was not yet known. Was he trying to recruit new personnel to the MIT? That was one theory, certainly. Perhaps he was just pining for his former days as a DCI when he'd headed up different investigations, not just ones that were categorised as class As? He'd put a few DIs' noses out of joint last summer, taking an undue interest in different cases of homicide, though in the end he seemed to have made more friends than foes amongst his more junior officers. Whatever the reason, Mairi found that she was intrigued to meet the legend that was William Lorimer to see if the man measured up to his reputation.

'Boys, this is Detective Superintendent Lorimer,' she said, smiling at the three young lads who were sitting in the family liaison officer's room. 'He'll want to ask you lots of questions so mind what I told you, eh?'

There were glances between the boys and the FLO and a few nervous looks at the man who stood towering over them all. Lorimer was sure that Falconer was more than capable of handling the lads but sometimes it paid dividends to attend an interview like this. And it would not be the first time that he had pulled rank and sat across a table in an interview room, his years of experience and particular manner giving him an edge over many of his colleagues.

Lorimer gave the DS a smile and sat down next to the boys.

'Right, who do we have here?' he asked in a cheerful tone intended to put the youngsters at their ease.

Again, all three pairs of eyes turned expectantly to DS Falconer but she shook her head and grinned at them in mock despair. 'Go on, introduce yourselves.'

Lorimer waited patiently, knowing that this was all part of the adventure for these lads, something else to tell their friends at a later date.

'Jayce Barnes,' one boy said, holding the detective's gaze for a fearless moment.

'Jason?'

'Naw, Jayce. Spelled J.A.Y.C.E,' he replied, a tinge of pride in his voice as though he'd put one over already on this big guy. Then he shrugged as if he was trying to appear nonchalant, though his rapidly tapping foot gave away his inner excitement.

'Okay.' Lorimer's eyes flicked to the boy sitting next to Jayce, a thin wee lad with scuffed trainers and holes in his jeans that were not a designer statement but more likely the result of wear and tear. Seeing the detective's glance shift, Jayce elbowed the boy in his side.

'Gary Kane,' he mumbled, ducking his head and squirming awkwardly in his seat. The lad was pale, Lorimer noticed, and wondered if this was the one that had been sick.

'You all right, son?' he asked kindly.

Gary nodded, one swift glance towards the detective then back at his feet.

'Spewed his load when we found it,' Jayce commented, 'didn't you, Gary?'

Again, just a nod, but there was a flush to his cheeks now that spoke of sheer embarrassment. Or perhaps anger at the other boy's words. Would there be a stramash after this was all over? Lorimer wondered. Gary lashing out at his pal for being put down like this. Or was Jayce Barnes the leader of these lads and keeping them in some sort of check?

'And who are you, young man?' Lorimer asked, deflecting attention from Gary and turning to the third boy who was seated on the other side of DS Falconer.

'That's Ryan the bairn,' Jayce blurted out with a mocking laugh.

'Jayce, Ryan can introduce himself,' Mairi told him, her warning tone making Lorimer realise that the FLO had had her work cut out already with this trio.

'I'm Ryan Hastie,' the wee lad said, his piping tone giving credence to Jayce's sarcasm.

'How old are you, Ryan?' Lorimer looked at the boy, wondering why on earth he was part of this group of school dodgers. His white shirt was reasonably clean and the red jersey had the school crest emblazoned on it. Unlike the other boys clad in jeans, Ryan wore a pair of grey trousers, admittedly muddied at the knees, and a pair of black leather shoes with Velcro straps.

'Eight,' the small voice replied and Lorimer saw a wobbling lip as the boy looked up at him.

'Your mum's on her way, Ryan. Detective Superintendent Lorimer can't ask you any questions till she gets here. He's just getting to know you, that's all,' Mairi Falconer soothed.

It was clear to Lorimer that the FLO had placed this youngster apart from the others, not just for his own protection but also to offer her support as a kindly adult. He was certain the moment that Ryan's mother walked through the door there would be a flood of tears.

'I've got their names and addresses here,' Mairi whispered, handing Lorimer a sheet of paper.

The boys all lived within a few streets of one another in Ferguslie Park, an area of Paisley that Lorimer visited occasionally when his favourite team was playing away to St Mirren FC. The reputation of Feegie Park, as locals termed it, was one of long-term deprivation though there had been stalwart efforts in recent years to put some heart back into the community along with a programme of refurbishing the houses. It was a long walk for the boys to have sauntered through the town and up the Braes where they had found the burned corpse but, looking at Jayce, with his defiant chin in the air, Lorimer doubted whether the boys worried much about that. He could imagine the thrill they'd enjoyed under Jayce's leadership: skipping school, walking past shops and giggling at their own bravado before setting out to climb the hills on the outskirts of Paisley.

'Ma'am, this is Ms Barnes . . . ' A young uniformed constable had the door open but was swept aside as a large blowsy woman wearing a too-tight red dress and black leather jacket barged past him straight up to her son.

'Right, youse!' she declared, ignoring the two detectives. 'Whit've ye bad wee toerags bin up tae noo? Jist you wait till we're home, boy!' she added, glaring at Jayce whose grin simply widened, apparently impassive to her tirade.

Lorimer stood up and took a step forward, extending his hand courteously.

'Detective Superintendent Lorimer. And this is my colleague, Detective Sergeant Falconer. Do take a seat,' he said pleasantly, waving a hand towards one of the spare chairs beside Ryan Hastie.

'Ah . . . ' The woman's mouth fell open as she looked up at the tall detective and his smiling companion.

'The boys have been very helpful and we are grateful you have spared the time to come in and be here so we can ask them some questions.'

'Well . . . ' She shook her head slightly as if unsure what to say then meekly walked to the chair along by Ryan, giving the wee boy a beaming grin.

'Ye awright, wee man?' she asked, nudging the youngster. Ryan merely nodded, a quick glance towards Jayce as if to see the other boy's reaction. It was clear that Jayce's mother was familiar with his pals and that Ryan was a favourite, despite her outburst. Lorimer suspected that she had her hands full with her own boy and wondered now if this was not the first time Jayce had seen the inside of a police station.

'We're just waiting for Mrs Hastie and Gary's gran to arrive,' DS Falconer explained, glancing towards the constable who still stood hovering at the doorway then back at Jayce's mum. 'Would you like a cup of tea? The boys have had drinks of water.'

'Aye, okay,' Ms Barnes agreed.

The constable gave a nod and disappeared, closing the door behind him.

'Well, this is a right turn-up. Being called frae ma work jist like that,' Ms Barnes grumbled.

'It is necessary to have you here before we can question your son,' the FLO explained. 'If they are under age, we are not permitted by law to do more than ask their names, addresses and suchlike.'

'Aye.' The woman gave a sigh and sank back in the moulded plastic chair with the dubious grace of a deflating balloon.

Once more the door opened, admitting an anxious-looking woman who made straight for Ryan, followed by a middle-aged woman in a beige padded jacket not much older than Jayce's own mother. As he'd anticipated, Ryan broke down as soon as his mum's arms had enfolded him, gulps and wails filling the room.

'I'm Nancy McLelland, Gary's gran,' the older woman said, heading towards Lorimer as he rose to greet the women.

Lorimer made the introductions once more and soon they were all seated in a semicircle with Ryan snuggled onto his mum's lap.

'Thank you all for being here,' he began. 'It was a big thing that the boys did, calling the police as soon as they could.' He glanced approvingly at the three lads in turn. 'Good work, boys. Even though you should have been in school, we are glad that you did the right thing. Always remember that. The police are here to help you, no matter how hard it might be to talk to us, okay?' He smiled encouragingly.

'Whit's goin' on, onywey?' Ms Barnes growled in a gravelly voice that sounded as if she was a fifty-a-day smoker.

DS Falconer took the initiative to explain. 'The boys

dialled 999 when they came across a dead body up in the Braes. We need to ask them some questions about that,' she said firmly.

Jayce's mum remained silent but her open mouth made an O of astonishment.

'Oh, you poor wee soul.' Mrs Hastie held Ryan more tightly than ever as if hearing these words was somehow more awful than the experience her son had already undergone.

'Best get on with it, hen,' Nancy McLelland sighed, raising her eyebrows in disapproval at the young woman rocking her son back and forwards like a baby.

'Jayce, you first,' Mairi Falconer said, taking the grandmother's hint. 'Tell us in your own words what you did today.'

The boys then took it in turn to describe their walk through Paisley and up the Braes, Jayce's eyes shining when he described the moment they had stumbled on the body. 'Ah seen it first!' he declared proudly then turned to Gary as he took over the tale.

Gradually they pieced together the adventure, not forgetting Gary being thoroughly sick (no murmurs of sympathy from the scowling grandmother), and, by the time they had finished asking questions, Lorimer was certain that the taped interview would hold a reasonable amount of information for DI Brownlee and his team to work with.

'If you touched the body, we need to take your fingerprints,' Lorimer advised them.

'Dis that pit them oan wan o' they databases? Like a permanent record?' Ms Barnes blurted out.

Lorimer shook his head. 'The boys have done nothing criminal,' he assured her. 'On the contrary, they have been good witnesses and their answers will be very useful in our subsequent enquiries.' Too much *CSI* on the TV, he thought. That was where most of the public seemed to get their impression of police work nowadays.

Once the boys had trooped out with their mums and gran, Lorimer sat back and shook his head. 'Amazing how little we really know about what they did,' he said, turning to DS Falconer. 'Wouldn't put it past Jayce or Gary to have done a wee bit of a recce of the shops, lifting a sweetie or two. And, as for hauling Ryan along, what was all that about?'

'Happens all the time,' the FLO told him. 'A wee impressionable kid from a decent family makes the rest of a group look good if they ever have to explain themselves. "Oh, we were with Ryan." See? That suddenly shows the others in a better light.'

'He's not even in their class at school, though, is he? How did he come to tag along with characters like Jayce and Gary?'

'Hero worship? Tired of being mollycoddled by his mum, perhaps?' Falconer shrugged as they both rose from their chairs.

'Maybe this will be a lesson to him, then, not to keep company with that pair.'

'Hmm,' was all the reply he received from the family liaison officer who had clearly seen much more of underage kids and their development than the head of the MIT.

CHAPTER FOUR

'Yorrite, son?'

Daniel turned around, key in hand, to see a short plump woman standing, arms folded across her ample chest. Despite the cold she was dressed in a knee-length black skirt and garish red jumper with diamanté sparkles, her bare feet pushed into a pair of fake sheepskin slippers.

'Hello?' He took a step back as she approached, unsure whether this was friend or foe. She was a granny, was his first thought as he stood looking at her. Not like the grannies he knew, faces split in grins that showed their white teeth, bright cotton shawls wrapped around to hoist up the latest small member of their family. But, still. Daniel could see something of them in this female, her white curls blowing in the breeze eleven floors up in this multi-storey block.

'See me, son,' she said. 'Ah'm no wan o' they racist types, know whit ah mean?' She unfolded her arms and stuck out a hand. 'Netta. Next door but wan,' she added, tilting her head towards a red-painted door two along from the flat that Daniel had been allocated.

'Nice to meet you,' Daniel replied politely. He turned towards the scuffed wooden door and stifled a sigh. The number 8 of flat 118 was hanging by a single nail, making him wonder how long it had been since the previous resident had vacated the place.

'Jist movin' in, then?' the woman asked, pointing at his case and backpack then shuffling a little closer.

It was obvious that he was so he nodded and stood for a moment, wanting her to go away so he could see the place for himself yet intrigued by her thick Glasgow accent and the way she was looking at him with such frank appraisal.

'Course you are, son. Don't let me keep ye back. But come on through for a wee cuppa when ye've got yersel sorted. Okay?'

Daniel nodded, somewhat mystified by the torrent of words, catching just a few. 'Wee cuppa' must mean tea or coffee, yes? But did she mean today or at another time more mutually convenient?

'Where is it yer from?' she asked suddenly. 'Ye dinna look like wan o' thae Syrian refugees we had last year. Africa, ah'm guessin'. Right?'

'Yes,' he replied. 'Zimbabwe.'

'Oh, ah ken a' aboot thon place,' Netta told him, wagging her head in a manner that reminded Daniel more and more of the elderly grannies from his village. 'Whaur thon bad Mugabe wis, aye?'

Daniel nodded again then looked meaningfully at the door key clutched in his hand.

'Ye goat a name, son?'

'Pardon?' Daniel frowned. Goats? What did goats have to do with anything?

'Goat a name?' Netta repeated, poking his arm. 'Ah cannae jist ca' ye Mr Zimbabwe, can ah, noo?'

A smile spread across his face as the words began to make a sort of sense.

'Daniel,' he said, swapping the key into his left hand and holding out his other hand. 'Daniel Kohi.'

Netta shook his hand up and down, nodding a little as though she was finally satisfied.

'Awright, Daniel son. Come away ben the hoose wance yer ready. Kettle's on.' Then, with a wave of her hand the woman turned and headed back through the red door, adding, 'See ye in a wee while.'

Daniel blinked as she disappeared, leaving the corridor suddenly empty, the silence only filled with the sound of his sigh as he turned once more towards the flat. So, he thought, fitting the key into the lock, this was a regular safe place for refugees, was it? Syrians the previous year, the woman, Netta, had said. And, as the door swung open revealing a darkened hallway, he wondered how many lost souls had found it a place to hide from whatever demons had chased them across the world.

It smelled stale when he closed the door behind him, as if the air inside had been trapped for a long time and was too weary to make an attempt at freedom. Daniel wrinkled his nose but there was nothing offensive, no stink of rubbish or even cleaning fluids, merely the suggestion of layer upon layer of dust. Straight ahead was another door and he pushed it open to find himself in a rectangular room with a large window opposite. A sagging settee had been pushed against one wall, a single armchair and small wooden table with two mismatched chairs against the other, a dog-eared calendar pinned onto a wooden background. There was an ancient carpet on the floor, cigarette burns and marks where things had been spilled, patches worn and scuffed.

He'd been told that there would be basic accommodation. A furnished flat. But despite all the places he'd already been in, Daniel's expectations had been a little higher than this. He'd return to gaze out of that window later, but first he needed to see where he would sleep and what the other facilities were like.

Back in the corridor he saw two further closed doors, one on each side. A quick glance as he pushed open a white-painted door let him see a small bathroom, its toilet and washbasin side by side. He pulled on a light cord by the door and immediately a whirring sound made him look up to see an extractor fan set into the ceiling. Well, something was in working order, he told himself, trying to summon up a vestige of enthusiasm. The bare light bulb swung a little as though he had brought in a draught of air.

Leaving the light on, Daniel took a couple of steps back across the corridor and into the adjoining room where a single bed sat in the middle of the room, a pile of neatly folded sheets and towels beside a lumpy grey pillow. Someone had prepared that, at least, he thought. The only light was from a glazed window that looked out onto the landing, a dingy net curtain that had been white at some stage in its existence hanging from a thin metal rod. There

29

was a mirrored wardrobe, its glass foxed around the edges. It creaked, protesting, as he slid it half open, a jangle of metal hangers suspended from the faded brass rail.

It would do for now, Daniel told himself, a weariness descending on him that had nothing to do with his journey to this northern city, or the hard seat he had been forced to occupy as the harried-looking woman in the office had asked him question after question. She had demanded to see his papers as though Daniel was keeping her back from something else despite the fact he had arrived there exactly on time, her sighs and shaking of her head making Daniel feel as though he should feel guilty for disturbing her at all. She had thrust the envelope at him, the key inside it, told him to call if there was a problem then glared at him as if that was the last thing she wanted him to do.

He had been offered nothing there, not even a glass of water, and now he realised how thirsty he was. Coffee. A large cup, he thought, imagining himself back in the church hall with his British friends. A puzzled frown crossed his brow. Where was the kitchen? Looking around, he saw no other door so, retracing his steps, Daniel found himself back in the big room with the window.

He had missed it first time around, a partition door on hinges, between the table and armchair, that he had mistaken for part of the shabby décor.

Pushing it gently along aged runners revealed a square kitchen with pale grey units, a washing machine backing on to the wall that separated this from the bathroom, and an empty refrigerator whose door was kept open with a brick laid on the floor. There was a square window that looked out onto the outside corridor but there was nothing to see, only darkness.

Daniel moved back through the lounge and walked towards the window, laying his hands on the cold sill. He looked out over the city, imagining he could see a view of distant hills beneath the darkening clouds. A sudden shaft of light pierced the gloom, a ray escaping from a hidden sun, then it was gone, the violet-coloured mass moving swiftly across the horizon. Below he could see a myriad of lights twinkling either side of a highway where cars snaked along, their red tail-lights hesitating now and then as the rush hour traffic slowed everything down.

Red. That was the colour he had seen back in that narrow alleyway. A fleeting glimpse on a blade. A man pushing past that door then retreating once more.

Daniel Kohi felt a shudder down his back as he closed his eyes and recalled the moment over again.

Would he return there? Try to make sense of what he had seen? He'd been warned repeatedly to be careful, to stay out of trouble. But, as he'd known for a long time, it was trouble that had a way of finding Daniel Kohi.

CHAPTER FIVE

W eeping achieved nothing.

She had found that out very quickly, the searing pain in her chest changing to a rage that fuelled Shararah's every waking thought. The image of her beloved Kalil swaying from that noose was one that refused to leave her mind, though in truth she had not been there to see his body, then or afterwards. Rising from her prayer mat, she resolved to maintain both her strength of spirit and the calm demeanour that concealed her inward hatred.

For months she had been setting up the necessary steps to complete their plans, her unique position affording them access to so many secrets. That, combined with a powerful command over others in their cell, gave the woman some consolation in her grief. The money was in place, the equipment ready, and now all that remained was to prepare for the day itself.

They might need some new recruits, however. Not every one of her men was so steadfast in their aims as she had wished. The lure of Western ways corrupted some, money and the stuff it could buy being of greater importance than the cause. She had been trying to find replacements but that was proving very difficult and they might need to be less selective now when bringing in some muscle.

The woman stood at the washbasin gazing at her reflection through narrowed eyes then, looking down, she saw that she was rubbing her hands together, an unconscious gesture as if to remind herself of the time spent washing off that blood. She drew back with a shudder. Hadn't Lady Macbeth been haunted by the deed she had committed, urging her husband on to murder? She shook her head defiantly. Nothing was going to intrude on her plans, and she was made of sterner stuff than the Shakespearean character who'd descended into madness. Yet, like that same woman, hadn't she drawn back from taking that knife into her own hands, using her feminine wiles to ensure that another person committed the act instead?

There was no question but that the man had to die. He had learned too much and had been on the point of shattering all her plans. And they would go ahead now, thanks to her determination.

The woman heaved a sigh. When the boy detonated the device, he would send his soul to paradise, destroying hundreds of these Christian infidels on the eve of their festival.

Shararah's brow furrowed for a moment as she remembered what Christmas had been like in her childhood: presents piled beneath the tree, uttering squeals of delight as she unwrapped the gifts her adoptive parents had left for her. They had been well-meaning people, she conceded, but her heart was hardened against all that now, the zeal of her newfound conviction outweighing any residual gratitude she felt for them.

CHAPTER SIX

Maggie Lorimer turned over the calendar with a smile. The first of December, the start of Advent. It was a season that she loved, not only for its religious connotations but also because of the heightened pleasure that it gave to her as a schoolteacher. Sure, there was always pressure on the seniors as exam time loomed nearer but there was a lot of fun, too, the school show being held close to the end of term and lots of Christmas themed pieces chosen by her for English lessons. Christmas itself was going to be a little bit different this year, too, with an invitation from their friends, Erin and Flynn, to have dinner with them in their new home.

Joseph Alexander Flynn had been shown the greatest hospitality by Lorimer in years gone by, given sanctuary in their home following a near fatal accident after being chased by one of Lorimer's own officers. Now an established land-scape gardener with a thriving business, he had met DS Erin Finlay during a case that had started when Flynn had turned up a body buried in a country garden. This unexpected beginning had led to a romance that delighted both Lorimer and Maggie and now the pair were living together in a small cottage near Carmunnock, high above the city.

Maggie shook her head. *Time to get a move on*, she told herself. Bill had gone ages ago, his habit of arriving early in the MIT at Helen Street meaning that they rarely took breakfast together on weekdays. Today was Tuesday and she had to help with the Scripture Union club at lunchtime, something she'd enjoy, especially today as Advent began. She grabbed her coat, stooping briefly to pat Chancer, their ginger cat, on the landing as he sauntered towards their bedroom, fluffy tail erect, in the hope that the recently vacated bed would still be warm.

'See you later, lad,' Maggie murmured as she hastened downstairs. In moments she had locked up behind her and was in the car, ready to drive to Muirpark Secondary School across the city and begin her day. It was still dark and drivers needed their headlights on at this time of the morning, daylight yet to creep like a reluctant thief across the horizon.

The figure watched as the red tail-lights disappeared around the corner. Mrs Lorimer was gone, then, and the house would be empty until she returned from work. A quick glance had shown the burglar alarm high above an upper window. It was to be expected that a senior cop like Lorimer would have all the bells and whistles that security could provide. Still, there was no harm in keeping an eye on the place until some way could be found to get into that house.

The detective superintendent could prove a stumbling

block to their plans and the person watching his home right now had been ordered to conduct a complete search of this particular villa in Giffnock. Getting access to his personal computer which they hoped to find here in Lorimer's house might tell them exactly what was going on. Besides, any information meant more money passing through several hands and the hooded figure standing in the shadows of next-door's hedge was already calculating how much that might be. A slow walk along the curving avenue and a rapid glance upwards were enough to take in the details. A door with two locks, the burglar alarm, modern double-glazed windows that were most likely locked from inside. A small movement made the figure pause and look once more. But it was just a ginger cat sitting on the upstairs window sill, regarding the outside world with a haughty stare that would have done justice to the Sphinx itself. A slow smile crossed that shadowed face. If the cat had free run of this house during the day, then chances were that the alarm was left off, the external device merely for show.

At the end of the cul-de-sac the figure turned and retraced its steps, hood pulled down to obscure any features that might be caught on a residential camera. The large haversack slung over one shoulder gave an impression of business so that anyone staring out of a window would assume that the flyers recently dropped through their door had come from that very source.

Nobody remembered the invisible people, after all: the assistant helping at self-service checkouts in a busy super-market, the dog walkers who passed them by or the delivery drivers who left parcels in the front porch. And the figure taking a last look at the house with the yellow-flowered creeper arching around the door felt as secure there and then as if a magic cloak of concealment had been cast around their shoulders.

CHAPTER SEVEN

'This could be the biggest one yet.'

David Mearns, acting chief constable of Police Scotland, regarded his two colleagues with a grave expression on his face. 'We know enough to think that an attack is planned for the city centre but exactly where, when and, more to the point, by whom are details we need to find out. And time is against us.'

His deputy, Caroline Flint, turned to Detective Superintendent Lorimer and caught his glance. She could see his jaw tighten as he acknowledged the CC's words. As head of the Major Incident Team, Lorimer had been asked to join these two senior officers and he was well aware that the approaching Christmas season could make Glasgow a target for a terrorist attack. The security services had given them that much information and more had been filtered through from undercover officers tasked with rooting out whatever cell was planning this latest atrocity.

Lately, however, things had become messy with the

suspicion that someone was feeding information directly from the heart of Police Scotland to the terrorists. Not only that, but the cover of several officers tasked with gathering intelligence had been blown in a dramatic fashion, their identities splashed across the papers.

Mearns had warned them that if there was one thing to be expected, it was that they would not find it easy to identify the person they were seeking. *Every barrel has its rotten apples*, the chief constable had told them, shrugging as if it was something that he'd seen elsewhere than in Police Scotland. Trouble was, no amount of rattling any particular barrel had resulted in producing the officers behind the current problem. Centralising the force all those years ago had gained a modicum of control but with it they had relinquished the familiarity that different squads around the country had with their particular patch.

A female officer, possibly a crime scene manager or senior investigating officer, had been suggested at one of their preliminary meetings with MI6, following information from the security services.

It was a difficult time for the senior officers who sat in that office with William Lorimer. Not only was the force without a permanent chief constable but an inquiry into recent difficulties with a now depleted undercover department had left a bitter taste in many mouths, particularly when a unit from the Met had been entrusted with looking into that department's failings. There were political feelings running high, too, in parallel with the wave of nationalism across the country, some officers resenting what they perceived as the London unit's interference.

These particular problems, for all that they presented a delicate background against which to work, were peripheral to the main reason that Lorimer was seated beside Deputy Chief Constable Caroline Flint and Acting CC David Mearns, former chief constable of Cumbria.

'Thanks for coming in today,' David Mearns said, nodding towards his deputy and detective superintendent in turn. 'Hopefully we'll manage to get to the bottom of this before Christmas and then you can concentrate on appointing your new chief.' Mearns had made it quite clear from the outset that he did not covet the top job himself, happy for now to take the reins till the post was filled. However, there was history in Scotland of looking south to find the right candidate and Lorimer hoped that Caroline Flint's bid for the job would not meet a barrier of opposition from those ardent nationalists (some of whom had a tendency to be a bit anti-English) keen to see one of their own in place. Flint's background as an undercover officer in the Met had stood her in good stead for this particular investigation and, since her appointment here in Scotland, she'd found a good ally in William Lorimer.

Mearns clasped his hands across the file on his knees, looking from one of his officers to the other, a smile now crinkling his eyes as though he were genuinely glad to be discussing matters with them. Lorimer had watched the man several times on TV, expounding on different topics to do with Police Scotland, and he admired the relaxed way he dealt with the press, fielding questions with good humour and an innate intelligence. He would have made a fine politician, someone had remarked, but Lorimer felt that although Mearns had a genuine desire to serve the public, he lacked the brutal cut and thrust that seemed a prerequisite for modern-day politicians. In short, their temporary chief constable was a man of integrity to whom uttering the smallest lie would be anathema. It had taken some persuasion from Flint and Lorimer to allow the current subterfuge. Nobody was actually telling porkies to the different divisions, simply allowing rumours to develop so that they might create a sort of smokescreen.

The bottom line was that somewhere in the force (and they had narrowed it down to the central belt) somebody was risking the lives of their fellow officers by passing information into the wrong hands. It was not just a lucrative source of money from a journalist anxious to have a story, though that was bad enough. They had suspected for some time now that big money was being made by some officer on the take, letting criminal bosses know that they were being spied upon by a cop in their own organisation. Undercover operatives had a hard enough time of it, often away from home for months on end, their personal lives on hold until a case drew to its conclusion. Already three officers had been forced to change their careers, taking jobs that were far less demanding, in the wake of their identities being splashed across the front pages of the papers. All of them were expected to quit the force before long and there was a dire need to recruit more officers to replace them. There was now a very small number of officers being deployed and right now the intelligence they were providing was of the utmost importance to national security.

'Intelligence has led us to believe that the person we seek

is probably Scottish and female. That covers around half of our population but what about officers? Any further forward?' Mearns began directing his question to Lorimer.

The detective superintendent shook his head slowly. 'Looking at DS Morris's background certainly was one idea,' he said. 'She's married to an Asian chap.'

'He's squeaky clean as far as we can tell,' Caroline Flint murmured. 'Had some bother when he married her, though. Family not happy at all to see their boy taking a non-Muslim, white Scottish wife. But there doesn't appear to be any radical element in their midst. Security services have assured us of that.'

'Hmm, we need to look at the bigger picture, of course, but step softly. One hint of racism and the press will land on us like a ton of bricks,' Mearns warned. 'What do you think, Lorimer?'

'As a scene of crime manager, she's the first line of contact at a locus, knows each and every one of the team from pathologist down to SOCOs, given every piece of information right from the start of a case,' he replied. 'There can't be many in an investigation team other than the SIO who keeps track of every single bit of what is ongoing. And even the SIO isn't always kept up to scratch,' he added, pulling a face as though to remind himself of past cases where review teams had been put in after the senior investigating officer had been found wanting. He'd headed up a case like that himself, down in Inverclyde, one that had ended with tragic consequences.

'Caroline?' Mearns shifted his eyes to his deputy.

'She'll know a lot of officers,' she agreed. 'But how would

she have found out the identity of undercover cops? That's nowhere near her brief.'

The two men nodded silently. It was still a mystery how these officers' details had been leaked to the press.

'Only our Intelligence Division has their names on file. And Counter Terrorism, of course,' Mearns agreed. 'Here are details of our officers, past and present,' he said, handing over sheets of printed paper to the others.

Lorimer swept a glance at the names and addresses of past and current undercover officers, frowning a little as he noticed that several of them lived in the Paisley area and one in Barrhead. All within easy distance of Glennifer Braes Country Park. A coincidence? Or something he needed to worry about? His thoughts were interrupted as Caroline Flint looked his way.

'It will do no harm for a scene of crime manager or her SIO to find the head of the MIT hovering at their elbow, I suppose,' Flint said. She gave a sly grin as she looked at Lorimer. 'And it's doing this one a favour. I can always feel you itching to get back out there.'

'Any inklings so far?' Mearns asked.

Lorimer shook his head. 'Just the sense that there is some-one playing a very dangerous game with us; an officer who appears to abide by the rules but is leading a double life.'

'Someone knows every last detail of what goes on in this area,' Mearns went on. 'Otherwise we'd have been turfing out these Islamists long before now.'

'Are we certain that's who they are?' Lorimer asked cautiously.

'Yes, just one of the things we learned from our officers

before their cover was blown,' Flint confirmed. 'That and the fact that they were sure it was a female passing information directly to the leaders of this terrorist cell.'

'Well, whoever she is, she's doing a good job of disappearing in plain sight,' he sighed. 'Almost as if she were undercover trained herself.'

Caroline Flint raised her eyebrows and gave Lorimer a questioning stare.

'Don't worry.' He grinned. 'None of us in this room has anything to worry about.'

'We have three undercover officers currently deployed in the Glasgow area,' Flint said. 'Two men and one woman, and whatever else we do it is imperative that we keep them all safe.'

'And each of them working on finding the source of millions being spent on bringing terrorists into the country,' Lorimer murmured. He knew that the woman had been given the job of infiltrating a city law firm that they suspected of being a hub for money laundering.

'One thing I think we all ought to do is keep a very careful check on these discussions. Any emails or texts between us could be compromised if we aren't scrupulous about their security.'

'What do you suggest?' Mearns asked.

'Carry your personal laptops with you at all times. Have them under lock and key in your own homes, just in case . . .'

Mearns raised his eyebrows. 'Is that really necessary?'

'I think we cannot be too careful, given the way these undercover officers were ferreted out,' Lorimer agreed.

'We've been careful to keep dialogue between us off

email for now, at any rate,' Flint agreed. 'If you don't have a safe place to lock your computer away, David, then I suggest you order one. Police Scotland will pay for it, of course.'

Mearns gave a nod. 'Okay. But the rented house we're in is pretty secure as it is. Still, it makes sense not to leave that sort of thing lying around. I'll see to it today.' He made a note on the pad on his desk then looked up at them both.

'Are we sure it is something major planned for Christmas?' he asked.

Flint nodded. 'MI6 have a good idea that something big will happen in the city centre. It's what terrorists do, of course,' she added. 'They look for the biggest crowds enjoying themselves, totally unaware of a danger in their midst.'

'And definitely Glasgow?' Lorimer asked.

Flint nodded. 'That's what intelligence tells us.'

'At least the homicide rate showed a remarkable dip this past month,' Mearns said, giving Lorimer a sympathetic look. 'You must be pleased about that.'

'Of course,' Lorimer replied. And yet there was something he left unsaid, something that had been a source of concern to him. It was a statistical anomaly to have one single homicide on his calendar, wasn't it?

What if that was not really the case at all? What if there had actually been more murders taking place on Scottish soil than they realised?

And where were the bodies to be found?

CHAPTER EIGHT

He was back in the city centre, heading towards the same place where he had stood and stared a few days before. Glasgow and its different streets were becoming a little more familiar now, though each office Daniel had sat in since his arrival looked pretty much alike. He had repeated the same things over and over until he felt that the words almost belonged to a different person. Nobody had smiled very often, no one asked how he felt, just question after question about why he had fled his native land. Sometimes he wondered if it was a plot to see if he deviated from his story.

What happened to those men and women after office hours? he wondered. Did these official people meet up and discuss his case? Try to find a hole in his claims for refugee status? Or were they so tired after a dreary day that they simply took themselves to wherever they called home? Sometimes he thought back to discussions he'd had with other displaced people. The accusations about being set up by those in authority had sounded fanciful to Daniel's ears. Did they genuinely think that these civil servants were trained to deliberately catch them out? Some of the stories he'd listened to had filled him with dismay. *It could never happen to me*, he'd repeated to himself, willing it to be so. Besides, his own story lacked much of the horror he had heard elsewhere, his grief and pain almost commonplace beside the torture and beatings some men had faced in order to reach these shores. And, once in the UK, their expectations had been thwarted by suspicion and mistrust that had made many of them both fearful and bitter about the men and women who now held sway over their lives.

They'll give you refugee status, his church friends had assured him. *And in time you'll be a settled person. Britain isn't like other places.*

Daniel stopped at the entrance to the lane. He was not sure that he really believed that any more. Human beings felt the same things the world over, the desire for wealth and power too often overcoming any inherent goodness they might once have displayed. Why should this country be any different?

The lane was empty today, the cobbles slick with earlier rain. He glanced at his watch, the only thing he had left to remind himself of the woman who had bought it for him. Yes, this was the same time, all right. If anyone was in the habit of leaving that building halfway along, then perhaps they would open the heavy metal door and emerge into the open.

He recalled the man stepping out, the glint of metal then ...? Had he turned and looked at Daniel? Or was that something he had imagined? He closed his eyes and tried hard to recapture the moment. The sound of traffic in the background faded as Daniel conjured up a picture in his mind.

No, the man had not turned his head. That was something he would definitely have remembered: a look, an expression, some small communication between strangers in a dark place. Well, that was to his advantage, he decided, walking slowly and carefully into the narrow lane.

The heavy black door was firmly shut, no sign of a handle or anything that would allow a person entry from here. So, he thought, raising his eyes to the rooftop high above, it would be some sort of emergency exit, security demanding that the door could only be opened from within.

He looked left and then right, calculating the distance from one end of the lane to the other. It was almost midway along. A small smile of satisfaction tilted his lips as he walked through the lane and emerged in Renfield Street, hardly noticing the buses and taxis slowly making their way towards the next set of traffic lights. With a bit of luck he would soon know a little bit more about what lay behind that closed metal door.

The block stretched from one corner to the next, each main door accessed from street level by a set of stone steps. There were window boxes full of what looked like purple cabbages and evergreen plants, things that appeared strange to Daniel's eyes. A moment of longing swept over him for warm skies full of weaver birds twittering and fine streets lined with jac-aranda trees, their *bhuruu* blossoms a shade of purplish blue impossible to describe in English. The blast from a car horn startled him out of his reverie and he turned his attention once again to seeking out the building he wanted.

For a moment he hesitated on the pavement, gazing at the doorway. A row of brass plaques was set just inside on the left, too difficult to make out unless he climbed those stairs and committed himself to going further. Just a few steps to see, he told himself. No need to do any more, not yet.

There were six floors to the building, offices belonging to different firms. Daniel read them all, memorising their names, a skill that had been honed in all his years investigating matters where such details were important.

'Can I help you?' Daniel looked up to see a man in uniform standing, hands behind his back, regarding him with polite curiosity.

'Thank you,' Daniel began, realising that this was some sort of concierge in charge of the building's security. A quick glance over the man's shoulder showed a marble-floored hallway with a long, curved desk at the far end and a reception area for visitors, a well-lit staircase to one side. He gave the man what he hoped was his most disarming smile.

'Thomas Bryson,' he said, stating the name on the top floor that he remembered.

'Lift's just round there,' the man replied, walking Daniel along and pointing to a door. 'Saves you a long walk up those stairs,' he added with a chuckle.

'Thank you,' Daniel replied, breathing a silent sigh of relief that the concierge seemed perfectly happy to admit a stranger into this building without any trace of suspicion, and wondering what sort of business Thomas Bryson conducted six floors up in West Regent Street.

Once inside the lift, Daniel studied the names again and noticed that, not only were there six floors of business addresses, but that the lift also took passengers to a lower ground floor. His heart beat faster, anticipating the moment when he might step out in the place where he had seen that man with the bloodied knife. But not yet. First he would ascend right to the top and spend some time looking around. Who knew if the concierge's prying eyes were following the progress of this lift to see if the stranger had made it to his chosen destination?

Thomas Bryson's offices proved to be a firm of solicitors, their name etched on a smoked-glass door. A large tub sat in one corner near the entrance, a small evergreen tree surrounded by shiny-leaved plants full of red berries. Daniel would not ring the bell set to one side of this door, however. Instead he crept quietly towards the stairs and made his way down, stopping at each level to examine the names and occupations of each business. There was no need to write them down, his mental images of them were fixed in a memory that had always enjoyed this peculiar trait. A photographic memory, one of his uncles had joked when Daniel had been a small boy but so it had proved. School had never presented a problem for the boy and his career thereafter had been a good choice for one possessing such a talent.

He would not emerge at the ground floor, of course, provoking that concierge's curiosity. He needed to leave a respectable amount of time to make it appear that he had indeed had an appointment with a solicitor on the top floor and so Daniel retraced his steps upwards once more, having given each of the named occupants of the building his fullest attention. The lift on floor six opened with the faintest of sighs and he stepped inside and pressed LG. If anyone was watching, he could claim to have made a sight error, he decided.

Luckily nobody else stopped to enter and he watched the numbers change from level to level as the lift descended to the very bottom.

The doors opened and Daniel stepped out into a shadowy area, the bright lift behind him a patch of light in the gloom. Then, as the doors behind him swooshed closed once more he was left looking around at the place where a man must have stood several days before, his hand clutching that bloodstained knife.

He made out the dim shapes of packing cartons piled up to one side, their dusty sides fixed with brown tape. Too large to be wine crates, he thought, giving the one at shoulder height a small shake. Nothing within rattled and it felt heavy, so filled with something, all right.

There was no obvious reason why anyone might have been wielding such a thing; a caterer preparing food might have been taking a short break, of course, and Daniel had no way of knowing what facilities might exist at the back of these offices. However, the figure he'd seen had not been wearing kitchen whites, but a dark suit with collar and tie. Besides, there had been a furtive look about the man, as if he had wanted to leave by the lane then changed his mind.

Daniel had his phone in one hand, its torchlight casting thin beams across the cement floor, stepping closer and closer towards the exit. Then, hunkering down, he examined the area nearest the door. He peered closely then stopped. Was that a trail of bloodstains he could see? Dried and darkened now, of course . . .

A noise from the lift made him turn swiftly and he stood up, pocketing his phone. In two silent strides he was behind the crates, bending as low as possible.

The lift doors opened then closed once more as Daniel stared into the gloom.

Footsteps drew closer then stopped. Daniel held his breath, fearful of discovery. Then he heard a metallic clang as the emergency bar was pushed and the doors swung open, daylight streaming into the darkened basement.

For a brief moment the man's face was illuminated and Daniel caught his breath.

He saw the figure step outside and heard the footsteps walking away down the cobbled lane.

Slowly, slowly, he rose from his crouching position and crept towards the door. But, when he risked a peek outside, there was no one to be seen.

With a sigh that was only partly relief, Daniel retraced his steps, entered the lift and pressed the button to take him back to the ground floor, heart beating a little faster than normal.

There was no need to acknowledge the concierge this time as nobody sat behind the lobby desk and he was on the pavement in seconds, walking swiftly uphill, his mind replaying what little he had seen.

The sight of that retreating figure was fixed in his brain. A fleeting image, perhaps, but Daniel Kohi was certain that it was the same person he had seen almost a week before, though this time there was no knife in his hand and anyone watching him walking through that lane might have taken him for a city businessman.

He stopped at the next corner and took out his phone once more, eyes flicking down to the steps up to those six floors of offices. He would stand here, apparently absorbed by his screen like half the world but waiting for that figure to reappear and walk back into the building.

But no one appeared. Daniel turned into the lane once more, walking this time towards Hope Street. The cobbles were uneven beneath his shoes and once he almost stumbled as he stared at each back door along this block. He stopped when he reached the black door. A notice on one side read FIRE EXIT, and on the other KEEP CLEAR, as if to warn any motorists stupid enough to take a shortcut through this lane. Each side of the black metal door was a security gate, a flimsy-looking affair in iron mesh, but the padlock attached to a hasp was solid enough to mean business. These were details that Daniel squirrelled away in his mind, things that might add up to make sense of what he had seen the day he'd arrived in this city.

How often had he done something like that in the old days? Watched and waited for someone who had crossed an invisible line. But that had been part of his life. So why, when this was none of his business, was he letting his curiosity take him into a situation that might ruin his already precarious future?

CHAPTER NINE

The sensible thing to do would be to call the police. But Daniel had been warned to keep out of any sort of trouble and that included sticking his nose in where it did not belong.

He knew what he had seen, though, and the image would not leave him in peace.

Today the bitter east wind had dropped and there was stillness in the air, frost carpeting the ground. Looking out from his window, Daniel could see distant hills glittering as the morning sun cast its rays across snowy peaks. Despite the freezing temperature he was seized by a sudden urge to be out of doors, climbing up the sides of those hills. Grabbing his jacket, he headed for the front door and swung it shut behind him.

'Ye goin fur yer messages, son? Gonnae get me a pint o' milk?'

What? Daniel swallowed the word as he spun on his heel. His neighbour's words bounced off the cold walls.

'Messages?' he said at last, a puzzled frown creasing his brow.

'Aye,' Netta replied, looking at him and shaking her head. 'D'ye no' ken whit ah mean? Mess-ah-jies,' she said, enunciating each syllable as though that would help him. Then, as he continued to look bewildered, she began to chuckle.

'Goad help us,' she cried. 'We've a right one here. Messages, son. Grocery shoapin, a'right?'

Daniel nodded, understanding at last. The woman thought he was off to purchase groceries. Messages? Was that a Scottish name for them? Odd, he thought. Very odd.

'No, I was just going to go for a walk,' Daniel explained.

'In this weather?' Netta exclaimed. 'Withoot a dacent coat on yer back? Son, ye'll catch yer death, so ye wull.'

Daniel shrugged. He had no warmer garment than his fleece-lined jacket.

'Here.' Netta summoned him inside. 'Ah've goat wan o' ma auld man's still. He'll nae be wantin' it ony more whaur he is.' She gave a sudden whoop of laughter as she shambled back into her warm hallway, Daniel following her as meekly as a lamb.

'Where is your husband?' Daniel stood for a moment, uncertain if the woman was trying to sell him another man's garment.

'Roastin' in hell, I expect.' Netta grinned. 'Dead these past fower year. Nasty auld bugger, so he wis. Cannae think why I didnae pit oot thon coat alang wi' the rest o' his claes,' she muttered, pushing open the door to her bedroom.

Daniel hesitated, reluctant to follow the older woman any further. Was this some sort of ploy to entice him there?

Netta turned and stared at him. 'Ye gonna staun ther like an eejit?' she demanded. Then, as he took a tentative step towards her, she slid open her wardrobe door and rummaged inside, pushing garments along, the metal rail screeching in protest.

'Ah, therr it is!' she announced, and, with smile of triumph on her face, she pulled out a garment bag and handed it to Daniel.

'Might be okay if the moaths huvnae goat it,' she grinned.

Daniel stood looking at her, still uncertain of what sort of transaction was taking place.

'Well.' Netta stood, arms crossed, looking at him steadily. 'Open the damned thing up and see if it fits, eh?'

Daniel unzipped the bag and took out a thick black coat buttoned up to the neck.

'Ma man wisnae as tall as ye are, son, but it was always ower big fur him onyway,' Netta declared. 'Go on intae the living room and try it oan.'

Then, as though impatient to see her neighbour wearing it, Netta tutted and took it from him, unbuttoning the garment then handing it back to him.

It was a good fit, he had to admit, as Daniel wrapped it around his body and fastened the buttons.

'I don't think I can afford—' he began.

'Tsk! Who said onything about me sellin' it to ye?' Netta bristled indignantly. 'It's nae loss whit a freen gets, son,' she declared, leaving Daniel to blink once more. The translation of her words might be utterly beyond him but he had caught their gist: Netta wanted to give him the coat, plain and simple.

'Thank you,' he said gravely. 'This is a very generous thing that you do for me.'

'Ach, away wi' ye,' she replied brusquely. 'Jist bring us back a pint o' milk, okay?'

Outside, the crisp, sharp air was a welcome contrast from the previous day when the wind had whipped sleety rain under his jacket, soaking his trousers. Daniel drew up the coat collar and thrust his bare hands into the capacious pockets. His fingers closed around a piece of stiff paper and, curious, he took it out and stopped to see what it was. Unfolding it, he saw an order of service for the funeral of one James McTaggart. A grainy black and white photograph showed the face of a man with white hair smiling at the camera. The inside displayed familiar hymns, the twenty-third psalm and 'Abide With Me', and, on the reverse of the card, another photograph, this one in colour, the late Mr McTaggart holding a pint glass in one hand and a blue rosette in the other. Something significant to celebrate in a life of . . . Daniel read the dates given on the front . . . sixty-nine years.

So, had Netta's own husband last worn this to his friend's funeral? Or was James McTaggart a relative, perhaps, worthy of the purchase of a new coat, its Marks and Spencer garment bag hung up on the bedroom rail afterwards? It was indeed a generous gift and Daniel thrust the card back into his pocket, determined to do something in return for the kindness of his neighbour.

Everything seemed quieter today as if the cold air had tamped down harsh sounds and even his footsteps made little noise as he strode away from the high flats and headed towards a row of shops that included a mini-market, an Asian takeaway that would not open its metal shutters till later in the day and the ubiquitous bookmaker's that never seemed to close at all.

The Asian boy looked at him as Daniel handed over the milk carton and counted out his money instead of using the ASPEN card that guaranteed him almost thirty-eight pounds each week. He still possessed a handful of coins from the gift of money he'd been given by his church friends before travelling to Glasgow, but these were precious. There was no knowing when he'd be granted settled status, never mind permission to work and earn money again. Yesterday that same lad had given a disdainful sniff when the tall black man had appeared in the shop but today he did not appear to recognise him, a sort of doubt creeping over his features.

'Thank you,' Daniel said as he took the milk.

'Aye, see you later,' the boy said, a throwaway remark that was probably his standard reply to all his customers. Had he realised that this was a previous customer? Or did the big coat make such a difference, giving Daniel the appearance of a more prosperous figure worthy of some little respect?

Once again, the moment took him back to a different place where young boys stopped and stared, not daring to whistle after him but creeping into the shadows in case he spotted their misdeeds. Daniel Kohi had not been a man to suffer fools gladly and the good folk in the townships would nod courteously to him whenever he passed them by.

Always stand up for what you believe, his mother used to tell him and even as a small boy Daniel had stuck to that principle. In time to come, of course, that very maxim had been his undoing.

A blast from a horn made him stop suddenly to see a driver skid to a halt as a cyclist swung across the road, wobbling a little then speeding away over the opposite pavement. There was no need to hear the angry words hurled at the cyclist, one look at the driver's expression said it all. Was that what had happened to him? One little deviation from how they had expected him to behave resulting in a rage that had consumed . . .

Daniel shut his eyes tightly, the scenes reappearing in vivid colours: crimson tongues of flame burning, burning . . .

When he opened his eyes it was a street in Glasgow that lay before him, the traffic moving past, people going about their daily business.

Daniel swallowed hard, clutching the carton of milk in his hands. He would not go to that place in his mind where nightmares lurked, waiting like monsters to swallow him up.

CHAPTER TEN

Sylvie felt the eyes on her back and knew without turning around that she was being watched. It was a sixth sense that people in her world developed over time, something few talked about but acknowledged just the same. *A prickling of hairs on the back of my neck*, one man had told her before he'd been career-changed, a phrase they used amongst themselves. That was the expression used for trainee guide dogs that didn't make the grade required to assist a blind person. And in a lot of ways their jobs were the same, walking beside those unable to see them or know of their superior skills in detecting danger. Being an undercover officer was full of pitfalls and it took a person with heightened sensitivity as well as the ability to melt into crowds to do the job and do it well.

Despite long hours spent in surveillance, watching darkened windows in obscure city streets or listening to subversive creeds being spouted from fanatical mouths, Sylvie Maxwell loved her job. And it was one that suited her well. A woman of average height, her shoulder-length hair easily adapted to become a sleek chignon or dyed black to merge in with the rent-a-mobs that were intent on causing trouble at any sort of public rally, Sylvie was happiest being disregarded by those around her.

The case she was presently involved in had meant spending weeks with the sort of people whose day-to-day lives were very different from her own as a serving police officer, something she had to subsume in her everyday dealings with them. Her degree in Economics and Information Technology followed by her police training had led to several placements in offices where she was able to obtain information relating to financial irregularities and pass that on to the appropriate authority within the Fraud Squad. Currently, Sylvie Maxwell (which was not, of course, the name on her official birth certificate) was employed in a sixth-floor office in one of Glasgow's more desirable streets where she spent hours ostensibly drawing up balance sheets for a firm of solicitors but in reality looking for anything in their accounting systems that might lead her to the hidden millions that were funding some serious criminal activities.

She had recently reported back about one significant change: the absence of one of the junior partners who had simply failed to come into work one day. It had been the presence of Carter that had led Sylvie here in the first place, an ex-con in a solicitor's office flagging up some interest. Yet, despite his chequered past, Derek Carter had been a chatty type of fellow, warm and witty, and Sylvie had enjoyed his banter over the water cooler or in the communal kitchen. No real explanation had been given for why he was no longer in the firm. She had enquired innocently about the missing man to her immediate boss, Vincent Burns, but had been given no satisfactory answer, feeling instead a sense of disquiet emanating from the senior partner. He hadn't liked Derek, Sylvie decided. She'd heard them arguing once as she'd passed Burns's office but Derek had just shrugged it off when Sylvie had questioned him about it.

'All right, Ms Maxwell?' A familiar voice made her stiffen, the man bending so close to her that Sylvie could feel his breath on the back of her bare neck.

She swivelled on her chair, a ready smile simpering on her lips.

'Oh, Mr Burns,' she gasped, one manicured hand raised to her mouth. 'You startled me!'

She saw the man's eyes bore into her for a moment before dropping her gaze as though too modest to meet his own.

'Keeping busy?' he asked, in a whispering tone that might have held a threat.

'Oh, yes,' she assured him, turning back to her desk. 'Always plenty to do here.'

There was a silence behind her as she let her hand hover over the mouse as though to continue working, then she felt his hand squeeze her shoulder briefly in one strong grip that would surely leave a mark.

'Good,' Vincent Burns said, then walked away, leaving Sylvie with the distinct impression that something was not good at all and that she had been tested and found wanting.

Once she was sure that he had left the room, she gave a long sigh. She was not the first officer to worry whether or not her cover might be blown but for now she would remain here unless her superiors ordered her to quit. In recent weeks there had been others who had left their posts in different cases after months of painstaking work to infiltrate different organisations, the mystery of who had sold their secrets to the press baffling the entire force.

There would be no extra hours worked this evening, searching files for data that might help root out the sources they needed to find. No, she would leave right on the dot of five o'clock, take the lift down to reception and walk out into the bright city streets with their Christmas lights, just one more office worker on her way home. Though, like any good undercover police officer, Sylvie Maxwell would not take a direct route to her home, an address that was rather different from the one presently lodged in the personnel files of Thomas Bryson, Solicitors.

Vincent Burns watched the woman as her boot heels clipped smartly across the marble floor, down the flight of stone steps that led to street level and turned in the direction of the town. His car was waiting in the parking area out in the lane, a small cobbled square chained off for use by the senior partners, but tonight Vincent would take a walk first, his curiosity piqued by the woman who had worked in his office for these past months. It was nothing sexual, of course. She was not his type at all, too skinny, too plain for his liking. And too old as well, in her late thirties according to her CV. Yet, as he kept his eye on her retreating back, he saw a figure that was lean and fit, her footsteps quickening as she approached the junction, ready to cross on a green light. What was her hurry? Did she have a bus to catch or a particular train?

Once, as she turned into Nelson Mandela Place, he saw her looking at her watch, hardly breaking her stride. He followed her right down Buchanan Street, the silvery-blue row of Christmas trees a dazzle of light, and stared at her retreating figure as she turned into Princes Square.

Once inside, Vincent paused beside a kiosk selling expensive chocolates wrapped in beribboned boxes of gold and red, watching his employee descend on the escalator to the basement area where a huge Christmas tree dominated the entire centre of this glittering mall. He saw her march purposefully into the Everyman Cinema and disappear out of sight. So, that was all, he told himself. She had been hurrying to catch a movie. Perhaps meeting a friend inside. He looked around as a pair of well-dressed young women, their fur collars turned up against the cold, passed him by, chattering happily. His gaze lingered on them for a few moments, admiring their sleek blonde hair and the sort of clothes that only a lot of money could buy; much more his type of female, Vincent thought, dismissing the notion that dowdy Sylvie Maxwell could possibly be any threat to the business that he had built up. He was overly careful, that was all, he decided, taking another look at the goods on offer in the kiosk and wondering if any of them would be an appropriate gift for a particular lady friend. Ms Maxwell had been in the habit of clocking up overtime and Vincent had wanted to know why. Looking around him at the baubles and the glitter, Vincent saw his answer. It was Christmas soon, he reasoned, and she had probably been trying to make a bit of extra money, that was all. Still, he'd keep an eye on Sylvie Maxwell. It did not do to have too many strangers in their midst, no matter how good their office skills.

She sat in the darkness watching the adverts on the big screen, aware of every movement around her. Mostly there were twin seats, couples snuggled up together, glasses of wine on their tray tables, but in the back row where she had chosen to sit as close to the exit as she could there were still some empty seats. She would sit through the featured film then return home, once she had taken time to be certain that Burns was no longer following her. And then? A phone call was in order tonight, reporting back to her own boss and maybe, just maybe, alerting her to the worry that Sylvie Maxwell might have to disappear for good.

CHAPTER ELEVEN

It was one of those winter mornings that were made for setting off out of the city and heading for the hills. The crisp air made Lorimer imagine snow-capped peaks an hour's drive away, Ben More and Stob Binnein near Crianlarich. He saw them in his mind's eye, their tops thrusting upwards against this bright blue sky, the clear air letting any climber see the panoramic view for miles around. Perhaps, if he found time once this case was wrapped up, there might be the chance of a few days' leave, he thought with a sigh of longing. It was always dependent upon the weather, of course, and who knew what lay ahead now that December was upon them. And, with each passing day, he was more acutely aware of how time was against them, the threat from those terrorists becoming more vivid in his mind.

Instead of standing on the top of one of Scotland's Munros, Lorimer was out above the town of Paisley looking down from the roadside that was adjacent to the place where three young schoolboys had stumbled across a dead body.

The scene of crime officers had completed all their work and samples were being analysed painstakingly back in the labs but for now Lorimer wanted to feel a sense of place, wondering who had dumped that corpse and what had made the killers choose this particular locus. They knew it would have taken more than one man to carry a dead weight and Lorimer tried to imagine what that must have been like. It was a dark time of year, the daylight hours rapidly waning towards midwinter, and up here on the Braes few vehicles cast their headlights along the winding road. It was, he admitted grudgingly, an ideal spot to dispose of a body, particularly in the gully that was unseen from the nearby road. Glennifer Braes was a country park whose hillsides swelled high above the town, a blaze of yellow gorse in summer and often snow-clad in the winter months. Wee boys liked an adventure up here, he knew, and, given the names of places near the reservoir like Fairy Fall and Witches Corner, who could blame them? As he had suspected, the lads had all touched the man's corpse. Their prints would be eliminated from the case in time, of course, since no evidence had been found of them starting the blaze that had consumed the dead man's body.

But someone had. And whoever that was must have thought that their deed would lie undiscovered much longer than this. Had they expected the depredations of hungry creatures like foxes to finish off their grisly work? Lorimer cast a glance at a crow wheeling past, its ragged wingtips stretched out as it balanced against a sudden gust of icy wind. He shivered, any notion of hill climbing for pleasure vanishing as a dark line of clouds rolled in from the east. It was time to go, he thought, his boots crunching on the frosty grass as he walked towards his waiting car. There were other minds than his that might make more sense of the choice of where this body had been laid. Lorimer's mouth curved in a smile as he thought of one in particular whose expertise he was about to seek.

Professor Solomon Brightman had left the city of London several years ago, Glasgow becoming much more to him than a place of work. His academic career in psychology had not only taken him into the world of criminal profiling; it had also rewarded him with a wife and family. Solly had encountered the petite blonde pathologist during a case where he had been called to assist DCI William Lorimer, now superintendent and head of the Major Incident Team. The unlikely friendship between the bearded psychologist who paled at the sight of blood and a woman who cut up dead bodies for a living had blossomed into a lasting romance. Now Rosie was head of the Department of Forensic Medicine at the University of Glasgow, Solly's own office just a few hundred yards away.

The tap on his door made Solly rise from his seat next to the large bay window where he had been reading an essay by one of his first-year students. He laid the script aside with a sigh and headed across the room.

'Lorimer!' Solly beamed at the tall man standing there. 'What a surprise. Come in, come in.'

'Hope I'm not disturbing you, Solly,' the detective apologised, heading towards the pair of comfortable armchairs that were angled towards the window, a place where they often sat together.

'Some tea?' Solly offered, adding hastily, 'I do have some ordinary stuff one of my postgrad girls brought me. Builder's tea, she called it, but it says something quite different on the packet.' Solly frowned, already searching in a cupboard beneath an enormous bookcase that stretched to the ceiling. 'Ah, here we are. No, it says Yorkshire ...' He broke off, studying the label.

'Grand,' Lorimer replied, smiling at his friend. 'You have your healthy option, Solly. Cat's piss on a gooseberry bush or whatever it is,' he joked. 'Give me a cup of strong tea any day. The sort that builders like.' He glanced at the bearded psychologist who was now switching on the kettle and peering at an array of mismatched mugs to find a couple of clean ones.

'Biscuits,' Solly said, scratching his curly dark hair. 'I'm sure we had biscuits this morning during a seminar ...' His eyes fell on an old-fashioned wicker waste basket, its contents revealing a crumpled wrapper. 'Ah, sorry. Those hungry young folk must have polished them off.' He shrugged and popped the teabags into a couple of mugs. 'Nearly lunchtime anyway. Do you want to go out for a bite to eat?'

'Not me,' Lorimer replied. 'Actually, I was hoping to talk to you about something. If you can spare the time.'

The two men sat sipping their respective brews, a companionable silence falling between them. Lorimer had outlined the story about the find out on the Glennifer Braes and how he had wondered about the location of the body.

'The wee lads came from Ferguslie Park, but that isn't exactly nearby,' he explained at last. 'There's a mix of housing much closer, like Glenburn,' he added helpfully.

70

'Ah.' Solly nodded. 'One of our professors lives in a very large property near there. A beautiful house in Thornly Park. Rosie and I attended a Christmas party a couple of years back. Huge garden. Gorgeous interior. All the original cornicing and fireplaces. Mmm, yes. A desirable area, one might say,' he mused.

'I'm looking for someone who might know the Braes well. Someone who could have been a long-time resident in the area, perhaps, or who was used to walking up there with a dog.'

Solly gave him a tired smile. 'You want me to map a murderer?' he asked quietly. 'But how can I do that when there has only been one fatality?'

Lorimer sighed. It was true that the psychologist had taken places on a map in the past and examined them for a common point from where a killer might begin. It was something he had thought about, standing up on the cold windy hill this very morning. 'It's the only homicide we've had in the whole month of November,' he agreed, setting down his empty mug on the carpet. 'But there's a curious pattern beginning to emerge in a completely different sphere of interest.'

'More burned bodies?' Solly's bushy eyebrows rose in astonishment.

Lorimer shook his head. 'Nothing like that,' he replied. 'It concerns something that you will not have heard about. Though you may have caught a bit about them in the papers.'

'Oh?' Solly laid down his tea, gazing at his friend with renewed curiosity.

'It's about the undercover officers whose stories were

leaked to the press by an unknown source,' Lorimer told him. 'Do you remember that?'

Solly nodded. 'Go on,' he said.

'There are three so far whose identities have been made known and who have had to be taken off those particular sorts of duties for what remains of their careers.' His face twisted in an expression of disgust. 'Two are desk-bound now for the most part and the third quit, though they'll all likely want to seek early retirement and gainful employment outside the force.'

'And this is a pattern ...?'

Lorimer shook his head. 'It's to do with the body on the Braes. And where some of those officers live.'

'Let me guess,' Solly said, looking at him intently. 'They are all a stone's throw from Glennifer Braes, am I right?'

Lorimer nodded. 'It could just be a coincidence, of course ...'

'But you're the man who doesn't believe in coincidences,' Solly finished for him.

'And there's more. We have an undercover officer currently placed in the city,' he sighed. 'And, yes, she lives in Paisley. I can't say where, of course, but it's not so very far from the Braes.'

'And like the others, within a short drive to where you found that body,' Solly finished.

'Yes. Now, there is a very discreet internal inquiry going on that I'm part of,' Lorimer explained, his voice lowering instinctively as if to keep his words from being overheard. 'Someone from within our own force is suspected of selling out these officers, either to the press, or – and here's where

I must insist that you keep this strictly to yourself, Solly – we suspect that they are being paid by criminal enterprises, particularly the people-trafficking side of them.'

Solly let out a soft whistle. Lorimer had put other gangsters away in prison before, but as soon as one outfit was broken, others seemed to arrive from elsewhere.

'We're pretty certain that money from an unknown source is being used to fund organised crime on a very big scale indeed,' Lorimer explained.

'You think someone is being paid to blow the whistle on these officers,' Solly said slowly.

'And not just that,' Lorimer added, lowering his voice. 'This is in the strictest confidence, Solly. We have intelligence that a great deal of money is being poured into a terrorist cell. These officers were tasked with infiltrating it before their cover was made public.'

'And now you find a body ... Unable to identify it, I assume?'

Lorimer nodded. 'The post-mortem shows that death occurred long before the man was set alight, thank goodness, though I did wonder when I first saw it ... ' He shuddered.

'You think this murder may have something to do with one of your former undercover officers?'

Lorimer sighed. 'I don't know. It's odd, though, that they are all within easy distance of the Braes. One of them lives over in Barrhead, close to Cross Stobs Inn. Do you know it?'

Solly shook his head. Being neither a drinker nor holding a driving licence, he was not used to frequenting village pubs.

'He could walk up to the Braes from his bungalow,' Lorimer said. 'No bother at all. And,' he smiled ruefully, 'he does have a dog so it would be natural for him to know his way about these parts. However, it is a very long walk from that part of the hills to where the body was found.'

'And the others?'

'One of them is married to a schoolteacher and they live in Stanely Avenue, a nice residential part of Paisley and much closer to where we found the corpse. Maybe a ten, fifteen-minute walk to Potterhill. She's the one that left the force. All the publicity sickened her and she's working in a care home. Such a waste of talent.'

'Perhaps those she's caring for won't think so,' Solly mused. 'That is a worthwhile job in anybody's reckoning.'

'Well, the other two are still serving officers, though as I said, tied to desk jobs meantime. They'll never revert to being undercover, that's for sure.'

'Didn't one of your officers used to be undercover? The tall blonde lady?'

'Molly Newton? Yes, she was. Almost came to grief in a case.' Lorimer raised his eyes to heaven. 'Think she's much better suited to her job with us in the Major Incident Team, frankly.'

'And the third officer? You mentioned the dog owner in Barrhead and the lady in Stanely Green, plus the one who is still undercover. But who is the last one?'

'Ah.' Lorimer nodded. 'She's the one that interests me most. You see, she lives in Glenburn itself, Hillcrest Avenue, right beside the road up to the Braes.'

Lorimer reached down and drew out a sheaf of papers from his briefcase. 'Here,' he said, handing them to Solly. 'It's all there, the stories about them in the press. They didn't submit to having their photos taken so the journos had to make do with ones taken at a distance. They're a bit grainy but you can see them better here.' He swooped down once more and took out a plastic folder. 'That's their official police photos, though they are kept separate from the normal database of officers' pictures for obvious reasons. And I've copied out details of their home addresses and other factors.'

'Are you allowed to do things like that nowadays? To former officers, I mean? Isn't there some sort of code to protect their privacy?'

Lorimer looked at him, his eyes narrowing. 'That is exactly what I am trying to do, Solly,' he said, a bitter note creeping into his tone. 'Someone took these details and sold them to the press. And we think that same someone may well be receiving generous payments from a criminal source. Whoever it is, their intention was to stop that undercover work. And we must find them. It's not only our own officers that are in danger, Solly. These people mean to create something devastating in Glasgow.'

Solly threw him an anxious look. 'That's dreadful,' he replied, shaking his head. 'I should be inured to the atrocities human beings can perpetrate on one another, but the capacity for things like this never fails to shock me.'

He looked up at Lorimer as though a new thought had come to mind.

'You think this body may be a police officer?'

'No. There's no missing person amongst our own, thank goodness. But I do think whoever killed him wanted to make completely sure that he was never going to be identified. And that,' he added sourly, 'is exactly the sort of thing I would expect from a gang like this.'

Solly sat back in his chair, tapping the files on his knee but not yet ready to open them. 'It's all a bit tenuous, though, isn't it? These undercover officers were not working together, were they?'

Lorimer nodded. 'Well, they were involved in the same operation but in different locations. They know one another, all right, and now thanks to our newspapers, some of them are only too well known to the general public.'

It was not until the children were both in bed and Rosie and he were alone at last that the professor managed to slip into his study and take the police files from his own ancient leather briefcase. He sat facing the window, the frosty darkness outside suiting his mood, reading the notes that Lorimer had given him earlier that day. It was, as his friend had said, a terrible waste of resources to have three undercover officers exposed in this way. The schoolteacher's wife, Mandy Richardson, was now working in a nearby home for the elderly, a caring profession that, however laudable in itself, had surely resulted in a huge drop in her income. Teachers were not as highly paid as they deserved, though Solly did note that Phillip Richardson was a principal teacher of guidance, a promoted post that would at least offset what might be a hefty mortgage. Property in Stanely Green didn't come cheap. Their two children were both at the local primary school so perhaps Mrs Richardson was glad of her more sociable working hours, something that Lorimer might not have appreciated. Lorimer and his wife Maggie were godparents to Solly and Rosie's two children, a role that was special to them both since they were a childless couple. Sometimes it took knowing about family life to truly understand its pressures, Solly thought.

Turning the pages over, he came to the officer who lived in Barrhead, Douglas Hutton. This chap was older than the rest and so it might make sense for him to try to work out his thirty years' service to obtain a full police pension. Hutton was currently employed in Mill Street HQ as one of the back-room boys whose job it was to supply information to a team on an active case. Not a bad job at all and still well paid. Hutton, Solly noted, was a widower with no family, the post-war bungalow owned outright. So, he mused, no need to worry overmuch about money. Why had that come to mind? Was he imagining that one of those officers had actually shopped their fellow officers? Solly frowned. It was hard to believe, though Lorimer felt that it was someone from within the force who had wrecked three careers. Now he was concerned about a possible involvement with that corpse found high on the hills above Glenburn. Still, the psychologist had to take every factor into account and money, he knew, often played an important part in motivating a human being to carry out the ultimate crime.

On his desk, held open with a paperweight, was an A to Z of Glasgow and its surrounding areas. He glanced at the large green spaces that showed Glennifer Braes Country Park. Hillcrest Avenue was at right angles to a zigzag white line against the green, the road that must have taken that body to the lonely gully where it had been found. Did DS Hazel Cochrane, the third undercover officer to have her career ruined, gaze up at those hills and wonder about the body that had been discovered? It was just a matter of time until the press got hold of this titbit of news. Despite their best intentions, someone would blab, probably one of the family members of those wee lads or, more likely, the boys themselves, unable to keep from boasting about it in the playground.

And what, he wondered, was DS Cochrane doing right now? Her old job had been torn from her and she was, like her colleague, desk-bound at Mill Street for the foreseeable future. Unlike Hutton, Hazel Cochrane was young, single and, if her photo was anything to go by, a very attractive woman. Would she stay in the force? Lorimer hadn't thought it likely, Solly reminded himself. And so, would she be eager to try and find out who had shopped them all before she moved on to a completely new career elsewhere?

Solly closed his eyes, thinking about these strangers whose photographs lay side by side on his desk; strangers who were unaware that he was trying to make sense of what had happened to them, their profession as officers of the law now in shreds.

But there was another thought that refused to leave him: what if one of them had taken that very law into their own hands?

CHAPTER TWELVE

If Sylvie Maxwell noticed the man standing opposite her office building, she gave no sign of having seen him. It was a wet day, most pedestrians sheltering beneath umbrellas tilted against a persistent downpour or, like Sylvie, cocooned in a padded raincoat, its hood pulled down across her brow.

Daniel stood in the doorway opposite garnering a few curious stares from the office staff as they arrived for work. He paid them little apparent heed, years of asserting his authority by his mere presence paying off despite the fact that now he was a stranger in a strange land. Had anyone stopped to take a long hard look at the black man standing there just inside the portico they might have noticed how still he was, intent on gazing out at the street ahead, his eyes fixed on something only he could see. In fact, Daniel Kohi was watching the stairs that led up to the offices he had already visited, examining each and every person whose steps took them into that particular building.

Nine o'clock came and went but still he stood there,

gazing now at the short flight of stairs and wondering why the person he sought had failed to arrive. There was, he reasoned, a fairly simple explanation: the man he had seen twice (once with a bloody knife clutched in his fist) might be in the habit of entering the building from the basement door at the rear of the building. An earlier stroll through the cobbled lane had given him time to see the spaces between the offices that were reserved for a few parked cars. Senior staff members, Daniel had surmised. So now he was ready to walk quietly back, retracing his steps through that lane and making a note of whatever vehicles might be there. He glanced at his watch, realising that he had been standing on this spot for over an hour. Unlike the offices across the road, there was no reception desk on this level, only a trio of lifts that took passengers upwards to their different places of work plus a corridor that snaked around to a door at the rear, giving access to a restaurant-cum-tearoom on two levels that did not open till later in the morning.

Clutching his coat collar closely around his neck, Daniel slipped quietly down the steps to the pavement and headed to the corner of the street. It was surprisingly busy at this time of day, he thought, as folk bustled alongside him, waiting for the green light to cross at this junction. Christmas shoppers, he guessed, from the large bags that were being carried and the chatter of a nearby pair of women sharing a brolly, their faces animated. He'd spotted poinsettias in the windows of various shops, an instant reminder of the scarlet hedgerows back home, the so-called Christmas plants growing prolifically. He closed his eyes seeing poinsettias, flame

80

lilies, colourful flowers that conjured up an image of what home had been like . . .

The insistent beep of the crossing signal made Daniel blink then move swiftly, the moment past. Then he was walking downhill a little, turning sharply into the darkened lane, away from the Christmas lights swinging high above the city street, their bright colours reflected like shards of stained glass on the puddles.

He passed a bay where cars were cordoned off by chains, a padlock swinging heavily to one side. Looking up, he saw an enamelled sign on the wall indicating that this was not for the occupants of the office he had visited but the one next door. Daniel stopped when he reached the middle bay, his eyes picking out a similar sign. Yes, as he had suspected, this was the designated parking area for senior staff cars allotted to Thomas Bryson. These premises had belonged to that particular firm for some time, Daniel reckoned, staring at the white sign with its dark blue writing, nail holes on each corner rusted over the years. Then his eyes fell on the cars parked there: three side by side facing the wall and one turned side on. It would be difficult, he thought, to access this area with those large vehicles, little space for a turning circle. Last in, first out, he realised, his gaze now on the large black 4×4 that was taking up the bulk of this car park.

It was an easy enough job to slip under the chain and look at the other cars in turn: the silver Mercedes in the far corner next to a white rain-spattered Audi and a low-slung grey Jaguar. Daniel drew a small notepad from his inside pocket and jotted down each registration number, though in truth he could probably have remembered every one.

As the chain rattled across his back when he stooped to bend under it, Daniel became aware of another noise above the persistent hum of nearby traffic. The metal door, just feet away, was beginning to open, a scraping sound that grated on his ears.

In moments he was out of the lane and back in Hope Street, collar turned up to hide his face.

Daniel stood still, leaning against the corner of the wall, peering through the gloom as a man wearing a high-vis yellow jacket emerged from the basement, pushing a dustbin into the lane. It was only a janitor, he saw, his heartbeat slowing down to normal once more. An older man, his grey hair cropped short as he bent down to pick up a piece of litter that had escaped from the big industrial bin. Daniel heard the lid closing then the man disappeared inside, the metal door clanging shut behind him.

What now? A huge sigh escaped him as he walked uphill, his steps taking him towards a square of gardens he'd discovered on a previous recce. It was a little oasis within the bustling city, its trees leafless yet alive with birds chattering their own peculiar messages. Daniel stood there, transfixed, as they fluttered from branch to branch, bright red patches beneath their wings. He had no idea what these were, brown birds that might be migrants like himself, seeking sanctuary in this northern city.

There was no possibility of work, he'd been told. Nothing until he had been resident for much longer, but of course there were opportunities to volunteer, one young woman at the Home Office had told him brightly, as though she were doing him a great favour.

'You were a police officer in Zimbabwe?' she'd asked, casting a brief glance at the file in front of her.

'A detective,' Daniel had replied, not adding that he had been Inspector Daniel Kohi, firstly to the people of his township, then to the citizens of Harare where his reputation for honesty had grown in direct proportion to the corruption of too many of his fellow officers.

The question lingered in his mind now, not just what to do about the man he had seen, and the bloody weapon clutched in his hand, but also how to fill his days in this cold, dark place.

He looked up, watching the flock of redwings sweep skywards as if in response to some unheard signal. Perhaps that was what he needed, Daniel thought: the fellowship of men like himself, outcasts from places once called home. There were places in Glasgow where he might find them . . .

His attention was drawn away from the garden and the empty trees as two uniformed police officers passed him by, a woman and a young man. They looked his way and smiled as Daniel caught their gaze and he nodded, a wave of nostalgia sweeping over him for the times when officers had acknowledged Inspector Kohi, saluting him as they passed by.

No, he had no desire to seek out those drifters from other lands, Daniel decided. If he were to volunteer in any capacity, surely there was something he could usefully do within the police force here?

CHAPTER THIRTEEN

Lorimer stepped out of the car and stood for a moment, distracted by the sudden movement. A flock of redwings, he decided with a smile, his birdwatcher's keen eye appreciating their flight towards the treetops in Bellahouston Park, probably arrivals from Iceland, searching for food as they travelled further south. They would stop and strip berry bushes and trees, gorging themselves as the colder months set in. There were three pairs resident in his own garden, an annual occurrence that he and Maggie waited for each winter. They roosted within the branches of an ancient holly, emerging to peck at the ripe red berries, the tell-tale yellow eye stripe and red patch underneath their wings distinguishing them from other passerines.

His earlier visit to Gartcosh, the Scottish Crime Campus, had not been as successful as he had hoped. Neither of the top brass had taken his concerns about the residences of those undercover officers seriously. Had Solly? he wondered. Today there was a chance that he might be sent the post-mortem results from that burned body, the tests due back from the lab. Any residual tissue could be used to find DNA, something the team was anxious to learn. If the dead man's DNA was on a database and they could put a name to him, then perhaps this case might move forwards.

It had taken more than one person to put that body in the hidden gully, for sure. But how many had carried it there and where had they started out on their grim journey? The scene of crime officers had taken tyre prints and other samples from the surrounding area but had anything transpired from these that might tell part of the story?

Smiles greeted him as he opened the door to the boardroom and he sensed an electric tension in the air: something had come up.

DCI Niall Cameron stood up and walked towards him as Lorimer shuffled off his coat and tossed it onto a chair by the window.

'We have a result from the PM,' Cameron said, his tone further emphasising the general atmosphere of anticipation in the room. He handed his boss a piece of paper and watched as Lorimer read the report.

'Well, this is a turn-up and no mistake,' he remarked, his eyebrows raised as he glanced over the top of the report. If his face registered shock at the name on the paper, he was quick to hide it.

'No enquiries about him being a misper,' DS Molly Newton put in. 'Ex-wife lives down south and there were no kids, so ... ' She shrugged.

'Neighbours? Colleagues?' Lorimer shook his head as if in pity of the situation. It wasn't the first time in his years as a police officer that he had come across a dead man (or, more rarely, a woman) whose body had lain unidentified in the city's mortuary unbeknown to their family members. Sometimes it happened because that person had been estranged from them or had been a bit of a loner, but no matter the reason he always felt a wave of sadness: unloved and unmourned, that made even more of a poignant end to someone's life. 'What do we know so far?' He took a seat at the end of the oval table. He had to pretend that he had no prior knowledge of this victim, act as if this was news.

'Apart from what is in the PM report and his police record, we've found that Derek Carter was a junior partner in a legal firm in the city,' Cameron replied. 'There's more information here,' he added, turning his laptop towards Lorimer so that he could read what was on the screen.

In the hours he'd been in Gartcosh Lorimer saw that the team had uncovered a fair bit about the late Mr Carter. They now knew that he'd been thirty-nine, divorced from his wife, Amanda, a decade ago, he had continued to live in the family home in Ralston, a quiet, respectable suburb off Glasgow Road on the edge of Paisley, close to a well-known golf club. He had only recently joined Thomas Bryson, his previous work having been with another established firm of solicitors whose modern offices dominated the Glasgow skyline, their circular windows overlooking the river and beyond.

Lorimer swallowed hard. Thomas Bryson! Sylvie Maxwell had been there for several months now but only her most recent report had mentioned the name of Derek Carter. Few were aware of the woman's current task, to infiltrate the lawyers' office where intelligence had led them in the search for money being secretly passed from sources overseas and the whereabouts of a terrorist cell in the city.

'Nobody in Bryson's thought to call us when he didn't turn up for work?' he asked, keeping his voice as neutral as possible. None of his team must suspect that he already had a dossier on Carter, but for very different reasons.

Molly shook her head. 'I spoke with their HR woman this morning,' she told him. 'Seems he had been on a fortnight's leave, so they had no reason to be anxious about him.'

Lorimer nodded. Something had happened here, a story where he could only read the ending, but that snippet of information made him wonder where the story had actually begun. Had Carter, an ex-con, been involved in some shady dealings, taking time off from work to carry them out? And, strangest of all, why hadn't their undercover officer, Sylvie Maxwell, known about this?

'We need to get on to his colleagues as soon as possible,' he decided. 'See what he'd been working on, what tale he'd told them about where he was going to spend this leave.' *But do it with kid gloves on*, he thought, turning to the tall blonde woman who herself had once been an undercover police officer. She knew what the score was. 'Molly, see me after this meeting,' he said, then turned back to DCI Cameron who was scrolling down to show what else had been learned about the man whose body had been found up on those lonely moors.

'Carter was done for dangerous driving,' Molly told him as they sat together in Lorimer's office. 'Did his time and sacrificed his driver's licence for a year after he came out. Not all he seems to have lost,' she added.

Lorimer raised his eyebrows questioningly.

'His wife left him,' Molly said drily. 'Here's the draft of the divorce settlement.' She handed him a sheet of paper.

'Hmm, she certainly got what she asked for,' Lorimer remarked, speed reading the document. 'He was left with the house but also with a hefty mortgage, given that she took her share in cash.'

'Yep.' Molly gave no indication of what she thought about that. Who knew what sort of relationship had existed prior to the night Derek Carter had taken away the lives of two people through his reckless drink-driving?

'I want to tell you something, but it goes no further than this office, Molly, okay?' Lorimer shot her a sharp look. 'There's an undercover officer in Bryson's,' he said slowly. 'Goes by the current name of Sylvie Maxwell. Do you know her?' He slipped a hand into his jacket pocket and produced a colour photograph.

Molly gave a smile as she caught sight of the woman's image then nodded. 'I think I know who you mean. She worked on the Clarkson case,' she replied. 'Back in 2015, I think it was. Long hours of sitting in a car watching a row of windows over in Bellshill. I took over when she went on furlough. We never actually met. I'm guessing she's changed a bit since then.' Molly took the photo and examined it more closely.

Happily, so have you, Lorimer thought to himself, remembering the case that had almost finished the woman's career.

'I think, DS Newton, it's time we sent you out to do a bit of undercover work once again.'

*

It was a ten-minute journey from the MIT in Helen Street, a straight run along Paisley Road West, past the dark red Lourdes Secondary School and the huddle of four-in-a block homes, then rows of shops before Lorimer slowed down at the corner of Newtyle Road where Derek Carter had lived. He stopped opposite the semi-detached house, wondering just when the man had last been here and if the forensics team might find anything inside that would help to determine what had happened to its last resident. There was a garage at the far end of the driveway. Would they find Carter's car inside? He held that thought as he and DS Newton crossed the road and strolled past the entrance to the house. A paved driveway with gravel on either side led him to the garage. At his height of six feet four, Lorimer had little need to do more than peer into the cobweb-covered garage window.

'Yep, I can see a vehicle inside,' he told her. 'Blue saloon, possibly a Honda from its shape though it's hard to see it clearly from this angle.'

Stepping away, they continued around to the back of the house that was sheltered on two sides by a tall hedge of leylandii, a wooden fence dividing the property from its adjoining twin. A square of grass and a few shrubs sufficed for a back garden, a bare-branched maple tree swaying in the corner nearest to the fence, its scattered leaves blown across the lawn like scarlet confetti. Three dustbins stood side by side against the wall of the house next to a row of steps that led to a glazed back door. Lorimer and Newton raised their lids with gloved hands, knowing that any contents would be thoroughly examined by the members of the forensic team in due course.

It was a still, windless day now and the only sound was the distant thrum of traffic from nearby Glasgow Road. Lorimer looked at the green sward that rose upwards beyond the garden wall; Carter had been lucky to live here in this peaceful enclave so close to the city. But perhaps the very quietness of his home had been a contributing factor for his killers. They might know these things soon enough, he realised, hearing a van stop at the end of the driveway. The forensic team had arrived and now it was up to them to find evidence of Derek Carter's final hours here.

Or, Lorimer thought, anything that might tie him to the illegal entry of several terrorists whose presence in Glasgow was a threat not just to the city, but to the entire country. Someone had wanted Carter out of the way just at the time when enquiries were being made about the connection of Bryson's to these people. But whose side had he been on? And, was there something Sylvie Maxwell wasn't telling them?

It was harder than he had thought, leaving the building by that basement door, the memory of so much blood making him pause for a moment. *It was necessary*, these were the words he had been told and certainly it had been too dangerous to let Carter live. Drawing on his calfskin gloves, he pulled open the heavy door and emerged into the dark lane. One flick of his key fob and the car responded, winking its lights as if to greet him. He would be home soon enough, and she would be waiting for him, just as she had promised. A sigh escaped him as he turned out of the parking space and joined the traffic, just one more vehicle heading out of the city.

There were things he needed to tell her, worries that had begun to creep into his mind that only she could solve. *Once it is over, we will be together for good* – wasn't that what she had told him? The thought of their future should be enough to blot out what had happened back in that dingy basement. Listening to her soothing voice had persuaded him before and he knew that it would do so again.

So, why was it that he felt such a sinking feeling in the pit of his stomach?

CHAPTER FOURTEEN

Sylvie Maxwell sat in a cubicle within the ladies' toilets, mobile phone clutched in her hand.

Derek Carter was dead.

She blinked again as she read the message from Lorimer. *Identity confirmed*, it said. *Forensics at his home now. Be in touch later.*

The woman heaved a long shuddering sigh. Nobody had a right to take away the life of an innocent man. *But*, a small, insistent voice asked, *was he really so innocent after all?*

Sylvie had spent months trying to identify any of the staff here who might have been involved with the perceived terrorist threat. Intelligence had suggested that somewhere in this office there was evidence of money being filtered from an unknown source directly to a terrorist cell in Glasgow. It was partly through scrutinising the audits in their books and partly by listening carefully to anything that was being said, especially behind the closed doors of the partners' offices, that she hoped to gain information. She had a knack for passing by and stopping to fix her hair or bending down to tie an errant shoelace, pausing just long enough to catch a word or two any time there appeared to be some sort of crisis that was being discussed in private. So far she had gleaned snippets of conversations, little pieces of a jigsaw that were still to be put together.

She slipped her phone back into the inside pocket of her Radley bag and flushed the toilet. Then, as she washed her hands, the undercover police officer looked at her reflection in the mirror. What did she see? Tired eyes, certainly, the harsh overhead strip lighting emphasising lines that no amount of concealer would hide.

Derek was dead. And, of course, not so innocent or his name would not have appeared on a police database, something of which Sylvie had been quite aware. The junior partner had been her way into the firm in the first place, notification of his past misdeeds flagged up on their system. A student prank, some might have called that initial criminal act of defacing a billboard poster. However, the military had not taken it lightly, their recruitment campaign sullied by Carter's attempt at protest. *Join the Army and Become a Man* was a fair enough slogan; however, Glaswegians in the locality of Strathclyde students' union would probably remember it for the insertion of the renegade adjective *dead*.

Carter had been reprimanded in court and, though his DNA had been taken off the database in due course, a further brush with the law had meant that it had been retained once more. The accident that had resulted in the deaths of an elderly man and woman was something Sylvie knew that Carter had deeply regretted and his time in custody and subsequent divorce had coloured his outlook on life. If Sylvie had not known more about the background to the car crash, she might have suspected a long-held desire for revenge on the part of the old couple's family. But there had been nothing like that. These were good Christian folk whose very forgiveness of that awful accident had reduced Derek Carter to seeking out ways of apparently making amends for that terrible night. Stints at a food bank, helping in refugee centres, the latter eventually bringing him to the attention of the Counter Terrorism department at Gartcosh.

Nothing will ever bring them back. She'd read Carter's words in an archive copy of the *Gazette*. *And I will endeavour to seek ways to make up for what I did.*

And it looked as though he had. Until he'd joined Thomas Bryson. That, and Carter's involvement with refugees, was why the intelligence branch of Police Scotland was currently taking an interest, sending Sylvie Maxwell to dig deeper, to see if Bryson's was involved in helping to fund the trafficking of illegal immigrants of a type that might prove a danger to the UK.

Why would an outwardly respectable firm like that take on a solicitor who had done time? Not everyone was so forgiving nowadays, and law firms were especially old-fashioned about employing anyone who had even a whiff of the dark side about them lest they be tainted by association. Some of them were corrupt however much they managed to hide it, and it was clear that whoever was behind this steady entry of foreign agitators had to have a respectable front like a law firm to hide behind. And now the question was: had Derek Carter been a victim of that very organisation?

She'd liked him, perhaps a little too much on some occasions, that much Sylvie would admit to herself, though she was under no illusions that criminals could be as charming as those men and women whose intentions were as pure as the driven snow. And now he was dead, murdered by persons unknown, his body burned to a crisp and left out on that lonely hillside. A shuddering sob issued from her and Sylvie reached for a tissue to blow her nose, hoping that she would not appear in any way touched by this news. A deep breath and a toss of her head, then, straightening her back, she marched purposefully back to the office to resume her work, thankful that the years of dissembling had helped to create this ability to put a mask over her real feelings.

For a moment she paused to stare out of the window, casting a glance down at the street below where folk were scurrying against the rain. Then she blinked as one particular figure caught her eye. A man dressed in black, his face turned upwards. She drew back instinctively then moved towards the window again. Surely he was not staring up at her? For a moment it was as if their eyes met then he bent his head and began to walk uphill. Sylvie craned her neck, watching till he was out of sight.

Who was he? she wondered, shivering slightly. Then, giving herself a mental shake, she sat back at her desk. It was the shock of hearing about Derek, that was all. She'd been temporarily taken away from the persona that she assumed each day in these offices, allowing herself a moment of genuine emotion. The man was probably staring up at the building, taking an interest in Glasgow's architecture, something many visitors to the city enjoyed. But, as Sylvie

Maxwell resumed her daily tasks, the image of him, hands thrust deep into his coat pockets, continued to haunt her.

Daniel had seen a tiny pale face at one of the windows, staring down at him. It would not do to make himself quite so visible, he thought, moving briskly uphill and heading once more for the sanctuary of Blythswood Square.

He stood at the gate watching the different birds on the bare branches of trees, his thoughts still on that office block and the face at the window.

'Waxwings. No' bad, eh?'

Daniel turned to see a man wearing a dark uniform under a yellow jerkin, his peaked cap banded in blue reminding him of the police officers he'd sighted in the city.

'Pardon?'

'Waxwings. Over there.' He pointed. 'Did you not see them? Here, haud a wee look with them,' the man replied, fishing in a bag slung over his shoulder and producing a set of field glasses. 'High definition, these are. Go on, you'll see every wee detail, so you will.'

Daniel put the binoculars to his eyes and swivelled around until he could make out the tree with the twittering birds his companion had indicated.

Sure enough, there they were, small bright birds with the tell-tale blob of red that gave them their name.

'Thank you,' Daniel said politely, handing back the glasses. 'I don't know your British birds very much yet.'

'Not from round here, are you?' the man asked.

'Africa,' Daniel confirmed. 'Zimbabwe.'

'Over here for a holiday?' his companion queried.

Daniel shook his head, wondering how to reply. People here in Glasgow were friendly, he'd discovered, but sometimes they expected to share life stories and Daniel Kohi was not ready to do that. Not yet.

There was an awkward silence then, 'Sorry. The wife always says I'm a nosy so-and-so but, hey, there's no harm in having a chat, eh?'

'What is it you do?' Daniel asked, looking pointedly at the man's uniform.

'Traffic warden,' his new companion said proudly. 'When I was laid off from my last job a few years back I decided to do something completely different.'

'Oh.' Daniel did not quite know what to say so he looked around at the cars parked around the square. 'That isn't a job the police do, then?'

'Aye, there are traffic cops, right enough, but it's our job to spot any vehicles illegally parked. Cops have enough to do as it is,' he added.

This was his chance, Daniel thought. Tell this man about what he had seen, let him pass on the information. But still he hesitated, knowing the first words he uttered might bring him into contact with the very authorities that might cause trouble for him in the future.

'Used to meet a cop here. Birdwatcher, like myself,' the warden told him. 'The old HQ was just down that way.' He turned and indicated a street that sloped away from the square. 'Pitt Street. Used to see him strolling up some lunchtimes. Big tall guy.' His brow creased in a frown. 'What was his name again?' He shook his head. 'See my memory . . . ?' Then he clicked his fingers, looking at Daniel with a smile.

'Lorimer. That was it. Detective Chief Inspector Lorimer.' He grinned and looked back at the birds, evidently relishing a memory. 'We would tell each other about the different birds we'd seen,' he added, a faint smile of reminiscence on his lips.

Daniel said nothing, suddenly reluctant to divulge what he had seen to this man, a traffic warden, not an officer of the law as he'd first thought. The silence between them grew, as some silences do, uneasy and awkward when only one person is really contributing to a conversation.

'Well, better get on. Hope you enjoy your time here. Weather might be lousy but the Glesca folk are all right,' the warden chuckled, touching the edge of his cap in a friendly gesture then moving along past the railings of the gardens and looking carefully at each car windscreen.

Daniel continued to stare after him, wishing now that the man had stayed a bit longer. There were plenty of people around, some leaving a nearby hotel, a liveried footman helping with luggage, others walking briskly to a destination only they could know. Daniel stood still. He had nowhere to go, no purpose, unlike that traffic warden or those travellers.

The rays of the fine winter sun fell onto his skin, a mere trace of warmth, reminding Daniel of what he had lost. The encounter with that stranger only served to show him how alone he was in this city. And how desperately he longed to be with his own people, just like that flock of birds chattering in their tree.

CHAPTER FIFTEEN

'How do you feel about it?' Lorimer asked the woman beside him.

Sylvie blew across the surface of a full cup of tea that was clasped in her hands. For a few moments she was silent as though considering his question.

Then a sigh escaped her, and she drew a hand across her brow.

'Sad,' she said. 'He was a nice man despite everything that had happened in his past.' She looked up and met Lorimer's blue gaze. 'I thought he was trying to make a go of the job at Bryson's. But there were things . . . ' She shook her head as if annoyed by a passing thought. 'Things that I remember now. Things that make more sense now that he's dead.'

'Go on,' Lorimer encouraged.

'Well, he was always friendly, ready to share a joke, talked a lot about politics, but not in a serious way, more as if politicians were put on earth to be the butt of a comedian's humour. But sometimes . . . ' She tailed off again to take a sip of the hot tea. 'Sometimes he was more serious. I remember once he said that he was waiting for the right moment to quit his job and move on. I told him he was in a great office. Asked him what he would do if he left.'

Lorimer waited to hear what the woman told him next.

'He said he wanted away from Glasgow. Said that he would feel happier somewhere warm. I took that as a slight against our awful weather, but now that I think of it, Derek seemed a bit uptight when he told me that, not his usual flippant self.'

'The HR folk say he was on annual leave.'

'That's right, but nobody else seemed to know that and I have to say, Derek would have told me if he was going to be off on holiday. He was chatty like that. Liked to share things.' Sylvie shrugged. 'Us singletons can be a bit wearisome, I guess, when we start talking. No one at home to confide in,' she added, giving Lorimer a self-deprecating grin.

'How much did he know about you?'

'Nothing. Though he swallowed the cover story about Sylvie Maxwell all right.' She smiled, a sad sort of smile, and Lorimer could see how the strain of keeping up a façade might take its toll on officers like this detective sergeant.

'And you never saw him after his final day in the office?'

'No. Whatever happened to him then is as much a mystery to me as it is to the scene of crime folk.'

'Well, we are beginning to untangle a bit of that already,' Lorimer said. 'The pathologist is putting time of death not that long after he was last seen in the Glasgow office.'

Sylvie frowned. 'You don't think he was killed at home?'

'There are no signs of anything untoward out in the

Ralston house. However,' he paused for a moment, wondering just how much to reveal, 'some things don't add up. From what we've seen in Derek Carter's home, it looks as if he never actually returned there at all. In fact,' he looked straight into Sylvie's eyes, 'you might be one of the last people to have seen him alive.'

He heard the small intake of breath, saw her jaw tighten, but that was all. He shook his head and gave a brief smile. 'Don't worry, we aren't looking at you as a suspect.' Lorimer watched as the woman visibly relaxed. Perhaps this was the right time to divulge their latest findings, let her think over their implications.

'Carter lived alone and at first it looked as if there were no signs at all of another person having been in his home.'

She looked up at that, a tilt of her head showing renewed interest.

'Forensics made a thorough examination of the entire house and it wasn't till they reached the bathroom that they found it.'

'What?' she asked, leaning forward slightly.

'Sets of fingerprints high up behind the shower and a very small device that had been planted out of sight in a corner of the shower cabinet. They found three more elsewhere in the house. Someone had been keeping tabs on Carter, wouldn't you say?'

'Not one of mine,' Sylvie retorted immediately. 'I've never been in his house, anyway. We were just office buddies, no more, in case you wondered.'

Lorimer nodded his agreement. But the faint flush of pink on the woman's face gave the lie to her words. She'd liked him, perhaps stepped over a line and made Carter more than a friend. He would have known if there had been any instructions to plant a bug in Carter's home and he hadn't really suspected this woman of doing that, though it was interesting to see her reaction.

'The prints have not been identified,' he began, 'and we are now assuming that there was another agency keeping tabs on Carter.' He looked at her intently. 'Did he ever mention a female friend? Someone he was dating?'

Sylvie frowned as if she were thinking hard. 'Not that I can recall,' she said. 'And I would have put anything like that into my report. If he was seeing someone, then he kept it a secret.'

Why would he want to do that? Lorimer wondered.

'There were traces of a particular perfume in the bathroom,' he continued. 'The house doesn't have an en suite toilet so any visitors would use that.'

'What sort of perfume?' she asked.

'Forensics matched it with a very expensive brand,' he said. 'Baccarat Rouge 540, it's called.'

Sylvie raised her eyebrows. 'Someone has a lot of money or else a generous boyfriend.'

'That doesn't ring any bells with you?'

She shook her head. 'Don't know if I'd even be able to identify it,' she admitted. 'But I'll visit the perfume counter at John Lewis to get a whiff, so I'd know it again.'

Lorimer nodded. If the undercover officer caught a trace of it within the office, then perhaps that might lead them to their mystery female.

It didn't do for the woman to be seen fraternising with a

cop for too long, particularly one as well known as the head of the MIT, and the rendezvous for this meeting had been chosen well out of Glasgow in a small garden centre opposite a country church. A line of parked cars outside the adjoining hall and a sign stating CHRISTMAS FAYRE TODAY showed that for now, at least, they would not be disturbed. No doubt Santa and his elves were busy inside the old building, parishioners enjoying their festive snacks there rather than in the garden centre's café. There were few customers here on this cold dreich morning, two young mums with toddlers sharing coffee and cake and an elderly couple in the corner by the wall heater.

It would be a nice place to come in summertime, Lorimer reflected, glancing around at the shelves filled with craftwork for sale, the ubiquitous holly garlands and fairy lights making the walls glitter. The coffee was good, too, and if he'd been here at a different time, the soup of the day advertised on a chalkboard might have appealed. The staff had been friendly and welcoming but had not lingered overmuch by their customers' table. Opposite the car parking area outside was a large field where he'd spotted several alpaca and three miniature ponies grazing, wisps of hay scattered across the grass from an earlier feed. He looked across at the senior citizens, his mind wandering from the woman sitting opposite. Would he and Maggie come here in years to come, once they were both retired? The thought vanished as he picked up his coffee cup and gazed at the undercover detective.

'Nobody has given you any cause to worry?'

Sylvie glanced at him briefly then dropped her gaze.

That'll be a yes, then, he thought, reading her body language as easily as if she had actually spoken.

'One of the senior partners followed me into the city centre,' she admitted. 'I lost him in Princes Square, but I am certain he was trying to see where I would go, what I was doing.' She bit her lip and raised her teacup so that it hid part of her face.

Lorimer suppressed a sigh. They needed this woman there right now to see what was going on in that firm. Intelligence had led them to believe that someone in Bryson's had been linked to people trafficking on a large scale and, short of a raid on their premises, there was nothing more they could do.

'Who is he?'

'Senior partner. Name of Burns. Vincent Burns. I don't like him much, though to be honest I've found nothing on him. Incidentally, he and Derek didn't always seem to get on very well. Heard them arguing once but couldn't find out what that was about. Still, Burns appears to be clean as a whistle. Member of the Western Club. Lives out in Newton Mearns. Golfs at weekends.' She shrugged. 'I haven't had any problems with him in the office. He's not a sex pest like some men I've encountered on other jobs so . . .'

'So, you think he's suspicious about you?'

'And that makes him a person of interest.' Sylvie looked him straight in the eye, her lips widening in what might pass for a smile.

Lorimer nodded. 'It's always a risk staying on when there's the slightest chance your cover could be blown but leaving abruptly would only confirm anything this guy suspects about you. No,' he took a sip of his coffee, 'stay put meantime but begin to throw out the occasional hint that you might be going away over Christmas. Skiing, perhaps.'

'I do ski, as it happens,' Sylvie mused. 'What did you have in mind? A sudden accident off-piste?'

'It would do as a story if we need to pull you out,' Lorimer agreed. 'Right, if that's everything you can think of, we'd better make tracks. I bet this place will get pretty crowded after the Christmas fayre finishes.' He grinned, glancing up at the wall clock where the time was ten minutes before noon. 'And I'm sure you have things to do on a Saturday.'

Vincent Burns stepped back, driver in hand, as he watched the golf ball rise into the air, a satisfied smile on his face. It was a good shot and he might make the green in three, stealing a birdie to give himself a decent lead over his opponent. He leaned on the golf club, staring at the other man who was lining up his own shot. Gerry was a keen golfer, like himself, a friend from way back whose determination to win was only equalled by Vincent's own. Being members out here in the Renfrewshire countryside gave them the opportunity to catch up at weekends, conversation only turning to business once they had shaken hands on the eighteenth green and headed back to the clubhouse.

As Gerry shuffled his feet and began to line up at the tee, Vincent looked at the view across the River Clyde. The hills over on the far shore were a bit misty and rain would no doubt be falling by the time they turned to leave. The morning had begun cold and damp, but without a wind, perfect golfing conditions for this time of year. It had been a morning like this when he had been instructed to set out for the Braes, a recce to see just where to dump an unwanted burden. It had been the perfect spot, or so they'd thought, early nightfall hiding that task some hours after the deed had been done.

Vincent Burns shivered suddenly. *A goose went over my grave.* The phrase came to him and he tried to dismiss it with a frown. The ground up there had sloped away to a grave-like hollow as if it had been waiting for a body to enfold. Nobody would ever find it, he'd told Gerry, believing his own words even as he'd uttered them. His guys would be sure to make a decent job of burning the corpse, leaving not a trace to identify their victim, he'd boasted. And that was what the men had told him, money changing hands between them under the cover of darkness.

'Good shot,' he called out as the other man's ball described an arc against a sky that was as pale as a bloodless corpse. They would walk in silence, find their golf balls and con-centrate on their next shot. Was Gerry's mind full of what was not being said, Vincent wondered, or was he focusing on which iron to use to make the sixteenth green? He glanced at the man by his side; he was a couple of inches shorter than Vincent, but with a stockiness to him that suggested phys-ical strength. Gerry O'Neill had the sort of stamina to walk all day and never tire. And, looking at the gloved fist that clutched the handle of his golf cart, Vincent was reminded of what other things it had held, back in the day, things that had wreaked violence on human flesh.

One dead man had been a hard enough thing to stomach, Vincent realised, but the thought of hundreds of bodies strewn on the ground was more than he could take. He'd

106

already tried to explain this to the woman whom he loved to distraction, but she had simply told him to talk to Gerry.

He opened his mouth to say something but closed it when he saw the man's face already turned away to concentrate on the next shot.

As they split to walk to the places where the small white balls lay, Vincent suddenly knew that Gerry O'Neill was going to win this match. And that, unless he chose his words very carefully, the conversation they would have afterwards might lose him a lot more than a golf partner.

CHAPTER SIXTEEN

He'd been lucky to find a parking space in the Buchanan Galleries, Lorimer thought as he walked through the overpass above the railway station. Beyond the windows he could see snaking lines of metal rails glinting in a late afternoon sun, the city beyond mere outlines of buildings under a haze of cloud. It would be a good opportunity to sample that perfume for himself, he had decided after leaving the undercover officer back at the café. At this time of year there was nothing suspicious about a man buying perfume for his wife in the big department store. He'd have a sniff of that Baccarat Rouge, make a show of debating over different scents, then buy Maggie's favourite Chanel Number 5.

There was a small crowd around the perfume counters, and it took him almost a quarter of an hour to test the samples before making his eventual purchase. Happily, the girl at the Baccarat counter had sprayed a sample onto a piece of card which now nestled inside a folded handkerchief in his coat pocket. Something for him to think about, should he ever come across that scent again.

He was back in the Lexus and heading through the town at a snail's pace, Christmas traffic slowing everything down, when Lorimer received the call. He flicked the button that gave him hands free access to his mobile.

'Lorimer.'

'We've just had the report from Robinson, the tyre prints expert,' Niall Cameron told him. 'It's as we expected. Most likely a van, given the tread width. Hard to say what type but if we ever find it, there are some particular aspects of the tread that would create a match. Robinson says it's likely to be a transit van of some sort. Probably the kind you can hire from Arnold Clark any day of the week.' Cameron sighed.

'Okay, thanks, Niall. That's another tiny bit of forensics to add to what we have. Nothing ever goes to waste,' he said encouragingly.

Lorimer rang off and concentrated on the flow of traffic as the lights ahead changed to green. This had been a difficult case from the start, especially given his own parallel inquiry into the threat of a terrorist attack. He looked out of the window as the car turned into St Vincent Street, crowds of Christmas shoppers thronging the city, the air of anticipation almost palpable. An attack here at Christmas was unthinkable; the casualties involved possibly in their hundreds if the intelligence from MI6 was correct.

For a moment Lorimer thought of a case in Glasgow that had been his previous contact with Special Branch. A man calling himself Drummond had been in the city working with them to prevent an equally horrific incident at the opening of the Commonwealth Games. He'd taken Lorimer aside afterwards, asking if he would consider giving up his job with Police Scotland and joining the spooks at MI6. It hadn't taken much thought, of course, Lorimer content to be in Scotland as a senior detective, but now he wondered what life would have been like had he switched to that side of public service. He shook his head, his thoughts returning to the here and now.

Some woman was behind it all, they'd been advised by the security services. But whoever that was remained a mystery. Was it the same person who had planted the listening devices in Derek Carter's home? Had the dead man been having an affair with her? Or had she slipped into his house unseen, leaving only that trace of expensive perfume behind?

It was dark by the time he reached home, lights from nearby gardens a welcome sight. Hidden in the boot of his car were several packages, wrapped beautifully by the staff at John Lewis, hidden under a tartan travelling rug till he took them out on Christmas Eve. Lorimer whistled as he locked the Lexus and stepped towards his front door. He was a lucky man, he told himself, putting his key into the lock. Behind that door Maggie would be waiting, his home bathed in warmth and light, a meal prepared for them to enjoy.

'Hi,' he called out and closed the door behind him, shutting out the darkening night and every thought of the terrors that threatened the safety of his fellow citizens.

When the lights went out, Daniel clutched the arms of the chair, blinking into the sudden darkness. It took a little effort to stand up and grope his way across the room to the window, carefully planting his feet on the worn carpet. His fingers reached out and grasped the wooden sill. There before him lay the city, shimmering in the darkness of an early winter's night. Down below, at street level, all was shrouded in gloom, not a single lamp illuminating this particular area.

A power cut, he realised. These things happened, of course, and he had experienced it often enough in his own home back in Zimbabwe.

The sound of his front door being rapped on made Daniel look up, a frown creasing his brow. An unexpected visitor was an unwelcome guest in his book and his hands were bunched into fists as he stumbled along the hallway, trying not to bump into things. He fumbled for his mobile and switched it on, aiming the thin pencil of torchlight straight ahead.

One look through the spyhole changed Daniel's expression at once.

'Netta, come in,' he said, opening the door wide, admitting his elderly neighbour. He glanced down at her, the light in his hand showing carpet slippers worn at the heels, white cotton socks covering swollen ankles.

The woman struggled in, bearing a large cooking pot in both hands.

'Seize a haud o' this, son,' she panted, and Daniel eased the handle from her grasp. It was, indeed, very heavy.

'What . . . ?'

'S'ma Christmas pudding,' she declared with a broad grin, giving Daniel a small push. 'Gonnae pit it oan yer hob? Ah ken ye've goat a gas wan. Ah'm a' electric, so ah am, an' it needs tae steam fur anither hour.'

Daniel looked at her, frowning. What on earth was she talking about?

'Go on, son, it's jist another hour. Ah'll pay ye back when ah get ma pension the morra.'

Daniel hefted the pot and carried it through the darkened hallway and into the kitchen, beginning to understand the drift of her request. She wanted him to cook whatever was in this pan for an hour, yes?

His hand found the box of matches exactly where he had left them and breathed a sigh of relief as the spurt of flame illuminated the kitchen for a moment. It was easy enough then to light the gas and place the cooking pot on top, and Daniel sensed Netta at his elbow watching him with her hawk-like gaze as though this were a matter of considerable importance.

'Takes me weeks tae save up fur a' thae ingredients,' she told him, in confidential tones. 'Widnae like tae have the hail thing ruined at this stage, eh?'

'A Christmas pudding?'

'Aye.' Netta nodded. 'Ye no' dae Christmas where ye come frae, son?'

Daniel began to smile. 'We celebrated Christmas every year, yes, but we didn't cook it in a pot,' he explained, a quizzical expression on his face.

The older woman gave a hoot of laughter. 'It's a pudding,' she said. 'Fur the big day, get it? Ye huv tae steam it oan the actual day itself, like, but it needs tae cook fur hours noo then be pit away again. See, ah'm awfie late this year.

Shoulda had it in the closet weeks ago. But . . . ' She gave a shrug by way of explanation, leaving Daniel no wiser but suspecting that the expense of cooking a huge pudding was a bit beyond his neighbour's means. Netta was leaning against the wall of his small kitchen, arms clutched around her cardigan as though to preserve some little warmth. The old lady was cold, he realised, and the electricity had cut out, facts that suddenly disturbed him.

'Would you like some tea?' he asked. 'I can boil water in a pot . . . ?'

'Thanks, son, appreciate it,' she murmured, giving him a shy glance of gratitude. The woman's face looked older tonight, lines Daniel had not yet noticed etched heavily on the skin around her eyes and mouth; a trick of the peculiar blue light coming from the gas burner, perhaps? It was the sort of detail that Daniel Kohi noticed, a small yet significant thing to be stored away for future use. He looked at her more closely, trying to catch her eye, but Netta seemed mesmerised by the blue flames and did not return his gaze. Why, he wondered, would his neighbour go to the expense of undertaking this apparently massive cooking project when she clearly did not have the means to do it? Lifting the lid of the pot a little showed him a large ceramic bowl covered with white cloth and secured with string. The water it stood in was beginning to bubble and Daniel turned to see Netta following his glance.

'Dinna let it bile oot,' she advised, stretching her hand to adjust the gas knob so that the boiling water became a mere simmer.

'Okay.' Daniel smiled and lifted a small pan, filled it half

113

full with water then set it on a back burner. 'I also have some instant coffee.' He nodded towards a jar on his countertop, a precious farewell gift he'd been given by his friends down in England.

'Ooh, get you, son,' Netta teased. 'Na, jist tea if ye dinna mind. That'll be grand. Right cairry oan this power cut, in't it? Last wan wis five oors. Day afore ye moved in,' she snorted.

Soon they were seated in his living room like two ghosts peering through the darkness, Netta's gnarled hands clasped around her mug of tea.

A sudden noise made them both turn in the direction of the front door.

'What's that?' Daniel stood up, hearing voices and thumping coming from out in the corridor.

'Oh, my goad, it's them! Look, son. I need tae go.' The old woman thrust her cup into Daniel's hands. He caught a glimpse of her face as she sped past him, alarmed to see an expression of fear.

'What's happening?' He followed her, but she was out of the door before him and then he heard the raised voices once again, some foul language being directed at the old lady then a bang as his neighbour's door was slammed. Daniel stood at his own door, anxious for the old woman, uncertain what to do. She had been in a hurry to meet these people, whoever they were, though clearly upset at their arrival. It was a mystery and one he needed to solve.

In minutes Netta's door opened again and two men bundled out.

'See ye next week, auld yin!' one of them called as they turned away and set off along the passageway towards the stairs, unaware of Daniel standing watching them in the pitch dark. He listened to the sound of their voices and the clang of the lift, then there was silence in the building once more.

Daniel took the few steps that separated his flat from Netta's and knocked on her door.

'Whit're ye wantin noo . . . Oh, it's you, son!' The woman's belligerent tone changed abruptly as he looked down at her.

'You haven't finished your tea, Netta. Come back in, won't you?'

They sat in silence in the darkened room, the visitation from these men lingering like a bad smell.

'Are you all right, Netta? And who were those people?'

'Ach, it's jist the loan men. Noisy pair, so they are. Ah forgoat they were comin' the night what wi' this power cut.'

'Loan men?'

'Aye, gombeen men, ma mammy used tae call them, but then she wis Irish.'

Daniel looked at her, mystified yet again by some of her words. But he was quick enough to realise what she was trying to tell him.

'You are not in thrall to a loan shark, are you, Netta?'

He sensed rather than saw that shrug of the shoulders as she remained silent.

'You did not accept any money from me for that very good coat,' Daniel began, 'and yet you are making what seems to be a very expensive sort of pudding.' He frowned, hoping that he did not sound as if he were interrogating the old lady. 'May I ask why that has happened, Netta?' he continued gently.

The old lady looked down at her tea and he was close enough to see her eyes filling with tears. 'It's a long story,' she said, lip trembling.

'I have plenty of time to listen,' Daniel told her, 'and it will take an hour to complete the cooking of your Christmas pudding,' he pointed out with an encouraging smile.

'It's mebbe different where you come frae,' Netta began. 'But ower here, ye dinna argue when the man tells ye tae pay up or else.'

'What man?' Daniel frowned. 'There were two here just now.'

'Naw, naw, they're jist his boys. The wans that collect fur him. The man wi' the book doesnae come aroon,' Netta said. 'See, every year it's the same carry oan. Ye get a wee loan frae the man tae buy presents fur the weans then it gets so ye cannae make ends meet ...' She gave that shrug again as though to say *that is what life is like and what can anybody do about it?*

'You borrowed money?'

'Aye, that's no' a crime.' Netta bristled suddenly.

Daniel bit back a response. In his old life he had handled similar cases of loan sharking, men threatening vulnerable folk with all sorts of violence if they could not make regular payments in return for a debt. Sometimes he had bundled such men into the back of his van and dealt with them properly. But, more often, such people were in control of the very powers that Daniel had tried to implement. Was it the same here, then? He shuddered at the thought.

'How much do you owe them?' he asked quietly.

'That isnae your business, son,' Netta retorted. 'And ony-weys it's no fur very long cos we get oor Christmas bonus frae the government this month, don't we?'

Perhaps it was because of the darkness in the room hiding her embarrassment, but soon the whole sorry tale came out. Yes, Netta admitted, she was in trouble with the gombeen man, his rates so high that there was now a weekly payment that stretched from one Christmas to the next, despite the cash injection of the pensioner's annual bonus, something she took pains to explain to Daniel.

When the lights came on as suddenly as they had gone out, Netta stood up quickly. 'How long has the pudding been on fur?' she asked, brushing past Daniel and heading into his kitchen. He followed her quietly, sensing that the brightness of the overhead light had somehow shamed the old lady, her confession putting a rift between them. The kitchen was warm, a fragrant aroma of sweet spices coming from the huge pan, steam making a cloud above their heads.

'I want to help you, Netta.' Daniel clasped the old lady by her shoulders. 'I want these men to stop troubling you,' he said as she patted his hand.

'Nice of ye, son, but ah hae ma doots ye've less in your purse than I have, a refugee like yerself.' She switched off the gas burner under the pudding. 'Must hiv been an hour at least,' she murmured.

She turned and gave him a tremulous smile. 'See and bring the pot back when it's cooled down, eh?' And with that she walked past him and left the flat, the subject of her money problems closed.

Daniel stood looking at the old cooking pot, wondering what he could do to help his neighbour. She was right about his own finances and he had no means of earning any money, the terms of his present stay in the city denying him anything other than voluntary work. But perhaps there were other ways of helping her, keeping those men at bay.

CHAPTER SEVENTEEN

Maggie smiled as she turned into the driveway, glancing along the curve of houses. When they'd first moved into their home there had been Christmas trees in every front window but over the years fashions had changed and now there were lights everywhere, festooned along rooflines or draped amongst leafless trees, candle branches on window sills as well as huge fir trees displayed behind bay windows. It was tasteful here, though: no inflated snowmen, or Santas billowing in the stormy winds, or garish lights flashing on and off like visual rap music. Their own home's decorations were modest in comparison to many, Bill happy enough to bring down their artificial tree from the loft and Maggie enjoying decorating it with the baubles and trinkets they had picked up on several holidays. The lights were on a timer and now, when she returned home from school, she could see them twinkling in the front window.

Once indoors she would switch on the candle branch lights on their kitchen window sill and enjoy their reflection against the glass. She pressed the key fob for their new garage door and watched as it rose slowly upwards then drove in and parked. It was a small luxury that Bill had insisted upon when they'd had the old wooden garage demolished and a sturdy concrete one erected in its place and Maggie was glad not to have to heave and pull the door again. Carrying heavy bags of books was bad enough and her lower back was beginning to ache again. 'You need to see the doctor,' Bill had told her, and Maggie knew that was true but had prevaricated owing to the busy schedule that this term demanded. 'I'll make an appointment for during the holidays,' she'd promised and now, feeling the ache become more of a sharp pain, Maggie thought it was time to see her German friend, Dr Annett Schmautz, at their local surgery.

A cry made Maggie look down at her feet as she inserted the key into the door.

'Chancer!' she exclaimed, smiling as the old orange cat reared up on his hind legs, paws against her leather boots.

Cat and woman entered the house and Maggie dumped her bags, heading straight through the big open-plan room that was both study and dining area with one cosy corner where they could sit by the fire. The kitchen beyond was where Chancer had padded swiftly, the familiar expectant look from his green eyes something Maggie knew well. Feeding time took precedence over human desires and so it was not until the cat's head was down in his full bowl that Maggie filled a kettle and gave a sigh.

It was good to be home and soon she'd be off for two whole weeks. If Bill had taken her hints about Christmas presents, then Maggie would be sitting down here by the firelight reading some new books that she'd had her eye on for a while. But meantime there was marking to do, reports to write and a reading test to devise, all part of her remit as an English teacher. She poured the Earl Grey tea into a favourite blue and white china mug then slumped into the old rocking chair by the hearth. A twinge of pain made her gasp and she shifted a little, remembering her resolve to visit Annett. Nothing to worry about, the GP would probably tell her, and Maggie would feel the guilt that came from taking up appointment time for someone that really needed it. And yet ... she'd promised Bill and Maggie Lorimer was a woman who kept her promises.

Sipping the fragrant tea, she rocked gently back and forth, gazing at the tree in the window. How lucky they were! Two professional people with jobs they both loved, no money worries and the prospect of a good break together over Christmas. Maggie did not dwell on their childless marriage or the heartache she'd experienced losing her beloved mother; instead she thought about the shoebox appeal to which the kids at school had responded. She'd given a little speech at morning assembly a few weeks back and highlighted the plight of the poorest people whose Christmas was destined to be without all the material things the pupils took for granted. The head teacher had read out a letter from the charity just this morning, praising the number of shoeboxes filled with warm hats and small gifts that had been donated and thanking the pupils of Muirpark Secondary School for their generosity.

Maggie closed her eyes and thought about the needy people these boxes would reach. They had so much, and millions had so little. There were displaced folk all over the world now, refugees heading to Britain in desperate search for a new life. She was a practical woman, giving her time and talents to help charities like this, but sometimes she also felt the need for prayer. So many people were in need and a plea to their Heavenly Father would surely not go unheard.

Daniel stood at the window, the chill making his breath cloud the glass. He'd never become used to this godforsaken climate, he thought, shivering. Night after night he'd been woken by the intense cold, face freezing so that he pulled the duvet over his head. Sleep had eluded him again tonight and so he'd risen, wrapped himself up in the coat Netta had given him and padded into the living room. Okay, it was winter and he'd yet to experience a Scottish summer, but the thought of this numbing cold year after lonely year made him pull back from the window and gaze instead into the room. A couple of colourful cushions covered in cheap Indian patchwork with little mirrors that danced against the light caught his eye, another gift from Netta. There had always been colour back home, a bright orange batik bedspread in his childhood room, his mother favouring yellows and scarlet in her dress, reminding him of the sun that warmed their bodies.

He closed his eyes, trying to conjure up images that would shield his soul against the blackness of despair, but they seemed dim and distant now. It was no use. The battle against the *kufungisisa*, the Shona word that conveyed this deep depression, would continue. He had always been guilty of *thinking too much*, the inner meaning of the word, and that, combined with a zeal to rid his country of the corruption that had torn it apart, was what had driven him here, far, far away from the land he loved. Daniel shivered again, fatigue and loneliness overwhelming him, memories crowding into his brain. And it was so cold . . .

Yet there had been times in Zimbabwe when he'd felt chilled like this, Daniel remembered, thinking back to days spent in the bush. A quick glance at his watch told him that it was nearing four a.m., just before sunrise in Africa. His face grew still, and he closed his eyes once more as the words from a poem returned to mind.

> *The moon shines over the vlei*
> *full and golden.*
> *Watchful deer crouch over their patch of warmth.*
> *Bitterly cold, this dawn,*
> *cold as the pearly sky.*
> *Sunrise, moonset,*
> *no struggle, simply a fading balance*
> *one sliding faintly to earth,*
> *the other rising in the chill*
> *through wreaths and trails of mist*
> *where antelope stay quiet.*
> *Even the bullfrogs' croaks have ceased*
> *and few birds sing.*
> *Yet somewhere, still as carved stone,*
> *The lion waits*
> *for sun to stir his frozen prey*
> *into their daily motion.*

A deep sigh funnelled through his body. He would sleep now, Daniel thought, walking quietly back to the bedroom, these images fixed in his mind.

Yet it was the thought of other dreams that might ambush his sleep that made him shiver once again; but this time it was not from the cold.

CHAPTER EIGHTEEN

Was he clutching at straws? Lorimer wondered, setting down papers that he'd read over several times. The four undercover officers were like hawks in his mind, circling over the Glennifer Braes, all coming from different locations but close enough to have converged at that place hidden in the lonely gully. It didn't feel right, though. Surely if one of them had wanted to sell their story to the papers, it would have been splashed across the front pages as a 'cop tells all' feature. Had they come to some agreement with the press to maintain a sort of credibility in order to come out of the whole thing looking like the injured party?

Or . . . had they gone rogue and tracked down the person responsible for those revelations? Sometimes, he thought, coincidences were just that and no more. These officers may well have had a good underlying reason for choosing where they lived and, after all, the outskirts of Barrhead and the Potterhill area were pretty far apart when you considered it, even though it would have taken very little time for any of them to access the crime scene.

Which brought him back to Derek Carter and the signs he had picked up from Sylvie Maxwell. Little things she'd been unable to hide that made Lorimer wonder if she'd become closer to Carter than she was letting on. The woman calling herself Sylvie Maxwell was someone he had trusted. And yet ... Molly Newton was preparing to shadow the under-cover officer as best she could in order to eliminate her as a suspect either for being involved in Carter's murder or for failing to disclose information that would lead them to the terrorist cell. DS Newton had expressed surprise when he'd tasked her with this, but Lorimer had seen a gleam in the woman's eyes too: a return to her old job of surveillance was a challenge she'd relish.

Today he'd be heading to Bryson's with the SIO from Mill Street, just as an observer, he'd assured the officer in charge. The man had let a silence play between them over the telephone call and Lorimer had sensed a certain animos-ity emanating from his voice when he spoke at last. *Yes, sir,* he'd replied in a clipped tone. He was unable to reveal why he was poking his nose into other officers' cases, the real reason being to find whoever was leaking information both to the press and to anybody connected with a terrorist group. (Anything deemed suspicious about an officer involved in even a routine crime scene might be worth following up, they'd been advised by Special Branch.) So he would be his most charming self, letting the SIO ask the questions and watching the reactions and body language of those being interviewed. Judith Morris, the crime scene manager, had introduced him to DI Graham Brownlee after that morning up on the Braes, and Lorimer had been struck by the younger man's authority and no-nonsense approach. But, even then, he'd felt a frisson of something else: a suppressed irritation that a senior officer was walking his size tens all over his patch.

Lorimer gave a sigh as he glanced at the calendar. In about two weeks Maggie would be stopping for the holidays. If they could root out the source behind these newspaper revelations, find whoever was feeding information to these terrorists and discover Derek Carter's killer before Christmas, he would be a happy man.

Graham Brownlee had dressed more smartly than usual this morning, choosing his shirt and tie carefully, wondering if making a good impression on the detective super was something he'd expect. Rumour had it that Lorimer was looking around for new blood to join him at the MIT. Brownlee knew of at least two officers at Helen Street whose retirement was on the horizon. Both of these older officers were DIs so did that mean Lorimer was casting around for someone like DI Brownlee? He'd swallowed his initial resentment at the head of the MIT turning up at the crime scene that morning even before he'd arrived himself. He needed to stay polite and professional and not allow anything to colour Lorimer's opinion of the SIO. Focus on the case, he'd told his team and that was something he needed to do as well, not let any personal issues of ambition cloud his judgement.

Now, walking from where he'd parked his car in Blythswood Square, Graham Brownlee rehearsed the questions that he would ask the members of staff at Bryson's about their late colleague. Had they known about the man's police record? What had Carter been like to work with? Had there been any cause for concern with the man's financial dealings? A question that might lead to evidence of drug use, perhaps? He'd been instructed by Lorimer not to march in heavy-handed, given that the very people he might question could be among those they sought. No, he would let them think the police were more interested in a motive for Carter's death, something completely outside the victim's place of work. Suggest, he thought, recalling a course on the psychology of interviewing he'd taken recently. Make it seem he was looking in one particular place whilst he was actually focused on another. Throw them off the scent and behave in as polite a manner as possible, obsequious even, should the interview require that. Criminals who assumed the cop asking questions was a bit dim were inclined to dismiss them in the belief that they'd never be caught. And that was an advantage to a keen mind like Brownlee's. And Lorimer, a man whose techniques in the interview room were legendary, would be watching and listening.

Brownlee was waiting inside the building near to the foot of the stairs when Lorimer arrived. He raised his hand in a casual greeting and smiled.

'Right,' he said, giving the younger man a nod. 'Let's see what waits for us upstairs, shall we?'

They did not speak as the lift ascended six floors, Brownlee apparently absorbed in his own thoughts, Lorimer apparently reluctant to indulge in small talk before they arrived, though his real reason for remaining silent was the fear of being overheard by any hidden devices.

The frosted-glass door was opened after Brownlee had pressed a buzzer and a fair-haired young woman stepped aside to admit them both to a reception area that was dominated by a pale wooden-fronted desk topped with a huge poinsettia.

'DI Brownlee, Detective Superintendent Lorimer to see Mr Burns,' Brownlee told her, showing his warrant card.

'Please come through to the boardroom, gentlemen,' she told them, turning on her patent leather heels and clacking across the marble-floored foyer towards a panelled door with a security pad. A few clicks from her manicured fingers and the doors slid open, revealing a wide corridor with doors on one side and an open-plan area where several people sat at desks behind their computers. They followed the woman to the end of the corridor that was carpeted in plain beige, a neutral shade to accentuate the paintings adorning cream walls. Lorimer lingered a little, recognising some contemporary artists and wondering if any of them were prints or if these were in fact original works. There was a Jolomo he'd never seen before, though there was no mistaking his style of painting: the gable end of an old whitewashed cottage under deepening skies, a splash of colourful flowers in the foreground.

He quickened his pace as the receptionist turned a corner, Brownlee by her side. He'd just caught them up when she stopped at another door and once more tapped in a code to let it open silently.

'Do come in,' she said, a polite smile on her face. 'There's tea and coffee on the tray,' she pointed towards a large oval table, 'help yourself to biscuits. Oh, and the mince pies are just out of the oven.'

'Thank you ... Miss?' Lorimer beamed at her but did not yet enter the room, content to carry on a conversation in the corridor.

'Fiona,' she replied, a pink tinge reaching her cheeks. 'Fiona MacKellar.' She hesitated a little as she looked up at Lorimer. 'You're here about Derek, aren't you? It's just awful,' she whispered in hushed tones.

'Dreadful business,' Lorimer said, a serious frown on his face. 'I expect he'll be badly missed by you all.'

'Oh, yes, he was well liked,' the girl agreed eagerly.

'And his girlfriend ... ?'

She gave a frown and shook her head. 'No. There wasn't a girlfriend. I think you've got that wrong. I'm sure Derek wasn't seeing anyone. He would have told us if there had been a new woman in his life,' she assured him, wide-eyed. 'Derek was like that, you see, never could keep a secret.' She sighed. And, with that, Miss Fiona MacKellar left the two officers and disappeared back along the corridor.

'Tea? Coffee?' Lorimer asked, stepping into the room and glancing at Brownlee who had listened to the conversation with interest.

'Er ...'

'I'm having coffee. And those mince pies look good.' Lorimer grinned, leaning across and lifting a plate from the silver tray.

'Oh, right,' Brownlee said at last, clearly nonplussed by the preparation that had gone into greeting their arrival. 'Er, coffee, please, sir.'

'They're trying to soften us up,' Lorimer laughed, pouring black coffee from a thermal jug. 'But I can see it'll take more than this to disarm you, DI Brownlee.'

Brownlee gave a faint smile that failed to reach a pair of anxious eyes, but he came around to Lorimer's side and waited until he'd filled two bone china mugs. Unlike his senior officer, Brownlee declined anything to eat but Lorimer munched on his mince pie and took a second, imagining what Burns would think when he saw the detective superintendent making himself at home.

Relax, he wanted to tell the younger man. The lawyer they were to meet had deliberately left them here alone rather than meet them and escort them to the boardroom himself. He'd already spotted a tiny camera angled in one corner of the ceiling and guessed that someone was watching their every move. Was this a sign of the man they'd come to meet exerting authority over the police officers? And, did it bear any relation to the device found in Carter's home?

On the other hand, it might be standard practice to have security cameras in an office like this where confidential matters might be discussed. Perhaps leaving the two police officers alone for a while had no sinister connotation at all and they were simply too busy to discuss a case of murder? Or had he wanted to make a show of offering hospitality in order to ingratiate himself with them? Would Brownlee pick up on any of those ideas? Lorimer wondered, watching the DI sip his coffee and make nervous glances towards the open door.

Lorimer hung back when Vincent Burns strode into the

room, arm outstretched to greet them. Brownlee's mug was on the table in a split second, his hand grasping the silver-haired lawyer's.

'DI Brownlee, we spoke on the phone,' Burns said. Then, turning to the tall man who was wiping sugar from his lips with a paper napkin, he gave a slight frown.

'This is Detective Superintendent Lorimer,' Brownlee said, making the introductions. 'Mr Burns is the senior managing partner here at Bryson's.'

Was that a flicker of recognition in those deep-set eyes? Lorimer wondered as Burns came around the table.

'Great mince pies,' Lorimer said, rubbing his hands together as though to shake off the crumbs. 'Good to meet you, Mr Burns.'

The man shook his hand and met Lorimer's eyes, holding his gaze just a fraction longer than was necessary, something Lorimer squirrelled away for future scrutiny.

'Please, take a seat, gentlemen,' Burns said at last, ushering them both to the far end of the highly polished table next to long windows that overlooked the streets below.

Brownlee sat opposite the lawyer but Lorimer fussed a little over the coffee pot, pouring himself another cup and grabbing yet another mince pie before walking round the table and sitting with his back to the window, his chair pushed out a little so that he was sitting at an angle where he could watch both men. From the corner of his eye he caught the detective inspector exchanging a glance with the senior partner, one that seemed to say, *Don't worry, I'm in charge here.* Lorimer suppressed a grin, wondering if Brownlee had already cottoned on to his own dim cop act, allowing him to conduct the interview while the detective superintendent observed every little detail.

'Derek Carter,' Brownlee began.

'Terrible business, just terrible,' Burns responded, shaking his head as though the death of his junior partner was a personal blow.

'Tell me how you came to recruit him,' Brownlee said calmly.

'Oh.' Vincent Burns sat forward a little and folded his hands on the tabletop, a frown beginning between his bushy white eyebrows as if the question had thrown him somewhat. 'Er, well, that wasn't down to me,' he said, shuffling uneasily in his seat. 'Our human resources department would have all the information you need, however. I can ask them to come in if you wish ...?' He began to rise from his chair, but a wave of Brownlee's hand stopped him.

'That won't be necessary, sir. We can of course speak to your people in due course. Were you aware that Mr Carter had a police record?'

'Well, of course not!' Burns exclaimed, tossing his head indignantly. 'That only came out after he was ...' The rest of his sentence hung in the air as though Burns were reluctant to utter the word *murdered*.

'What did you think of Mr Carter when you first met him?' Brownlee continued.

'Well ...' Burns gave a sniff and looked away thoughtfully. 'I'm not sure I remember what I thought. He's been with us for a while, you know,' he said, looking at Brownlee as if that was a sufficient answer.

'Was Carter a reliable employee?'

'Oh, my goodness, yes! We only have staff here that can cope with our sort of work, you know. Never have time for hangers-on or time-wasters,' he assured the DI. 'No, Carter was fine, just fine.'

Lorimer noted the man biting the edge of his thumbnail, his legs crossed and uncrossed as he sat a little back from the table. His body language was beginning to reveal a man that was rattled in some way and that in itself was interesting.

'You told me on the phone that Mr Carter had taken time off,' Brownlee continued. 'Is that correct?'

'Yes,' Burns replied, his jaw relaxing a little, this sort of question evidently much more to his liking.

'Was this a planned holiday?'

'I wouldn't know,' Burns replied smoothly, examining his fingernails. 'Not my part of the ship to deal with employees' time off.'

'So, he didn't talk to you about any plans he had?'

'No, not at all. Our relationship was purely professional, Inspector,' Burns said. 'We were not ... friends.'

'But not enemies either?' Brownlee retorted with a knowing smile.

'Ha ha!' Burns raised an admonitory finger. 'No indeed. None of our employees had any worries about their relationship with the senior partner,' he laughed. But it was a mirthless sort of laugh and Lorimer noted a certain coldness in the man's eyes. As if he did not appreciate Brownlee's small insinuation.

His designation of Carter as employee rather than junior partner was interesting, thought Lorimer.

'Was there anything in Mr Carter's manner recently that

might have suggested he was worried about anything?' Brownlee continued.

'No, nothing at all. Derek was a happy-go-lucky sort of chap as a rule. A bit of a chatterbox, in fact. If there was anything to complain about, it was the length of time he spent blethering at the water cooler, I suppose,' Burns replied, sitting back and folding his arms.

'Would he have confided in you if there had been a problem?'

'What sort of problem?' Burns frowned again.

'Financial difficulties? Anything that might have had him anxious about his safety?' Brownlee suggested.

Burns shook his head slowly. 'No, I doubt very much if Derek Carter would have come to me with a personal problem. As I said, we were not on such terms. Good enough fellow, of course, but we didn't see one another outside work, you know. Not really my type of golfing companion,' he added carelessly, his attention drawn once more to his fingernails as though it were beneath his dignity to associate with a junior partner at weekends. However, that was possibly a ploy to avoid eye contact with either of the police officers.

'When was the last time you saw Mr Carter?'

Burns sat forward again. 'Didn't I tell you this already?' he asked, his tone a trifle acerbic.

Brownlee drew out a notebook from his inside pocket. 'I think we established that it was the day Mr Carter was last in the office, sir,' he said, apparently looking at a page of the notebook. 'Late in the afternoon, I think you told me.'

There was a silence in the room as Brownlee waited for

an answer and Lorimer wondered just what was going on in the mind of Vincent Burns.

'We have reason to believe that was the same date Derek Carter was killed,' Brownlee said slowly and deliberately.

'Oh, how dreadful,' Burns replied, licking his lips nervously and glancing for the first time towards Lorimer. 'You mean I may have been the last person he spoke to that day?'

'Oh, no, sir, that would be the person who murdered him,' Brownlee said firmly, drawing the man's attention back to himself.

Vincent Burns sat motionless, staring at Brownlee as though he could not think of a suitable response. Yet there was a muscle working on the man's jaw that made Lorimer wonder just what turmoil of emotions was going through the mind of a man who claimed to have had no strong link to an employee who had become the victim of a horrendous crime.

'Good work,' Lorimer said as they reached the line of cars outside Blythswood Hotel. It had been two hours since their arrival at Bryson's and Lorimer had listened as Brownlee had interviewed several more of Carter's colleagues, including the human resources lady and Sylvie Maxwell. The undercover officer had not once glanced Lorimer's way after the necessary introductions, he'd been pleased to see. Like Fiona MacKellar, none of the staff believed that there had been a lady in Carter's life. Nor had Lorimer noticed any of the women wearing the expensive scent lingering on that scrap of card in his pocket.

'That Burns is a hard nut,' Brownlee commented grimly.

'Think there was more going on between him and the deceased than he's letting on.'

'I agree,' Lorimer said. 'Any chance we can get a warrant to search the offices?'

'On what pretext?' Brownlee wanted to know.

'Oh, I'm sure you'll think of something, Detective Inspector,' Lorimer replied with a smile and one raised eyebrow. 'I might be very interested in the paperwork you find. Especially anything relating to large sums of money.'

Brownlee stared at the detective superintendent for a long moment.

'You're not just here to oversee a murder inquiry, are you, sir?' he said softly. 'There's more to it than that, isn't there?'

Lorimer tapped the side of his nose and smiled as reply.

'Maybe we could have a drink some time, Graham?' he suggested, his blue gaze fixed on the other man's eyes.

Brownlee nodded silently. 'Yes, sir, I think that might be a good idea.'

Lorimer sat in the Lexus, wiping a tissue across his mouth. Those sugary mince pies had been a bit much though they'd served to give an impression of a greedy cop who was more interested in stuffing his face than being part of that interview. And, it had worked. DI Brownlee had handled the interview well and Burns had seemed just rattled enough to commit more time to raking up his junior partner's background. What sort of impression had that lawyer hoped to present to the police officers? Lorimer wondered, setting off from the city centre at last.

*

'They've gone.' Burns turned to gaze at the closed door, telephone pressed to his ear.

'And? Any awkward questions asked?' a voice demanded.

'Nothing I couldn't handle,' Burns retorted.

'So, everything back to normal now?'

The lawyer drew a hand across his white hair and blinked as a shaft of sunlight stole through the window of his private office.

'Everything's fine,' he said, hoping that his confident tone belied what he was really feeling, the acid churning in his stomach making him feel more than a little sick.

CHAPTER NINETEEN

He couldn't help it, Daniel told himself as he stood once more outside the entrance to that cobbled lane. It was as if his feet had brought him back to this spot almost against his will and certainly against his better judgement.

Once a cop, always a cop, he thought. If he'd been back in Harare with his old team, before it all went wrong, what would he have done in a situation like this? He'd have sped down that lane and wrestled the knife from the man's hands, for a start. Daniel gazed along the lane, remembering the moment as though he were watching it on a screen, the replay facility of his photographic memory bringing the incident into focus.

And now? He had no back-up team, no way of calling in an extra officer or two to charge into the building and see where that man had come from. Would he have found a blood-soaked person in that basement? Injured? Or dead?

Daniel looked back down Hope Street, recalling the rain that had flooded the gutters that day, soaking through his trousers.

Today was bright and cold, the sunlight filtering through the spaces between these tall buildings. There was nobody he could call, he realised. Nobody who would listen to his story.

With a heavy heart, Daniel walked uphill again, keeping to the outside of the pavement, careful not to bump into any other pedestrians who all seemed to have bags full of Christmas shopping, some even wearing red Santa hats. Was it their splash of colour that made him think back to the birds in Blythswood Square Gardens? What was it the traffic warden had told him about the bird-loving cop? He was a senior officer somewhere else in the city, but perhaps Daniel could find him. Then, as if he had heard it spoken, the man's name came back to him loud and clear: Lorimer.

Daniel Kohi quickened his step, the decision made. Somehow, he would find this man and try to engage him in conversation. And then . . . ? Well, that would depend on what sort of man he was. After all, hadn't Inspector Kohi been betrayed by fellow officers he'd trusted? He'd have to proceed with care if he wanted to remain here in Scotland, biding his time until he was granted settled status and could pick up some of the threads of his former life.

The Mitchell Library was a lot larger than Daniel had expected it to be, the building looming up as he walked down the last few yards towards the pedestrian crossings. Its green copper dome rose proudly from pale grey stone, rows of windows gazing down on the noisy motorway below. A flight of steps took him up and inside then he paused to gaze at the winding marble staircase, the hush from the interior a welcome contrast to the traffic outside.

'Can I help you, sir?' A genial-looking man in a dark uniform stepped closer to Daniel.

'I ... just wanted a quiet place to look up some information ... ' Daniel replied.

The man's smile broadened. 'Come to the right place for that, sir,' he commented. 'Is it your first visit here?'

'Yes.'

The man smiled at him. 'Biggest reference library in Europe, this is!' he exclaimed proudly. 'You'll find anything you're looking for here. Do you have a visitor's card? Or do you wish to register as a borrower?'

'Thank you,' Daniel said. 'Perhaps I can do that while I am here, but for now I just want to find a quiet corner.'

The man nodded and pointed along a corridor. 'Just turn right along there, through the swing doors and you'll find plenty of wee quiet places. There's a restaurant downstairs too. And the loos are along that way,' he said.

'Thank you.' Daniel gave him a faint smile.

'No bother. Anything else you need during your visit, just come and ask. There's always someone on hand to give you help.'

Daniel stepped along the wood-panelled corridor, his spirits lighter from the friendliness of the encounter. Not every official in this city was tired of being helpful. This was a place that people loved, he guessed, his attention to detail making him notice several things as he turned a corner: the black and white chequered floor, the gleaming brass handles on doors and the faint scent of furniture polish as he pushed his way through a set of swing doors.

There were several people at desks and in small break-out

141

corners, most with laptops open, the muted sounds in the big open area reminding Daniel of the university back home. He cast his gaze around until he saw a table in the corner, a pink padded chair next to it. That would do perfectly, he thought, heading towards it and noting that the people next to it would have their backs to him.

Daniel sat down and took out his mobile phone and the small worn notebook that he kept beside his wallet. The search for Lorimer threw up a few surprises, like a famous Scottish architect and a football player of yesteryear, before Daniel refined his search to include the officers of Police Scotland.

And, there he was, thumbnail photographs of a dark-haired man looking out at a camera, some showing him smiling, crinkles around his eyes, but most of them giving the impression of a serious police officer whose craggy good looks were marred by deep lines around his mouth and between those startling blue eyes. Daniel blinked as he gazed at one particular picture. It was as if the man himself was staring out at him, challenging him somehow, and he felt a shudder along his spine. Not a man to mess with, he thought.

There were several press items about Detective Superintendent William Lorimer and Daniel read them slowly, his admiration for the man's track record increasing as he scrolled down. There was one from several years back announcing the officer's appointment to the Major Incident Team in a place called Govan. *Such a strange name, Go-van,* Daniel thought as he scribbled down a few details then began to search for the exact location of this MIT headquarters.

The kindly steward's words came back to him: *you'll find anything you're looking for here.* And, had he? Glancing back to the picture of William Lorimer staring out from his small screen, Daniel wondered if this senior officer would dismiss him for wasting his valuable time. After all, who was Daniel Kohi now? Not Inspector Kohi any longer, but a mere refugee fleeing from an uncertain past with no discernible future.

A hollow rumble from his stomach made him decide to take a look at the prices in the restaurant the steward had told him about. A pot of tea and a sandwich then he would think more about finding the red-brick building he'd glimpsed on his phone.

The wind was sweeping a shower of hailstones along the road beside Bellahouston Park, the white ice pebbles rattling on the tarmac as he walked, head down, collar up, feeling the blast against his dark curls. Ahead of him Daniel could see a modern building, its red brickwork and chequered sign exactly as he'd seen on the internet. As he approached, he saw cars parked to one side and, presumably, all the way around the rear of the police station. One of these might belong to William Lorimer, he thought, regarding them all with a renewed interest. There were several 4×4s and family-sized hatchbacks but one long silver vehicle made Daniel pause for a second look: a Lexus that was badly in need of a wash. Who'd spend that kind of money on a car? Daniel pursed his lips, remembering some of his former colleagues whose purchase of Mercedes cars had raised a few eyebrows. The corruption within the force had escalated to such an extent by then that nobody dared speak out. Nobody except Inspector Kohi. Which was one of the reasons he was here now, wondering if he had the courage to speak to this Lorimer or not.

There would be CCTV trained on him right now, Daniel imagined, so he stepped around the building until he reached a set of steps leading to a front door.

He swallowed nervously, grasping the bright blue rail on one side, a sensation of nausea gripping him suddenly. It only took a moment to push through the doors and enter the warmth of the police station.

There was a uniformed officer behind a desk who looked up as Daniel stepped forward.

'Yes, sir, how can we help you?' the man asked, giving Daniel an appraising but not unfriendly look.

His throat seemed to close over as Daniel opened his mouth to speak.

The officer waited patiently, Daniel wondering just what was going through the man's mind: is this guy an English speaker? Has he just wandered in out of the cold?

'Can you let me speak to Detective Superintendent Lorimer?' Daniel said at last, his voice coming out a little rough. 'I believe he is here in Go-van,' he added.

The officer smiled. 'You mean Govan,' he corrected. 'Well, you got the location right, at any rate.'

Guvin, that was how this man pronounced the place, Daniel realised, filing away yet another scrap of linguistic knowledge.

'Do you have an appointment, sir?'

Daniel shook his head.

'I'm sorry, you will have to call the Major Incident

department if you need to speak to him,' the officer explained. 'Make an appointment with one of the admin staff.'

'Oh, I see,' Daniel replied, suddenly feeling rather stupid for presuming he could simply walk in and demand to speak to a senior officer of Lorimer's standing.

The officer had folded his hands on top of the counter and was looking at Daniel with a sympathetic expression on his face. 'Is there anything I can do to assist you?' he asked, speaking more quietly as though to encourage this stranger who had appeared from nowhere.

'I . . . ' Daniel bit his lip. 'I really think I need to speak to him myself,' he murmured.

'May I take your name, sir?' the officer asked. 'Perhaps Detective Superintendent Lorimer knows you were looking for him?'

Daniel was tempted to agree with him, tell a lie and weasel his way past this first hurdle, but his innate sense of doing what was right and proper prevented him.

'I'm Daniel Kohi,' he said instead. 'Inspector Daniel Kohi, formerly of the Zimbabwe Republic Police.'

CHAPTER TWENTY

'There's an African fellow downstairs. Says he wants to talk to you. Name of Kohi. Used to be with Zimbabwean police,' the voice on his internal line explained.

'Have you looked him up? Checked his story? Could be anyone,' Lorimer replied.

'Aye,' the officer replied. 'There was a Kohi in that force, the ZRP, some time back. Could be the same fellow.'

'First impressions?'

'Looks nervous, but then I guess if he was wanting to talk to the head of the MIT, he might feel a bit of pressure,' the officer chuckled.

'Hasn't said what this is about?' Lorimer frowned. He was busy, but that was a perennial state of affairs in his job. Especially when his mind was turning more anxiously each day to the threatened attack on his city.

'Nothing. He wants to talk to you and to you alone.'

Lorimer drummed his fingers on the desktop. 'Can you get him a cup of tea and ask him to wait?' he said at last. 'See if someone can get him to explain why he wants to speak to me and not to another officer.'

Inspector Kohi. Zimbabwean police. There were no bells ringing at all. A past case involving child slavery from Nigeria was the only connection Lorimer had ever had with that particular continent. Nonetheless he was curious about this random visitor.

'Tell him I'll see him,' he decided. 'If he can wait about an hour or so.'

The room where they had escorted him was so warm that Daniel removed his coat and folded it carefully on an adjacent chair. The door was left ajar and he listened to every set of feet passing along the nearby corridor, straining to hear if one of them was slowing down to enter this place.

He was grateful to accept the cartons of weak tea that were placed before him but now Daniel was beginning to wonder if this was all a huge mistake and his case worker would regard it as a bad mark against him.

He looked up expectantly as a smiling female officer entered the room.

'Not long now,' she assured him cheerfully. 'The detective super's just on his way down.'

Lorimer walked briskly along the corridor, a nod to one of the DIs from CID downstairs as he met the woman's glance. Everyone in this building knew who he was, and the detective superintendent experienced a small rush of pleasure at this thought. He was in a place where he belonged, unlike the stranger waiting for him in a small room normally reserved for family liaison purposes. Who was this man? And why had he sought him out? Those questions buzzed around his head as he pushed the door wide and entered the room.

The man stood up abruptly and for a moment Lorimer had the impression that he might offer a salute. His first impression was of a black face and large dark eyes regarding him with a serious expression. It was a handsome face but there was an air of weariness that seemed to lie on his shoulders and for a moment he found himself wanting to know this man's story.

'Inspector Kohi.' Lorimer stepped forward and grasped the man's hand, feeling a firm grip under his own, three brief shakes before he released it.

'Please call me Daniel,' the man said, his sing-song voice a strange mixture overlaid with an English accent that might be tinged with just a trace of Glaswegian. 'I am no longer an inspector, sir,' he explained. 'I am a refugee now, finding escape from ... ' He hesitated and looked away from Lorimer's gaze.

'From a difficult situation?' Lorimer supplied.

Kohi nodded.

'Please, sit down.' Lorimer gestured to the two chairs on opposite sides of the table but, as Daniel Kohi took the seat he had been in, Lorimer picked up the other chair and carried it so that he was sitting closer to Daniel. No confrontation required, he decided, no need to put a barrier between the two of them.

'So, what brings you over here to Govan?' Lorimer asked, getting straight to the point.

He saw the man study his face for a few moments as

though trying to read his inner thoughts. As a police officer, had Kohi done this very thing with suspects, looking for clues in a man's demeanour?

Then, as though he had reached a decision of some kind, Kohi raised his hand and let it fall again with a sigh.

'I wanted to find someone that would listen to me. And I heard about you,' he said.

Lorimer raised his eyebrows, his curiosity piqued even further.

'The day I arrived in Glasgow I saw something,' Kohi began. 'It was a small moment.' He paused and looked to one side as though he were seeing whatever it was once more. 'A man with a bloodstained knife. In an alleyway,' he told Lorimer, his gaze back on the detective superintendent's blue eyes. 'It was just one moment, but there was something that told me the person holding that knife was looking to get rid of it.'

'And . . . ?'

Kohi shook his head. 'I do not think he noticed me. I was standing at the mouth of the lane and we did not make eye contact. No . . . ' He tailed off thoughtfully. 'It was as if he had decided to go back in again. As if the lane was not a safe place to be in daylight.'

'Where exactly was this? Can you remember?'

He saw a faint smile twitch at the corners of his mouth as Kohi nodded slowly.

'I remember everything, Detective Superintendent,' he replied sadly. 'That is my God-given gift but also my misfortune.'

Lorimer frowned. 'Are you telling me that you have a photographic memory?'

'That is correct,' Kohi sighed. 'I cannot forget details. Sometimes that makes life very hard.' He shrugged. 'But other times it can be useful, you know?'

'Tell me about this,' Lorimer said at last. 'Date, time, place ...'

And, giving another sigh that seemed to come from his very soul, Daniel began to recount the incident that had brought him to seek the man that was head of the MIT.

'I'm bringing someone back for dinner, is that okay?'

Maggie Lorimer smiled. 'Fine. Anyone I know?'

'I didn't know him myself till an hour ago,' her husband replied. 'He's from Zimbabwe. Former cop. I think you'll like him.'

Maggie put down the telephone and wondered what this man from southern Africa would like to eat. There was a pot of soup already on the stove, plenty for them all, and some nice Italian bread that she'd picked up from the deli in Giffnock. Luckily she'd taken out a venison casserole from the freezer last night and all she needed to do now was peel a few tatties and serve them as mash. That would do, surely? What if he was vegetarian? Maggie bit her lip. Could she whip up an omelette? Or, maybe he was vegan? A quick stir-fry in her wok, she thought, mentally going over the contents of their cupboards and fridge.

She hesitated by the larder door, glancing towards their wine rack. Maybe uncork a nice bottle of red? Och, they could decide once they were around the table. There was beer in the fridge, would the chap like that instead? Maggie shook her head, wondering why Bill was bringing home a stranger she'd never heard of on a weeknight. Well, she'd be as hospitable as she knew how. After all, in this season of Advent her thoughts turned often to the days of feasting that lay ahead and it would be nice to share a meal with someone new from a different country.

Daniel looked out of the car window, seeing the city lights as a blur against the deep darkness. He'd been taken aback when Lorimer had led him to the Lexus and had glanced nervously at the tall detective.

'Nice car,' he'd remarked, not meeting Lorimer's eyes.

'Too good for a cop?' Lorimer grinned as if he had read Daniel's thoughts. 'I can afford it, luckily. No kids and two salaries. Didn't buy it new, of course. I'm not made of money.' He chuckled, slipping into the driver's seat and buckling his safety belt.

Daniel said nothing, digesting this snippet of information and wondering about the man beside him. He'd been surprised when he had been invited back for dinner to the detective's home and yet there was something in Lorimer's manner that had made him inclined to accept right away. He'd given Daniel a knowing smile as if he could see the loneliness inside and those bright blue eyes had brooked no refusal of the invitation.

Now he sat back, feeling the warmth spread out beneath him from the heated seat, a small luxury that he'd never experienced before. Luxury cars driven by cops back home smelled of dirty money, but this man was different. He noticed the worn leather steering wheel and the dusty wooden fascia. No, this man did not see his car as some sort

151

of status symbol. It was, rather, a car he would use to race to a scene of crime, its comfort an added bonus.

Lorimer stared straight ahead, Daniel's words ringing in his head. He had asked for dates and times, his face impassive though inside he was experiencing a frisson of excitement. The day Daniel Kohi had witnessed that strange incident was the day Derek Carter had been murdered and this time the detective superintendent was not going to put that down to coincidence. The solicitors' office was on the top of that selfsame building and he thought about how Kohi had described his venture inside at a later date, hiding from sight in that basement and seeing the same figure that had held a bloodstained knife in his fist and possible traces of blood on the floor. There was a lot to do now, including taking a witness statement from Kohi, though the former cop had seemed reluctant to put his name to anything that might jeopardise the terms of his asylum. Perhaps, he thought, the man might agree to talk to him about why he'd left Zimbabwe and what it was that he still appeared to fear. For, if he had read him aright, there were things deep down that he was trying hard to suppress.

Daniel looked out into the darkness as they turned off the motorway and headed through tree-lined streets, houses flashing past, their windows bright with Christmas lights.

'Here we are,' Lorimer murmured, turning the wheel and parking outside his home.

Daniel looked at the house, a pretty Glasgow villa with a wreath of red berries on its door.

'Come on in,' the tall man told him, striding towards the house, a bunch of keys in his gloved hand. Then that door was flung wide and Daniel hesitated, wondering for a moment what on earth Mrs Lorimer must think of a stranger being dragged into her home on this cold winter's night.

'Come on and meet Maggie,' Lorimer told him, turning back and beckoning Daniel with a smile.

The door closed behind him as Daniel stepped into the light. The smell of cooking wafted through the large room, making him realise how very hungry he was. A small movement by his feet made him start then he laughed softly to see a fluffy orange cat rubbing its head against his ankles.

'You're privileged,' Lorimer remarked. 'Old Chancer here doesn't often make a pass at folk he doesn't know.'

Daniel bent down to stroke the soft fur and the animal reared up a little, purrs of appreciation throbbing through its body.

'Hello, there.'

The woman's voice made Daniel straighten up and he saw a slim woman with dark hair that curled past her shoulders.

'I'm Maggie and you must be Inspector Kohi,' she said, putting out her hand and touching his arm. 'I see Chancer's met you already,' she added with a smile as they both looked down at the cat that was winding itself around his legs. 'Come on through. Dinner's ready.'

Lorimer's wife led them through the long room, past the Christmas tree by the window to a table that was set for three. Daniel noticed some comfortable chairs on the other side of the room and a kitchen area beyond a breakfast bar, the source of these good smells. As he sat down at the table, he saw a candle lit in the middle of a nest of golden tinsel and paper napkins decorated with flying reindeer placed on each side plate, small reminders of the Advent season. This time last year Daniel had come home to things like that, the anticipation of a family Christmas filling him with a joy that was now gone for ever. He swallowed hard, sudden tears filling his eyes.

'I'm glad you could come,' Lorimer's wife said, touching his hand, and he glanced up to meet her eyes. She was looking at him intently and for a moment it was as if this woman could see into his very soul.

'Thank you,' he murmured. 'I appreciate it very much.' He looked at Lorimer who was pouring water into three glasses. 'I hope it's not a bother . . . '

'Maggie's a great cook,' he told Daniel. 'Always makes enough for an army,' he chuckled. 'Sorry, never asked if you had any food issues. Any intolerances?'

Daniel's face split into a grin. 'I love my food,' he assured him. 'And no, there's nothing I cannot eat.'

He sat back as Maggie brought a bowl of soup and laid it before him.

'Butternut squash and pumpkin. Help yourself to parsley,' she said, indicating a plate of chopped herbs.

Later Daniel would tell Netta all about that meal, the hearty stew and vegetables, the apple crumble and cream, then sitting with the husband and wife by a warm fire, a mug of tea cradled in his hands. But he found it hard to explain about how the shyness he had felt had fallen away as these people had welcomed him as a friend more than an unexpected guest. Perhaps it was the way that Maggie Lorimer had smiled at him, a sadness in her eyes that was all sympathy and kindness for his situation, that had made Daniel recount his story, something he had never mentioned to his elderly neighbour. Or, perhaps it was the realisation that they too were alone without children as Christmas approached that had made him begin his tale with a shuddering sigh.

'Why am I here, seeking the status of a refugee?' Daniel asked, though neither Lorimer nor his wife had voiced the question. 'Since Mugabe has gone everyone thinks Zimbabwe is a different country and that it will be like it was in the old days.' He shook his head. 'I was brought up to respect the elders and to know right from wrong. I was not a wild boy, but I did love to play football with my pals as well as study for my school exams. I did well.' He shrugged. 'First at training school when I was a police cadet. I was going to change the world. Make it a better place.' He gave a rueful grin and caught Lorimer's blue gaze, seeing him nod. 'You too?'

'Aye, we were all full of great intentions, weren't we?' the detective agreed. 'Still, it's good to look back at some cases where our actions did make a difference, brought perpetrators to justice.'

Daniel heaved a sigh. 'My career was good to begin with and promotion came quite quickly but then things went wrong.' He looked down at his hands, wondering just what to tell these people. 'Corruption seeped through every aspect of my chosen profession,' he said quietly. 'And, like a fool I tried to resist it, change what it was into what I knew it ought to be.'

'And suffered the consequences?' Maggie suggested.

He nodded. How could he tell them? He hung his head and closed his eyes, seeing the flames devour the house, hearing the roar as the roof collapsed.

'I lost everything,' he whispered. 'They killed my wife and my little son. Set our house on fire and left them to die ...'

There was silence as he sat there by their hearth, head bowed. Then he felt a hand on his shoulder and Maggie Lorimer was clasping his hand in hers, a gesture that spoke far louder than any murmured words of comfort.

It had all come flooding out after that, his anguish as they'd held him back from rushing into the fire, the protection of the church elders who'd hidden him from his oppressors and given him a route out of his own country.

'I can never go back,' he had said at last, looking up at the man and woman sitting by his side. 'Nothing has changed enough to make it safe. I would certainly be killed.'

'And now?'

'I'm almost there,' Daniel smiled. 'Asylum seeker becomes a refugee of settled status quite soon. I hope,' he added.

'And that will make a difference?'

'Oh, yes,' he assured them. 'Once I achieve this status, I can hope to have a new life in a couple of years, even get back to some sort of work.' He glanced at Lorimer as if for acknowledgement of this.

The tall detective nodded but said nothing, the pact between them kept a secret for now. But there was a look in those bright blue eyes that warmed Daniel Kohi and for the first time in many months he experienced a feeling of hope that he thought he had lost for ever.

*

It was time, the killer thought, turning over in bed and catching sight of the light flickering through the curtains. All their plans had been well thought out, but human frailty had been the unforeseen stumbling block that had thwarted them so far. Carter had become too suspicious of his boss but, despite having left bugs around his home all those weeks ago, there had been absolutely nothing that had shown him to be a threat.

It was the final confrontation between them that had spelled out the man's fate. That, and his overweening desire to become a better man in the eyes of society. Well, that was never going to happen now.

And he had not been the only one to be sacrificed for the greater good. Cowardice and greed were the twin crimes that carried a death sentence and, as the figure turned once more, away from the light, there was not a trace of remorse in their mind.

CHAPTER TWENTY-ONE

Vincent Burns let out a curse as he saw the slight angle of his Jaguar.

A flat tyre! Not what he needed on a morning like this, he thought, casting a sour glance as the heavens spilled heavy flakes of snow from a leaden sky. It might be his own fault for not putting it away in the garage last night, of course, but he suppressed that thought, anger rising in his chest against whatever wee neds had taken the valve out.

Clenching his teeth, Burns crouched down and peered at the wheel. It was difficult to see small details in this thick gloom, mornings becoming ever darker as the month approached the shortest day of the year. He could feel cold moisture from the driveway seep into his trousers as he balanced against the wheel arch, one gloved hand on the ground.

There was neither sound nor shadow as he bent there, peering at his tyre, nothing to tell the man of approaching danger.

A sigh of frustration escaped Vincent Burns.

It was the last sound he ever made, the blow to the back of his skull killing him instantly, mouth still open as he landed face first on the icy ground.

The killer looking down at him stayed motionless for a few seconds, observing the victim, then bent and felt for a pulse, the latex gloves leaving no trace for those who would come later. Satisfied, the figure rose once more and stepped back into the whirling snow, disappearing as silently as it had arrived.

The house in Newton Mearns was a post-war villa surrounded by established trees and lawns, its curving driveway leading to the street where the paper boy made his deliveries. From there it was a short drive into the city, perhaps twenty minutes or less pre rush hour, the time it seemed Vincent Burns had intended to leave. It was a big house for one man, Lorimer thought as he looked back. Six bedrooms, three bathrooms, one added as part of a more modern extension, and a large conservatory at the rear. This December morning it was shrouded in white, the dark roof tiles completely covered, blunt roof edges softened by the constantly falling snow. To one side of the house was a stand of Scots pines, their tops coated like a layer of thick icing; elsewhere, bare branches reached towards the heavens as wave after wave of snowflakes descended.

'Burns? Dear Lord!' DI Brownlee sat back at his desk, openmouthed in shock. 'What happened?'

'Someone whacked him over the head, first thing this

morning,' Lorimer told him. 'Paper boy on his rounds had the sense to call it in. We've got a team here now. Thought you'd better join us.'

'Right,' Brownlee replied. 'Be there in fifteen minutes.'

Lorimer stood under the shelter of the forensic tent that had been erected around the body of the dead man and ended the call. It was only right that he should have Brownlee here. After all, he was SIO in the Carter murder and this, surely, had to be related to that? Outside, snow was still falling heavily, carpeting the ground as well as the roof and bonnet of the big car which was now separated from the body by one side of the tent. There was a flat tyre on the Jaguar's near side, a fact that had already been noted by the scene of crime officers as well as Lorimer, and he wondered just what had happened to cause that. Later the car would be taken to a lab where forensic scientists would examine every inch of the vehicle for traces. But for now, the ever-falling snow was making their job increasingly difficult, obliterating any signs of footprints that might have given them a clue as to what had happened earlier this morning.

'Boss?'

Lorimer looked up as DS Davie Giles appeared at the entrance, two paper cartons of coffee in his hands.

'Cheers, Dave,' Lorimer said, stepping under the tent flap and emerging once more into the blizzard. Hot black coffee, just how he liked it, he sighed, grateful for his detective sergeant's thoughtfulness.

'Who's on call?' Giles asked, sipping his own drink as they stood side by side, the snow whirling around them.

'Rosie Fergusson,' Lorimer told him, naming the consultant forensic pathologist who was a good friend as well as a colleague. 'She's on her way. Don't think there will be too much to add to what we already know, mind you. Someone cracked his skull good and proper. Must have taken a bit of brute force to lay him out like that.'

'Maybe they knew exactly where to hit him?' Giles suggested.

Lorimer nodded. The same thought had already occurred to him. This was a planned attack, he'd decided. Though why carry it out so close to the victim's own home? Whoever had committed this murder had surely known the risk they were taking. And, he reminded himself, knew the daily routine of the late Vincent Burns.

The man's front door was just a few yards from the crime scene and he and Giles now retreated into the porch, sheltering from the snow that seemed to fall endlessly from a chalk-white sky. Inside the house other officers were already searching, looking for anything that might give an answer to the question of why Burns had been killed. The man's house keys had been in his overcoat pocket and that in itself provided one significant fact about what had taken place earlier that day. Burns must have locked up, prepared to leave for the city, when he had noticed the flat tyre.

'Need to do a house-to-house as soon as possible,' Lorimer said. 'Who saw what? Or, maybe, who went out earlier?' He looked across at Giles, eyebrows raised.

'You think a neighbour might have committed this murder?'

Lorimer shrugged. 'Someone knew his comings and

goings. Burns lived alone. The paper boy arrived at this street same time every day. He'll know a bit more about these residents, perhaps.'

'Poor lad was shivering with shock when the uniforms arrived,' Giles told him. 'He's still in the van.' He nodded towards a large Police Scotland vehicle that was parked several yards along the drive.

'Is he a minor?'

Giles shook his head. 'Don't think so. Said something about having to get to school, but I think he's a senior. His father was coming to pick him up.'

'And his bike,' Lorimer added, looking at the cycle that lay abandoned by the side of a snow-covered bush.

As he slid into the back seat of the van, Lorimer could see the young lad was still shivering, a blanket draped around his shoulders.

'I'm Detective Superintendent Lorimer,' he said, nodding at the boy who'd discovered the body.

'Ian Chalmers,' the lad replied. 'Do I have to stay here when my dad arrives?' he asked, blinking back tears that were not too far away.

'We won't keep you much longer, Ian. Sorry you've had such a horrible experience,' Lorimer replied gently. 'But right now, you are a really important person to us. First on the scene. Someone who knows the area. Accustomed to delivering papers here every day. There will be lots of questions we want to ask you.'

The boy drew back, eyes widening.

'No need to worry, we don't think you had anything to do

162

with this,' Lorimer assured him. 'But any information you can give us could be very, very helpful indeed.'

'Will I need to go to a police station?'

'Your dad can come with you if you want,' Lorimer said. 'How old are you, Ian?'

'Seventeen,' the boy replied.

'Okay, you don't require to have another adult present, but I don't mind if Mr Chalmers comes along if it makes you feel better.'

The lad nodded and pulled the blanket closer to his chin.

'The officers in charge will get you something to eat and drink soon as you get there.' Lorimer smiled. 'Bet you've not had breakfast, eh?'

Ian shook his head and gave a tentative smile, his watery grey eyes meeting the detective's.

Trust, that was what was needed here first and foremost, Lorimer realised. And seeing to the needs of this traumatised young man would help establish that.

He lifted his phone and pressed a number.

'Lorimer here. Can you make sure that Mr Ian Chalmers gets a decent breakfast as soon as he and his father arrive? Thanks.' He snapped the phone shut and smiled across at the lad.

'Sorted. I may see you later, Ian. Thanks again for calling this in so promptly,' he said, leaning across and shaking the boy's hand.

He would return here again, Lorimer decided, but right now his place was back in Helen Street where he would continue to instruct each member of his team to discover what had taken place earlier. Any relatives of Burns must be found and informed first, of course. Then he would drive into the city to talk to the employees at Thomas Bryson, particularly the woman known to her colleagues as Sylvie Maxwell.

CHAPTER TWENTY-TWO

Daniel looked out onto a world that had been transformed overnight. He had seen pictures of snow-covered mountains in *National Geographic* magazines and on television programmes about places like Nepal. But nothing in his experience had prepared him for the hypnotic quality of this cascade of snowflakes swirling and tumbling from a milk-white sky. Down below his window everything had changed, no grey streets to be seen, no pavements either, the line between both disappearing beneath this blanket of snow. His gaze shifted to the heavens and for a moment Daniel felt a dizzying sensation as if the whole world was tilting further on its axis.

He opened the window and leaned out as far as he could, stretching out a hand and catching the soft flakes that instantly melted on his skin. Logically he knew that this was simply water in a different form but that did not stop a grin of childlike delight spreading across his face. Johannes would have loved this, he told himself, the smile disappearing as fast as the melting snowflakes. If only he had been home in time, hauled them out of that burning building ... all three of them might be here now living a new life in Scotland.

Daniel closed the window with a bang and turned the handle. He would not go there, he told himself firmly. It had been enough to tell the good people last night about the reason why he was here; dwelling on it further would achieve nothing except to plunge his soul into an abyss from which he might never escape.

It had been a special evening, Daniel thought, recalling each and every small detail of his visit to the detective superintendent's home: the sparkling Christmas lights, the warm food, Chancer, the fluffy orange cat that had sat on his lap after dinner ... And, of course, he would not forget the conversation with Lorimer as they had sat in his big car outside this flat. It was a strange proposition that the tall detective had made and he was not to make an instant decision about it, but even as Lorimer had told him what he had in mind, Daniel Kohi knew that he was going to accept it. There would be no contravening the issue of not working for pay, Lorimer had told him; this was purely voluntary and a private agreement between the two men. Also, if things turned out well, it might enhance Inspector Kohi's chances of renewing his career as a police officer.

'I can't and won't give you any money, Kohi,' Lorimer had said, turning those piercing blue eyes on Daniel. 'But we can certainly help with transport. A car filled with petrol could be made available to you. And a few food parcels wouldn't go amiss, I'm sure,' he'd added. 'After all, as Maggie said earlier, it's the season of goodwill to all men, eh?' And he'd patted Daniel's shoulder to emphasise his point.

There were other things the policeman could do for him, Daniel decided, practical things like topping up the credit on his mobile phone. If he wanted the former detective inspector to be his eyes and ears, then they needed a way of being in touch at all times.

He turned away from the window feeling a renewed sense of purpose. Nobody might pass him by on these Glasgow streets and call him boss, but Daniel Kohi would take a pride in being part of an investigation that had begun the moment he had caught sight of that bloodied knife.

Sylvie Maxwell was hovering towards the back of the reception area when Lorimer and Brownlee strode in, a brief glance between them the only sign that she knew what was happening.

'Detective Superintendent Lorimer, DI Brownlee,' he told the blonde behind the desk as the two officers showed their warrant cards. 'We need to speak to whoever is in charge today.'

'Oh.' The young woman appeared suddenly flustered. 'I'm afraid Mr Burns hasn't come in today,' she stammered. 'We tried his mobile, but it seems to be switched off and nobody knows if it's the weather that's held him back.' She gave a shrug.

'Are any other senior partners available?'

'Well, there's Dominic Fraser,' she replied doubtfully. 'He's in today.'

'Can you arrange for Mr Fraser to meet me in the

boardroom right away, and also your head of HR,' Lorimer said, directing a steady gaze at the woman.

He turned to see if the undercover officer was still there, but she had gone, discretion being of greatest importance right now.

Dominic Fraser proved to be a tall man in his mid-forties with thinning hair, a pair of bright red designer spectacles perched on his beaky nose. His handshake, a brief but firm once-up-and-down, gave Lorimer the impression of a no-nonsense sort of fellow, and the quizzical stare that he gave the two officers as they introduced themselves showed curiosity rather than any sign of nerves.

'Sorry, our head of HR isn't available right now, so you'll just have to put up with me,' he began. 'It was a dreadful thing to happen to Carter.' Fraser waved a hand to usher the detectives into his own office.

'That is not why we are here today, Mr Fraser,' Lorimer said quietly, closing the door behind him. 'I'm afraid we have further bad news. I think you had better sit down.'

Dominic Fraser stared at the two men on the other side of his desk, his lips parted as though to utter words that simply would not come. He shook his head in disbelief as Lorimer broke the news about the senior partner's death.

'It wasn't an accident? You said he was beside his car . . . ?' Fraser looked from one man to the other, his face pale as he processed the facts.

'I'm sorry,' Lorimer said. 'There is still to be a post-mortem examination, of course, but the initial signs are of a sudden attack on Mr Burns.'

'But who . . . ?' Fraser shook his head. 'Who would . . . ?' He took a deep breath, the unspoken words lingering in the air.

'That is what we will do our utmost to find out, sir,' Brownlee assured him. 'And we will need all your cooperation meantime.'

'Of course, anything . . . Oh, God!' Fraser heaved a sigh and glanced around his office. 'They'll be big shoes to fill,' he murmured. 'I never really thought . . .'

Lorimer waited, wondering what was going on in the lawyer's mind.

'I was planning on taking a sabbatical,' Fraser sighed. 'Write a book about contemporary Scottish law. I never saw myself stepping into the senior partner's role.'

'Are there any other partners that would take that on instead?' Lorimer enquired.

'We're a fairly small outfit these days, Superintendent,' Fraser explained. 'Most of the staff are my age or younger. Vincent . . . Mr Burns . . . was managing partner as well as senior partner. Several of the old guard retired in the past few years, leaving me as second in command.'

'I'll need to ask for a thorough look at every scrap of paperwork in the office. I expect most of that is currently stored in computer files.'

Fraser frowned for a moment. 'Just a minute,' he began, 'we have confidential files pertaining to clients that I would not be happy to hand over without their say-so.'

'And we have a warrant to search this entire premises, sir,' Brownlee put in firmly.

Fraser slid a hand across his scalp. 'First Carter now Vincent Burns,' he murmured. 'Is our firm being targeted by somebody, do you think?' Then he swallowed hard, an expression of alarm crossing his face. 'Could anyone else be in danger?'

Was that genuine fear of being next on some killer's list that had made the lawyer's face blanch with fear? Or was there something Dominic Fraser wanted to keep hidden? Lorimer was certain that the lawyer was not feigning shock at the news of Burns's death and it was perfectly within his rights to try to protect client confidentiality. No, if he had to make a snap judgement, he would say that the man now rising from behind his desk was *a decent and honest citizen*, a phrase that Sylvie Maxwell had used to describe him in one of her earlier reports.

'We need to let the rest of the staff know about this,' Lorimer said. 'And, no matter what or who is detaining your HR person, we need them right now. Please can you have them all brought into the boardroom?'

Sylvie stood at the window, looking down on the snow-covered railings, and gave a deep sigh. She was not sad about this latest death, only curious to see what Lorimer might make of it. He had called her on his way here, giving Sylvie a chance to collect her thoughts and disguise any feelings of animosity that she still felt towards the man. It was never wise to speak ill of the dead. Later she would be asked questions and she must prepare herself for that, too. Perhaps her days here were numbered, in any case, the police now visibly taking over with no further need for an undercover officer.

It had been too much of a risk to develop the relationship she had enjoyed with Derek; the nights spent together initially to gain information turning into something far more personal. And, after all, what had she found? A nice man with a deep social conscience who volunteered in refugee centres. What was it he'd said in that last voicemail message? That he *hoped to make a difference in the world. I'll tell you more tomorrow.* But then he was gone and now she would never know just what he had meant by that.

She would not miss this place, Sylvie told herself, casting a glance around the room where she stood; too many unhappy memories lingered here.

Both he and Brownlee scrutinised the faces of every staff member for their reaction as Dominic Fraser introduced the two senior officers and listened as the acting senior partner broke the latest news. He knew, of course, that another pair of keen eyes was watching, Sylvie Maxwell positioning herself in a corner where she might more easily observe her colleagues. There was silent shock, of course, and a few gasps from the women as they took in the enormity of what had happened to their boss. Glances between some of them were noted too, but then that might be normal human reaction to see how others were taking it.

'I want everyone to remain here this morning while Detective Superintendent Lorimer and Detective Inspector Brownlee conduct their enquiries. You may be asked to surrender your laptops, too,' Fraser told them, his voice gaining a little strength as he took charge. 'This is an unprecedented thing to have happened in our firm.' He glanced across at the two detectives. 'There is no doubt that this is a case of murder?' he ventured.

Lorimer shook his head, his eyes still taking in the various expressions on faces around the table. 'There will be a police presence here all day and possibly for several days to come,' he told them. 'You will be required to answer questions but most of these will simply be for a process of elimination or to enhance our knowledge of Mr Burns's background. I expect some of you will be free to leave earlier than the usual time once you have signed statements for our officers. As Mr Fraser says, this is a case unlike any other that has taken place in the city, certainly to my knowledge. Two lawyers from the same office found dead within a short space of time ...' He let his words hang for a moment. 'I would urge you not to talk to the newspapers about this. For your own benefit as well as for your co-workers' sakes.' Lorimer could almost feel Sylvie Maxwell's eyes boring into several faces, in an effort to see what sort of reaction was produced by these words. Had there been anybody in this office staff involved in blowing the cover of her fellow officers? He would be interested to hear what she had to say later, Lorimer thought. But, for now, the staff were being dismissed, returning in ones and twos to their workstations or private offices.

He had seen no sign of anything but real shock, a few faces simply too stunned to register any emotion, but footage in the small camera that was angled in a corner of the ceiling might yield a little more. Forensics would be here too, taking samples from those bloodstains Kohi had remarked upon in the basement. And, if they were found to be those of Derek Carter, then one piece of the puzzle would be put into place. If Carter had been murdered here, in this building, then someone in this firm might know about it and was keeping their mouth firmly shut.

It was just after lunch that he heard from the undercover officer, a telephone call put through to his private number.

'Anything?' he asked, more in hope than expectation.

'No, sorry. There was no visible reaction from anyone and the aftermath of that meeting was only what you'd imagine. A bit of hysteria from his PA and a lot of speculation, but nothing concrete.'

'No whispering about anything to link it with Carter?'

'Not really,' Maxwell replied, then there was a pause that Lorimer recognised. There was something she had picked up, after all.

'If folk can't explain something, they sometimes make it up,' she began. 'But more than one person speculated that there was something fishy about Burns being killed so soon after Derek Carter.'

'Go on.'

'Well, I overheard one of the women saying that there was no love lost between Carter and Burns. And, like I told you, I did hear them arguing.'

'You never heard what they were arguing about, though?'

'No. And I must admit that Derek never bad-mouthed his boss in any way. Not to me, at any rate.'

'So, it was something else that happened a good while back? Something to do with Carter's past, maybe?'

'I can always try to dig a little deeper. I think the women are so traumatised by this that they'll open up to me without a second thought.'

'Do that,' Lorimer told her. 'What was said after we left?'

'Most of us were just shocked. General comments about how awful or how bizarre it all was. Some were a bit scared, I think, to find murder happening so close to their own place of work. The atmosphere was pretty tense, I can tell you. Nothing like that has ever happened to these people before, I guess.'

'Still no trace of any lady friend of Carter's?'

'Nobody mentioned anybody and under the circumstances they would have spoken about a girlfriend. Though this latest news has overtaken Derek's death.'

Lorimer nodded as he listened. 'Be careful not to distance yourself from the rest of the staff,' he said. 'You need to have as much to say about Carter and Burns as the rest of them.' He thought for a moment. Sowing the seeds of a rumour must come from somewhere and why not from Sylvie Maxwell?

'It wouldn't be a bad idea to suggest that Carter and Burns were up to no good. A little financial mismanagement, perhaps? That would go down easily while the team are trawling through files and computer data, don't you think?'

'Well . . . ' There was a tone of doubt in the woman's voice.

'Cast a stone into that pond and see where the ripples take it, eh?'

'Okay. I'll do my best,' she replied. 'I'll check in with you same time tomorrow unless there's something to report.'

Lorimer listened as the line went dead. Why had she hesitated at his suggestion? Was there something else that Maxwell was keeping from him? He had guessed that Carter's death had affected the woman far more than she was letting on. So, had he been more than a cheerful work colleague to Sylvie Maxwell? Lorimer picked up his phone once more and tapped out a different number.

'Molly? There something I'd like you to do,' he said.

CHAPTER TWENTY-THREE

Trudging through several inches of wet snow was not Molly's idea of a good walk. However, it was not too far to the garage where she had to pick up the car and the roads at least were beginning to clear, brown slush in the gutters replacing the heaps that had been dumped by the snow-ploughs earlier in the day. A weak sun was emerging from thinning clouds but there was no warmth, a chill wind biting at her cheeks as she headed further into the city.

Lorimer had given no indication about why he needed another vehicle or why it had to be kept secret from the rest of the team. Molly knew when to keep her mouth shut, however, and do what the man told her. He'd earned her respect ever since she'd joined the MIT and if his methods were a bit unusual at times, well, he got results. Once she'd delivered the vehicle to an address over in Maryhill she would be free to follow up the next part of her duties and that, Molly told herself, was going to be far more interesting.

Investigating an undercover officer was not something

Molly had ever been asked to do before and her first task would be to find out exactly where Maxwell had been on the morning of Vincent Burns's death. CCTV cameras close to Potterhill Avenue in Paisley might help but that was not terribly likely in such a residential area where a car might take several different routes to avoid them. Lorimer had not disclosed his reasons for wanting this intelligence, but Molly felt there must be something behind it, some grudge that the Maxwell woman had held against the lawyer. Or – and here it became a tad more interesting as Molly speculated – had it been necessary for Sylvie Maxwell to get rid of the senior partner of Bryson's for some other purpose? She smiled at her thoughts as she crossed the road to the garage. A bit fanciful, perhaps, but Lorimer evidently wanted one of their own scrutinised. Just to eliminate her from any suspicion? Or to consider her as a person of interest? You set a thief to catch a thief, she told herself, but did the same rule apply to one former undercover officer shadowing another?

Daniel was waiting outside the flats, eyes fixed on the road. *A red Ford Focus*, Lorimer had texted him, *should be with you before it gets dark*.

He'd checked that his driver's licence was valid for the UK and read the online regulations about driving in this country. His greater concern, however, was where to keep the vehicle safe. Any inner city was fraught with danger from petty criminals and young hoodlums and the last thing he wanted was to cause trouble for Lorimer or for himself.

At last he saw a red car approaching and slowing down. The driver was wearing a hooded top, but he could see that it was a woman, sunglasses hiding eyes that might be summing him up right now. He'd need a pair of those himself, Daniel thought, the glare from a winter sun so low in the sky that it could almost blind when reflected off the banks of snow.

'Hello.' He came forward. 'Are you delivering this car to me?' he asked as the woman swung her long legs out from the driver's seat.

'Who's asking?' came a swift rejoinder.

'A friend of Lorimer,' Daniel replied. 'I'm Daniel Kohi. Was Inspector Kohi once upon a time.' He smiled ruefully as the woman removed her glasses and stepped closer.

'Here.' She held out a set of keys. 'Tank's full of petrol and Lorimer says to fill up on his account at this address,' she said, taking a folded piece of paper from her pocket and handing it to him. 'He didn't tell me who the car was for, so you needn't have given me your name.'

Daniel smiled. 'I'm guessing you are a colleague from his place of work?'

'You guess right,' she replied and returned the smile with one of her own. 'But I'm not about to share any more with a stranger from a strange land,' she added, her smile becoming wider as Daniel took the keys from her hand.

'Perhaps we may meet again, though,' he suggested. 'In the line of work.'

The woman tilted her head and looked into Daniel's eyes as if to read what lay behind his words, but he knew better than to divulge what Lorimer had in mind. At least for now.

'That would be nice,' she said smoothly, 'if it's meant to happen.'

Then, with a small wave of her hand, she turned away

and headed towards the city centre, not looking back as she made her way along the icy pavement.

Daniel watched her till she turned a corner and was finally out of sight. He let out a sigh. Another cop, someone in Lorimer's outfit. He was only on the edge of things, he reminded himself, but, oh, how good it would be to be part of a real operation, discussing actions with like-minded colleagues, something that he hadn't done for a very long time.

Daniel got into the car and made to shift the driver's seat but there was no need: the woman's long legs had made it perfect for him to drive straight away. He closed then locked the door and looked for the car's manual. *First things first, Kohi*, he told himself. Once he'd found everything there was to know about this particular vehicle he'd go for a drive, test its roadworthiness in these conditions. Then, he thought to himself, it might be nice to see a bit more of the outskirts of the city. Possibly with another woman by his side.

Later, headlights now switched on against the encroaching twilight, he parked in an empty bay at the back of the flats and breathed a prayer that come morning the car would still be there along with four wheels and a satnav system intact. Tomorrow would begin a new chapter, Daniel told himself, flicking the locks shut and walking towards the entrance to the high-rise tower that had become his new home.

'Thought we might have a pizza tonight,' Maggie remarked as Lorimer threw down his car keys onto the table. 'No leftovers after last night.' She grinned. 'Not that I'm complaining. Daniel seemed a nice man and he's been through such a lot.'

'He appreciated it,' Lorimer told her, taking Maggie in his

arms and giving her a kiss on her neck. 'He really enjoyed his evening here.'

'Will he come back? I did ask him.'

Lorimer smiled and shook his head. 'We'll see,' he replied. 'And pizza sounds great.'

He retreated from the kitchen and headed upstairs to wash away the day and change into jeans and a warm jersey. Maggie knew not to ask too many questions and he'd already hinted that former DI Kohi was going to be an asset in one of the ongoing cases, but to keep that secret for now. Perhaps, if the Zimbabwean refugee made some progress with the investigation as well as being a witness to something on that back lane at Bryson's, he might manage to find him some sort of permanent job in Police Scotland. He would need to have him brought in to meet DI Brownlee, however, the sighting of that bloodstained knife a possible lead in Derek Carter's murder.

Where had Lorimer found that dishy-looking black guy? Molly asked herself as she sat on the underground train on her way home. He'd stared at her with huge eyes as if he wanted to ask lots of questions and for a second the detective sergeant had been tempted to lower her guard and indulge in a normal conversation. But, whoever he was, ex-cop or not, he was off limits, someone Lorimer wanted to keep under wraps, and Molly Newton knew better than to ask just why that was. Still, maybe he was only over here for a short time? Something to do with an ongoing case. But, if that was so, why not bring him to the MIT and share his expertise with the team?

She'd kept a close eye on the undercover cop after leaving Kohi with his hired car and made certain that Sylvie Maxwell had gone straight home by train after work. It had been a bit of a trudge following her along the streets till she'd turned into Potterhill Avenue but then it had been difficult to keep her eye on the woman, every window filled with twinkling Christmas trees demanding to be admired, but she'd kept her head down and walked steadily on, glancing as Maxwell fitted her key in the lock and disappeared indoors. After that Molly knew she was free to retrace her own steps and head back into town. Still, her night wasn't over yet, she told herself as the train hurtled through narrow tunnels. Waiting for her on her laptop would be copies of CCTV records to trawl through to see if she could spot the woman leaving that nice house of hers on the morning Burns was killed.

CHAPTER TWENTY-FOUR

Daniel stood outside the door and waited till he heard the footsteps approaching.

'Aw, it's you! Come away in,' Netta said, gasping a little as though she was out of breath.

It had only taken a split second to see the change in her expression: fearful anticipation disappearing as relief washed over her. Had she expected to see the two loan sharks standing there?

'Nice and warm in here,' Daniel remarked, rubbing his hands as he passed into the house and peeped into Netta's kitchen.

'Tray o' mince pies jist oot the oven,' she remarked, laughing. 'You must've smelled them, son. Fancy a wee cuppa tea?'

Soon they were seated in the overcrowded living room, Daniel taking his first tentative bite of a Christmas pie. Not minced meat but sweet dark things like raisins, he guessed.

'Are you busy this morning?' Daniel asked.

'No' really. How?'

Daniel smiled at her reply. It seemed a typically Glasgow expression to substitute *how* for *why*, something he found amusing. *How no'?* Netta had asked him once, meaning *why not?*, and he was beginning to become used to her odd way of phrasing things.

'I've got a surprise,' he told her. 'But I need to ask you to keep it a secret.'

The older woman frowned. 'Hope you've no' been up tae somethin', son,' she said, wagging a remonstrative finger at him.

'Nothing bad,' Daniel assured her. 'I've made a friend here in the city, a connection with my old job,' he added, knowing that however tenuous, that was not a lie. 'Get your coat on and come downstairs with me.' He set down the empty plate and mug on the table.

'In the name o' the wee man!' Netta gasped as Daniel stopped beside the red car. 'Ur ye sure ye nivver lifted it?'

Daniel laughed out loud, understanding Netta's meaning. 'No, Netta, this is not a stolen vehicle. My friend has lent it to me for a while, that's all.'

'Nice friend,' Netta began, doubtfully. 'Plenty o' money if he can afford tae dole oot a wee beauty like this.' She ran a mittened hand across the car's bonnet.

Daniel took out the set of car keys and flicked the door open. 'Fancy coming for a drive, dear Netta?' he grinned.

To see his elderly neighbour exclaiming as they whizzed along the motorway made Daniel Kohi feel a sense of delight

183

that he had thought never to recapture. He had asked Netta where she wanted to go and the prompt answer had been 'Largs', wherever that was. Luckily the satnav would show the way and for now Daniel was happy to listen to the unseen female voice guiding him as well as the woman in the passenger seat who was constantly pointing out places she knew. It was good to be driving again and the Ford was an easy car to manage.

'Ye're a guid driver,' Netta remarked as they followed the signs for Glasgow Airport and Greenock, the M8 motorway taking them away from the city. 'Is it no' awfie hard tae drive on th'ither side o' the road, but?'

'We drive on the left in Zimbabwe,' Daniel told her, 'so I'm used to this.'

'Oh, look at that!' she exclaimed, pointing straight ahead as they sped past the airport runways and headed west. Straight ahead of them were snow-capped mountains gleaming in the sunshine, the pale blue skies clear with no threat of further blizzards. 'Picked a grand day fur a drive.' She dug him gently on the arm with her elbow. For a while she was silent, possibly lost in admiration for the scenery passing them by, the River Clyde to their right and bigger hills and mountains marching into the distance.

To Daniel it was his first real sight of the west coast where the river opened out into a wide firth before reaching the Atlantic Ocean, towns clinging like limpets to each side. He read their names as they passed through: Langbank, Port Glasgow, Greenock ... some of them in Gaelic, Netta explained when he asked about the different words beneath the signs. A quick glance at the satnav showed they had a way to go yet before reaching their destination, but he was in no hurry to get there, enjoying his companion's evident pleasure in the drive itself. Lorimer had told him to take the car out and have a run, get to know the outskirts of the city, and he was glad to be able to share these few hours with his kindly neighbour. Later he would meet up again with the detective superintendent and his colleague, tell them both in detail what he had seen on that fateful day when he'd first arrived in Glasgow, but for now this was a time to forget about death and despair.

'Aw, this is jist amazin', son,' Netta sighed, licking the ice cream cone she had bought, insisting, despite the chill in the breeze, that he have one too. 'Cannae come a' the way tae Largs and no hiv an ice cream frae Nardini's!'

Daniel smiled down at the old woman by his side. She'd told him tales from her past, courting days when she'd been taken to Largs for a day out or 'doon the watter', as she termed it, to a place called Rothesay, that turned out to be a town on a little island not far from the shoreline where they now sat side by side. It was a place that had been chosen to welcome several Syrian refugee families, Netta had informed him. He listened to her stories, mentally filling in the gaps when she had raised her five children and coped with her husband's not infrequent trips to jail. Hers had been a hard life, he realised, and now, all these years later, she was still struggling to pay her rent in that high-rise flat, none of her family apparently bothered to take her in to live with them.

It was so different back home, Daniel thought. The townships were full of extended families, grannies living with children and grandchildren, something his own mother might have done if she'd wanted to come to stay in Harare with them. He heaved a huge sigh, thanking whatever fate had kept her in their old home with his sisters and their families. If she'd been with Chipo and Johannes that night . . .

'Ye orright, son?' Netta was looking at him with an anxious expression on her face.

He forced a smile. 'I'm fine, Netta,' he assured her. 'Just remembering my mother.'

'She still in Africa, then?'

Daniel nodded.

'You should send her a Christmas card,' Netta advised. 'Tell her how you're getting' oan, eh?'

Daniel was silent. It was not a good idea to be in touch like that, any mail from the UK carefully scrutinised by the authorities. If they thought his mother was in contact, then it could only harm her and he was not prepared to risk that.

He shook his head sadly.

'How no'?' she demanded with a frown. 'Sure she'd be glad tae hear frae ye.'

Daniel took the older lady's hand in his for a moment then began to explain as best he could, without mentioning his own personal tragedy, why he could not send any mail back home.

'People there should not know my whereabouts, for, if they do, I fear that may put my mother and other family members in danger.'

'Well,' Netta said at last. 'If ye cannae get word tae her, how about I dae it? Kind o' clandestine, know whit ah mean? Say I wis her pen pal frae Scotland an' I dropped a few wee hints aboot ye, no' naming ony names like?'

186

She looked at him, an eager expression on her face. 'Wid that work, d'ye think? Mind, it'll huv tae go airmail noo afore the last postin' date.'

Daniel gave her a smile and shrugged. 'Perhaps,' he replied. 'Let me think about it.'

It was quieter on the journey back, Netta dozing in the passenger seat, the strong sea air working its soporific magic. They had left behind a fine day, the sun-dappled sea bright under a blue sky, but he could see clouds gathering and Daniel felt as though the carefree time they had spent was over. The memory of that hand clutching a bloodstained knife seemed to be growing ever clearer as they approached the city boundaries.

Daniel dropped his neighbour in the city centre and then headed back across the river once more, the satnav directed to the red-brick building in Helen Street where he had first met Lorimer. This time he parked in the same place he had spotted the silver Lexus, a sense of pride tugging at his mouth as he drove the red car into a space beside vehicles belonging to other police officers. Okay, he wasn't exactly an inspector again, but he was here on genuine police business and any fear he'd had in sharing the incident with Lorimer and his colleague had disappeared. Nobody in the Home Office would have any idea that he was involved in a live case and, besides, his role today was as a witness, not as part of an investigation team.

DI Graham Brownlee stood up when the door of Lorimer's office opened to admit the man they'd been expecting.

Brownlee stretched out his hand as Lorimer made the introductions, hiding his initial surprise at Daniel whose firm handshake and ready smile was nothing like he had anticipated. A refugee, Lorimer had told him, and somehow Brownlee had created an image in his mind of some thin, downtrodden creature, not this handsome man in an expensive-looking overcoat whose intelligent dark brown eyes were regarding him with interest.

'Daniel Kohi,' he heard Lorimer say. 'Former Inspector Kohi of the Zimbabwean Police,' he added, making Brownlee raise his eyebrows in a gesture of astonishment that even he could not conceal.

'You're a police officer?'

Kohi smiled and sat down beside him on one of the chairs Lorimer had brought into his office. '*Was* a police officer,' he replied, and Brownlee noticed something else in the man's face, a strain around his mouth, the way he looked down for a moment, as if unwilling to meet Brownlee's own gaze. There was a story here and one that the man did not wish to share with a stranger. A refugee, Brownlee reminded himself, with a good reason to seek asylum in Britain. Something he was not going to mention unless Kohi wanted to.

'You'll be accustomed to being on the other side of an interview like this, then,' Brownlee said. 'Though I'm intrigued to hear what you have to tell me.'

'Yes,' Kohi admitted. 'Plenty of times I conducted enquiries into serious crimes, but . . . ' he heaved a sigh and drew a hand across his brow, 'those days are past now,' he said quietly.

'It was such an odd thing to see,' he began. 'I had just

arrived in Glasgow, was making my way up Hope Street, when I happened to look down this particular narrow lane.'

'Why did you stop there?'

I was carrying my baggage and simply stopped to shift it from one hand to the other, a few moments, that was all. Then . . . ' he drew in a deep breath, 'then I saw it.'

Brownlee watched the man's face as the jawline tensed and his eyes took on a faraway quality as if he were seeing the entire scene in his mind once more. He listened carefully as Daniel Kohi related the incident that he had seen.

The man had perfect recall, it seemed, was even capable of what was known as having a photographic memory, something that must have come in useful when he'd been a cop himself. That second visit to Bryson's and seeing the man slip out of that basement had been related in detail and, when he'd produced a photograph of the late Vincent Burns, Kohi had nodded.

'Yes,' he said, pointing one finger at the image. 'That was the man I saw on both occasions. First holding that blood-stained knife and second when I was hiding behind those boxes in the basement area of the building.'

'You know this man is dead?' Brownlee asked him.

Kohi nodded, glancing towards Lorimer.

'I told him,' Lorimer confirmed. 'It looks as if we need to do a great deal more digging into Burns's past. We mustn't jump to conclusions but the fact that Burns was seen holding a bloodstained knife the day that Derek Carter was mur-dered obviously suggests that he may have been involved in his colleague's death. And we now have the lab results confirming the bloodstains in the basement are a match for Carter's.'

'So, it looks as if Burns may have killed Carter down in that basement. And then someone wanted Burns out of the way,' Brownlee said. 'For what reason? To avenge Carter's death? Or because his continued existence was a threat of some sort?'

Lorimer kept his face completely impassive. There was no way he was going to divulge the high-profile investigation into what lay behind the unmasking of several undercover officers and a terrorist threat to their city; no, for now that must be kept completely secret. These two deaths were cases that the MIT would focus on, with Brownlee co-opted for the duration. The DI might well be persuaded to throw his cap into the ring if a vacancy appeared here in the upper floor of Helen Street but meantime he was there to help and as far as Brownlee was concerned former Inspector Kohi was simply an eyewitness.

Lorimer stood up and shook Kohi's hand. 'Thanks for coming in today. We really appreciate it.'

'Yes,' Brownlee added. 'It's been very helpful indeed.'

Lorimer saw the DI smiling ruefully as he continued, 'Pity we couldn't have you as an officer in Police Scotland, but I gather you have to have settled status first and a period of non-working, is that correct?'

All credit to Kohi, he did not glance Lorimer's way or hesitate as he smiled and nodded.

'Perhaps one day when the time is right,' he murmured and then turned and left the two detectives looking after him.

'Well, that was a surprise and no mistake,' Brownlee

commented. 'I can see why his natural inclination was to follow up the incident in that back lane.'

'And we ought to be grateful that he did,' Lorimer put in. 'Now, where do we go from here?'

That had gone better than he could have anticipated, Lorimer thought as he sat alone once more, fingers steepled under his chin, a thoughtful expression in his blue eyes. Brownlee had what he wanted, an eyewitness who could identify Burns and confirmation that the African had spotted him with that knife the day Carter had died. Easy enough, if he'd had some help, to haul a body from the basement into the boot of a big car opposite that back door then drive up to Glennifer Braes, they had agreed. Burns's Jaguar was already impounded and now being examined by a team of special forensic experts to see if that theory was correct.

Kohi had been great, he told himself, giving nothing away about their arrangement and saying little about his own background. Lorimer heaved a sigh. He agreed whole-heartedly with what Brownlee had said: he too would have Kohi on the force in a heartbeat if circumstances allowed. However, there were ways in which the former inspector could still make himself useful and Lorimer intended to initiate one of them right now.

He picked up his mobile and dialled a number.

'Kohi? It's me, Lorimer. Meet you in half an hour? Here's where you're going.' He reeled off the postal code that he knew by heart.

CHAPTER TWENTY-FIVE

The watcher in the van pulled the hood further across a shadowed face.

The schoolteacher's car was back first as usual and it would only take a matter of minutes once she'd parked to whack her over the head and drag her into that garage. One gloved hand began to pull open the door then, as a second car came around the corner, clicked it shut again.

It was a red Ford that turned into the Lorimers' drive and, not waiting to see the occupant of the vehicle (a friend by the looks of it as no delivery driver would park right behind the schoolteacher's car), the watcher accelerated away from the pavement and drove out of the avenue, muttering curses that were mercifully unheard by any living soul.

'Daniel, what a lovely surprise!'

Maggie turned from the garage and flicked her key fob, letting the door shut behind her. 'I wasn't expecting to see you again so soon. Come on in and I'll put the kettle on.'

Daniel followed the dark-haired woman into the house and waited until she had turned on the Christmas tree lights before he spoke.

'Your husband sent me here,' he told her. 'He gave me navigation coordinates but until I drew up, I didn't realise this is where he was sending me.'

Maggie chuckled. 'Perhaps he wanted to surprise you,' she suggested. 'Or maybe he was being ultra-cautious? Who knows what goes on in that mind of his sometimes,' she said. 'Here, let me take your coat, Daniel. Sit over there and I'll put the fire on. Tea or coffee?'

Daniel watched as she bustled about the long room that was divided into living room and kitchen. It was obvious that she was pleased to see him, however unexpected, and he felt a familiar sense of home as the gas fire was ignited and he warmed his hands by its blue flames. Women like Maggie Lorimer were the same the world over: glad to show hospitality to strangers and ready to feed them with whatever resources they had. She reminded him of Aunt Hannah back in the township, the youngest sister of his late father, who was known for her kindness and loved nothing more than cooking up a huge pot of squash to feed the menfolk in her family plus anyone who was in need of a hot meal.

He had scarcely put the coffee cup to his lips when he heard the front door opening and Lorimer's voice calling.

Daniel rose to his feet as the detective superintendent entered the room.

'Hi, Daniel, glad you could make it,' Lorimer told him. 'We'll have a cup of something together upstairs. Is that all right with you, Mags?' he called.

'Suits me,' his wife replied. 'Gives me time to fix something nice for dinner.'

Daniel followed the tall detective up a flight of stairs that turned onto a landing then found himself ushered into a large room that overlooked the front garden. Outside he could see twinkling fairy lights shining from the adjoining properties until Lorimer switched on the overhead light and pulled a cord, drawing dark velvet curtains across the windows.

'Thanks for coming in today,' Lorimer began as he motioned Daniel to take one of the comfortable chairs that were angled around a long low table. 'Brownlee was impressed,' he added. 'And your statement will be extremely helpful in pushing this case forward. However, that isn't why I wanted to talk to you here, in private.'

Daniel immediately recognised a new note of seriousness in the detective's voice.

'Look, I know this might seem an imposition, but I wondered if you could help me.'

'Of course,' Daniel began, but Lorimer had already raised his hand.

'Don't agree till you hear me out,' he said. 'This is something that could put you in a difficult position.'

'Go on,' Daniel said, curious to learn what was coming next.

'I had an idea,' Lorimer began. 'I thought that you might begin to mingle with other refugees that have arrived recently to the city, talk to them, see if there is anything that makes you suspicious that they are here under false pretences.'

'Why? What is it you are looking for?' Daniel asked. He stared at Lorimer, noting the way he bit the edge of a finger, anxiety revealing itself in that one small gesture. Had he debated long and hard with himself before summoning up the courage to ask for his help?

Lorimer shook his head. 'I'm not at liberty to discuss the details,' he replied. 'Suffice to say we are expecting something big in the city. This Christmas.'

Daniel's eyes widened. 'A terrorist threat?'

The detective superintendent merely stared at him, his blue eyes unblinking. To answer that question might put Lorimer in a tricky position, Daniel realised at once, so it was better that the idea come from Kohi and be left hanging, neither denied nor affirmed.

'I know this is a big thing to ask, Daniel. And, to be honest, it would be entirely between us both, no one else involved.'

Daniel watched as he took a deep breath then continued.

'Can you be our eyes and ears in places where any of our own officers would find it hard to mingle?'

Daniel swallowed. He had no taste for being amongst the poor souls he'd spent many months with, their harrowing tales of torture and betrayal far worse than his own. Yet, if this was his way back to becoming Inspector Kohi once again . . . ?

'Yes,' he replied, his voice a little husky. 'Tell me what you want me to do.'

Lorimer stood at the door as the hired Ford drew away and Maggie waved her hand. He had taken bigger risks than this in his career but if things all went wrong, he might be facing more than a disciplinary hearing.

*

Netta chuckled as she signed the Christmas card. Daniel could give her the address tomorrow and then she'd close the envelope and seal it with the Guide Dogs for the Blind sticker which had her name and address. Every mother should have a card from their bairns at Christmas, she told herself fondly. Even if hers only came around for a wee while on the day itself, it was keeping in touch that mattered.

She sat in the sagging armchair, cradling the card in her hands and wondering about Jeanette Kohi, the woman in Zimbabwe who might be thinking of her boy at this very moment.

'Dinna ye worry, hen,' she said softly. 'Ah'll see he keeps in touch even if it's me that's writin' the letters.'

CHAPTER TWENTY-SIX

'That's it!' Lorimer punched the air as he read the forensic report. Traces of Carter's blood had been found in the boot of Burns's car, despite someone's attempt to bleach the entire surface area. Partial fingerprints in and around the boot seemed to match those of Burns plus another unidentified person, and hairs from an unknown source had been gathered along the headrest of the passenger seat. Burns might have taken the Jaguar to be valeted and given the boot a good clean-out himself but that had not been quite thorough enough to hide some evidence. *Every contact leaves a trace*, Locard's principle insisted, and so often that held true to the satisfaction of officers pursuing a case like this.

Now it was time to piece together exactly what had happened on the day of Carter's death and take steps to trace the vehicle that had transported his body to the Glennifer Braes. He was in no doubt now that Vincent Burns had been involved in Carter's death, either by wielding that fatal knife himself or disposing of it and the body. Just why Carter had been so brutally murdered remained a mystery, though that, and Burns's subsequent death, were surely linked.

Lorimer tried to envisage the scene: had Burns lured Carter to that dingy basement on some pretext only to thrust a knife into him several times, a brutal attack that was surely premeditated? The pathologist's report had shown that the weapon used was possibly a large kitchen knife, not something that would have been easy to hide. Had Burns secreted it in the basement then taken his colleague by surprise? Or had there been more than one attacker, the basement door lying ajar as Kohi had seen it. It would have been difficult for Burns to haul a dead body into the boot of his Jaguar by himself, after all. No, Lorimer thought, there had to have been a second person there. Someone from Bryson's? And when had Burns cleaned himself up afterwards? So, under cover of late afternoon darkness, had Burns and his accomplice bundled Carter's body into the car and driven straight back to the villa in Newton Mearns?

Lorimer breathed out a long sigh of relief. He hadn't wanted to believe that any of the officers whose details he'd given to Professor Solly Brightman were involved with Carter's murder and still hoped his mind would rest easy on that score. If Carter had been killed just before Kohi had spotted Burns in that alleyway, then it would have been before clocking off time for Cochrane and Hutton at the Mill Street Division in Paisley. That left Mandy Richardson and Sylvie Maxwell. However, if Richardson had kept to her usual pattern, she would have been at home with the kids after school. Sylvie? No, he told himself, that was an absurd idea. She had shown genuine grief about Carter's death and he was certain she had no knowledge of what had transpired that fateful day, though he still felt there was something the undercover officer was hiding from him.

Still, it was a bit strange how all four of the specialist officers lived close to Glennifer Braes. He shrugged and shook his head.

Now he had to figure out Vincent Burns's death in all of this, and that meant returning to Newton Mearns, he decided. He had to hear what the crime scene manager had to say and find out if any progress had been made in the house-to-house enquiries.

The big house lay silent, the scene of crime officers long gone. So far there were no reports of anything incriminating being found on the man's laptop or iPad that had been recovered from a downstairs study, but Lorimer wanted to have a look around, see what sort of lifestyle this man had enjoyed before being bludgeoned to death. He unlocked the storm door with gloved hands then set a Yale key to the inner door, lifting a couple of newspapers from the porch as he went. Perhaps the lad had simply been following orders from his shop if Burns had paid till the end of the month? Lorimer frowned. Odd thing to do when he knew there was nobody there to read them.

He paused for a moment, an idea forming in his head. Had Burns really been all alone in this big house? Or was there a regular stay-over visitor, perhaps? A woman, maybe? Forensics would pick up signs and traces if that had been the case. And that would explain why newspapers had been left here for somebody to pick up. Once he'd had a chat with the officer in charge of house-to-house enquiries that might become clearer. For now, he'd walk around, look at the place with the eyes of a detective.

Inside was warm, the central heating no doubt on some sort of timer during these cold winter months, and he was glad to feel the change in temperature. The house was in darkness, however, no twinkling lights from a Christmas tree, no smell of fresh pine. What had the man's plans been for the seasonal holiday? he wondered. Lots of single people he knew liked to get away from these icy shores to sunnier climes: Florida with golf courses in every residential area, or the islands of the Caribbean where life seemed more relaxing. Perhaps, like Sylvie Maxwell, Burns had planned to have a skiing break. Looking around at the total lack of Christmas decorations, it did seem as if the senior partner at Bryson's might have hoped to get away from this big empty house.

It had been loved and looked after at one time, Lorimer reckoned as he moved from the solid oak kitchen with rows of patterned plates lining the shelves of a large Welsh dresser. Someone had picked these out several years ago, he told himself, seeing a woman's hand in such touches. It was spotless, no doubt due to the ministrations of the cleaning company Burns had employed, and yet it lacked a genuine feeling of homeliness. Despite the expensive furnishings – copper pans hanging from a pulley above an island table, a sleek set of knives arrayed against a metallic strip (none apparently missing) and matching appliances in cream and chrome – there was something lacking. No plants, no little jugs or bowls on the wide window sill of the sort that Maggie loved to collect. Would the rest of the house have that neglected air? he wondered, strolling back to the reception hall with its dark wood panelling and subdued lighting.

The main lounge downstairs did not look as though Burns had used it on a day-to-day basis, the dark leather corner suite and sheepskin rugs centred around a vast glass-topped table, a gas fire on one wall concealed behind a smoked glass panel. There was no sign of a newspaper or a book here, not even a waste bin with crumpled sweet wrappers. Had this been a place where Burns had entertained visitors, perhaps? Lorimer stood beside a glass-fronted cabinet, neat rows of crystal lined up in order of size and shape. Below, hidden behind a set of sliding wooden doors, he found racks of wine and champagne plus every sort of spirit he could imagine. He turned once more to gaze at the table but there was no sign of a ring mark and no coasters laid out either.

The room to the back of the house proved to be the one where Burns must have spent most time, he reckoned, a large flat-screen TV against one wall and a side table heaped with golfing magazines and back issues of *Private Eye*. Signs of the man were everywhere: a box of tissues on the carpet next to a recliner chair and several remote controls for the TV and DVD player. Forensics had lifted all the personal stuff, of course, but so far there was nothing to suggest he had had any recent company, female or otherwise, so the detective superintendent headed up the wide staircase that led to a half landing then up to the next floor.

The main bathroom was immaculate, beige stone tiles on every wall and floor, sleek chrome fittings gleaming from the walk-in shower and freestanding bath. He ran a finger under the taps and shower head; everything was bone dry. Breathing in, all he could smell was a faint scent of lemon, possibly from a cleaning product. Out in the corridor, he walked into what appeared to be the master bedroom, a vast space with a king-sized sleigh bed, stripped to its mattress, and a door opened to reveal the en-suite bathroom.

Here his nose told him two things: one, that Vincent Burns had enjoyed a splash of expensive Christian Dior cologne and two, that the faint fragrance he could smell on one of the towels hanging by the side of a green glass basin was one he had recently come across. He picked the sample from his pocket and laid it near his nostrils. Yes, it was the same scent, Baccarat Rouge 540. So, Burns may have had female company not long before the morning he was killed, the same woman who had left the listening devices in Carter's house in Ralston, perhaps? And that, Lorimer decided, was another reason for finding out what the neighbours may have seen or heard in the days before the murder. He'd have to contact the forensic specialist who had picked up that trace of perfume in Carter's home. They'd missed that bathroom towel, he thought, but the scent was so faint that only someone like himself who'd been carrying it about in his pocket may have discerned its aroma.

'The paper boy was a real help,' DC O'Brien told him as they sat side by side in the warmth of the Lexus, her own car parked a little further along from the crime scene. The officer was a woman about his own age, Lorimer knew, and he thought he remembered her from lectures they had both attended for the Scottish Medico Legal Society. She looked tired, heavy circles beneath grey eyes, but that determined jawline showed her compulsion to dig into this case no matter the unsociable hours or the intense cold outside.

'He delivered papers to everyone in the street,' she went on, 'and the householders can vouch for the time he usually arrived.'

'Helluva shock for the poor lad,' Lorimer commented. 'But I'm glad he's been able to help you. Any reason why the papers have still been delivered to the house?'

The DC raised her eyebrows. 'That hadn't been noticed. I'll ask at the newsagent's, though.'

'Pre-paid bill so carrying out their obligation, maybe? Or expecting someone to be in the house?' Lorimer suggested. 'What about the other neighbours, any joy there?'

'There are sixteen houses on this particular street, eight on each side,' O'Brien continued. 'Few of the residents were in the habit of leaving their homes as early as Vincent Burns, unfortunately, so we only have a couple of people who could confirm they sometimes saw his car leaving the drive and turn onto the main road.'

Lorimer nodded, waiting to hear more.

'One is a girl who went swimming early each day. Sharon Jackson. She's on track for a Commonwealth medal, it seems, so she trains before going to school. She's seventeen, got her own licence. And her own brand new Mini Cooper.' O'Brien wrinkled her nose in a gesture that was intended to convey her feelings about over-privileged teenagers. 'Anyhow, she says that Burns left the house really early on several occasions recently when she was just setting off for the swimming pool.'

'How early?'

'Around five a.m.'

Lorimer gave a whistle. 'What the heck was he doing up at that hour? Their offices don't open till seven when the cleaners arrive.'

'Think he was off doing something we want to know about?' O'Brien asked, her eyes twinkling.

Lorimer said nothing, just gave a slight nod. If Sylvie Maxwell was right about Burns being suspicious of her, then perhaps he had something to worry about? And maybe that same something had taken him off for early morning trips somewhere. Or . . . ?

'Did this Jackson girl say if he was alone in his car?'

'Oh!' O'Brien's face reddened, giving away the fact that this was something she had failed to ask.

'Which is her house?' Lorimer asked and O'Brien turned to point along the street at a white two-storey house that was just visible behind a row of bare-branched poplars. He would go there later but first needed to hear everything else that had been gleaned from the house-to-house visits.

'Apart from the Jackson girl and the paper boy the only other resident who saw Vincent Burns regularly was an old dear across the road. It's the smallest house on the street.' She pointed out a cottage that was closer to the road than its neighbours, a much smaller garden separating the home from a low perimeter stone wall that ran beside the pavement. 'Mrs Alicia Milroy. Eighty-three years young and sharp as a tack.' She grinned. 'Up with the lark every morning to do her yoga and stands there at her open bedroom window to breathe in the fresh air, so she told me.'

'And . . . ?'

'And she sees Burns some mornings when his car turns out of his drive, the headlights on at this time of year, she told me, but in the springtime she "sometimes saw him leaving as the dawn chorus was in full flow". Her words, not mine,' the woman added, her eyebrows raised.

With a female companion? Lorimer wondered. Someone who wanted to be away from Vincent Burns's house before anyone might spot her? Had the man been conducting an affair? Could these sightings have been no more than a top lawyer hiding his indiscretion? Or, and here was the real question, had Burns been hiding something far more sinister on these early morning journeys?

Burns had been married once, many years before, his wife having left him for another man, and since then there was no record of any further permanent relationship. That was not to say the man had been a hermit, that faint scent in his en suite bathroom giving a hint of some female presence. And the impression Lorimer had been given during their meeting at Bryson's was of a man who was pretty much in control of himself, somewhat arrogant, perhaps, the type who might see a woman as a person to control rather than as an equal partner. Sylvie Maxwell had felt threatened by the man and she was not some wilting creature but a strong-minded and well-trained officer who did not suffer fools gladly, be they men or women.

Lorimer lifted the phone and tapped out a number then waited. A male voice gave his name.

'Lorimer here. Any results yet on the items taken from the

scene of crime? Vincent Burns? I'm particularly interested in anything you discovered on his bedding.'

There was a throaty chuckle then the forensic scientist asked Lorimer to wait for a moment while he consulted his notes.

'Yes,' came the voice once more. 'Is this what you were hoping we'd find? Traces from the bedclothes. His *and* hers. DNA's been done on both and, before you ask, there isn't anything on a database to identify the female who'd shared his bed. Sorry.'

'You might want to take a hand towel from the en suite,' Lorimer told him. 'There's a faint scent that I recognised. Same perfume that was found in Carter's bathroom.'

'Oh,' the scientist replied. Lorimer heard the fellow sigh. 'Would have expected all of the towels to have been brought in for examination. I'll get onto that right away.'

'And ask someone to pick up the kitchen knives from there while you're at it,' he said. 'I'd like the pathologist to have a look at them.'

Lorimer nodded to himself as the call ended. Well, he'd not been wrong about his thoughts on a female in Vincent Burns's life. And, since nobody that fitted such a role had come forward to express grief at his death, Lorimer decided to make it one of his tasks to find out who this woman was and why she had remained a secret till now.

Mrs Milroy, he thought, gazing across at the little cottage. An older lady whose habits included early rises might well be the sort to remember details that could lead to finding out about the mystery female.

CHAPTER TWENTY-SEVEN

L ark Cottage was a simple pre-war bungalow with a dark slated roof and creamy roughcast walls, its diamond-paned windows showing the sort of pebbled glass that had been fashionable several decades ago. Café curtains at the front gave some privacy to the householder, otherwise passers-by might have gazed straight into the downstairs rooms. Lorimer rang the old bell push, heard a trilling sound reverberating beyond the glazed front door then waited patiently. An eighty-three-year-old might take her time to arrive at the summons of a bell despite her regular fitness regime, he reckoned. However, he soon heard footsteps and a shadowy figure appeared.

There was a rattle and the door opened just wide enough for him to raise his warrant card to a pair of pale blue eyes that looked from him to his identification.

'Hello, Detective Superintendent Lorimer, Police Scotland,' he called out.

Seemingly satisfied, the woman released the chain and stepped aside.

'You'd better come in,' she said. 'It's freezing outside.'

Lorimer looked down on a tiny old lady, not more than five feet, he reckoned, who was smiling up at his own six foot four inches. Her white hair was twisted into an elaborate knot at the base of her neck and the face that looked up at him was smooth and hardly wrinkled except for laughter lines around her eyes.

'My, you're a big lad,' she commented. 'Your ma must have fed you porridge from an early age.' She laughed then beckoned him along a short corridor. 'Come into the kitchen. It's warmer there and I can put the kettle on. Coffee, I suppose? That's what all the TV cops seem to drink, anyway, isn't it?'

Lorimer followed Mrs Milroy along to a large kitchen that looked as if it had not been upgraded since the house had been built. A large Raeburn stove belched out heat and the flagged stone floor had a couple of rugs laid carefully by the Belfast sink and beside the stove. A black cat was curled in its bed beneath a circular wooden table, which was draped in patterned oilcloth. A William Morris design, he saw, the familiar fruit patterns in muted greens and apricot picked out elsewhere in the room: sage-coloured curtains at each of three windows and a row of bright orange cast-iron pots lined neatly on a long shelf. The room was cosy and welcoming, a scent of something sweet that suggested Alicia Milroy had recently been baking.

'Thank you,' he said. 'That's kind of you and yes, coffee will be fine, just black, no sugar.'

'Watch you don't bump Maori,' the old woman told him. 'He's an elderly creature and easily offended.'

'We've got an old fellow at home. Big ginger tom,' Lorimer

offered. 'No idea how old he is as he came years ago as a stray. Nobody knew where he'd been, and he wasn't micro-chipped, so we ended up adopting him.'

'Really?' Mrs Milroy turned and smiled knowingly. 'I always think they choose us rather than the other way around.'

She set two porcelain beakers on the table and a plate of biscuits that were still warm from the oven then sat facing Lorimer.

'Now,' she began. 'You're here about Mr Burns, aren't you? And even though that nice young policewoman asked me all sorts of questions you think I might have something to add?'

Lorimer did not try to hide the grin that spread across his face. My, this one was as sharp as O'Brien had said. Straight to the point and not a single sign of making a fuss about "my poor neighbour" as so many in her place might have done.

'You knew him quite well?' Lorimer asked, blowing across the surface of his coffee to cool it a little.

'Hardly that,' she replied. 'Folk round here tend to keep themselves to themselves. Easy enough when they are hidden away at the back of those long curving drives. It's a wealthy area now,' she mused. 'Used to be a row of cot-tages belonging to the estate, but they were all sold off for development. Except ours,' she added with a tilt of her chin. 'Someone made a packet back then, all right. Plots went for a fortune and each buyer built a house of their own choos-ing. Not like modern estates elsewhere in the Mearns,' she sighed. 'All the same, row after row, hardly a decent bit of garden for children to play in.'

Lorimer followed her gaze and looked out of a window

to see a large lawn surrounded by mature trees and shrubs, dormant now during these cold winter months but probably bursting with colour come springtime.

'I might not have known Vincent Burns too well but I did see him coming and going, Detective Superintendent.' She smiled and tapped her head. 'I may be old, but I have good eyesight and a grand memory. Plus,' she gave a sudden hoot of laughter, 'I'm a nosy old woman!'

Lorimer smiled at her. 'The sort that make the best witnesses,' he said drily. 'Perhaps you might tell me something.' He leaned forwards and lowered his voice. 'Did you ever see him with a woman?'

'Ah, so that's why you came to see me? Yes, I did, and, though I could not give you her name I can tell you what she looked like.'

Several ginger biscuits and a refill of coffee later, Lorimer had detailed notes based on what Alicia Milroy had told him. A woman much younger than Vincent Burns, 'old enough to be her father,' the old lady had snorted derisively, but obviously in a different type of relationship, from what she had observed. 'Fair hair cut in a bob, pert little face; pretty when I saw her smiling, clever-looking girl. Maybe in her thirties? Much taller than me, almost Vincent's height, possibly five foot seven or eight?'

Lorimer had scribbled down these and other facts as Mrs Milroy had sat, eyes closed as if to better remember such things. For a moment she reminded him of the Zimbabwean with his photographic memory.

'I think she was afraid of being seen with him,' the old

lady said at last, looking Lorimer directly in the eye. 'She always had to be away so early from that house and, of course, there was never another car. He took her home, wherever that was.'

'Do you think she was married?'

Mrs Milroy shook her head firmly. 'No wedding ring,' she assured him. 'I looked, of course,' she added with an impish smile. 'Binoculars always handy for birdwatching, you know. Us old dears never miss a trick.'

Lorimer smiled back, glad to have a witness of this calibre.

'Did you see anyone coming to the house on the morning he was found dead?'

'The other officer asked me that,' she sighed. 'And, no, I'm sorry. Think the snowfall must have blotted out sounds so much during the night that I wasn't awake as early as usual.'

'And did you see anything unusual the evening before that?'

She shook her head. 'It's dark so early. I tend to have my tea around five-thirty then watch the six o'clock news till seven. Besides, there's nothing much to see at that time, just cars going past as the residents return home from work.'

'Were there any other visitors to the house across the street recently that were unusual, perhaps?'

The old lady wrinkled her brow. 'I don't think so,' she began. Then held up a finger. 'Wait a minute, there was a big van.' Her frown deepened. 'I remember now. It went up the drive after Vincent's own car. Thought it might be a workman of some kind. But it was still there after midnight when I was out in the garden calling for Maori.'

'Can you remember what sort of van?'

She gave a sigh. 'It didn't have any lettering on the sides, more like a hired van. A dark colour. It looked maroon under the streetlight as it turned into the drive. But of course, these new lights make colours a little bit strange, don't they? And,' she added, jaw tensed, 'before you ask, no I haven't a clue about its registration number. It was gone when I woke up. I can see right down the drive from my bedroom window and there was nothing there at all. I expect Vincent had put his car away in the garage as he usually does.'

'Why do you say that?'

'Oh, well, I spotted him leaving that morning. About seven-thirty, I think. I guess he was just going into work as usual, trying to beat the rush-hour traffic.'

'Can you remember what date it was that you saw the van arriving?' Lorimer asked.

'Oh, yes,' she assured him. 'You see it was my birthday, November the twenty-seventh.'

Lorimer sat very still. This was the same day that the pathologist reckoned Derek Carter had been murdered, the day Daniel Kohi had arrived in Glasgow.

Was it possible that this unmarked van had been used to transport his body from the house in Newton Mearns to that lonesome gully up in Glennifer Braes? And, had this keen-eyed old lady been witness to something that had culminated in the death of Vincent Burns himself?

CHAPTER TWENTY-EIGHT

He wasn't worth mourning, the woman decided, tossing the newspaper aside. Vincent had had his chances and, like the greedy man he'd always been, he'd blown them in favour of amassing more money than he could ever have spent in a lifetime. And, despite the promises he'd made to share that future lifestyle with her, it was not enough to spare him from his fate.

There would be an obituary sometime, no doubt. A half column of obsequious drivel about his perceived achievements and none about his failures. Meantime, his name was being splashed across the front pages as another death in the city's business sector, poor Derek Carter's demise dragged up for inspection once again. Her jaw clenched in frustration at the memory of the listening devices she had planted, not one of them proving to be of any use. He'd never had a single visitor apart from herself to his home.

She looked at her reflection in the window and sighed. They had come so close to everything being perfect, plans laid out in detail, but human frailty had been the unforeseen factor that had cast them aside for now.

And Lorimer was still sniffing around. True, a double murder at Bryson's merited the attention of the MIT but why had he appeared at other crime scenes? And what was he looking for? It was more than ever imperative that his home was searched carefully to find an answer to that question. He kept a laptop there, of that she was certain, evening emails flying back and forth from a source other than his smartphone. Their people had checked. And he was away from his Giffnock residence a fair bit now that he'd taken on this latest murder inquiry. Her other source of information from within Police Scotland had dried up, much to Shararah's fury, but she would bide her time in the hope that someone might make a slip and she could seize her chance to find out exactly what they knew. Meantime, they had to target the detective superintendent's wife.

It was time to act. And the sooner the better.

She lifted her phone and pressed a few numbers.

'It's me. I want you to go there now. I think there's a good chance that she'll be on her own this afternoon. In and out as fast as you can. And no slip-ups. We don't want it to look like anything other than an opportunistic robbery. With not *too* much violence,' she added, a thin smile across her lips.

The car radio was playing 'Troika', one of Maggie's favourite Christmas tunes, part of the *Lieutenant Kijé* suite as she turned the car into their drive. It was too nice to switch off just yet, so she let the engine run, smiling happily as the heater blasted out warm air and Classic FM entertained their listeners with the music.

She was blissfully unaware of the shadowy figure lurking around the edge of the garage, unseen but waiting.

As the final strains died away, Maggie flicked the key fob towards the door and watched as it rose up silently. In seconds she drove forwards into the garage, parked in her usual spot and turned off the ignition.

There was no sound as she opened the car door, nothing to alert her to the presence of another person creeping up behind her.

All that Maggie Lorimer knew was a sudden pain on the back of her head then darkness. Her body landed with a dull thud onto the floor, arms outstretched, the thick duffel coat breaking her fall.

Swiftly, the attacker prised the car keys from her hand, searched in her coat pocket for the house keys that nestled there then, as silently as it had risen, the garage door was closed, leaving William Lorimer's wife lying unconscious on the cold stone floor.

It was late when he drove the Lexus into the drive, smiling at the sight of the twinkling Christmas tree in their bay window. Maggie would have been home for hours by now, his text message telling her to go ahead and have dinner without him, not an unusual occurrence at this stage of a major inquiry.

'Hi, I'm home!' he called out, peering into the darkened hallway. He frowned as no voice answered his greeting. Apart from the tree lights on their timer, the whole downstairs was shrouded in gloom. Even the candle branch on the kitchen window sill had been left unlit.

'Maggie?' he called, starting up the stairs to see if she was in their lounge watching TV or had turned in for an early night.

He switched on the stair light, puzzled. It was not like Maggie to leave the house in such darkness, rather her habit was to turn on several lamps downstairs and keep this stair light switched on till he came home.

'Maggie?' he called again, entering their bedroom and approaching the bed, fearful of waking her. A small sound greeted him and, as he blinked, the shape on the bed became Chancer, their orange cat, stretching himself with a yawn.

'Where is she?' he muttered, more to himself than to the cat.

The lounge was also unlit and, as he strode towards the television and put out a hand, he could feel its cool surface. Nobody had watched a programme here in the past few hours, Lorimer reckoned.

Had he forgotten something? Was there a date he'd missed, something on their kitchen calendar that showed Maggie out with a girlfriend or at a school function?

He sped back downstairs and headed straight through the long room, Chancer following him with plaintive miaows.

'You not been fed?' he asked, his frown deepening as he approached the calendar fixed to their kitchen wall.

There was nothing written on today's date, he saw, no meeting with friends, no school Christmas concert till next week.

For a moment Lorimer stood still then turned to look at

Maggie's desk where her laptop sat. Perhaps she had written a note in her online diary?

But, when his eyes came to rest on the place where the device was kept, all he saw was a blank space and wires pulled out.

A cold feeling crept over him as he took in the objects around the room. His own laptop was safely stowed in the briefcase he'd brought home. And there was no sign of Maggie's school bags or her precious iPad, things she would have dropped off at home before going back out for the evening.

Retrace her steps, an inner voice suggested and, a bunch of keys in his hand, Lorimer stepped out of the house then pressed a small blue button.

He watched, mouth opening in horror as he saw, first Maggie's car, its driver's door still open, then his wife's inert body sprawled across the floor.

The two men sat huddled together, one casting worried glances at the other as he stared at the screen in front of him.

'Have you found anything?' Mohammad asked, unable to bear the silence any longer.

Qasim looked up for a moment into the younger man's anxious eyes but said nothing, his face stiff with an inner fury that was all the reply Mohammad was going to receive.

'I did everything she told me,' he whined, rubbing his hands together and then giving a shudder. 'Tell her I'm not to blame.' He tried to catch Qasim's glance. 'Nobody saw me. We're quite safe,' he went on, his voice full of apprehension. 'And maybe you'll find what she wants in there,' he added, pointing to the open laptop.

The long drawn out sigh from the older man made Mohammad shrink back into his seat.

Something had gone wrong and he might be to blame.

Would they take him away like they'd done to the last guy? He shivered, wringing desperate hands beneath the table top.

Shararah was ruthless in meting out punishment and Mohammad feared the woman's ill favour far more than the sharp words Qasim might utter if this laptop did not hold the secrets they had hoped for.

It was five a.m. and pitch black outside the room where he sat, holding her hand, his heart pleading with her to wake up. *Severe concussion*, the doctor had told him. *Onset of hypothermia.*

If he hadn't come home for several hours more … The doctor had shrugged and left Lorimer to imagine a worse fate for his beloved wife than a broken wrist, a badly bruised head and a few hours of complete oblivion. The call had gone out for an ambulance first then to DCI Niall Cameron. A break-in at his home and an attack on his wife were too important to leave to the local cops, he'd decided straight off. He'd followed the ambulance, its blue lights flashing in time to his beating heart, and called Caroline Flint on his hands-free phone to alert her to what had happened. Could it be that whoever had broken into their home had something to do with the investigation that was known only to a handful of senior officers? And, if so, what had they been looking for?

A soft moan from the bed made Lorimer turn to gaze at his wife, her head swathed in bandages, bruises showing on her cheek and mouth where she had fallen. Luckily her gloved hands and heavy coat sleeves had cushioned the worst of Maggie's fall. As it was, her lips and eyes were swollen, and her left wrist had a hairline fracture that had required a plaster cast.

He watched intently as the dark eyelashes began to flutter then she stared at him, blinking as if awaking from a dream.

'What . . . ?' Maggie croaked, her throat dry after the time she had lain on that cold stone floor. She stared at her husband then caught sight of the drip attached to her right hand.

'Oh . . . '

'It's okay, love. You're all right,' he soothed.

'What's happened?' Maggie's voice was a whisper, her sea-grey eyes trying to focus on her surroundings.

'You're safe now,' Lorimer assured her. 'How are you feeling?'

A faint sigh came from the woman in the bed. 'Did I have an accident? Is the car all right?'

Lorimer bit his lip. She didn't remember, then, but the doctor had warned him that the actual events might not return at once.

'The car's fine,' he assured her. 'And it wasn't a traffic accident, darling.' He paused for a moment. Better to tell her the truth than leave her worried. 'Someone thumped you and broke into the house,' he said at last.

'What?' Maggie stared at him, wide-eyed. 'A burglary?'

'Looks like it,' he admitted.

'Goodness. A burglary? Really? I don't remember . . . '
She tailed off, a confused look in her eyes. 'Oh, no! Is there much damage?'

'They took your laptop,' Lorimer said. 'Other than that, nothing. No mess, no sign of vandalism.'

'Maybe they were disturbed?' Maggie ventured.

He nodded, agreeing with the idea for now. If she thought this was an opportunistic burglary, then that was fine with him. No need to worry her with any further details.

'My laptop? That was all?' She tried to sit up but lay back down again, groaning as the pain kicked in.

'That was the only thing they took,' he confirmed.

'Can you find it? My story's on that machine,' she said. 'Backed up, of course,' she added with relief.

In recent years Maggie had gained a modest reputation as a children's author, something that she enjoyed just as much as her teaching career.

'Of course, we'll try,' he promised.

'Should be able to trace it. It's protected that way ... ' Her voice faded in a yawn then her eyes began to close once more.

Lorimer watched as Maggie's breathing became softer and more regular, sleep taking her to a place where pain was banished for a while at least.

If he wasn't involved in the case, then this would never have happened, he told himself. Being a police officer brought risks, of course it did, but his work should never have posed a danger to his wife. Lorimer bit his lip. *Perhaps it is time to retire*, a small voice suggested. *Let others take over.* Niall Cameron would make a fine head of the team, his experience well worthy of promotion. He was almost at his thirty years' service, after all. Nobody would blame him for handing over the job to a younger man. But ... He sighed.

There was always a *but*, wasn't there? Unfinished business that only he could handle right now, caught between the clandestine investigation into a possible terrorist attack and the two murders that were like flies trapped within an invisible web. No, he would carry on meantime, take care that Maggie was safe in their own home and track down whoever had injured her.

His thoughts turned to the practicalities of the attack and theft. Of course, they could put a trace on the laptop, find out exactly where it was, and then? Well, that depended on what the thief had done with it. He doubted very much that Maggie had been coshed in the garage just for her laptop. She was making a name for herself in the world of children's fiction but Margaret Lorimer was still far from becoming a household name, one whose work in progress was hardly worth stealing. If it had been a proper burglary, there would have been far more items missing than that.

No, it was more likely that whoever had taken it was unaware that it belonged to *Mrs* Lorimer and not to the detective superintendent, though once their mistake was apparent, they might simply ditch the device and scarper.

'A *what*?' The woman clenched her fists in a moment of fury.

'A ghost story. She's a children's writer . . . '

'*She?* You mean . . . ?'

'It was the wife's laptop. The only one in the entire house, I told you.' The voice on the telephone sounded a whining note. 'Looked everywhere. He doesn't keep any of his own stuff there.'

'And Mrs Lorimer?'

There was a slight pause as she imagined the person on the other end shrugging his muscular shoulders.

'She'll live. Just gave her a knock on the head. That was all.'

The woman cut him off, her face a mask of rage.

They had spent weeks planning this night, watching and waiting for the right moment, certain that something would have been found in the detective superintendent's home. But he'd been too clever for them, it seemed, and now they were back to where they had started, wondering why William Lorimer had been turning up unannounced at different crime scenes and poking his nose into other officers' business. If, as rumours had it, he was simply looking around for likely candidates to fill upcoming vacancies at the MIT, then all was well.

But, if he was part of a clandestine operation to root out their plans, then everything could collapse.

She drummed impatient fingers on the table in front of her. Perhaps it was time to change things a little, alter the date that had been agreed all those months ago. After all, maximum damage was the desired outcome and most evenings in the run-up to Christmas would see the city centre packed with revellers.

Kalil had instilled into her the need to plan carefully in order to carry out their mission. His teaching would not be in vain, Shararah promised him, silently. This was a crusade against a people who deserved no mercy and this Christmas was one that Glasgow would not forget in a hurry.

'Paisley town centre,' Lorimer was told, several hours after he had left the Queen Elizabeth Hospital. 'Thrust into a bin and covered up with fish supper wrappings. Only damage seems to be the grease all over the casing.'

'And, any traces?'

'Clean as a whistle. They got into it, mind. Some clever hacker managed to bypass the safety screening. But they left no trace. Keys sprayed with some fluid and not even a partial print on the screen or the casing. This lot knew what they were doing all right,' the forensic scientist at Gartcosh told him.

'Okay, keep it for now, of course. Maggie has everything backed up and she doesn't need it just now,' he said, half to himself.

He had left his wife after watching her take a little breakfast, helping her to drink some weak tea and wiping her bruised lips with a soft handkerchief. Forensics had been and gone to their Giffnock home and, as he now expected, there was no trace of the intruder except for some footprints on the garage floor. He had spilled some sand there after that last snowfall, keen to clear the icy drive, and now there was at least one piece of evidence that might be used to trace the suspect's footwear, though both Lorimer and the forensic scientist tasked with this job doubted it would be enough to catch him.

There was no way he was going to leave Maggie on her own in this house, however, and his thoughts turned to someone who might offer to come and stay in their spare room once she had been discharged from hospital.

CHAPTER TWENTY-NINE

J ack of all trades, master of none, Molly Newton thought, applying some fresh lip salve and examining her face in the mirror. It was nice to be asked a favour, even if it had meant abandoning the original task of shadowing Sylvie Maxwell. The undercover officer appeared to be going about her business as expected, travelling from Paisley each day by train to the city centre and spending her days working at Bryson's. Fair play to her, Maxwell had spent long hours of overtime since the death of the senior partner, poring over any files that had not been taken away by Police Scotland for closer examination. Her willingness to be helpful had charmed Dominic Fraser who seemed to be perpetually harassed in his new role as head of the firm, the undercover officer had reported. No, a few days away from overseeing Maxwell's movements would be fine; at least that was what Lorimer had told her.

Now it was a different sort of babysitting job that her boss had requested, looking after his wife when she came home from hospital today. *This was no ordinary burglary*, Lorimer had told her, his keen blue eyes narrowing as he nodded. But, with no more to add to that remark, it was down to Molly to imagine just what he meant. Someone had been looking for something more than hardware they could flog around the pubs to make a few quid for Christmas and Molly Newton was curious to know what that might be. The files at the MIT were all secure and Lorimer toted his personal computer back and forth each day in his battered old leather briefcase. Nobody had ever asked him why but now Molly was beginning to wonder what it was that the detective superintendent had to hide even from his fellow officers in Govan.

He had been up at Gartcosh a bit more often than usual, she knew. Could there be something afoot that was too big for the Major Incident Team to handle? Or, and here Molly paused as she flicked back her hair, eyes crinkling thoughtfully, was there someone rotten inside the force that he needed to find? The debacle over these undercover officers' identities being splashed across the Sunday papers had come and gone again, as all stories did. However, the reverberations were still being felt within the force and Molly was beginning to suspect that Lorimer might have been tasked with the job of rooting out the person behind it all.

'This is really kind of you, Molly,' Maggie said as the taller woman helped her into the car. 'I'm sure I could have taken a taxi, but Bill wouldn't hear of it.'

She looked behind at the hospital. Two nights spent there seemed more like weeks but still Maggie could not remember anything after she had left work that fateful December afternoon.

'No trouble at all, Mrs Lorimer.'

'Oh, Maggie, please! It's only classes full of school pupils who call me that,' she laughed. 'And, after all, we're going to be housemates for a while, though honestly, I think I could manage fine on my own for a few days.'

'No bother.' Molly smiled. 'And I think your doctor was pleased you were having somebody with you.'

'Well. I'm sure he was. They've all been so kind.' Maggie sighed. 'What would we do without our NHS, eh?'

'Right,' Molly replied, then swung her car into the lane that would lead them to the motorway and the fastest way home to the Lorimers' home in Giffnock.

Bill had fussed too much, Maggie thought. It wasn't as if she was in any danger of an incident like that being repeated. After all, statistically speaking, wasn't right now the safest time for her to be alone at home, officers patrolling the area several times a day? The doctor at the Queen Elizabeth had given her strict instructions to take the rest of the term off but Maggie was already chafing against that stricture. What about the end of term dances? The school carol concert? The last day of term when her friends on the staff left early to enjoy a slap-up lunch at a favourite restaurant? Maggie frowned then sighed as the pain in her head throbbed. Well, things happened, and she would simply have to put up with it. Besides, DS Molly Newton seemed like a good companion to have and Maggie began to imagine the pair of them sharing present wrapping and listening to Classic FM as it played her favourite Christmas music.

*

Molly turned with a start as a noise came from behind her.

'Oh, it's just you,' she gasped as Chancer the cat leapt up onto the rocking chair by the fire. Maggie Lorimer had gone upstairs for a rest and last time Molly had looked the woman was blissfully asleep. The orange cat jumped up onto her knees and before she knew it, Molly's fingers were stroking its soft fur, rhythmic purring reverberating under her caress.

She must have dozed off, Molly realised as Maggie put a mug of something sweet smelling on the table beside her.

'Oh! Sorry, I didn't mean ... '

Maggie smiled down at her. 'I thought a mug of *glühwein* might make us both feel a little bit more festive,' she said. 'It's been a strange few days and I'd almost forgotten that Christmas is just around the corner.'

Molly nodded and picked up the steaming mug, aware that the cat was no longer curled on her lap and that it was already dark outside, lights from a twinkling candle branch reflecting its own image on the kitchen windowpane.

She watched as Maggie moved across the room to turn on the radio then she came and sat beside her. 'A little music will help us to capture the festive spirit if this doesn't do the trick.' Maggie grinned, lifting her mug carefully in her right hand.

It was not a radio channel that Molly normally tuned into, nevertheless the Christmas carols were a pleasant distraction and she had to admit they enhanced the mood that Maggie Lorimer was evidently trying to capture.

Molly's eyes were closed as the strains of a familiar tune began, though she'd forgotten its title.

'Nooo!'

She jumped up, startled, as Maggie stood up suddenly, mouth open and eyes wide, the contents of her mug spilling in a red arc.

'It's okay, I'll fetch a cloth,' Molly began, but Maggie waved a hand to stop her, face chalk white as if she had suffered a shock.

'What . . . ?'

Maggie looked down at the detective sergeant. 'Shhh . . . listen . . . ' She raised a commanding finger to her lips as the strains of the music continued.

Then, the colour slowly spreading across her cheeks, she gasped aloud.

'I *remember*,' she began. 'I was listening to "Troika". Sitting in the car till it finished.'

Molly watched as the woman's face lit up.

'I was just sitting there. Then I drove into the garage . . . got out of the car . . . ' She looked at Molly. 'That's when it must have happened,' she said, her hand feeling the back of her head. 'Someone must have been waiting for me out there, crept up behind me, then . . . '

'Coshed you,' Molly finished grimly. 'Look, why not sit down and I'll clear this up,' she said. 'Think back to that moment, see if there is anything else you remember, okay?'

She watched as Maggie sank into her chair, an entranced expression on her face. Could she recall anything more? Or had that tune simply conjured up the moments before the attack?

Sylvie closed the front door and sighed. Still nothing, she thought, her mouth turned down at the corners. Despite her

228

best intentions, there had been no sign of any paperwork that could lead to signs of money laundering in Bryson's.

She flung her keys into the dish on the hall table and made her way through to the kitchen at the back of the house, switching on lights to banish the shadows.

What was it that Derek had wanted to tell her? Their friendship had deepened into something more and Sylvie had been keen to eliminate him from any suspicion during her searches. He'd talked a little about the refugee charity where he volunteered at weekends, even hinting that she might like to join him there for a coffee. Refuweegee, Byres Road, he'd said. But Sylvie had hesitated, reluctant to be seen with him in such a public place.

Would there have been a future for them? She would never know, and perhaps it was a lesson well learned not to let her emotions become entangled with her work. After all, she had a job to do and she would carry it out to the bitter end.

CHAPTER THIRTY

The music from the speakers in a corner of the room was a mixture of brash pop interspersed with soulful ballads, most of which Daniel had never heard before.

The big room was decorated with garlands of paper chains hanging from the white ceiling and an artificial Christmas tree stood in another corner, tilted somewhat drunkenly to one side under the weight of its garish decorations. There were several small children on rugs by the tree, playing noisily with some plastic toys, their antics searing Daniel Kohi's heart as he tried not to watch them.

It was the fifth place that he had visited in recent days, each time being warmly welcomed by different volunteers, some of them former asylum seekers who had made their home in this city. Daniel had listened to the tales of many journeys and months spent waiting, waiting . . . the strain of being suspended between hope and despair showing in so many faces. He had not found anyone that fitted Lorimer's description of a potential terrorist in these centres, however.

Folk had been more than happy to share their stories and praising their Scottish hosts was a common refrain.

This refugee centre, like these others, was a godsend no doubt for many families new to the city, their journeys fraught with so many difficulties more tragic than Daniel's. He had been given a leaflet on the day he'd arrived, an open invitation from this charity to drop in at any time. But until Lorimer's suggestion he had resisted spending time with fellow refugees, afraid to hear any more of their harrowing stories. Instead he had chosen to remain cocooned in his own little world of Netta, his small flat and the long walks into the city centre, the impulse to revisit that narrow lane drawing him back time after time.

But now things were different and coming here had a purpose, one that was more in keeping with a man whose powers of detection were being valued again.

A couple of men had looked up as he entered but, affecting not to notice them, Daniel collected a mug of coffee then sat down opposite the slight figure of a man who was watching the children intently. Syrian, he guessed, by the look of him. Daniel had met a few like him down south, waiting in crowded rooms for decisions to be made, that familiar expression of hopelessness in so many eyes.

'Hello,' he said, leaning forward and extending his hand. 'I'm Daniel.'

The Syrian lifted his head a little but merely nodded then returned to gaze at the little ones playing on the mat.

'Your children?' Daniel asked cautiously.

The man looked at Daniel and nodded. 'The little one. He is mine.' He was blinking as though to hold back tears.

There was a story here, Daniel thought, and not one with a completely happy ending.

'You're staying here, in Glasgow?'

The man frowned, looking around him as if he had only just realised where he was.

'No.' He shook his head. 'We leave tomorrow. If boat sails.'

'You're going back?'

The man shook his head again but this time a tentative smile flitted across his narrow face.

'We go live on island,' he explained, then, looking out of the huge picture windows that overlooked the busy street where litter was being tossed skywards in a gusty wind, he pointed upwards. 'Boat no sail today. Storm,' he added.

Daniel nodded, relieved that his first thought had been wrong. He had met so many refugees in places throughout the UK who had been under some sort of threat: detention, being sent home, no hope of achieving immigration status. His own journey had been far easier than most, he knew, the church in Liverpool liaising with the Home Office on his behalf.

'You are fortunate,' Daniel told him. 'You will have a new home before Christmas.'

The man raised his watery eyes to Daniel and sighed. There was no answer to this, he thought. The past, whatever it had been for this man, was still large in his mind and heart; the future an unknown place.

'You can work once you gain your settled status,' Daniel continued. 'That is something to hope for. What did you do back home?'

The man seemed not to have heard Daniel, his gaze focused on the children by the Christmas tree.

'I was a teacher in Aleppo,' he said softly. 'To little ones like these,' he added with a wistful look.

'You can't go back?' Daniel asked. The ancient city had been freed from its years of turmoil and thousands had returned from refugee camps to begin the monumental task of restoring the place to some form of normality.

The man gave a slight shake of his head then looked at Daniel.

'No safe for me,' he replied simply, holding out his hands in a gesture of weary defeat. 'People here will give him a new life,' he added, looking down at the small boy who turned and gave the man a wide grin.

And what will you do? Daniel wondered. The child would learn the ways of this new country while the father waited patiently for the time when he could do some meaningful work. Teaching? Daniel wondered how many children inhabited this island and if there would be any need for this man's skills.

Whatever his story had been it wasn't over yet. Daniel nodded and began to stand up. 'Good luck for tomorrow,' he said.

There were only so many free cups he could consume before drawing attention to himself, Daniel decided, pouring hot coffee from a big thermal jug. Several groups of men and women sat at tables around the big room, mostly looking towards the children who were playing contentedly with one another, as children will do no matter that they may have met for the first time.

Don't intrude, he told himself, looking around for anyone

alone, like him. *They won't necessarily stand out*, Lorimer had said. *They're encouraged to blend in. So, don't go looking for the silent ones. Look for the those who are comfortable chatting to strangers.*

The two men who had caught Daniel's eye were seated on one side of the room, their backs against a wall. Their position commanded a view not only of the entire room but also of the street outside, watching people passing by or looking up as someone new pushed open the glass door bringing in a draught of chilly air, and the door was only a few paces away should they need to make a hasty exit. He had clocked them as he'd come in, their choice of seats exactly what he would have selected back when he'd been a cop. To sit beside them as soon as he had arrived was a bad idea, however, and it had taken Daniel a while to work his way around to their table. They looked up at his approach, a silent stare that Daniel interpreted as more than mere caution. The older man had a dark beard laced with grey, his salt and pepper hair shorn close to his scalp, a haughty expression in his deep brown eyes. His companion was thickset, muscular rather than fleshy, someone that reminded Daniel of the toughs he'd encountered in too many cases back home. Arabs, certainly, but from which conflict had they fled?

'Hello,' he said, setting down the brightly coloured mug that bore the charity's logo. 'I'm Daniel.' He nodded to the pair. 'I'm new to the city. Woman gave me a leaflet. Said it would be good to find other people.' He shrugged as if finding other people was not really on his wish list.

'Where you from?' the older of the two asked.

'Southern Africa. Zimbabwe,' he replied. There was no

point in trying to hide behind a lie, he'd decided. And, if he were to ferret out the people Lorimer wanted to find, then the more truthful he was, the more likely it was that he would be trusted. He would not reveal his previous occupation, however. Even back home that had sometimes had a negative effect. And, if they should find that out, well, the corruption within that police force might make him look like a bent cop, someone who broke rules and took risks.

'You?' he asked, glancing from one man to the other.

The older man shifted a little in his seat and for the first time Daniel saw a thin walking stick tucked in against the wall.

'Syria,' he said. 'We came across by boat ...' There was a shrug and a half smile as if to indicate that theirs was a familiar story. 'Detention for many months, of course.'

'And now? What happens here, in this cold city?' Daniel gave an impressive and not altogether false shudder.

The younger man glanced at Daniel then at his friend as if to calculate what the answer might be. It occurred to Daniel that he probably had a poor command of English and was relying on the other to speak for him. Or was there something else? Something that ought to remain unspoken?

'We take coffee here every day,' the older man said slowly. 'Mohammad, my good friend, likes the company.'

He said something to the other man in Arabic and he nodded, grinning at Daniel, showing a mouth full of broken teeth.

'I don't know anybody here,' Daniel muttered, slouching in his seat and gulping down the coffee. 'Not sure why I came.' He tried for a tone that might make him sound like a malcontent.

'I am Qasim,' the older man said, stretching out his gnarled hand and offering it to Daniel.

He took it, feeling the bones beneath his fingers, but also the strength in the man's sudden grip.

'Now you are not alone any more, Mr Daniel. Now you know us!' He sat back and raised his arms then laughed.

Daniel grinned at them both in turn. Perhaps it might pay off to find out a bit more about this pair, he decided. Two men who chose to sit and watch. And wait, he guessed. He had taken covert glimpses of them both as he'd sat with the Syrian father near his child, wondering at their continued interest in what was happening outside and how their eyes rarely left the door.

He felt the stream of cold air as the glass door opened, but was wise enough not to turn and stare, looking rather at the two men on the opposite side of the table. Whoever it was that had pushed open the door made the one named Mohammad sit up, an expression of excitement spreading across his podgy features. The slight dig in his ribs from the older man made him mutter something and he fell silent, his eyes darting from Daniel to the person who had come in.

'More coffee?' he asked, indicating their empty mugs.

'Thank you, yes,' Qasim replied with a polite little bow then he sat back, one hand slowly feeling for his stick.

Daniel stood up and turned away, striding towards the table that held an assortment of empty mugs and the flasks of tea and coffee. They were off somewhere, he thought, hearing a slight noise behind him that might have been the scrape of a stick across the wooden floor.

When he brought back the mugs of coffee, the seats where

they had been were empty, no sign of either man walking along the pavement outside.

In two strides Daniel had grabbed his coat and was in the street peering left and right, the sudden chill making him shiver.

The older man was walking briskly enough for someone who needed a stick, Daniel saw, the bigger one by the edge of the pavement. But what was more surprising than their hasty exit from the refuge was the woman who now strode between them, her hair swathed in a pale grey scarf.

Daniel ducked into a doorway as she turned to look behind her, evidently keen to see that they were not being followed. And, in that moment, he could see that she was not an Asian woman as he'd expected, but pale-skinned, the oval face framed by the headscarf one he would not easily forget. What, he wondered, were these two refugees doing with this beautiful woman? And why had her sudden appearance made them leave the refugee centre in such haste? Daniel pulled his collar closer to his neck and followed the trio at a safe distance as they headed along the road, the throng of Christmas shoppers making it easier for him to bob and weave his way after them.

Perhaps there was nothing sinister about the men, but Daniel Kohi's instinct told him that there was something that the older man was intent on hiding.

When they turned into the Subway station, Daniel bit his lip in frustration, watching as they each tapped a turnstyle and descended a moving staircase. The queue at the ticket counter was long, making Daniel seethe with impatience, glancing repeatedly at his watch.

At last he grabbed his ticket, pushed through the barrier and took the stairs instead of the escalator, almost running. They were more than four minutes ahead of him, now. Would he catch sight of them? Be able to follow them onto the underground train?

A whooshing sound and a blast of icy wind met him as he rounded the corner, only to see the orange train disappear into a dark tunnel.

CHAPTER THIRTY-ONE

Daniel stood outside the entrance to Buchanan Street Subway station and looked around. Nobody paid him the slightest attention as they hurried past. It was long past lunch hour for city office workers, but Daniel could smell something warm and savoury wafting across his nostrils as a couple of young men passed him by, carrying white polystyrene containers of food. He breathed in the vinegary smell, a memory returning to him of the last evening with his friends in Liverpool when they had treated him to fish and chips from their favourite takeaway shop.

He watched the crowds moving along the pedestrianised street like a river of humanity, Christmas shoppers adding to the normal lunchtime rush. The church in Liverpool would be decorated by now, he supposed, services planned for Christmas Eve, the way that Christian churches celebrated the world over. His mother would be rehearsing with her choir for their annual concert, the women donning their brightest garments for the occasion. Last year had been so special, he remembered, he and Chipo bringing baby Johannes to his first Christmas service, the grannies cooing and clucking like so many chickens around their son. He swallowed, no longer feeling pangs of hunger from the smell of chips but a pain that went far deeper.

If only . . .

Daniel bit back the burgeoning moment of self-pity and began to walk downhill. He was alive and had a task to do now, something that might make him forget these things for a while. He thought of the Syrian father back in the refugee centre; whatever his story, there was no wife there either and only one little boy. How many members of his family had he lost back in Aleppo? And how long would it take for him to begin afresh in that island off the west coast?

He looked up. It was desperately cold, but the clouds no longer scudded so swiftly across the darkening skies so perhaps the Syrian and his son would find their safe haven tomorrow. The street was lined with leafless trees whose branches began to blossom with blue lights. Daniel turned and walked through an archway, pausing to gaze upwards at a net of golden stars cast across the rooftops. Somewhere, hidden beyond the deepening clouds, there were real stars wheeling on their course. Once, he had been deep in the bush and spent the night wide awake, his eyes fixed on the different constellations, too absorbed in their wonder to sleep. Would his mother think of him when she looked up at the stars? Or did she assume that he was lost to her for ever? He sighed and walked on, past the noisy square with its huge Ferris wheel and patch of ice where would-be skaters screeched as they pushed and shoved each other.

When he reached the station, Daniel sat down and took out his mobile phone. He was sorry he had lost the two men, but perhaps even his gut feeling about them might be enough to make Lorimer want to meet up? He found the detective's name and pressed the button then waited. But all he heard was a request to leave his name and a message. Daniel looked around him. Too many people here, he thought, rising to his feet and preparing to take the long walk back to the high-rise flats where he could say the words he needed to speak in private.

The lift was off, a notice slung across the door to the effect that an engineer would be there tomorrow, and so Daniel climbed the ten flights of stairs until he reached his own small apartment. Walking through the city had definitely improved his stamina, he realised, as he unlocked the front door. He glanced at his stout boots, another gift from his English friends. *They'll see you through the winter*, they'd assured him and so far they had, though there were stains on the black leather where the snow had melted. He stopped for a moment, thinking hard. His shoes back home had rarely needed much polishing, just a good rub to rid them of the red dust that blew across the veldt. Perhaps Netta ...

He retraced his steps, pocketing his key, and strode along to the nearby flat.

'Och, it's you, son. Come away in. Jist pit the kettle oan, d'you fancy a cup?' Netta beckoned him inside and closed the door behind him, fixing a chain across before she followed Daniel into her living room.

'Whit c'n ah dae ye fur?' she asked.

Daniel frowned for a moment, his brain trying to make sense of both the old lady's words and syntax.

'I was wondering if you had anything to clean these boots,' he said at last, pointing to them.

'Aye, sure. Wait a wee minute an' ah'll hiv a rake in the closet oot here,' she said, waddling past him and opening a cupboard door in the hall. Daniel peered in, seeing several shelves neatly arranged with old biscuit tins and cardboard boxes, no labels to show what they contained, but Netta evidently knew just where to find things. She lifted down a plastic box that was filled with coloured tubes and flat round tins plus a few small wooden-backed brushes.

'Here ye are, see whit's in that lot. Ah'll get yer tea. Fancy a scone? Jist oot the oven, so they are,' she added, wheezing a little as she thrust the box into Daniel's hands.

It was at that moment that he noticed the mark beneath her eye, a purple bruise that even a thick application of beige make-up failed to disguise.

'What happened ... ?' Daniel began but there was no reply forthcoming. Was Netta pretending not to hear him as she stepped briskly into the kitchen, her back turned abruptly? Something wasn't right, he decided. The old lady's torrent of words as he had arrived, setting the chain on the door, that mark on her face ... Did these point to a recent visit from those loan shark men? Who would strike a defenceless woman like Netta? Daniel wondered, gritting his teeth in anger. Evidently she didn't want to talk about it and so he would have to be careful to coax the truth from his friend, all his skills as an investigator being put to good use.

'Ah, that's better,' Netta sighed, setting down her teacup and then leaning back into her armchair, several cushions supporting her ample frame.

'These are very good,' Daniel told her, pointing to the crumbs of scone on his plate. 'You should be a professional baker, Netta.'

'Ach, get away wi' ye,' she laughed. 'Onybody c'n make a few scones. Mind you, ah've aye had a light touch. Same wi' pastry.'

'Someone had a heavy touch, though, didn't they?' Daniel leaned forward and gently touched Netta's face. 'Who did this?' he asked quietly.

The old lady dropped her gaze and he could see her chin trembling as she fought back tears.

'Was it the same men who were here last week?'

There was no answer, but she clasped his hand tightly as she nodded.

'Why?' Daniel asked, though as soon as the word was out of his mouth, he knew that was an impossible question to ask. For who could reason the capriciousness of a violent man? The old lady's mere vulnerability was enough to goad these types into abusing their superior physical power. He'd seen things like this too often over the years: brute force exerted against a weaker mortal for little or no reason, simply because they could.

'Said they'd be back,' she whispered, stifling a sob.

I want to help you, he thought, stroking the back of the old lady's hand as he saw the tears course down her wrinkled cheeks. The previous time Daniel Kohi had felt this anger growing inside him he had been helpless to do anything about it. But now, with a friend like Lorimer, perhaps there was something he could do to protect his neighbour.

'How would you describe this woman?' Lorimer asked.

Once again they were seated in his upstairs lounge, Daniel nursing a glass of whisky in his hands. Maggie had remained downstairs, content to read a book by the fireside, her left arm still in a sling. He'd brought home a takeaway from their favourite curry house and had made sure everything was cleared away afterwards. He could see the frustration in his wife's face as he'd laid out their meal; Maggie Lorimer loved cooking and the kitchen was very much her domain, but tonight she had been told to sit and let them take care of her for a change. Molly had gone home for the night and would return early in the morning before Lorimer left for work. She'd raised a questioning eyebrow as Kohi had followed her boss into the house, but had the discretion not to ask what he was doing there.

'A very beautiful woman,' Daniel said at last, his eyes taking on a faraway expression.

Was he seeing this scene all over again? Lorimer wondered, fascinated by the idea of a photographic memory.

'She had a scarf over her hair, but I could see that it was fair, blonde. Her face ...' He broke off momentarily, closing his eyes. 'Heart-shaped, very pretty. I think ...' He turned towards Lorimer and grinned. 'What was the name of that famous American actress? She married a prince, a real prince.'

'Meghan Markle? Oh, but she isn't blonde ...' Lorimer frowned. Maggie was the one for the cinema; his work often prevented him accompanying her to see a film.

'No, no, a long time ago. She was killed in a car crash. Very beautiful woman.' Daniel gestured around his face.

'You mean Grace Kelly?'

Daniel slapped his thigh. 'That's the one!' He grinned. 'This woman reminded me of her. Lovely face, though she was not smiling as she spoke to these two Syrian men.' He paused again. 'There was something . . . '

Lorimer waited. For a moment Kohi's efforts to summon up pictures in his mind reminded him of conversations with his old friend, Solly Brightman, the psychologist prone to subjecting him to lengthy pauses as he chewed over an idea.

'She was not happy with whatever it was these men were saying.'

'You told me that the younger one had no English.'

'That is what it seemed,' Daniel frowned. 'But he was speaking to her, all right.'

'So, either he was fooling you or she knew enough Arabic to carry on a conversation with them both?' Lorimer suggested.

Daniel nodded. 'I wasn't close enough to hear what was being said. Too much traffic noise and I had to stay back sufficiently not to let them know they were being followed,' he said.

Lorimer sat back, thinking hard. It was unusual to have a white woman who spoke Arabic and the headscarf also suggested a link to a different culture. Was this a real breakthrough or had Kohi simply witnessed two Syrian men meeting a woman who was there to help them with part of the refugee process?

'I could go back there again tomorrow,' Daniel suggested. 'See if they are in the centre again?'

Lorimer nodded. 'Yes. I'd like you to make friends with this fellow, Qasim. See if there is anything of the malcontent about him.'

Daniel frowned. 'What do you mean?'

Lorimer looked straight into the Zimbabwean's eyes. It was folly to burden this man with too many details but at the same time, he needed to know enough if he were to penetrate what might turn out to be a clandestine cell within the city.

'We're looking for troublemakers,' Lorimer said. 'Folk who are politically or culturally opposed to the British government. And who might actually do something rather . . .' he paused to find the word he needed, 'shall we say, stupid?'

Daniel nodded gravely. 'There may be refugees who are not happy to be here, do you mean?'

'Oh, I think they are glad to be here, Daniel,' Lorimer told him, with a sardonic smile. 'But for all the wrong reasons.'

It was late when Daniel saw the high-rise flats loom into view, a misty gloom settling across the city, rubbing out the tops of buildings and casting halos around the streetlamps. He had told Lorimer about Netta's unwelcome visitors and the detective superintendent had promised to contact some local cops he knew. For now he had to be content with that but as Daniel parked his hired car, he was still troubled about the elderly lady who had shown him such kindness. Surely there was more he could do for her?

His ungloved fingers were cold as he tapped in the code then heaved the outside door open enough to enter.

The sound of running footsteps made him turn in time to see two hooded figures thundering up to the entrance.

In a flash, Daniel recognised them as the pair that had threatened Netta the previous week.

Before he could slam the door shut, they were on the steps, elbowing him out of the way.

'Hey!' Daniel called out.

The two men turned as one and looked at him.

'Who's callin'?' one of them sneered, loping back towards Daniel, arms hanging by his side. 'You lookin' for trouble?' He smirked at his companion and gave him a nod. The pair approached Daniel, their intentions apparent.

It was not the first time he'd been confronted by a pair of thugs like this and a cold rage made the former DI stand quite still, his jaw tensing.

But he had little time to wait as the man lunged towards Daniel, a blade in his hand.

Daniel threw his weight forward, blocking the blow and grabbing the man's wrist so tightly that he cried out.

Then, as the other began to move forwards, Daniel drove his head into his attacker's belly, winding him and making him collide with his companion.

'Ah, ye . . . !'

Daniel heard the roar of pain and curses as the second man hit the stone floor.

He stooped down, grasping the knifeman's arm, and hurled him back down the steps at the front of the building.

The second man was sitting now, one hand at the back of his head, groaning.

Daniel hauled him to his feet and frogmarched him to the entrance.

'Get out of here,' he said quietly. 'And don't come back if you know what's good for you.'

Then he slammed the door shut and stood, breathing heavily, listening to see if they would attempt anything else.

At last muffled curses and dim footsteps told him they were heading back down the street.

Daniel breathed a sigh of relief. They might have been watching and waiting for someone to press the security code and he had been that person.

Straightening his shoulders, Daniel prepared to climb the ten flights of stairs, the adrenalin rush still fizzing in his veins. That pair would not forget him in a hurry, he thought. But, had he done something that might further endanger Netta? Well, if he had, then there was perhaps a solution to that.

Once indoors, Daniel immediately headed towards the front window where he had found the best signal for his mobile.

In just a few minutes the familiar Scottish voice answered his call.

'Lorimer? It's me. There's another favour I'd like to ask,' Daniel began, putting bruised knuckles to his lips and wondering how to begin.

It was not a lot to request. In fact, Daniel might well be offering more than he was asking, Lorimer thought, as he rolled over in bed and switched off the light. The city divisional commander had been after a particular loan shark for some time now and it sounded as if Daniel's elderly neighbour's predicament could provide the very opportunity they were seeking to flush him out. There would be no mention of a refugee two doors along from the woman, however; Daniel Kohi was under Lorimer's protection and that included keeping him well away from any official police business. For a moment he lay still. Was he asking too much of this former inspector? It could endanger the man, put his application for settled status at risk, too. Perhaps he ought to tell Daniel to back off now? Yet, the memory of the Zimbabwean's eager smile when he had accepted the task made Lorimer realise that Daniel Kohi would simply shake his head and carry on regardless.

That was something they had in common: a desire to see justice done as well as the need to protect so many innocent people from harm.

CHAPTER THIRTY-TWO

Who was the mysterious woman who had been seen leaving Vincent Burns's home? Lorimer's head ached from thinking of what Daniel Kohi had told him and how that might be a link to the person Alicia Milroy had spotted on several occasions from her windows in Lark Cottage. A blonde woman who had appeared pretty when she'd been smiling, possibly around the same height as the female Kohi had seen with the two Syrian refugees.

Bryson's solicitors' office had been subject to police scrutiny, intelligence having indicated that the firm might be the source of finance for the terrorist group they were seeking. And now, with two of their partners murdered, it looked as if someone may have been trying to shut them up. Had Carter and Burns been involved with these people? And, if so, was the woman who had been seen slipping in and out of the big house in Newton Mearns the link they'd been searching for?

Their initial intelligence had suggested that the person they were seeking was a woman, someone with far too much insight into the workings of Police Scotland to be a civilian; at least that was the idea that the chief constable had presented at their secret meetings. Perhaps if both Kohi and Mrs Milroy could come in and look at photographs of different female officers, they might find their source? It was certainly worth a try.

He heaved a sigh. It sickened him to think that it was one of their own who had been passing highly confidential information to a group of Islamic terrorists intent on wreaking havoc in his city. Yet that had been the information given right at the beginning when the identities of these officers had been made known to the press.

Lorimer drummed his fingers on his desktop. Were they really looking in the right places? And, if not, where else were they to find this treacherous creature?

Alicia Milroy shook Daniel's hand and smiled up at him.

'I've never visited Africa,' she said. 'Though it is one place I'd have loved to see,' she added wistfully. 'All those animals and birds. Such colour. And your music. A friend took me to hear a gospel choir in the Concert Hall,' she added. 'That marimba band! My goodness, what a sound!'

Daniel smiled down at the old lady. She was looking at him with keen, intelligent eyes.

'Zimbabwe is indeed a beautiful country,' he agreed politely. There was no need to tell her why he was here in Glasgow, however, and she did not strike him as the sort of person who would ask probing questions.

'Do you know him well?' Mrs Milroy asked quietly, nodding towards the tall figure of the detective superintendent who was standing in the doorway of the room where they'd both been asked to sit. Lorimer was talking to a uniformed officer who was listening to him and nodding her replies.

'I've not known him for very long,' Daniel admitted. 'But I think he is a good police officer who gets results.'

Alicia Milroy nodded, her silvery-white hair catching the light from a nearby window. 'He struck me as someone who would never be happy till he brought a criminal to justice,' she murmured.

'And you're here to help me do just that.' Lorimer smiled as he turned to look at them both. 'It may take quite a while, but we want you both to look at rather a lot of pictures. Each of you will be given a laptop and we want you to scroll through a set of head-and-shoulders images. If you think you recognise one of them, just click on the picture, all right? Mr Kohi, please come with me. Mrs Milroy, Sergeant Clarke will look after you,' he said, waving a hand towards the uniformed officer who was already smiling at the old lady and taking a seat at the table beside her.

Alicia Milroy nodded. Lorimer had been relieved that the elderly lady was unfazed by modern technology and so the exercise she was being asked to carry out should not present any difficulties.

'Don't worry if you cannot see the person we are asking you to identify,' he continued. 'That in itself might be helpful to us.'

Daniel glanced across at the old woman as he left with Lorimer. There was nothing in her manner that suggested nerves of any kind and he wondered at the sort of life she lived. Lorimer had told him nothing about her as he'd made

252

the introductions earlier but Daniel could not help but compare this smartly dressed old lady to his neighbour, Netta,
whose clothes were worn and shabby. Yet there was something they both had in common: an air of decency that he
could admire and respect.

It was late in the afternoon when Lorimer looked in to the
two small rooms where he had left Kohi and Alicia Milroy.

'I'm really sorry.' Alicia Milroy shook her head tiredly.
'And I am quite sure that I have not overlooked a single one
of them,' she added firmly.

Daniel had already trawled through the pages of photographs and reached the same conclusion.

'Don't worry,' Lorimer assured her. 'That is helpful in its
own way. Really,' he insisted as Alicia Milroy raised a scep-
tical eyebrow.

He walked them both to the door, shook their hands
then made sure her taxi had the correct address before
waving them off.

Well, that was a dead end, he told himself, stepping towards
the stairs that would take him back to his office. Alicia
Milroy's findings would be included in a report that DI
Brownlee would soon see. But Daniel Kohi's observations
were only to be shared with the two most senior officers
in Police Scotland. Whoever she was, the woman Kohi had
seen was not a serving officer nor was the mysterious female
who'd shared Vincent Burns's bed. Was that a relief? He
supposed so.

Kohi had been asked to give a detailed description of the
woman to one of their digital artists and so there would at

least be an image forthcoming to work on. Once Kohi was satisfied that it bore a close likeness to the woman with the grey scarf then Lorimer would take a little trip back out to Newton Mearns, just to see if this was the same pretty lady that Alicia Milroy had seen with Vincent Burns. Meantime he would report back to Mearns and Flint that the trail had gone cold and their original suspicion that a female officer was selling secrets might be completely unfounded.

Lorimer stopped outside his door. It was at times like this he felt the need to talk things through with the man who had helped him so much in the past and whose insight often differed from that of the police. He glanced at his watch. He really should be home for Maggie, but perhaps Molly Newton would not mind staying a bit later if he could pay for another takeaway dinner?

CHAPTER THIRTY-THREE

'You've had a time of it lately, haven't you?' Solly said, nodding across the table at Lorimer. 'How is Maggie?'

They were seated in a booth at the back of a small restaurant in Argyle Street, one of several in the up-and-coming district of Finnieston.

'Bored, I think,' Lorimer replied, picking up his water glass and taking a gulp. 'And she's missing everything back at school,' he added, making a face. 'Still, she knows that it will take a while for her injury to heal and the doctor has said she's not to go back to work till after the Christmas holidays.'

'Any progress about who attacked her?'

Lorimer heaved a sigh. 'Not so far,' he said, 'though we have a partial footprint that has been sent for forensic examination. Still waiting to hear the result of that.'

'Nothing else?'

Lorimer shook his head. 'Apart from recovering her laptop, not a thing. We think whoever it was hid from sight as Maggie opened the garage door and drove in. She remembers sitting in her car listening to some music before she opened the door.'

'So, there was time for the attacker to creep up. Plus, she wouldn't have heard his footsteps,' Solly murmured.

'Exactly.'

'And what about you? How do you feel about it?'

Lorimer avoided his friend's gaze and fiddled with the bread in his hands. 'To tell you the truth, it made me want to jack it all in for a while.' He looked up and met Solly's eyes. 'It came too close to home this time,' he sighed. 'Someone knows where we live and was prepared to hurt my wife . . .'

Solly said nothing but continued to wait for Lorimer to say what was on his mind.

'One of these days I'm going to have to think about what I'll do once my thirty years are up,' he said slowly. 'And, until this happened, I was quite content to stay on as head of the Major Incident Team.' He made a face. 'Dammit, Solly, it's what I'm good at. But now . . . honestly? I can't see a way forward in this case at all. If our intelligence was correct, then surely we would have uncovered the person responsible for creating this mess?'

'Depends who it is, surely? And with the attack on Maggie, the theft of her laptop, which presumably they thought was yours, it does look as if there is someone deep within the force that has been trying to access your personal files, no?'

Lorimer drew a hand across his brow. 'Nobody at the MIT, that's for certain,' he said. 'Many members of the team may well be aware that I carry my laptop to and from work at the moment. Though,' he allowed the shadow of a smile to cross his mouth, 'there may be a few wondering why that is.'

256

'Have any of them been asking questions about that?'

Lorimer shook his head. 'No. We're too busy dealing with our case load to bother about details like that.'

'And yet, the team is comprised of detectives skilled in observing such details.'

'Granted. But here's the thing, Solly. I know each and every one of those officers and would trust them with my life. And Maggie's,' he added, his thoughts turning to the former undercover officer who was with his wife at that very moment.

'You have inspired a great deal of loyalty over the years,' Solly observed. 'It would be a pity to have to throw that all away.'

Lorimer raised his eyebrows and nodded his agreement.

'Enough about me,' he said at last. 'I wonder, have you had time to think of these former undercover officers who live near Glennifer Braes?'

'You still think one of them might have something to do with the murder of Derek Carter?'

Lorimer did not respond at first then he frowned. 'I can't see it, Solly. Yet, we should never rule anything out till we have enough evidence to eliminate them completely. We know now that Burns had a large van driven into his property on the same date that Carter was killed. Traces have been found in his Jaguar that link him with Carter. So, it's a distinct possibility that the body was transferred to this van then driven up to the Braes under cover of darkness.' He went on to describe the findings in both the victims' homes, particularly the traces of expensive perfume.

Both men paused as a young waitress stopped at their

table and placed dishes of oil and bread between them. 'Ready to order, gentlemen?' she asked with a smile.

Once their order was taken and she had left them alone, Lorimer leaned forward.

'One thing I have put in place is someone to watch and listen to any troublemaking talk amongst the immigrant community.'

'An undercover officer?'

Lorimer shook his head. 'Too risky. We don't know who is aware of these officers' movements outside their covert operations, but someone could be. It happened to these other three and it could happen again. No,' he leaned forward, picking up a piece of sourdough bread and dipping it in the yellow oil, 'I've got a man who I hope will be completely above suspicion.' He grinned at the psychologist. 'You'll meet him some time. Think you'll find him interesting.'

Solly nodded, regarding his friend solemnly from behind his horn-rimmed spectacles.

'Your idea about these former officers might hold water, you know,' he said at last. 'But first I'd be interested to see what any of them might have to gain from becoming involved in a scheme that was so at odds with their previous commitment as police officers.'

'Motive,' Lorimer agreed.

'Means and opportunity might both be there, given their police training and where they all live, but, yes, motive is what I believe would drive them to a treasonable act such as the one you suggested.'

Lorimer glanced round carefully. Their booth was out of earshot and neither he nor Solly would be heard over the

258

music spilling out from wall-mounted speakers. It was not the usual Christmas carols or Michael Bublé on a loop but pleasant tunes from the past that instantly made him think of the Grace Kelly era.

'There's something else,' he ventured. 'We may be looking for a woman who is not, in fact, part of Police Scotland.'

'So, that would rule out the ladies near Glennifer Braes?'

Lorimer hesitated, his bread poised above the table. Had anybody checked if the undercover officers' images were included in the files that Kohi and Mrs Milroy had painstakingly studied? That was something to look into, he told himself, trying to remember if Mandy Richardson or Hazel Cochrane were indeed lookalikes for the late Princess Grace of Monaco. Had their photographs been added to the general database since their career change, or in Richardson's case, resignation?

'Possibly,' he began, 'though I'd like to take another look at their files.'

'I didn't find a single thing that would motivate any of them to betray their fellow officers. Or indeed anything that could be construed as a link to a terrorist cell,' Solly admitted. 'But then as you said, we are dealing with professionals who have undoubtedly had time to prepare and money behind them.'

'Yes,' agreed Lorimer. 'Brownlee's team have been going through the files from Bryson's with a fine-tooth comb.' He sighed. 'If it is there to find, then they should come across it.'

'Whoever is in charge of these organised crime gangs can't keep the money hidden for good, surely?'

'Unless it's secreted in an offshore account where we have

no jurisdiction,' Lorimer grumbled. 'That puts it out of our hands, of course.'

'So, at that stage it's a matter for the security services?'

Lorimer did not reply, looking up instead as the waitress returned with their meals. It was not a question he could answer right now. Only the chief constable and DCC Caroline Flint had the ear of those particular people. He'd come across them once before, during his involvement in a plot to blow up the opening ceremony of the 2014 Commonwealth Games here in Glasgow. Lorimer remembered exactly why he'd declined their offer to quit the police and join a different type of service knowing that his place was here in Scotland's largest city. Still, the memory gave him a renewed sense of value. He was still needed here and his time to hand over the job had not yet come.

Lorimer looked across at his friend. Solly's dark curls gleamed under the lamplight and he could see a distant look in his eyes as he sat motionless, fork raised part way to his mouth, his thoughts somewhere other than in this restaurant. Perhaps he had asked too much of the psychologist? After all, Solly was not being paid to look into this case. But the bearded man sitting opposite relished a difficult puzzle and was known for coming at such things from quite unexpected angles.

They had finished their meal and split the bill, though Lorimer had protested that it really should be his shout. Solly wiped his beard with the napkin and laid it on the table. It had been good to see him tonight, not just to reassure himself about Maggie's well-being, but to gauge Lorimer's current mood too. It was not unexpected that he'd had a moment of doubt about his career; under the circumstances who would not have such thoughts about giving up their job if it endangered a loved one? The question about who was behind the planned attack that the Counter Terrorism division had heard about, and the leaking of those undercover officers' identities, was of paramount importance. But were these senior officers really correct in thinking the source came from within Police Scotland? He pondered the idea as they collected their coats and headed out into the wet streets.

A slight drizzle was coming down, the sort that could soak a person in minutes.

'Here, hop in and I'll run you home,' Lorimer said, aiming his key at the big silver car that was parked opposite the restaurant.

Molly and Maggie were sitting side by side at the fire when he walked in, the sound of their laughter warming Lorimer's heart.

'There you are!' Maggie exclaimed. 'We've had a lovely evening here and Molly's been regaling me with tales from her past.'

The detective sergeant smiled and looked up at Lorimer. 'No trade secrets given away, honest, boss!' she laughed. 'Just a bit about my misspent youth.'

'Not misspent if you were helping to build an orphanage in Romania,' Maggie scolded.

Molly shrugged and rose to her feet. 'As I said, that was a long time ago,' she murmured. 'Right, time I wasn't here. See you two in the morning.'

'Why not stay the night?' Lorimer offered. 'It's pretty late and we both have an early start, after all.'

'Your toilet bag's still in the spare room,' Maggie urged. 'And it means we can have a proper nightcap,' she added, a wicked glint in her eyes.

Molly looked to Lorimer who nodded agreement.

'That's settled then,' he said. 'Who's for a whisky?'

Maggie had gone to bed early leaving the two police officers alone downstairs, seated by the fireside, Chancer snuggled up on Molly's lap.

'Something I wanted to run past you,' Lorimer began as he lifted his glass and examined the amber liquid under the lamplight. 'You know I'm working on this case, something that involves a security threat?'

'I'd gathered that much from the little you've told me,' Molly said, shooting him a curious glance. 'But I'm happy to hear more.'

Lorimer sat back and breathed in deeply. 'Sometimes it's hard to know whom to trust, especially when it seems as if there is someone within the force guilty of the deepest malpractice.'

Molly sat still, watching him intently as he swirled the whisky glass thoughtfully.

'You are one of those people I do trust, DS Newton,' he said at last, turning his blue gaze upon her. 'And what I am about to tell you must go no further than this room.'

She nodded, never taking her eyes from his face for a moment. A lesser person might have looked away, but Molly had that inner strength that had served her well over the years of her service, both as an undercover officer and as a member of the MIT.

'It all began a few months back when the chief constable had a visit from a man in the security services. No need to give a name, and anyhow, it was probably an alias just used for the occasion.'

'Go on,' Molly said quietly.

'Intelligence showed that there were various persons coming into the country under the guise of refugee immigrants but whose real intentions were to infiltrate different groups, stirring up trouble and amassing enough of a rabble to cause a great deal of harm. One they had their eye on was found hanged in his room at a detention centre. Probably suicide. That was back in July,' he added. 'Since then we have had snippets of intelligence and we deployed some of our officers to keep tabs on a couple of these groups. You know what happened then.'

'Their cover was blown, and the papers had a field day writing about them,' Molly went on.

'But not before they had a chance to tell us a bit more,' Lorimer said slowly, looking into the whisky glass as though he were addressing it and not the woman sitting opposite.

'We now have reason to believe that the person behind the threat is a woman,' he continued. 'Someone intent on causing a great deal of damage in the city centre, possibly around Christmas or New Year. At first I was looking at members of our own force.'

'A female officer in Police Scotland?' Molly's tone of outrage did not surprise him. 'Surely not?'

'We've been looking very hard but so far not a single person has fitted the description we have of a potential terrorist.'

'I can't believe one of our own would be capable of something like that,' Molly protested.

'Neither can I,' Lorimer said slowly. 'But the fact remains that whoever gave away the secrets of those officers must have had inside knowledge that we believed could only have come from a serving officer.'

'Surely the members of a terrorist cell would have wanted to do what they could to keep these officers onside, whilst pretending they did not know their real purpose?'

'I think they were too afraid to do that,' Lorimer replied. 'Or else wanted to create a diversion with selling their stories to the press.' His lips tightened. 'In retrospect, these officers might feel lucky to have escaped any physical harm. Whoever it was, we are beginning to eliminate serving female offices from our enquiries.'

'What about a husband? Boyfriend?'

Lorimer gave a slight nod. 'Maybe. Or at any rate someone who was clued up enough to get that sort of information.'

'A hacker?'

'Might be. They got into Maggie's laptop without too much difficulty, so they have IT professionals on their team.'

'But why? Why would anyone want to do a thing like that?'

'Money? Power? Or, maybe just sheer spite, who knows?'

'Is that why you were seeing Professor Brightman tonight?'

Lorimer took a sip of his drink and nodded. 'He has the ability to look at things from strange angles, you know? Lateral thinking taken to an extraordinary degree,' he murmured.

'Why are you telling me this?' Molly asked suddenly, sitting forward a little and searching his gaze.

Lorimer gave her a slow smile and set down his glass. 'I

think it's time that we had a little more help on our small team,' he told her. 'And, as I said, I need someone I can trust.'

Molly folded her trousers and hung them on the back of the bedroom chair. Their conversation had taken her into familiar territory, the world of undercover operations that she had left behind some years before. Now, however, her task was to stay within the MIT and use all of her expertise to try to find something that might lead Lorimer and the senior officers to the person who had spread their insidious poison into the very fabric of Police Scotland.

Of Kohi he had made no mention, but Molly was certain that the man to whom she had delivered that hired car was one more member of Lorimer's secret team, though what his role in all of this was she had still to find out.

CHAPTER THIRTY-FOUR

It was not too far to the nearest post office but by the time Netta reached it there was a queue snaking around the shop and she made a face as she joined the people waiting in line. Christmas cards used to be something she enjoyed writing but nowadays the postage was far too expensive, so she contented herself with buying a cheap pack to hand deliver to her closest family and friends. She'd kept one back to give to Daniel on Christmas Eve, the same design as the one she held now in her mittened hand. The words had come quite easily once she'd thought about them.

Wishing you a merry Christmas from your pen pal in Scotland. Having a good time in the lions' den so don't worry. Hope the New Year is good to you.

From,
Your friend,
Netta.

His mum would get the message, surely. Daniel in the lions' den was a story from Netta's childhood Sunday School days and Daniel had mentioned his mother being a regular churchgoer. It would be nice if she wrote back, just to know that she'd got the card and understood the cryptic message. She'd written down her email address too, though she doubted if the lady could send a message from whatever remote wee place she lived in Zimbabwe. She didn't know much about that part of the world, now she came to think about it.

Netta's thoughts served to fill in the time waiting for her turn at the counter.

'Where to?'

'Zimbabwe.'

'Put it on the scales, please.'

Netta did as she was bid then tried to hide her shock when she was told the price for the airmail postage. She gulped back an angry remark; wasn't the girl's fault that it cost so much, she told herself. Besides, if she couldn't give the lad a present, she might be able to connect him with his old mum back at home.

She still didn't know what had happened to make him flee that faraway place but deep down Netta felt that someone had done something nasty to her neighbour and she was reluctant to believe anything bad of him. He'd shown her courtesy and kindness, qualities rare in most of the menfolk in her life. But she was more curious than ever to find out about Daniel, especially since he'd turned up with that smart red motor car.

*

267

The lift was back on when Netta returned to the flats and she breathed a sigh of relief, pressing the button for the eleventh floor. Her stomach gave a rumble, reminding the old lady that breakfast had been hours ago and that she had a pot of lentil broth to heat up when she got home. Maybe the lad would like a bowlful?

The thought stayed with her as the lift ascended. Sending that card all the way to Africa had given her a connection to Daniel Kohi, so perhaps it was time that he told her a bit more about why he was here and what he was doing with that car.

By the time she reached her own door, Netta had made up her mind and so she took a few more steps and knocked on number 118.

'Netta, come in.' Daniel stepped aside, his ready smile showing his pleasure at seeing her.

'Naw, jist came tae see if ye fancied a plate o' soup. Far too much fur wan,' she said, trying to appear casual.

'Thank you, I'll just grab my jacket,' he said and disappeared for a moment.

Netta waited, then, when he reappeared, they walked side by side to her front door.

'Ye'll nivver guess where ah've been,' she smirked, casting a sly glance at him as they entered her flat.

'Sounds as if you are going to tell me, am I right?'

'Well, that all depends, son,' she said. 'Mibbe if ah tell ye ma wee secret then you can tell me some of your story, eh? Whit d'ye say?'

Daniel stood still for a moment, the smile dying in his eyes, and Netta clasped his arm.

'Sorry, son, dinna mind me. Ah'm jist a nosy auld besom, so ah am.'

Daniel shook his head slowly.

'You are my friend, Netta, and friends share their secrets. But I can only tell you so much of my story,' he said quietly. 'Some of it is not the sort of thing I want you to think about. But one day I shall tell you why I am here in Scotland, a refugee and not a member of the Zimbabwean police force.'

'A copper?' Netta gasped.

Daniel nodded slowly. 'I was,' he confirmed. 'But I had to leave when certain of my colleagues wanted me to agree to carry out some things ... things I did not wish to become involved with.'

'Bent coppers?' Netta said grimly. 'Could ye no' hiv telt the wans in charge?'

Daniel gave her a sorrowful look. 'They *were* the ones in charge, Netta. I'd been warned repeatedly that if I didn't do their bidding, follow a corrupt way of working, then they would make my life hell.'

The old lady's face was like stone as she regarded Daniel. 'And ye nivver paid them ony heed?'

'No.'

'What did they do tae ye, son?' she whispered.

Daniel simply took his friend's hands in his and shook his head sadly.

'Now, you, Netta, dear, what was it you wanted to tell me?'

It was time to return to the refugee charity in Byres Road and so Daniel walked briskly from the flats, collar up against the chilly wind that crept under his chin. As he had hoped, Qasim and Mohammad were there, sitting in the same place as before.

'My friends!' Daniel beamed. 'I missed you the other time. Now, shall we drink coffee together?'

The younger man slid an uneasy glance at his companion but Qasim returned the smile, extending his hand to Daniel.

'Welcome back,' he said simply. There was no offer of explanation why the pair had left in such haste, nor, Daniel was pleased to see, any reference to the former police officer tailing them all the way to Hillhead Subway station.

Daniel fetched three mugs of coffee and laid the tray on the table, sitting as he had done before, his back to the doorway and facing the two Syrians.

'Ach, this place,' he muttered, giving a dirty look towards the window. 'Look at them,' he added scornfully, pointing to the pedestrians passing by, many of them bowed against a spiteful east wind. 'Like dung beetles. Digging themselves into any shit-filled warm place!'

'You are not happy to be here?' Qasim asked, his dark eyes seeking out Daniel's own.

Daniel looked away as though embarrassed to be asked. If he gave off an appearance of guilt, then perhaps that might serve to ingratiate him to this pair.

'I cannot return,' he said with a shrug. 'But if I'd known what sort of place I was coming to . . . ' He let the words hang for a moment as if suggesting that he felt a particular animosity towards Glasgow. 'And I don't just mean the weather,' he added with a hiss.

Was that a look of complicity between the men sitting

opposite? Daniel took a gulp of coffee, eyeing them discreetly under the rim.

'You suffered at their hands, no doubt?' Qasim asked quietly.

Daniel nodded glumly. He'd spent time rehearsing the story he would tell, shreds and scraps of tales cobbled together from other refugees' stories: the time spent in detention, the deprivation and stonewalling experienced there, the constant threat of deportation.

He leaned forward, shuffling his chair a little closer to his new-found friends. 'It's like this,' he began, then gave them a fabricated account of his journey and the hell he had endured ever since arriving in the UK.

Qasim said nothing as they listened to the Zimbabwean's whining tones, simply nodding from time to time as though agreeing that such things ought not to be.

'Feel like I could give them something to remember,' Daniel said at last. 'But what can we do? They strip us of everything, leave us almost penniless and unable to ...' he hesitated, 'work.'

Would he ask the question that Daniel was dangling in front of him? He waited, eyes cast down, his face a mask of discontent.

'What is it that you did for a living?' Qasim asked, Daniel's bait swallowed up immediately.

'This and that,' Daniel replied, one quick glance then looking away as though to prevaricate. 'Not anything a nice pair of good citizens like you would approve of,' he added with a shamefaced grin.

Once again, the two men exchanged that look and

Mohammad burst into a spate of Arabic, casting glances towards Daniel as he spoke. So, he understood English, all right, but chose not to speak it, Daniel thought as Qasim raised an admonishing hand to silence his younger companion.

'We do not judge a man on what he has done in the past,' he said grandly, staring at Daniel and making the ex-cop look into his eyes. 'But at what he might do to win our trust.'

Daniel frowned. 'What do you mean?' he asked, his heart thumping. Was he about to be offered some sort of illegal activity that would put his refugee status at risk?

Qasim merely smiled and lifted his coffee towards his thin lips. 'Keep coming here and perhaps we will ask you to help us,' he replied.

'Help you? To do what?' Daniel asked crossly. 'Drink more coffee? Ha! That's not what I'd like to do.'

Qasim cocked his head to one side thoughtfully. 'Then, what is it you want to do, my friend?'

Daniel sniffed and rubbed his nose. 'Don't know,' he replied. 'Anything to give this place a bit of a fright. These people don't know they're living,' he complained, thrusting a thumb towards the window. 'Spending money on rubbish for their Christian festival. Huh!'

Once more Mohammad broke into a torrent of excited speech and once more Qasim silenced him with a commanding gesture.

'You are not of their faith?'

Daniel breathed a quick prayer of regret to whoever was watching over him before continuing with his biggest lie.

'Never!'

'Then, perhaps we can help grant your wish,' Qasim said, offering his hand across the table.

Daniel put on his best fake grin and clasped the older Syrian's hand. Trust was what it was all about, he'd told him, and now it looked as if he had gained entry into their confidence. But where was that going to lead? And would he really be able to carry out whatever crime they had in mind?

Caroline Flint was on her own when Lorimer arrived for the meeting at Gartcosh.

'David shouldn't be too long,' she told him. 'Here, have some coffee. Just brewed it a couple of minutes ago.'

'How are things progressing?' the deputy chief constable asked him as she poured the coffee.

'I have a few things put in place,' Lorimer admitted. He would not reveal Inspector Kohi's part in this just yet, his unorthodox offer to the Zimbabwean probably contravening several Police Scotland regulations. Yet it was more than that, he realised as Flint sat back and looked at him. He needed to keep Kohi a total secret and that meant not saying a word to either of these most senior officers. It wasn't as if he didn't trust Caroline Flint, but she had been an under-cover cop back in her Met days and there was a tiny ripple of unease in Lorimer's mind about that very fact.

'How's Maggie?' Flint asked. 'You must have got a real fright. Oh, here's David,' she said, looking up as the door to her office opened to admit the acting chief constable.

'Yes, how is your wife?' Mearns asked as he sat beside Lorimer. 'That must have come as a terrible shock.'

'I've got one of my team keeping an eye on her, sir,' Lorimer replied. 'And there was no lasting damage done. It really did look as though they were after a laptop, presuming it was mine.'

'But you don't keep yours at home?' Mearns asked.

'It's always in a safe place, sir,' Lorimer replied smoothly, not over-anxious to admit that he carried it about wherever he went while there was danger from some source within the police itself.

'Good, good. We all need to be vigilant right now, keep our personal places as safe and secure as possible.'

'You've got plenty of security set up at your own house?' Flint asked, looking at Mearns.

'Oh, yes, as soon as we moved in, I had the place rigged up with the lot. Paid for by Police Scotland, I might add. The rental people are quite happy to go with that,' he added.

'Coffee?' Flint asked and Mearns nodded. 'Same as usual, milk and two, thanks, Caroline.'

Lorimer blinked. The chief constable had taken on a property over on the south side of the city, he believed, though he was not sure of its address. By the new year there would be a few hats cast into the ring to compete for the top job, Caroline Flint's among them, and Mearns would retire with a decent pension, his final posting here in Glasgow completing what appeared to be an enviable career. Rumour had it that a gong might even be forthcoming for David Mearns in the New Year Honours list, something that he deserved, Lorimer thought.

But he'd missed something important just now, he realised. Something that one of them had said. He tried hard

274

not to frown as Mearns began the meeting, the moment lost for now.

'That guy who was here, the black fellow, a good friend, is he?' Molly ventured as she and Maggie sat at the dining room table, a Scrabble board between them.

Maggie looked across and saw a tide of pink appear on the detective sergeant's cheeks. Ah, so that was the way the wind blew, she thought.

'Someone Bill met quite recently,' she said. 'Used to be a detective inspector in Zimbabwe.'

'Oh, I did wonder,' Molly said, looking at the letters on her tray then back at the board.

'You've met him before, I take it?'

Molly shrugged. 'Just doing my job,' she said. 'Your husband asked me to take a car to this place in Maryhill where I handed over the keys to him.'

Maggie smiled. 'If Bill wants to tell you more about Daniel, then I'm sure he will,' she said lightly. 'But I can assure you he is a nice man. A widower, as it happens. Sad story, but not mine to tell,' she added firmly.

Molly glanced up and nodded. 'Okay, but I wouldn't mind meeting him again,' she admitted with a shy smile.

Maggie Lorimer breathed in a quiet sigh. If she were a fairy godmother, then she would wave her wand and make something happen between those two. The tall blonde detective sergeant was about Daniel's age, she reckoned, and it would be good to see a relationship blossom after the dreadful experiences that he had endured. Maybe it was time to suggest a foursome around this table for dinner,

Molly and Daniel getting to know one another in the safety of the Lorimers' home? It was Christmas time, after all, the season of goodwill, and Daniel had left everything and everyone behind him.

CHAPTER THIRTY-FIVE

Solomon Brightman fastened the straps of his briefcase with a sigh of contentment. The end of the university term had come at last and now he was free to stay at home with young Ben, sharing the day-to-day duties with Morag, their beloved nanny. Rosie was on call all of this week which meant that she could be asked to attend a scene of crime at any hour of the day or night, no matter what she was doing. He stared out of the large windows, their upper panes decorated with old-fashioned stained glass, a reminder of the age of this building and how many men and women had stood here over the years, their vocation to teach bringing them to Glasgow.

Even in the relatively short time Solly had lived in this city he had seen changes. Down towards Byres Road newer buildings jostled for space as demands for science and technology created different departments. In his own discipline of psychology Solomon Brightman had been part of a different approach to criminal behaviour, his work in profiling not just a help to police forces around the country but also gaining him a reputation as a writer and psychologist of note. The Christmas holidays might give him the opportunity to edit his latest manuscript, though if Rosie were working all hours, he was happy simply being Daddy to Abby and little Ben. He gazed back up towards the old buildings, cars passing up and down University Avenue. It was a fifteen-minute walk across nearby Kelvingrove Park to their top-floor flat and, with the storm clouds looming towards the west he would need to hurry if he wanted to avoid being soaked. Still, he stood, lingering for a few moments, contemplating his good fortune and wondering how much time he might spend later this evening thinking about the puzzle that Lorimer had presented to him.

A woman, a femme fatale, perhaps, young and beautiful. He saw many lovely girls and young women as they passed through this very room, earnest creatures for the most part, some refreshingly unaware of their own allure. He was still a student of human behaviour, and always would be, fascinated by the things one person could do to another, whether it be to steal their heart in a moment of desire or smash their skull with a blunt instrument. Had Vincent Burns lost his heart to a woman like that? One who possessed charismatic qualities that might overpower a man's reason? And, terrible though it might be to consider, had that same female predator wielded the fatal weapon? One of Solly's previous books about female killers had given him insights into things most people might wish to ignore. But the fact remained, however much statistics showed that a killer tended to be a male, there was no doubt that some women had the capacity not just to kill but to do so without any lingering sense of guilt.

He was looking for the psychopathic personality, Solly decided. A woman like some of those in ancient times who had slaughtered their menfolk in the most brutal fashion and gone on to savour their triumph.

What, though, was this particular woman's motivation? If the end result was to create carnage in Glasgow city centre, there had to be a driving force behind it. A religious fanaticism, perhaps? Or a deep-seated rage against something or someone that would make an intriguing study for a psychotherapist. But first, he told himself, stepping towards the coat stand in the corner and taking down his thick winter tweed, she had to be found. And stopped.

'We've found a new recruit.'

The woman listened as her caller described the African man that Qasim had met at the refugee centre. A disaffected type, the Syrian assured her. Ready to throw his lot in with them.

'I don't know,' she said at last. 'What's his background?'

'Mohammad and I reckon he's skipped from the authorities back where he came from. I can almost smell it on him, you know what I mean? He's been kicked out for some subversive activities is my feeling, though he's cagey about telling us the details.'

'Cagey is good,' she replied. 'It shows he's not a fool. Like some of them.'

Qasim risked a snigger. 'What is it they say about you? Not a woman to suffer fools gladly?'

'Hmm, well, I'd like to see him for myself, but I am not

ready to let him meet me. Let's arrange something where I can have a look and judge for myself before you make any promises to this stranger.'

'We were all strangers to you at one time,' Qasim reminded her.

'Yes,' she demurred. 'You were.'

She put down the phone and gazed thoughtfully out of the window of the room where she stood. Bare-branched trees were swaying in the rising wind but in here there was warmth and comfort, supplied by a man whose aim was to keep her happy whenever she chose to be in his house. When it was all over, they would leave this place and she would travel further from him once more, one task complete and others still to fulfil.

She glanced at her fingernails, slicked with pale gel, perfectly shaped as befitted a woman like her. There was no doubt that her beauty had captured men in the past and that she would use it to snare them in the future, so maintaining that veneer of perfection was a small price to pay, though she despised the nail technicians and beauty therapists who occasionally saw to her needs.

A Zimbabwean, she thought. Well, at least he would have English as a language and hopefully not have any understanding of the Arabic in which she was fluent. It had paid to speak to the Syrians in their own tongue, gaining their confidence and eventually becoming their leader. It had taken time here, in this cold city, but they were almost ready to carry out her plan, do her bidding. She'd tried for so long to find a replacement for the last one and now it looked as if her prayers had been answered. And, if she had an extra member of her team in this new recruit, she would be able to sit back and watch as it all unfolded, her hands apparently clean of any mortal stain.

'There is a place,' Qasim told him. 'We want to take you,' he added, catching hold of Daniel's sleeve. 'Will you come with us?'

Daniel forced a grin onto his face. 'Sure,' he said. 'Let's go.'

As before, the two Syrians headed for the Subway but this time Qasim produced money to buy Daniel's ticket.

'You have very little, I know,' he said as they descended on the escalator. 'It is a wicked thing to force a man like you into becoming a beggar, is it not?'

Daniel gave a shrug. The Syrian was evidently trying to show the UK immigration authorities as the bad guys and Daniel would play along with that as best as he could.

The little orange train roared to a halt by the platform, a sooty smell sweeping through the black tunnel. They sat side by side, not speaking, though any conversation over the noise of the Subway train was practically impossible. Daniel contented himself with watching the other passengers coming and going as each station drew the train to a screeching halt. Kelvinbridge, St George's Cross, Cowcaddens then their own stop, Buchanan Street. He rose with the other men and followed them silently up and out to the street where crowds of people surrounded a lone busker with his guitar and microphone.

Neither Qasim nor Mohammad paid the singer any heed, but Daniel felt a shiver down his spine as he heard the man's tenor voice rise in a familiar lyric.

'. . . but I long for yesterday . . .'

He swallowed hard, urging his emotions to stay under control. The words were so poignant, and he could wallow in their sentiment if he let them. But now was not a time to look back, Daniel told himself; now he had to assume the role of follower and see just where that might take him.

It was a surprise when the two men stopped by the big square opposite the City Chambers, a large ornate building where Glasgow's City Fathers went about their business. He had never yet stepped inside, though, as he had stood near the Cenotaph monument flanked by two huge white lions one day, a tourist guide in scarlet uniform had assured him that visitors were permitted.

'We're going in there?' Daniel asked, pointing across the square.

'No. At least, not yet.' Qasim chuckled. 'We are taking you to have some street food,' he said with a smile. Then, beckoning Daniel to follow, he led the way through the crowds until they reached a row of covered booths. The smells wafting from them made Daniel's mouth water and it was all he could do not to feast his eyes on the variety of food that was on offer. Yet, he'd been brought here for a purpose, he thought, not just to be given a meal and lured further into the Syrians' affections.

Daniel hung back a little, glancing this way and that, hiding his scrutiny of the crowd as he pointed to the different food on offer, nodding happily as Qasim chose things for him.

Most of the people pushing to get closer to the booth were dressed for the weather, dark coats and bobble hats, an occasional flash of scarlet, scarves wrapped around their necks to keep out the bitter wind.

It was easy to miss her, the pale grey scarf swathed across her fair hair, a long coat the colour of mud hiding her slim figure. But one look at her face was enough to tell Daniel why he had been brought here. She didn't see his glance, thankfully, the breeze catching the end of her scarf, making her look away for a second. He breathed a sigh of relief, turning back to nod to Qasim, ignoring her for now. They'd brought him here so she could inspect their potential recruit, he guessed. And that was fine by him. All he needed to do was play to their tune and let her overhear him. It was that easy, or so he hoped.

'Thank you, my friend,' Daniel said, giving a small bow to Qasim and stuffing his mouth with the hot spicy potatoes. 'We eat this food to give us strength for the job ahead, right?' He laughed, nodding his head in the direction of the City Chambers. Was he correct? Had Qasim's throwaway remark indeed shown him that the beautiful building was some sort of target? He tried not to turn around, convinced that the woman was staring at the back of his head, close enough to hear what they were saying but able to vanish into the crowds in a moment.

He would do, she decided, turning on her heel and merging with crowds gathering at the traffic lights near the corner of the square. Intelligent enough to do what he was told and strong too, by the look of him. A small sigh escaped the woman as she crossed the road and headed along a side street leading towards the river. It had been necessary to get rid of that last one. A bit of collateral damage. But this was a war they were fighting. And wars used mercenaries, men of no particular faith, lured by the promise of money. Wasn't that what Kalil had told her?

CHAPTER THIRTY-SIX

It was dark up here now, the afternoon light drawing to a close, sunset a memory as the last rays blinked against charcoal clouds then vanished. DS Douglas Hutton had taken the afternoon off to accommodate a workman fitting tiles onto the roof of the bungalow and was now making his way back across the slopes of the Braes. Gareth, his Labrador retriever, was roaming around the bushes, head down, intent on making the most of whatever smells were up here, yet still within shouting distance. Douglas pulled up the collar of his pea jacket, remembering other walks with the dog.

He'd been selected for one particular job because of Gareth, a dog walker required to seek out a person of interest, his cover the innocent animal that had befriended the target's spaniel. Dog walkers were themselves a breed apart, most of them content to exchange pleasantries, mainly about their respective mutts, but Douglas had managed to obtain a lot more from these excursions in parks and meadowlands than simply kennel pedigrees. The target would never know how he'd been found out, the last person on his mind a fellow dog owner. These early morning chats had been a rare interlude in the man's otherwise nefarious day, something of which DS Hutton had taken advantage.

Did that particular villain know now who had reported his movements back to Police Scotland? Douglas gave a sigh, his lips tightening with displeasure. The newspaper coverage had finished his career as far as undercover work was concerned and since then he'd been chained to a desk, still managing to provide useful work, but still, it wasn't the same as being out in the field.

'Gareth, here boy!' Douglas turned to peer through the thickening gloom, aware of the dampness descending. Soon the tops of the Braes would be shrouded in mist and he wanted nothing more than to be back by his own fireside, the dog fed and flopped out on the rug.

'Gareth!' he called again.

Where was that dog?

Frowning now, and beginning to feel a tinge of anxiety, Douglas retraced his steps, calling repeatedly.

A high-pitched whine made him turn abruptly towards the sound. The dark shadow of a rock loomed ahead, a narrow sheep track winding its way around the cliff edge.

'Gareth!' His voice was sharp, commanding, but the dog did not reappear. Instead his barks became excited and Douglas broke into a run, all his senses alert.

Shreds and tatters of mist obscured his sight as the cop followed the sounds, the path taking him steeply uphill between crags that were pitch black against the lowering sky.

His feet slipped and slithered as the track narrowed and then descended into a gully.

'Gareth!'

Douglas stopped for a moment, relieved to see the pale shape of his dog, tail wagging ferociously as he stood over something on the ground.

Then, relief changed to a different emotion, a smell wafting upwards that Douglas Hutton recognised only too well.

DI Brownlee stood shivering as the scene of crime officers made valiant attempts to cordon off the area. The man's body had been secreted between the banks of a stream, its icy surface obscuring the corpse. The torchlight showed him a partially burned figure lying face down, arms splayed out, the face disfigured by the depredations of some animal or other.

'Dumped here deliberately, you reckon?' he asked, turning to Hutton, the dog now firmly on a lead, panting by his side.

'Looks like it,' Douglas Hutton replied. 'Must have lain here for a while.'

'We'll know more once he's back in the mortuary,' Brownlee said firmly.

'Bit of a coincidence,' Hutton remarked. 'Two bodies on the Braes. Both of them burned . . . ?'

Brownlee nodded then looked up as a tall figure made its way down towards them.

'Aye. And if I know anything, that'll be a certain detective superintendent heading our way. Guy famous for not believing in coincidences,' he added grimly.

Douglas Hutton screwed up his eyes as the man appeared out of the mist. Big guy, he thought, watching him intently, noting the broad shoulders and the nimble way he traversed the narrow path. Used to hills, Hutton decided, not a slouch. Then, as the man came closer, he caught a glimpse of his face.

'Lorimer?' he whispered, turning to Brownlee.

'Aye, keeps turning up at crime scenes like the proverbial bad penny,' Brownlee growled.

Hutton said nothing in reply but raised a hand in greeting as Lorimer stepped nimbly over the burn and came to join them.

'This is DS Hutton,' Brownlee explained. 'Was out with his dog when they found the body down here.'

Lorimer gave Hutton a nod and a faint smile of recognition.

'It was Gareth that found him,' Hutton explained. 'We were on our way back from a walk when he hared off and I lost sight of him.'

'Where exactly did your dog pick up the scent?' Lorimer asked.

'Well, he disappeared below the ridges,' Hutton began. 'It must have been at the start of the track that goes over the top and down here to the Harelaw Burn.'

'Nearest road?'

Hutton frowned. 'Well, there's the main road that goes through Barrhead, past Cross Stobs where I live. Winds a bit towards the abattoir then onwards to Paisley. Nearest access from there would be Caplethill where a farm road turns up.'

'Need to get someone on to that as soon as,' Brownlee said, pre-empting the senior officer. 'Too dark tonight and besides, this fellow's lain here for a good while, I suspect.'

'There's access from the golf course over that way.' Hutton pointed through the dark. 'But you'd need to be pretty fit to cart a dead body all the way from there.'

'Perhaps he wasn't dead when he arrived here,' Lorimer murmured, gazing through the gathering dusk. Hutton and Brownlee exchanged glances behind his back as the detective superintendent stood motionless.

'Of Asian origin, five feet five tall, somewhere in his mid-twenties, I'd guess, and from the state of his teeth and how underweight he is, I'd say he's been neglecting himself.'

Rosie glanced up at Lorimer from behind her protective visor. The post-mortem necessitated use of a high-powered tool to saw into bone, fragments of which might hit the face or eyes of an examining pathologist. She was used to the noises of her particular trade, the whine of the saw, the scalpel ripping through dead flesh and the occasional gurgle as fluids settled within a cadaver. She could see Lorimer wincing at such sounds, though, as if affronted that a human body was being put through further indignities. It wasn't as if the man was squeamish, unlike Solly, her husband, who hated even the sight of blood, but Lorimer had a tendency to look further than a mere body and try to visualise what it may have been like when alive. That was his weakness, Rosie thought; an imagination that made him see deeper into things, feel the pain of others.

'I think these marks around his wrists were made from

twine,' she remarked, lifting the man's left hand and nodding towards his right.

'How can you be sure?'

'Had a closer look before you came,' she replied. 'The striations show a pattern similar to other types of binder twine I've seen before.'

'Nothing on his ankles? No binding marks?'

Rosie looked up, noticing the eagerness in Lorimer's voice.

'Nope. Think they walked him to the Harelaw Burn?'

He did not reply but continued to observe her movements carefully, his blue gaze fixed on the man's partially burned corpse.

'Forensic soil scientist will tell you what was on his shoes,' Rosie murmured, thinking at once of her friend and sometimes colleague, Professor Lorna Dawson. Lorna had helped in previous cases, though there were other soil scientists here in Glasgow that might be able to offer her particular kind of skills, allowing the substances to tell a story of where the wearer had been in the hours leading up to his death.

She continued the post-mortem, speaking aloud as each stage of the examination took place, a second pathologist taking note of everything for the record. Should the killer be found then it was a matter of certainty that Rosie would be called as an expert witness for the Crown, giving not just the details of this post-mortem examination but stating her opinion on the various possibilities that she could see from this medical investigation.

'Three knife wounds, one here on his upper arm, maybe a defence wound, another here on his shoulder and the one that undoubtedly killed him,' Rosie said. 'Severed the jugular.'

'He struggled,' Lorimer remarked quietly.

'It looks that way,' Rosie agreed. 'If his assailant had been aiming to cut his throat, the other two wounds might suggest that.'

It was conjecture, of course it was. Impossible to tell which blow had come first, but, as Rosie continued speaking as she worked, Lorimer's mind created an image of the small, thin man throwing himself this way and that as the killer stabbed with that fatal knife.

Lorimer left by the back door to retrieve his car and looked up at the entrance to the High Court of Judiciary. It never failed to make him give an ironic smile at the proximity of these two places: the Glasgow City Mortuary car park so close to those columns supporting the rounded portico where criminals and innocent alike entered to be judged. Life and death, he mused, wondering if Rosie Fergusson would one day change into the smart suit she wore to court and walk the few yards across that pale stone pavement to give evidence about the body of the man that had now been returned to a refrigerated cabinet.

Who was he? Like Derek Carter, there was nothing to identify the victim: no wallet or cards, nothing but the clothes he had been wearing that were even now being sent for examination by a forensic scientist. Painstaking details from so many experts might add up to something, he thought. Traces of soil on the footwear, the type of twine used to restrain him, anything that had been preserved from the attempt to obliterate the man's remains by fire, an attempt that had failed. Had it been too damp? Had he already fallen into that burn?

And how terribly strange that it had been DS Douglas Hutton who had found the body. Was that yet another coincidence? Or, and here Lorimer frowned as he sat in his car, was the ex-undercover cop somehow involved in these murders?

CHAPTER THIRTY-SEVEN

Vincent Burns had been a keen golfer, a member of an elite club close to his home, but perhaps he had enjoyed a round with friends at Fereneze Golf Club, the place Hutton had indicated beyond the Harelaw Burn. That thought had led Lorimer here to the Barrhead clubhouse and then across acres of rugged moorland, climbing steeply above the city. Today the sky was pale blue with swiftly shifting clouds and he could see the white peak of Ben Lomond from the hilltop where he stood. It was a popular course, he'd been told, and yes, Mr Burns had visited several times, signed in by a member, Gerry O'Neill. Lorimer had been given O'Neill's address and telephone number, despite a blustering protest from the club secretary about protecting the privacy of their members.

Lorimer had changed into his climbing boots before setting out on the course, taking care to avoid any greens. Hutton had given him a rough idea of the route a walker might take from the Barrhead clubhouse over the moor to the Harelaw Burn and so Lorimer had followed it for a while then climbed as high as he could to give himself a good vantage point. From where he stood, he could imagine the passage taken through the golf course and moorland of at least two men, one whose wrists had been bound, the other leading him to his certain death. Uniformed officers were still combing the area for anything that might give them a clue about what had happened, and in particular for a murder weapon that might have been discarded. Wintertime had advantages in that the foliage was thin on the ground and bushes bare of leaves though its big advantage to the killer was the dark days of this season. So far Rosie had given them an indication that it had been the same or similar knife that had been the murder weapon employed in killing Derek Carter. Had Carter been dumped first? Or had the unknown man been murdered here in that secluded spot, giving rise to the idea that Glennifer Braes made a good hiding place for unwanted corpses? It was now almost three weeks since Carter had last been seen alive, but what about this stranger?

Time of death was still a bit hazy and Rosie had refused to commit herself just yet but hopefully before the day was out, they might have an answer to that particular question.

Lorimer breathed in the cold air, tilting his face to a watery sun that gave no warmth, then began his descent, looking closely at the path that may have been taken by whoever had led this man to his death.

Gerry O'Neill was a retired *businessman*, that was all the golf club secretary had told him, a disdainful sniff suggesting that a mere policeman ought to watch his Ps and Qs when visiting the Fereneze club member. *Money doesn't talk, it swears* – wasn't that what Bob Dylan had written? And there were so many nowadays that measured a man's success by the noughts on his bank account, as if amassing great wealth were a mark of respect. Well, he'd met good men and some not so good who fell into that category and he would reserve judgement about Mr O'Neill till he met him, Lorimer thought as the Lexus rounded a corner and they arrived at the address he'd been given.

Thorntonhall was a pleasant little village in South Lanarkshire that had been transformed into an elite location for wealthy residents. Lorimer recalled one of his former bosses who had lived there fuming about the grand older houses being demolished to make way for what he termed 'modern monstrosities' but so far, he had not seen any that could be described as ugly. On the contrary, these were impressive well-built homes, probably individually architect designed, unlike so many contemporary estates.

'Some place,' DS David Giles remarked as they passed yet another palatial property. 'Lots of money here,' he added as they rounded the corner of the avenue and headed towards a large modern mansion at the end of a sweeping curve.

The tyres of the Lexus crunched as he drove slowly across the gravel drive and parked. It was huge, he had to admit, with two wings off the main building, one housing an internal double garage, a trio of pitched roofs giving the whole place a pleasing symmetry. Lorimer had already clocked a separate double garage to the left of the drive and now he noticed the sleek shape of a taupe-coloured Jaguar by the front entrance. The personalised number plate

GER0N showed that this was probably Gerry O'Neill's, another small status symbol that might be a mark of pride or simply a gift for the man who already had everything else of material value. A quick glance showed the usual security of burglar alarm and closed circuit camera; no need to be gated in this neck of the woods, perhaps, when you could see an intruder approaching. Or a senior police officer and his detective sergeant.

As if he had read Lorimer's thoughts, a white-haired man appeared at the front door and stood waiting for them at the porch. Lorimer's first impression of O'Neill was of a short, slightly tubby man whose penetrating gaze and unsmiling mouth reminded him of a particularly irritable science teacher who'd taught him in his teenage years and who'd been known for his dreadful temper. They were not welcome here, was the message that body language was sending out right now.

'Here we go,' Giles murmured under his breath as he stepped out of the Lexus and joined Lorimer.

'Detective Superintendent.' Gerry O'Neill shook Lorimer's hand and nodded as he introduced his companion, hardly sparing a glance at the younger man. 'Nice set of wheels you've got.' He nodded towards the silver Lexus. 'Like that particular model, myself, y'know. Had one that did over two hundred thousand when I was younger. Great car.' O'Neill turned to his visitors as if he had suddenly remembered them. 'Come in, come in. Far too cold to stand out here,' he commanded and marched back without another word.

Lorimer and Giles followed him into the house, the

detective sergeant's eyes widening at the huge reception hall and its massive Christmas tree by the foot of a winding staircase.

'Better come in here,' O'Neill told them, turning a corner and indicating an open door at the end of a wide corridor. 'Fire's on and I suppose you'd like a drink?' The question was fired over his shoulder, almost but not quite grudgingly as if his manners demanded that he offered refreshments to police officers visiting his home.

Lorimer dropped a wink at Giles before the detective sergeant could reply.

'That would be very welcome, sir, thank you,' he said as O'Neill took them into a large drawing room with picture windows overlooking grounds that were more like a private park than a residential garden.

'Tea? Coffee?' O'Neill's gruff accent began to intrigue Lorimer. It was a genuine Glasgow accent, all right, but overlaid with something else. Had he worked overseas? Picked up a different sort of tone to his voice?

Left to themselves, Lorimer and Giles stood by the window, Giles gazing outside while Lorimer had a careful look at the interior of this room. His trained eye took in the heavy silk drapes, a deep shade of coffee held back with contrasting gold ties, the fabric matching the two three-seater settees and bucket chair that were angled either side of a pale stone fireplace that housed a wood-burning stove. In one corner of the room another Christmas tree was artfully placed, its decorations all different shades of gold and silver, a massive array of gifts beneath, wrapped in shiny dark green paper and tied in gauzy golden ribbons. It was a far cry from his own modest home with the decorations they'd amassed over the years, each one a small reminder of happy times past.

Was this a happy home? Lorimer wondered, looking around the room. It was a tribute to some expensive interior decorator, he decided at last, wondering once more at his old boss's remarks. Had some treasured old property stood here years before? Torn down to make way for a rich man to stamp his own mark upon it? Trouble was, so far Lorimer could see nothing in this room that gave a clue to O'Neill's personality, just the fact that a great deal of money had been spent creating a lovely but impersonal room. Perhaps, he thought, that in itself might be an indication of some sort?

'Here you are.' O'Neill appeared once again, carrying a tray with three mugs of coffee and a plate of biscuits. 'Instant, all right? Help yourselves to milk and sugar,' he offered, setting the tray down on a long low table that was by the window.

'Now,' he said, settling himself on the middle of one of the settees and staring hard at Lorimer, 'what is this all about?'

'You were a friend of Vincent Burns,' Lorimer began.

'Correct. Terrible business, just terrible. Surprised you haven't got someone for that yet,' O'Neill growled.

'How well did you know Mr Burns?' Lorimer asked, taking a sip of his black coffee. It might only be instant, good enough to serve to mere coppers, but it was a decent enough coffee.

'Oh, we went back a long way,' O'Neill admitted. 'School pals, y'know? Lost touch for years while I was overseas a lot, but we met up again, enjoyed a few rounds of golf. I'm retired now, of course, so I get to play as much as I want whereas poor Vince ... ' He tailed off with a shrug.

'You're a member of Fereneze Golf Club?'

O'Neill gave a faint smile and lifted his chin a fraction. 'I am a member of several clubs, Superintendent. Do you play?'

Lorimer returned the smile but restrained himself from quoting the old adage about golf being a good walk wasted. 'No time for that, sir.'

'Too busy catching criminals,' O'Neill said with a dry laugh. He did not meet Lorimer's gaze as he spoke the words, however, and that made the detective curious.

'What line of work were you involved in, Mr O'Neill?'

'Oh, import and export. Big deals with oil-related companies. Worked in the Middle East for several years,' he said, his tone expansive though the statement itself was vague. Deliberately imprecise, so that anyone would fill in the blanks?

'Did you use Bryson's for any part of your work at all?'

O'Neill took up his coffee and drank slowly as if considering Lorimer's question carefully.

'Might have done at one time,' he conceded. 'Why do you ask?'

'Oh, we have to ask all sorts of little questions, sir, many of them just routine,' Lorimer assured him, still keeping his eyes fixed on the man's face.

'Yes, I think my wife might have consulted Vince about her late mother's property,' he said at last. 'Shall I ask her?' He turned to look at the door of the drawing room.

'If you don't mind,' Lorimer said. 'It is helpful for us to make contact with anyone who knew Mr Burns and if your wife was also a friend ... ' He let the sentence dangle.

'Right.' O'Neill scowled as he rose from his place by the fireside. 'I'll see if she's available, then, shall I?'

The door of the drawing room closed behind him and left Lorimer and Giles looking at one another.

'Wouldn't like to cross him,' Giles remarked as he picked up a chocolate biscuit from the plate. 'Seems a bit prickly about us being here, don't you think?'

Lorimer raised his eyebrows and merely smiled. He'd save the expression of his thoughts for when they were safely out of earshot and back in the car. But, yes, there was something defensive about Gerry O'Neill and he wondered if that was enough to merit a bit of digging into the man's business background to see if all these trappings of wealth had been hard earned in a perfectly legal manner.

When the door opened again, Lorimer and Giles rose politely to their feet to greet the slim, silver-haired woman who entered the room.

'My wife, Diane,' O'Neill said as she stepped forward to shake their hands. Diane O'Neill was a pretty woman in her sixties, wearing dark jeans and a fluffy cream sweater, her eyes crinkling in a genuine smile as Lorimer and Giles introduced themselves. Lorimer couldn't help but notice the huge diamond ring on her finger as she held out her hand, its single stone winking in the light.

'Oh, we were so very sorry to hear about Vince,' she began, taking the bucket seat next to the fireside and not, Lorimer noticed, next to her husband. 'Have you managed to find out what happened?'

'Our enquiries are still ongoing,' Lorimer replied. 'Did you know him well?'

Diane O'Neill shot a questioning glance towards her husband, as if asking for permission to reply. The almost imperceptible nod from O'Neill gave Lorimer an understanding about the relationship between this pair. She was a good-looking woman, possibly a second wife? And there was a definite air of deference about her manner, despite distancing herself from her husband.

'Yes, we did know Vince, at least Gerry did. I don't play golf with the chaps,' she said. 'But we did sometimes meet for lunch in the clubhouse.'

'Oh, any particular clubhouse?'

Again, that look towards her husband.

'Usually Whitecraigs. Vince was a member there,' O'Neill answered for her.

'That's right.' Diane O'Neill nodded.

'Never in Fereneze?'

'Where?' The word was out of her mouth before the woman could help herself and she actually put a hand to her lips as though to cover up a fault, Lorimer noticed.

'It's in Barrhead,' Lorimer said helpfully.

'Don't socialise there, myself,' O'Neill stated brusquely.

'But you do play there. Yes?'

O'Neill shot a dark look at the two police officers then nodded. 'It's a good enough course to play. Challenging. Scenic, if you like that sort of thing.'

'And you took Mr Burns there? Signed him in?'

'Done your homework already, haven't you, so why ask daft questions?' O'Neill snapped. 'Vince and I played several different courses. I'm a member over at Erskine – the old club, as well as Mar Hall – then there's Fereneze,

301

Whitecraigs and several others. Vince sometimes came for a weekend round with me, so what? Was he bashed over the head with a golf club?' He gave a mirthless laugh.

'Gerry!' his wife implored, frowning at him and shaking her head.

'We're not at liberty to disclose the details of Mr Burns's death,' Lorimer said firmly. 'We are interested in anybody who was recently with Mr Burns at Fereneze Golf Club, however, and of course as the member that signed him in your name came up, sir.'

O'Neill frowned. 'What on earth is all this nonsense about golf clubs? Vince was killed outside his home, wasn't that what the news report said?' He turned towards his wife for the first time and she nodded, sitting forward on the edge of her seat, clearly nervous and uncertain about what was going on.

'You will not have heard a news report with new developments yet,' Lorimer told them smoothly. 'However, I can inform you that we are investigating another death that may have taken place in the vicinity of Fereneze.'

'And what the hell has that got to do with me? Or Vince?' O'Neill's face was beginning to colour up, his tone belligerent, the signs of temper about to boil over.

'Again, I am not at liberty to discuss details, but it would be very helpful if we might have a look at your cars?'

'Certainly not!' O'Neill snapped. 'This is outrageous. Coming here and asking questions, wanting to know about our late friend and now nosing into things that don't concern you!' he blustered.

'If you would prefer that we returned with a warrant?'

O'Neill stood up, now bristling with ill-concealed rage. 'I'd prefer if you would leave,' he snapped. 'And I will have a word with your chief constable. Mearns, isn't it?' He smirked, striding towards the door and pulling it open.

Lorimer and Giles rose hastily and made their way from the room, but not before Diane O'Neill had cast an apologetic look their way.

O'Neill stood on the porch as before as the Lexus turned on the red gravel and headed back down the drive but this time there was no word of farewell, just an angry stare as he saw them off his premises.

'He didn't want us to see his cars, did he?' Giles said. 'And what's the betting he has them valeted before we can obtain a warrant to have a look at them?'

'You think he's a wrong 'un?' Lorimer asked.

'I'd bet my life on it,' Giles replied, then looked across at Lorimer. 'He's hiding something, don't you think?'

Lorimer nodded, but did not reply. There was something about Gerry O'Neill that demanded a lot more investigation, including where he had been on particular dates. That last round of golf at Fereneze between Burns and O'Neill had been as recently as November and now, what he wanted to know was the date on which Rosie Fergusson reckoned their unknown Asian man had been killed.

CHAPTER THIRTY-EIGHT

'The cops have been here.'

She listened to the man's spluttering invective as he outlined the morning's visit but all she could really hear was the fear in his voice.

'You say nothing. Clear up your own mess, do you understand?'

There was a sudden silence that she took for acknowledgement of her command.

'You have seen what happens when someone steps out of line. And I would hazard a guess that neither you nor your lady wife would wish to end up like that?'

She cut off the call and laid her mobile on the glass-topped table by her side. Perhaps it was time to groom that Zimbabwean fellow, make him aware of the services that would be required and the rewards that would come his way.

Netta listened as the footsteps drew closer then stopped outside her door. She had the money ready in an envelope, clutched in her hands, the door chained across so that this time no one would barge in and knock her about.

The thumps made the front door shake and Netta drew back for a moment as if she herself had been struck.

'Open up, ye auld bag!' a voice thundered. 'We know yer in therr!'

Netta unlocked the door with trembling fingers and thrust the envelope out before the men had time to push anything past the chain.

'It's all there. Now go home and leave me alone,' she called, pushing the door shut and bolting it fast.

A stream of invective and a kick on the lower part of the door were all she had in answer.

The old woman breathed out, her heart racing as she sank against the wall in the darkened hallway.

A sudden cry from right outside her door made Netta start. Then she heard running footsteps and yelling.

What the heck was going on?

Not daring to open her door again, she rushed into the kitchen and peered out from behind the curtains. It was hard to see further along the passage outside the flats, even craning her neck.

The sound of different thudding boots coming from the other direction made her turn to see a couple of uniformed police officers give chase to the men who had grabbed her loan money.

'Go on, boys,' she urged in a breathy whisper. 'Get the wee devils!' Someone had called the cops, another victim per-haps, not as terrified as she was with the threatened reprisals from the gombeen man? Heart beating rapidly, Netta stood at the window, half fearful, half excited by the appearance of these police officers.

When all was quiet again, she filled the kettle, deciding that a restorative pot of tea was needed to recover from the excitement.

A couple of raps on her door made Netta jump, spilling some water onto the work surface.

'Oh, ma goad! They're back!' she cried.

'Netta,' a familiar voice called through her letter box. 'It's me. Daniel.'

She struggled through the hallway once more, flicked off the chain and unlocked the door, letting it swing open.

'Oh, Daniel, son, come away in. You'll never believe what's been happening,' she began, ushering her neighbour inside and locking the door firmly behind him.

'Try me.' Daniel's grin made Netta stop and stare at him for a moment.

'You know? Did you see what was happening?' she asked, eager to find out if the police officers had caught up with her tormentors.

'Those loan shark people will not be bothering you again, Netta, dear,' Daniel told her.

'An' how do ye know that, son? You're a refugee, right? How come ye can say that to me? Ye dinna know whit these people are like,' she said, shaking her head at him.

Daniel's smile faded as he regarded her seriously. 'I wasn't always a refugee, remember,' he said at last. 'When I lived in Zimbabwe I was known as Inspector Kohi.'

'An inspector?' Netta's jaw dropped open in astonishment.

'Yes. I was indeed, with a team of men answering to me.

At least for a time,' he said, a note of sorrow in his voice. 'Now I have a friend here in Glasgow who has seen to it that these men will not trouble you any more for money. In fact, after today, I think the ... what did you call him? Gobbyman?'

'Gombeen man,' Netta corrected him, still wide-eyed with the revelation that her neighbour had not only been a senior policeman, *an inspector*, in a former life but had also taken it upon himself to sort out her problems.

'In the name o' the wee man,' she said softly and sank into the nearest chair.

'It's true, Netta. I was someone different back home, a respected member of society until ...'

Daniel knelt down and took his neighbour's hands in his own. 'You can't imagine what it was like. Finding that people I had known and trusted were doing the most terrible things. Then trying to do something about it. They threatened to kill me, Netta.' He stopped again for a moment, biting his lower lip to prevent the tears coming.

'They set fire to our home. Murdered my wife and our little boy,' he whispered huskily.

'Oh, son, that's whit ye couldnae tell me. Oh, Daniel, son, that's terrible!' Netta cried out and then she was weeping and holding his head against her chest, his own tears finally flowing.

Later, after the necessary tea and more explanation from Daniel, Netta listened as he told her of the incident at the front door of the flats and how he had packed off the two bullies who'd tried to force their way in.

'I have a good friend here in the police,' was all he would say; no mention of Lorimer's name and nothing about the vigilance of the local cops who had been given details of the loan sharking carried out against the old woman.

'So, let me get this right, son. You were once a top cop ower therr. Why can ye no' jist become a polis in Glesca? Eh? Can ye no' dae a transfer or something?'

Daniel's sorrowful smile and shake of the head made her sigh.

'Perhaps one day I will be a police officer again but like so many other professional people who have come to this country to seek asylum, I must follow the procedures.'

There was no way he would confide in this dear lady that he had begun a sort of police work already. It might be highly dangerous for his own life right now as he masqueraded as a disaffected type seeking some sort of role in carrying out a terrorist attack. But it could also jeopardise his future here in Scotland, if the authorities were to learn of it.

'Where is he?' Qasim muttered to himself, thrusting back the sleeve of his loose tunic and staring at his watch. It was an expensive make, not one that many refugees might still be wearing after the struggles and expense of fleeing their country.

Then, as if he had been called up by the Syrian's very question, Daniel appeared at the door of the refuge and slunk in quietly, glancing behind him as though fearful of having been followed.

'You're late,' Qasim accused.

'Am I?' Daniel's eyes widened in surprise as he glanced

at his own watch. 'Sorry, this is so old, perhaps the battery needs changing,' he apologised, holding up his wrist and showing the face to the man scowling at him. He was on his own today, Daniel saw, the younger Syrian absent for some reason.

'Well, get it sorted,' Qasim growled.

He leaned forward, fixing Daniel with a gimlet stare. 'If you are to be working with us, you need to understand that every second counts when it comes to carrying out our task.'

'I'm your man when it comes to getting things done,' Daniel assured him, tightening his lips in what he hoped looked like a grimace. He might be an amateur when it came to playing a part like this, but his police training had given him plenty of insight into putting on an act to fool criminals in the past. At this moment, all he really had to do was think of the men that had torched his home and murdered his family. That was enough to bring verisimilitude to his expression of antagonism. It was not any UK authorities that he was against, though with any luck this Syrian would never doubt that. No, Daniel Kohi's crusade was against any wrongdoers, whether they were greedy loan sharks intimidating an old lady or planning some outrage in his adopted city.

'Tell me more,' he said, eyes gleaming as though in anticipation.

Qasim made to rise. 'Not here,' he told Daniel. 'Come, there is somebody who wishes to meet you.'

She looked into the mirror, not seeing her own reflection but the room behind, its pastel colours chosen to give an impression of light. But there were shadows everywhere, the gloom of this midwinter day seeping into each corner. Glasgow was so different from the place where she had made her home, a land of searing heat and dust, endless horizons and a sky that could swallow you whole. Once this was over, she intended to return, though it would never be the same as before.

Did anything remain constant? The thought made her mouth harden. They had taken away the one person who had changed her entire life and now she would wreak her spite against his captors. An eye for an eye, the ancients had it, so different from these milksop Christians with their hybrid festival. Christmas, a birth of some Palestinian child, or so the old story would have you believe. But it was scarcely remembered amidst the frantic rush of Westerners to the altar of consumerism. Trees, baubles, cheap rubbish! Her lip curled in disdain at the thought.

It would be a Christmas to remember in this cold, dreary city.

The glass house was surprisingly warm inside, massive ferns and exotic greenery making Daniel look upwards. They passed by a shallow circular pool as Qasim led him further into the place, Daniel breathing in the scent of growing foliage as he followed the Syrian.

She was standing at the far end, near a set of metal stairs spiralling upwards, her back to them. As before, her blonde hair was swathed in that pale grey scarf, draped around her neck and hanging in two tails across her shoulders. There was a stillness about the woman that intrigued him. She was

310

not particularly tall, perhaps five feet six or seven, but she had a grace and alertness that reminded Daniel of antelope he had watched so many times: impala heading on delicate hooves towards the vlei, seeking water on the marshy edges of the bush. Even with her back turned to them, he could sense a watchfulness about her. It would not do to spook this female in any way, he thought, readying himself to become the obsequious thug he guessed she wanted him to be.

'You're here.' She turned as they drew closer and gave Daniel an appraising look. Close up she was more beautiful than he had first thought, her pale skin flawless, high cheekbones and a heart-shaped face. But it was the eyes that made him blink. Aquamarine, he decided as she continued to stare at him, siren's eyes with depths in which a man might drown.

'Daniel,' she said. 'Daniel *Kohi*. That's not a Zimbabwean name, surely?'

This woman knew about African heritage and that would be a small fact to squirrel away, he decided, impressed.

'My grandfather came from Tanzania. To work in the mines.' He shook his head as though in disapproval. 'White men's mines in the old Rhodesia.'

She nodded and then began to walk slowly around him as though he were an animal that she might purchase.

'You made money back in Zimbabwe?' she asked as she completed the circle and came back to the metal staircase.

'Enough,' he said sullenly.

'Ever been in prison, Kohi?'

Daniel looked down at the ground and shuffled his feet as though embarrassed or guilty. 'A few times,' he admitted, and though it was true, this woman must never suspect that it was to interview an inmate during his role as a police inspector.

'I can make sure you have plenty of money if you do what we ask you,' she said, her voice silky now, almost seductive.

Daniel's head shot up, his eyes gleaming in what he hoped was an expression of greed.

'I'd like that,' he said. 'All they gave me was this stupid card. Keeping you like a beggar on the streets!' he complained.

'We want you on the streets,' she laughed lightly, 'but not as a beggar. No, Daniel Kohi, we have much more use for you in the city, much more.'

She turned to Qasim. 'He isn't a Christian, you said.'

Daniel watched as the Syrian gave a slight bow, acknowledging her words.

'No religion,' Qasim assured her. 'That's right, isn't it, Kohi?'

Daniel nodded sullenly, hoping that his act was covering up the frisson of dismay that he felt inside. Raised in a Christian household, he had adhered to the faith of his family but right now he sent up a small prayer of apology along with a silent plea for forgiveness.

The woman smiled at them both. 'Well, perhaps we can begin by showing Daniel what will be expected of him.'

There was a taxi rank by the Botanic Gardens and it only took a signal from Qasim to alert a driver to draw into the kerb beside them. Once aboard, nobody spoke, the woman having given an address and sitting back, apparently looking out as they turned and headed back along Great Western Road and into the city centre. Qasim sat beside her, his eyes closed, Daniel opposite, staring at them both in turn and wondering what on earth he was going to be asked to do and if he could avoid anything that would result in him being thrown out of the UK.

The taxi took them past rows of brightly lit shops, past a church with an enormous spire (*Don't stare at it*, he reminded himself) and through a busy junction where he could see the sweep of a motorway and its overhead gantries. Everywhere he looked people seemed to be burdened with bags of shopping (messages, as Netta would call them) but the gaudy glitter on many of them suggested purchases of Christmas gifts. There would be none of that for him this year, though he would dearly love to buy a little present for his elderly neighbour. *No*, Daniel thought, *keep such ideas suppressed for now, give this female the idea that you disdain the very concept of Christmas*. He gritted his teeth, staring out at the crowds gathering at a set of traffic lights, mustering up as much false indignation as he could. Should she turn and glance at him, Daniel Kohi had to appear just as she wanted him to be.

They were dropped at one side of George Square and immediately Qasim led Daniel through the crowds until they reached a large glass-covered scene.

'You want me to bust that?' Daniel asked, jerking a thumb towards the Nativity figures that were displayed inside.

Qasim smiled and laid a finger to his lips. 'It will be broken, certainly, but not by you, my friend. We have another task for you, Daniel Kohi.'

He turned to look for the woman, but she had disappeared

313

from sight. Was she somewhere in this crowd, watching them? Daniel did not know and dared not risk searching for her.

'Where's . . . ? What's her name?' he asked Qasim. 'She seems to know enough about me but hasn't even said who she is.'

Qasim grabbed him roughly by the sleeve.

'If she wished you to know her name, do you not think she would have told you?' he hissed. 'Do not ask questions, Mr Kohi. Just do what we tell you and you will be rewarded. Is that not enough?'

Daniel gave a shrug. 'Suppose so,' he said. 'I didn't always know who my paymasters were back home.'

Qasim relaxed his grip, evidently reassured that their newest recruit had been part of some sort of gang, a bit of muscle paid to do what he was told.

'So,' Daniel said, giving Qasim a thoughtful look. 'What exactly is it you want me to do? And when can I expect my money?'

Qasim narrowed his eyes but Daniel continued. 'She said *plenty*, but, hey, how much is that and what do I have to do to earn it?' Putting on an act of a greedy conspirator was the way to play this, he decided, eyeing up the Syrian.

'You like money? Well, she will give you thousands, yes,' he said as Daniel's eyes gleamed, 'thousands to spend wherever you wish to go in this weary world.'

'Yeah? Sounds good to me.' Daniel grinned, rubbing his hands together.

Qasim nodded. 'Now, look around you. Tell me what you see.'

*

Afterwards, as he told Lorimer, he described the busy square with its funfair and ice-skating rink, the children running about and the people with bags full of Christmas shopping. He had searched the crowds for a fair-haired woman wearing a grey headscarf, but she was nowhere to be seen. Qasim had remained silent throughout, then, beckoning Daniel to the front of the City Chambers, he whispered in his ear, words that made his blood run cold.

'You're essentially there to be a lookout? Make sure that the boy is in the correct place?' Lorimer asked.

Daniel nodded. 'I have no idea who he is. The only ones I've met are the two Syrians and the female that seems to be in charge.'

'But this Qasim spoke of a boy?'

'I am guessing he is also Syrian,' Daniel said unhappily. 'Some youngster brainwashed by these people.'

Lorimer nodded his agreement. 'You need to find out more without scaring them off,' he told him. 'When do you expect to meet up with them again?' he asked, his mind already working on the best person to witness their rendezvous.

'Tomorrow afternoon, at the refugee centre,' he said.

'Right. Just carry on as if everything is normal. Leave the rest to me.'

It was too risky to involve any of the existing undercover officers or, indeed, any of his own team at the MIT. But perhaps there was someone that might be willing to provide eyes and ears, someone whose skills of observing human nature were far more advanced than most. He might have to pick up an old coat and scruffy trainers from somewhere to disguise the bearded man with horn-rimmed spectacles that he had in mind, Lorimer thought, already focusing on the scene as well as the danger of involving yet another civilian without telling Mearns or Flint.

CHAPTER THIRTY-NINE

'Let me get this right, you have intelligence that this act of terrorism is to take place in George Square right before Christmas?' Solly asked.

Lorimer nodded.

'Why not inform the security services? And why involve someone like me?'

'We think there is an insider, a woman who has access to either police files or perhaps someone linked with the security services. I'm worried, Solly. What if there is someone right at the heart of either of these establishments working with those terrorists?' Lorimer heaved a sigh. 'I know it was a terrible risk involving Daniel but I needed somebody that wasn't connected to the ongoing investigation. Now, I thought you too might play a small part?' He looked across at his friend then frowned suddenly.

'There was something . . .' He tailed off. 'I can't put my finger on it, but I thought either Mearns or Flint had said something that I meant to follow up.' He made a face. 'I was so intent on other things that it has now completely escaped my mind. Old age,' he said, giving a wry smile towards his friend. 'They say the more facts you absorb, the more begin to slip through the net of your grey matter. Is that right?'

'Tiredness, concern about Maggie, you have plenty of reasons to forget a small detail,' Solly soothed.

'It's the small details that often hold the clue to a big case, though,' Lorimer said.

'So, let me go over this again. At some time, close to Christmas, a young lad will set off a suicide device close to the Nativity scene in George Square. Maximum damage. Glass flying everywhere. Crowds gathered round. Am I correct so far?'

'Yes.' Lorimer nodded. 'Our initial intelligence from the security people was of a terrorist event, but they had no details of who was to be involved except a woman seems to have infiltrated police casework. We also strongly suspected that this same person had informed the press about several undercover officers because these particular officers were tasked with finding out about this terrorist cell. The same ones who all live in the Paisley or Barrhead area.'

'And Kohi has found the woman?'

'She is nowhere on our databases. Thank God. I'd have hated to be in David Mearns's shoes if she was one of our own. Speaks Arabic, may be the same female seen with Vincent Burns leaving with him from his house. Young, very good-looking, according to Daniel. A Grace Kelly lookalike, he reckoned.'

'Why?' Solly frowned. 'Why does a white woman plan

such an atrocity in the first place?' He turned to Lorimer. 'There has to be some very deep motivation going on here. Something that has brought her into contact with these Syrian refugees.'

'We've got the team looking into that as we speak,' Lorimer assured him. 'So far nobody of her description has been involved with any of the refugee charities and, of course, there are hundreds of other areas in which a refugee might have met her. Home Office, detention centres, you name it, we're searching every avenue we can think of.'

'You believe that the break-in, when Maggie was hurt, was an attempt to find your own personal files?'

'Yes.' Lorimer nodded. 'When this all started, we – that's Mearns, Flint and myself – all agreed to take our laptops with us wherever we went. Flint is very clued up about stuff like that. Her work in the Met included time as an undercover officer.'

'And your current chief constable?'

'Easy enough for him to tote his laptop around. He won't be with us much longer. They head back home for Christmas then we will be appointing a new chief some time in January.'

'They?' Solly's question hung in the air.

For a moment Lorimer seemed puzzled. 'I think he's up here with his wife,' he said at last. 'To be honest I've never talked to him about his personal circumstances. And he's never offered to socialise. Not a problem.' He shrugged. 'I rate him pretty highly, as it happens, Solly, and so do a great many others. Word has it he might be on the New Year's Honours list for a knighthood.'

'He's finally retiring then?'

'Yes. But I know it would be a real feather in his cap if we can prevent this threat from becoming a reality.'

'Yet you are still comfortable keeping both Kohi and myself a secret from the chief constable and his deputy?'

'I wouldn't say comfortable, Solly. But I felt it was important to involve individuals who could not be identified as police officers. Kohi is an intelligent man, not easily broken despite the trials he's been through, and he's keen to help.'

The psychologist gave a sigh. 'I could refuse, you know. I have Rosie and the children to consider. My family are coming here for Christmas this year and we are looking forward to being together.'

'Look, forget I asked you,' Lorimer said abruptly. 'I had no right . . .'

Solly held up his hand. 'I hope to have a wonderful time with my own children,' he said. 'But how can I enjoy myself if I failed to help so many other families that might be robbed of their little ones?' He lifted his dark eyes to Lorimer, a sad expression on his face. 'If I can do anything to help prevent this terrible thing, then I will.'

The ancient belted raincoat hid his warm sweater but Solly had put on his own cord trousers after rummaging through a bag that was full of old clothes destined for the playground recycling bin. The shoes he had chosen to wear were scuffed and worn, ones he used for playing football with the kids in the park. He hesitated as he approached the glass-fronted centre in Byres Road. It was not so very far to reach from his home across Kelvingrove Park or, in fact, from his office at the university and Solly's main worry was being greeted by any student who might not have returned home for the holidays. However, the raincoat turned up at the collar was a decent enough disguise, he decided, his hand on the door.

As instructed, he headed straight to the table where tea- and coffee-making facilities were spread out. A dark-haired young woman came forward to greet him with a smile, but not before Solly had glimpsed the pair of Syrian men sitting against a wall, gazing out at the street.

'Hello, you're new here, I'm Jackie.' She smiled. 'Help yourself to tea or coffee. There are biscuits here,' she offered, pointing to a round metal tin adorned with a picture of a robin on a holly wreath. 'Have you just arrived in Glasgow?'

Solly shook his head. 'I have been here for a while,' he whispered. 'But I have not been in this place before.' He nodded, hoping that the girl would take him for yet another refugee seeking some comfort in this place.

'Where are you from?' she asked.

'I was in London before . . . ' he told her truthfully, then shrugged as if too weary to go into more detail.

'Well, help yourself, sit anywhere you like. And if you want to have a chat, I'm always here.' She smiled again, giving him a small pat on his shoulder.

Solly carried a mug of tea and a home-made biscuit to an empty table close by the Syrians, his head down as though he were afraid to make eye contact. He had been genuinely shy when he was a boy, and it was the memory of a young Solomon Brightman that had given him the idea of behaving like this. As a scholar of human behaviour, Solly was enjoying creating this version of himself for others to see.

Sure enough, after giving him a cursory glance, the Syrians

continued to talk quietly as they waited for Daniel to appear. Now was the time to listen carefully, the device secreted under the folds of the raincoat recording their every word.

Solly nibbled the biscuit slowly, his fingers fidgeting on the tabletop as if he were nervous, a good sign to throw out to anyone watching. A refugee new to the city, that was the role he had chosen, and sitting quietly, head down, was part of that particular guise. The two men were conversing in a language he did not know but guessed was Arabic. That was no problem for a Police Scotland interpreter to translate, of course. So long as he sat and stared at the table, all would be well, he told himself, though, when the door opened and he saw two pairs of eyes turned towards the sound, Solly could not help but turn for one swift moment.

The black man sat down opposite the Syrians but not before Solly had taken a look at him. Mid-thirties, perhaps, average height and an intelligent expression on that handsome face . . . One brief look was all it took for Solly to process what he wanted. Lorimer had given him little background information about his fellow infiltrator yet Solly was encouraged by the feeling of strength in the man seated a few feet away from him. This one could handle himself, he thought, though it was something deeper than mere brawn, there was an inner power to Daniel Kohi, just as Lorimer had hinted.

At once the Syrians reverted to speaking in English, at least one of them did, Solly decided, listening to the voices.

'It will be on Christmas Eve,' he heard the older Syrian whisper. 'A big surprise present for the people of this city.'

Solly shivered inwardly. The evil that was in men's hearts . . . He suppressed a sigh.

'That's next week,' Daniel replied. 'Do you have more details?'

'Hush,' the Syrian rebuked. 'You will be told when this is to take place. All we need is for you to guide the boy towards the spot and leave him there.'

'Then?'

There was a low laugh followed by more words in Arabic then a sound of scraping chairs as the three men rose from the table.

Solly did not turn to stare at them but he could hear the door open and close then they flitted past the window, three dark shapes heading towards the Subway.

He was not to follow them, Lorimer had instructed, but simply to obtain what he could by recording their conversations.

When he was certain that none of the charity staff were around, he rose quietly from the table and headed out onto the street, collar up, head down, his ruined shoes taking him to the nearest taxi rank around the corner.

CHAPTER FORTY

'Your man by the stream was killed a few days before Vincent Burns,' Rosie told him. 'The cold air made things difficult to establish an accurate time of death, but we are thinking around November the twenty-seventh.'

'That was the date that Carter was killed,' Lorimer said at once, staring at the two calendars on his office wall. His former pride at a murder-free month was proving to be a hollow thought now. Two men had been murdered at the end of November, each of them dumped in different parts of Glennifer Braes.

'Any further ideas about who he was?' Rosie asked.

'No missing persons fitting his description. A young Asian chap from what we can see but we really don't know yet, though a reconstruction of what he may have looked like is being circulated to all the detention centres and points of official entry to the UK in the hope that there is a record of him somewhere.'

'There was something . . .' Rosie began.

Lorimer listened intently. Whatever she had found would be worth noting; Rosie Fergusson's observation and insight had helped him a lot over the years they had worked together.

'There was some odd bruising on his ribs. As if he had been crushed against a barrier of some sort. An unusual pattern, a bit faint now since it must have occurred a week or more before his death. I'm sending over some enlarged pictures to let you see. Maybe someone at your end can figure it out?'

'Thanks, Rosie,' Lorimer said. 'Ready to see them any time now.'

It was a matter of moments till the email pinged up on his screen and he could download Rosie's attachment.

Sure enough, there were bruises all across the man's ribcage and, as the pathologist had suggested, it might have been the result of being pressed hard against something. Had this young man been forced into a confined space, smuggled into the country with others, all fighting for breath, perhaps? Stories of terrible deaths in refrigerated lorries came back to him now. What terrors these poor souls had endured before they had landed here only to suffer worse and die, their hopes for a future smothered.

Lorimer scrolled through the images and then sat back, one hand stroking his chin thoughtfully. Perhaps these might be sent to Gartcosh to be examined by a counter-terrorism officer. There was something about the pattern of these bruises that the detective superintendent wanted to have confirmed. And, if he was correct, then the death of this young man, though sad, had been a lot less dramatic than it might have been.

*

'God bless technology,' Lorimer murmured. It was less than an hour since Rosie had sent the pictures, and now he was listening to the officer at Gartcosh.

'We've seen images like this before,' the woman told him. 'Happily, the public never know how many times a terrorist is apprehended before they can set off their device. A vest packed full of explosives would leave marks like this and so, yes, it is possible your victim was either a mule bringing it here or he had been wearing it for some other reason.'

'He was stabbed to death,' Lorimer told her. 'No ID. Nothing that can tell us much about him though we have a lot of feelers out in the right places.'

'Horrible,' the woman murmured. 'Wonder if he had been selected as the one to set it off then chickened out?'

Lorimer clenched his teeth and sighed. 'My thoughts exactly. Either way, he was fated to die.'

'Professor Brightman is here to see you, sir.' A smiling officer stood at his door then stepped aside to admit a scruffy-looking man in a worn raincoat.

Lorimer rose from his place and went towards his friend.

'Goodness, Solly, you fairly look the part. Makes me want to offer you a square meal and a change of clothes.'

'I'll settle for tea,' Solly said, taking off the coat and sitting down on one of the more comfortable chairs in the office. 'Mint tea, if you have it.'

Lorimer smiled as he bent to open a cupboard containing a couple of tins. One had some of Maggie's cranberry cookies and the other was stuffed with different sorts of teabags. The kettle in the corner of his room had not long been boiled and soon the two men were sitting side by side, mugs clasped in their hands.

'I liked the look of your chap, Kohi,' Solly began. 'He struck me as a courageous sort of man.' He threw a questioning look at Lorimer.

'I think he is,' he agreed. 'And it was his courage and integrity that made him a victim in his own homeland,' he added sadly.

'Perhaps he will tell me about that one day,' Solly said. 'But I do not wish to pry.'

'Did you manage to sit close enough to them?'

Solly nodded. 'I did. And here is the result.' He produced the device that had been hidden under his outer garment and handed it to Lorimer. 'Some of it will need translation but I can tell you one thing right now.'

'Yes?'

'They're aiming to carry out their plan on Christmas Eve.'

David Giles had been spot-on with his assessment of Gerry O'Neill and his collection of luxury cars, Lorimer thought, reading the detective sergeant's report. Not only was his taupe Jaguar missing from the premises but each of the other vehicles had been thoroughly valeted since the initial visit from the police officers. O'Neill had been smug, Giles had written in a postscript meant only for Lorimer's eyes, the warrant not making him fearful in any way. On the contrary, he had cooperated with the officers, showing them his classic cars as well as his wife's sporty Mercedes runaround. The Jaguar was in the garage for a 'service', he had told them, but they guessed that was a way of telling them gleefully that it was being deep-cleaned somewhere else and that there would be nothing to find when it was returned.

O'Neill had something to do with all of this, Lorimer was certain. His association with Burns, the membership at Fereneze Golf Club, it was all too cosy to be a mere coincidence. Members of his team were already hard at work to see just what sort of business O'Neill had handled in his past and, more than that, if it had any link to Bryson's. He sat back and closed his eyes. What was it Solly had said? Motive. Why had Derek Carter been killed? What had Vincent Burns done to deserve such a sudden death? And who was this beautiful creature who was a link to them both? Perhaps he ought to go once more and visit the old lady whose cottage stood opposite Burns's grand villa.

'Grace Kelly! You are right, Superintendent. That was who she reminded me of, but after looking at all of your pictures, my mind was quite jumbled up,' Alicia Milroy declared.

'Can you remember what she wore?'

The old lady sat and pondered his question for a few moments. 'I saw her in his car most often, sitting in the passenger seat. The car would turn out of his drive and pass by my window, so I had a clear view of her.' Her eyes clouded for a moment. 'She sometimes wore a long scarf over her head, I remember. Not a headsquare like the Queen wears, more the sort you can wind over your hair and around your neck,' she said, gesturing with her hands as if to show him. 'Grey silk, the sort of thing that makes you think of that particular era, you know? The Grace Kelly years. Though I never saw her smile. I think she would have been far prettier if she had. Always a serious look on that lovely face,' she told him.

Alicia Milroy glanced up at him, her eyes twinkling.

'Has she done something wrong?'

Lorimer shook his head. 'Not for me to say, I'm afraid. The lady is someone we would like to find, however. So, if you should happen to see her again, do let us know.'

'Do you think she would come back? Now that poor Vince is dead?'

'No, I don't. But a sharp pair of eyes like yours will be very helpful just in case she does.'

David Mearns rose from behind the chief constable's desk and stretched out a welcoming hand.

'Good to see you, Lorimer. Now, what is it you wanted to discuss with us?' he asked, waving a hand across at Caroline Flint.

Lorimer looked at the man and woman in turn, relieved to be able to share some news with them both. Mearns was seated once more, his desk top neat and tidy with a three-tier tray of documents and his laptop closed in front of him. There were no personal touches like photographs, but then he was really just passing through Police Scotland, Lorimer mused, wondering not for the first time about the personal life of this fine-looking man who was currently in charge.

'I hope it's something that will help resolve this matter,' he began with a serious look at Lorimer.

'I hope so, too,' Lorimer replied. 'More intelligence has come up since we last spoke.' He chose his words carefully. It would not do to reveal that he was using civilians to help this case along, but William Lorimer was a man to whom telling the truth was second nature and it went against the grain to deceive his colleagues.

'Looks like Christmas Eve is the date planned for the attack and we are focusing on George Square, particularly the area around the Nativity scene.'

'Dear lord, that's just days away,' Mearns declared.

'Security alerted?' Flint asked, getting down to the practicalities they needed to discuss.

'Yes,' Lorimer said. 'There ought to be enough bodies on the ground to oversee the crowds. And security checks will be made throughout the day.'

'Won't that put them off?' Mearns asked. 'Seeing such stringent measures?'

'They might just decide on a different place to carry out their plan,' Flint agreed.

'That's a chance we have to take,' Lorimer said. 'Until we have a better idea of the exact time this device is to be exploded then we have to make the safety of the public of paramount importance.'

'And, you think you might find out when they intend to set this in motion?'

Lorimer nodded. 'It's possible.'

'Well, there isn't a lot of time left till Christmas Eve,' Caroline Flint said, pointing towards a calendar hanging on the wall. 'And David had hoped to be away from here on the twenty-third, isn't that right?'

Mearns nodded, frowning. 'Sooner we get this sorted the better,' he said. 'And not just for my own personal convenience, you understand. I want to leave here with these perpetrators under lock and key. It's a horrible business. If they have their way, it'll be like Manchester Arena all over again.'

'All those children . . .' Flint said sorrowfully.

Lorimer said no more as the three officers contemplated the sort of carnage that could ensue in the centre of Glasgow.

'We do know that there is no female officer currently employed with Police Scotland that fits the description of the woman we're after and that includes DS Maxwell,' Lorimer told them.

'That's a piece of good news at any rate,' Mearns agreed. 'It doesn't bear thinking about that one of our own could be involved in something like this.'

'We are also investigating the death of a young Asian lad, possibly one of the same gang.'

'Oh?' Mearns looked up, interested.

'Here.' Lorimer fished in his briefcase and took out the images that Rosie had sent him. 'We think the faint bruising around his chest area may have been caused by a bomb vest strapped around him.'

Mearns gave a soft whistle. 'Good work,' he said. 'And what about the O'Neill fellow? Any joy there or is he just someone that happened to play golf with Burns?'

'He was pretty adamant that we weren't going to examine his cars,' Lorimer reminded them. 'And he's had the lot sanitised since our visit. Nothing to see but surely something to hide.'

'And, his background?'

'Still working on that, sir, but he was in the Middle East on different occasions in the past. Oil-related business, or so we are led to believe. But he may have had connections with some groups that are of interest to the security services.'

'Indeed?' Mearns raised his eyebrows. 'Well, if O'Neill is part of this outfit, I'll bet it's the money behind it.'

'What would he get out of it, though? Funding a terrorist organisation that was hell-bent on blowing a hole in his own city?' Flint demanded.

Motivation, again, Lorimer realised. The *why* behind a planned attack was surely something that they needed to discover before it was too late.

'I'll let you both know as soon as any further intelligence appears,' Lorimer promised, rising from his chair.

'How's that nice wife of yours?' Caroline Flint asked as she walked with Lorimer to the entrance.

'Still off school. Doctor is seeing her later today, I think. We asked for a home visit, given the circumstances.'

'Well, tell her I'm asking for her, won't you? Wives like Maggie are rather special.'

When the doorbell rang, Maggie made to rise from her chair, but Molly Newton was there before her.

'Oh, hello. Dr Schmautz?'

An auburn-haired woman breezed into the living room and gave Maggie a peck on her cheek.

'How's my favourite patient today?' she beamed.

'Annett, thanks so much for coming over. Hope it isn't too much trouble?' Maggie asked, then, turning to the detective sergeant, 'Molly, this is my good friend, Dr Annett Schmautz. Annett, DS Molly Newton who has been looking after me.'

'Well, you needed some looking after, lady,' Annett told her, sitting by Maggie's side on the settee. 'I'll have a look at your wrist in a minute but, tell me, have you still been getting the back pain you told me about?'

'Not such a lot since I've been off school,' Maggie admitted. 'Probably helps not lugging great loads of books about.'

'Yes,' the doctor mused. 'Our kids have these Chromebooks now; technology means far fewer things to carry back and forward to their classes.'

'Still to catch up with that at Muirpark Secondary,' Maggie told her.

The doctor proceeded to give Maggie a thorough examination then nodded cheerfully.

'You're right about your back. Though it would do no harm to see a good osteopath. Here,' she scribbled a number on the back of a prescription pad, 'this lady will see you all right. I can promise you'll feel the benefit once she's had a go at your back.'

'Sounds painful,' Maggie said doubtfully.

Annett shook her head. 'Not at all. I've visited her myself on occasion and can assure you she has magical fingers. Anyway, this is nice,' she said, turning to the kitchen area where little golden stars were strewn on loops from the lights. 'I love Christmas, don't you?'

'Usually.' Maggie made a face. 'This year I'm going to miss all the things at school. Bill has me virtually locked up here in case someone tries to thump me again.'

'That won't happen, surely?' Annett looked at Molly for confirmation.

'Certainly not while I'm here,' she promised.

'He won't let you out at all? But what about Christmas Eve? I thought we were all going into town to see the lights and join the carol singing in the square?'

'Golly, I'd almost forgotten about that,' Maggie admitted. 'And your kids love the German Christmas market, don't they?'

'Part of our heritage.' Annett smiled. 'Can't you persuade Bill to let you come with us? Matt and the kids are so looking forward to this.'

'What do you think?' Maggie turned to ask the detective sergeant. 'After all, if I'm with my own GP, surely I'll be safe enough?'

Molly Newton merely shrugged. The days here had been fine to begin with but now she was chafing to get back to some proper work, things she'd been trained to do, not come across the city day after day to keep her boss's wife company. There was no need to tail the Maxwell woman, either, Lorimer now convinced that she was beyond suspicion. Maybe it was time to return to Helen Street full time, and she'd suggest as much to Lorimer, Molly thought.

Daniel allowed himself to be led away from the square with its bright lights and noise then through a maze of streets that became narrower as they walked towards the river. It was a part of the city Daniel had not yet explored and his eyes soaked in the old tenement buildings, rows of small shops at ground level, each one decked with gaudy decorations of green and red tinsel, brash Christmas music floating out into the streets. They turned past a pub on the corner, the smell of greasy food making Daniel wrinkle his nose. Then he was being led past what looked like abandoned warehouses, some frontages hidden behind metal shutters, a few with TO LET notices pasted across their doors.

To their right was the River Clyde, its waters sludge-grey, reflecting the sombre sky above, a suspension bridge spanning its banks. He could see figures hurrying across, their dark shapes heading for the city. Daniel shivered, a feeling of dread stealing over him as they left the crowded streets behind, few pedestrians passing them by. Where was he being taken?

Qasim had said little but his determined expression showed Daniel that there was something significant to be found at the end of this journey.

Once, he caught sight of a mosque, its glass-panelled dome shining beneath a weak winter sun. Qasim followed his gaze and nodded.

'Glasgow Central Mosque,' he said. 'You have been there?'

Daniel shook his head. He had to remain in character as a godless atheist with no affiliation to any of the creeds. 'Your place of worship?' he asked diffidently.

Qasim nodded gravely. 'We will go there together when it is all over,' he said firmly. 'You will become a different man when you help us defeat the forces of evil.'

Daniel avoided his stare and continued to look across at the glass and metal structure. It had been his attempt to defeat the forces of evil that had destroyed his family, and all hopes for his future. Perhaps Qasim noted the bleak expression on his companion's face, as he touched Daniel's shoulder lightly.

'Come,' he said. 'We are almost there.'

*

A cobbled lane shadowed on either side by grey stone buildings led them to a series of lock-ups with huge wooden doors set on metal rails, some with the faded names of businesses on the front.

Qasim stopped in front of one that was bolted and shuttered, reminding Daniel for a moment of the back entrance to Bryson's.

The Syrian produced a key from his pocket and inserted it into the heavy padlock that held the hasp across a metal plate. Then, with a strength that surprised Daniel, the older man heaved the big door aside on its runners, revealing a dark space within.

'Follow me,' Qasim said, gesturing for Daniel to hurry inside. The door was pushed shut once more and Daniel stood blinking through the gloom until Qasim switched on a light. Ahead of them there were pieces of discarded machinery shoved to one side, the stone floor stained with old marks that might have been motor oil. Certainly, the place was big enough to house a lorry, Daniel realised, wondering if there had been such a vehicle secreted away here at one time.

There was another door, a smaller one, set against the back wall and Qasim headed straight towards it, another key ready to unlock whatever was behind it.

As the man opened the door Daniel could hear a voice singing, a thin piping tune. Was there someone actually living in this squalid place? Or was he hearing music from outside?

To his astonishment, a young boy of about thirteen leapt to his feet and, grasping Qasim around the waist, uttered a torrent of words that Daniel could not understand but that sounded as if they might be Arabic. He spoke Qasim's name and from the boy's questioning intonation Daniel heard another person's name: *Shararah*. It was the boy's expression, however, that made him stop and stare. His dark brown eyes were shining as he clutched the old man's sleeves and then he turned and stared at Daniel.

Whatever he was asking, it seemed to be a question and Daniel guessed that he was wondering who the stranger was that Qasim had brought to his den. For that was exactly what it looked like. There was a sofa covered in bright cloths, Indian cotton with mirrored shards inset in intricate patterns, a couple of thick quilts that seemed to suffice for a bed and in one corner a refrigerator and an opened carton beside it with packets of crisps and sweets.

His eyes travelled across the room and caught sight of a second door, slightly ajar, but the whiff of disinfectant was enough to make him see that at least the boy had toilet facilities. A prisoner? That had been Daniel's first thought but seeing the lad beaming up at them both, he was rapidly changing his mind. Besides, there was nothing malnourished about this youngster; in fact, he looked both healthy and content.

'This is Abdul Qahhar,' Qasim said at last, turning to Daniel. 'Abdul, this is Daniel. He will be our friend,' he said, then spoke what Daniel assumed were the same words in the boy's own language.

'Abdul is our prize, our hope,' Qasim told him. 'It will be our job to look after him until he commits himself to his quest.'

Daniel reached out to take the boy's hand, but the youngster pulled back a little and gave a deep bow instead.

It took all of his nerve not to lash out and strike the old man, grab the boy's hand and flee from this place. But his orders were to follow the woman's instructions until such time as the police could locate her.

The floor in this room was carpeted with colourful rugs and Daniel noticed a copy of a leather-bound book lying beside the couch. The Koran, he guessed. Was this lad a devotee of the fundamentalists' interpretation of his religion? Selected for his burning desire to destroy the infidel?

As if guessing his thoughts, Qasim turned to Daniel.

'Abdul Qahhar is named for a special mission,' Qasim explained. 'His name in English means servant of Allah. And, as such an important servant, he requires a bodyguard to protect him once he begins his final journey.'

The boy, Abdul, said something to the older man and both of them turned to look at Daniel.

'Stand still for a few minutes, my friend. Arms out, yes, like that,' he added as Daniel complied. 'Abdul has asked me to search you.'

Daniel swallowed hard but gave a silent nod.

Was it a weapon of some sort they'd expected to find on his person? he wondered as Qasim searched his pockets and felt under the waistband of his trousers. Perhaps a mobile phone? But they would find neither, the former cop only too aware of what that might provoke.

As the old man continued his search, Daniel gazed at Abdul, wondering what link he had to the woman. But there was one thing of which he was now certain.

This boy was the weapon they were going to use to commit the atrocity Lorimer had warned him about. Or, he would be once they had strapped on the explosives contained in a vest wrapped around his skinny chest.

'He stays here meantime?' Daniel asked, as Qasim finished his inspection and nodded to Abdul.

'For his own protection.' Qasim nodded. 'We must not let another person know he is here. And you will take him into the heart of the city when it is time. Understand?'

Daniel met Qasim's eyes and nodded. 'So long as I get away in time,' he muttered. 'Money won't be any good to me if I'm dead.'

Qasim threw back his head and laughed. 'Ah, you do anything for money? No conscience at all? I like that. A strong man with no principles. You will go far, my friend,' he chuckled. But there was no mirth in the Syrian's eyes as he regarded Daniel, merely a look of scorn.

CHAPTER FORTY-ONE

D I Brownlee sat staring at the man across the room.
'You're serious? A terrorist attack?'

Lorimer nodded. 'It's been on the cards a while, the threat of something big happening in the city centre. Only the chief constable, Caroline Flint and I have been made aware of it till now. The security services let us know back in October that there was a strong likelihood that information was being given to a terrorist group from someone inside Police Scotland. But, I'm glad to say that seems not to have been the case.'

'And why tell me now?' Brownlee failed to keep the irritation out of his voice.

'Because it is linked to the three deaths that your own people are investigating.'

Brownlee's expression changed, an understanding light in his eyes.

'That's why you were turning up at crime scenes? Looking for a bad penny?'

'Something like that. You were never on our list of possible moles, though, I hasten to add,' Lorimer assured him.

'You hinted there was something big going on,' Brownlee admitted.

Lorimer nodded, giving a sigh. 'We are still no further forward in identifying the source that blew their cover,' he began.

'The officers that were exposed in the papers?'

Lorimer nodded. 'We still have some people out there, but I cannot, of course, tell you who they are. Security has to be maintained at every turn if we are to stop this attack and find the woman behind it.'

'A woman?' Brownlee sat up, astonished.

'Aye, we had intelligence about her right at the start and were led to think it might be one of our own. But she is not a police officer.'

'A civilian working for us?' Brownlee suggested.

Lorimer shook his head. 'Been down that road a while ago. We have a visual description of her that doesn't match any female on our books.'

'Oh?' Brownlee raised his eyebrows, evidently curious to know more.

'We've traced her to both Derek Carter and Vincent Burns's homes,' he said. 'There's a forensic link. And we have a good idea that she might have been staying off and on with Burns before his murder.'

'Who on earth . . . ?'

'No name, just a description. A young Grace Kelly lookalike, one observer told us. Blonde, about thirty or so, medium height, slim, often wears a grey silk scarf over her hair.'

'Like a headscarf?'

Lorimer nodded. 'Perhaps. Not an actual hijab, though, from the description. She's been seen with a couple of Syrian refugees.'

'Why haven't you picked her up?' Brownlee frowned.

That was a good question, of course, and one that was going to be difficult to answer without revealing that the observer he'd mentioned was a civilian who had no right to be involved in this investigation at all.

'Let's just say that she is adept at disappearing,' Lorimer murmured. 'And, before you ask, we do want to apprehend her. If she is the main person behind this terrorist threat, then we have to stop her before it is carried out.'

'Do you know when . . . ?'

'Christmas Eve,' he replied. 'In the middle of George Square.'

'What do you want me to do?' Brownlee asked, sitting forward now, a serious look on his face.

'My team here at the MIT are turning over everything they can find about Gerald O'Neill. I'd like some of yours to keep an eye on him. See where he goes, who he meets. Manpower is what we are going to need in the next few days,' he said grimly, casting an eye on the calendar opposite. 'We have four more days, Graham. Four days to find her and stop this happening.'

It was not easy to find his way back to the flats without the shadow following him. Mohammad, Daniel guessed, or someone of his build, flitting between doorways, watching his every move. Qasim had promised to give him money but so far nothing had been handed over and Daniel was forced to walk back from the place where he had been shown that secret den all the way to the north of the city, his red Ford still parked in Maryhill. The rain that had threatened earlier was now replaced with hail and even the turned-up collar of his coat could not keep the icy water from trickling down his neck.

At last he turned to the high flats, a quick glance behind to see if his follower was still there. But the street was empty, pedestrians having no doubt hurried indoors once the violent shower had begun.

Standing in the lift, Daniel thought about what he had seen. A boy, just a kid, evidently brainwashed to the point where his fanaticism made him believe that his future in Paradise was assured. Where had he come from and what sort of life had he experienced that resulted in such beliefs? Abdul was willing, no, eager, to carry out his task, his Christmas Eve present the destruction of hundreds of so-called infidels. He ought to be disgusted, but all Daniel could feel as the lift doors sighed open was a feeling of pity.

Qasim did not know that he had a mobile phone, something Daniel had deliberately left in the flat before meeting them today, suspecting correctly that he'd be searched at some point. But now it was imperative that he contact Lorimer to let him know where he had been and what he had discovered.

'That's me packed, darling.'

Gerry O'Neill looked up from his perusal of the paper he was reading and made a grunting noise. She'd hung out his summer clothes in their dressing room and Gerry supposed he'd better do something about that before their annual trip across the pond. He shook the paper and dipped his head again, searching for the paragraph that he had been reading.

The share price index was really all that mattered at this particular moment and the figures were enough to make Gerry O'Neill give an added sniff of satisfaction. They were all fine and dandy here, he thought, sitting back in his recliner chair with a sigh. A couple more days and they'd be heading off to their place in Florida, sunshine instead of this interminable cold.

He gave a low chuckle. The police could look all they liked but they'd find absolutely nothing. Vincent had seen to that. His sigh changed to a frown. Pity the man couldn't keep his hands off that woman. His one weakness, O'Neill decided. But Burns had chickened out when she had told him what their plan entailed. Always had been too squeamish for his own good.

He was the lucky one, he told himself, watching his wife's retreating figure as she left the lounge. A good woman was above rubies, wasn't that the saying? Well, he had covered his in gemstones over the years, and deservedly so. She'd stuck with him even when these overseas trips had proved a bit too harrowing for her taste. Never did take to the desert heat, not like … He paused in his thoughts. What did she call herself these days? Shararah. Made her sound like something from a sixties band. 'Daft name,' he grumbled, unaware that he had spoken aloud.

He turned the paper and smoothed down the crease. Pity she'd needed to have this one big event here in Glasgow, all the same. But that was what the money had been all about, the source of it coming from some hidden place in Afghanistan via a couple of oil magnates and then to his own private account. Nice of Vince to have had it filtered through Bryson's, of course. But in such a way that nobody would ever find it.

Diane O'Neill sang softly to herself as she tucked the passport into her favourite handbag. Florida, she thought, imagining the villa with its azure blue pool and the friends they would meet once again at the Country Club. Far away from all of this awful stuff about poor Vince.

Diane's good humour deserted her for a moment, remembering the painstaking way the police officers had examined their vehicles. What on earth had they expected to find? Just being thorough, Gerry had consoled her. She ran a hand over her newly highlighted hair. Just forget it, he'd advised and so she would. She'd think instead of the fun she would have browsing the duty-free shops at Glasgow Airport. And, if the hints she'd been dropping had found his ear, then that was also a chance for Gerry to fill her stocking with some little things that he knew would make her eyes sparkle on Christmas morning.

'What did you say that name was?' Lorimer asked.

'Shararah,' Daniel replied. 'I'm certain it was a name from the way they were speaking. Does it mean anything to you?'

Lorimer typed in the word and in moments he had an answer to Daniel's question.

'It's an Afghan name,' he said at last. 'Means "a woman

who is burning like a flame". I think we may have found our beautiful lady.'

'She's not Afghani, though,' Daniel protested. 'She's a white woman, I told you that already.'

'And I believe you,' Lorimer assured him. 'But I think we need to dig a little further into any woman who may have had a relationship with an Afghan man here in Britain. Or changed their religion.'

A burning flame, he thought. A woman whose beauty may have lured a man to his death and who had no conscience about the murder of hundreds more.

'Tell me again about the boy. Where exactly is it they are keeping him?'

It would be fairly easy to take the youngster from that place and question him with the help of a translator but from what Daniel had told him, Lorimer guessed that the fanatical youth would give them absolutely nothing in return for his freedom. No, he decided, he would put it to Mearns and Flint that they continued to search for this woman, Shararah. If they could find her in three days, before Christmas Eve, then her plans would be finished. If not, they'd only be rescuing a lad from his death and putting the two Syrians inside. And somewhere else this woman would be making new plans to create the kind of misery that those bombers wanted.

'Annett and her family have asked me to join them on Christmas Eve,' Maggie said. 'Just for a couple of hours. What do you say?'

Lorimer smiled fondly at his wife. Maggie was so much better now, and he felt a little mean at having insisted she stay off school. Still, Annett had told her as much, hadn't she? Besides, if he had to hazard a guess, Christmas Eve might well see him in the city centre after finalising the actions for each member of his team.

'That's kind of them. Will they pick you up?'

'Yes,' Maggie agreed, putting one hand behind her back and crossing her fingers. Bill might not be too pleased to think of her in a crowded place in case she was pushed or shoved in any way but what harm could she come to with the Schmautz family looking out for her?

David Mearns straightened his bow tie as he looked into the wardrobe mirror.

'You're still a handsome dog!' a teasing voice called from his bedroom doorway.

'And look at you,' Mearns declared, eyeing his daughter with pride. 'Do a twirl for your old dad.'

Helena Mearns turned obediently, catching the pale rose silk of her dress then sketching a curtsy.

'Thanks for coming with me this evening, darling. It means a lot,' Mearns told her.

'Not a problem, Dad,' the young woman replied with a ready smile. 'A trip across to Edinburgh sounds fine to me, especially when I get time to spend with you.'

David Mearns turned back and fiddled with his tie again. He was a lucky man, he thought. It was not every grown-up daughter who would accompany their parent to an evening of classical music, but Helena had assured him there was nothing she'd like more than to hear the programme he'd mentioned. 'Scheherazade' was one of his all-time favourite pieces by Rimsky-Korsakov and, thankfully, Helena seemed intrigued by the story behind the music.

A clever woman weaving a spell over a powerful man, the basis for *The Thousand and One Nights* tales, of course, but it had chimed with her own particular thoughts about how a woman could manipulate a man for her own ends.

As they left the rented villa, Helena tucked her hand into her father's arm, casting a sideways glance at her reflection in the hall mirror. How easy it was for a beautiful woman with youth on her side to make men dance to her will.

Yes, undoubtedly Scheherazade must have known what that felt like, she decided, stepping into the waiting Mercedes and fastening her seat belt.

CHAPTER FORTY-TWO

'There's just two more days to go,' Lorimer told them, looking around the large room where the members of his team were gathered. As well as officers from the MIT, DI Brownlee was there, and Lorimer gave him a nod as he saw him gazing across. Brownlee would be offered the chance to fill a gap when one of his own retired in the new year, he had decided, impressed by the detective inspector's competence and ready understanding of this tangled web of a case. It was no longer a secret operation between the trio of senior officers and MI6 and Lorimer was thankful for the additional resources from Police Scotland, including his own team.

Outside it was pitch black, rain thundering down and beating the windowpanes. The previous day had marked the winter solstice, but it would be several more weeks until the season gave any sign of lengthening its hours of daylight. School was officially ended for Maggie and the children across their city, little ones no doubt counting the hours until Santa Claus appeared to fill their Christmas stockings. It was something they would never do, a childless couple like themselves, and occasionally William Lorimer felt a pang of regret for the babies they had lost. Still, if he could prevent this dreadful atrocity from happening, there was the satisfaction of having given something precious to thousands of children, a gift they would hopefully never have to know about.

He stood in front of the white screen, talking them through the plans to police the area around the square and the security measures that he had agreed with Mearns and Flint. It was not unusual for there to be a police presence at large outdoor gatherings of this sort and the mounted branch in particular had been alerted to what might take place.

Two more nights, he thought, as the officers left the boardroom. Two days to find the woman, Shararah, and stop her treacherous plan.

The team were still trawling through every university in the country that specialised in Arabic, in case the mystery woman was some sort of academic, though so far, no name had cropped up. Still, there was the chance that she might have learned the language overseas and returned here under some guise or other.

Mearns had given a short laugh when he'd been told the name, confessing that he was off to a concert in the Usher Hall to listen to 'Scheherazade'. *Another woman still burning like a flame, at least in Rimsky-Korsakov's wonderful music,* he'd told them.

Must have gone with his wife, Lorimer decided, a little grumpy that he had no time to spare for taking his own dear Maggie to a show over Christmas. Well, at least she was

350

having a night out soon with Dr Schmautz and her family, the German GP a good friend of Maggie's. But he wouldn't brood on things like that right now, there were more pressing concerns on his mind. Like finding every member of this cell. But, what if they couldn't?

They might have to let the woman go, he thought bitterly. Round up the boy, Abdul, and cut their losses. Hope that whoever brought the explosives would be caught in time before fixing them to that poor kid's body.

'Sir, a new report just in.' David Giles came into the boardroom again and handed over a sheet of paper to Lorimer.

'It's the third body. The one found beside the burn,' Giles added helpfully.

Lorimer scanned the paper and saw what the DS was referring to.

'Identified as an illegal immigrant. Name registered as Latif Karzai. Absconded from the detention centre down south during a major fracas,' Giles continued.

Lorimer read on, his frown deepening. 'Guy strung up . . . Just a minute, this is the same man the security services mentioned . . .'

Giles nodded. 'An Afghan man, suspected terrorist. Was due to be sent back and was found like that in his cell. Suspected suicide. Name of Kalil Durani.'

'Durani, yes, that's him. And, apart from this Latif chap, are there any other known associates mentioned that we might not yet know about?'

'There was a woman,' Giles continued. 'See over the page . . .'

And that was when Lorimer found the small matter of motivation that Solly Brightman had told him they needed.

'She's a British citizen, or was,' he told Mearns and Flint. 'Goes by the name of Shararah. Was in a relationship with a known terrorist, Kalil Durani. Who was found dead in his detention cell. Whole matter hushed up. Till now,' he added grimly. 'The detention centres were being targeted by several groups demanding freedom for asylum seekers and a suicide was the last thing they needed splashed across the newspapers.'

'Any ID given?' Flint asked.

Lorimer shook his head. 'But we can be pretty certain she's the one we're after. We've spoken to the warders that were on duty at the time. They were reluctant to say much, as you might expect, but one of them remembered a remarkably beautiful blonde woman who had collected his personal belongings.'

'The same woman?'

'I'd guess so, and that gives her a motive for carrying out this atrocity.'

'But, why here? Why in Scotland of all places when her man died in the south of England? That doesn't make sense, surely?' Mearns asked, drumming his fingers on the desk.

'It does if the money to fund her enterprise was being channelled through Bryson's,' Flint mused. 'Any further forward on that, Lorimer?'

'Still working on it,' he said. 'But we have found another link between Vincent Burns and Gerald O'Neill. One that doesn't involve a golf club.'

'Go on,' Flint encouraged.

'Rumour has it our Mr O'Neill had a few fingers in some dubious stuff way back,' Lorimer told them. 'We think perhaps an engineering business in the Middle East that wanted a legitimate British firm to launder their dirty money.'

'And?'

'I'm guessing that Vincent Burns was the partner who dealt with it,' Lorimer told them. 'And, we think that Derek Carter may have got wind of this somehow. Perhaps Carter's link with the refugee charity gave him some knowledge of what his boss was up to. Trouble is, we have no paperwork yet to back this up. Just rumours and speculations for now.'

'Why didn't he blow the whistle on Burns, then?' Flint wanted to know. 'He's been painted as a reformed character by your undercover woman, hasn't he?'

Lorimer nodded. 'But he also told her of his intention to give up his job and relocate overseas. And there was something else that he wanted to tell her, but he was dead before he had the chance.'

'Perhaps he knew too much and was afraid,' Mearns suggested.

'Or wanted a slice of the money Burns was undoubtedly getting from this source,' Flint said grimly. 'One way or another he had to be quietened for good.'

'Like Vincent Burns,' Lorimer reminded them. 'And they were both linked to this female.'

'We have to find her,' Mearns said seriously, a bleak look at Lorimer. 'Do everything you can. My God, time's running out and she's out there somewhere setting plans to blow up the city centre!'

'We're doing everything we can, sir,' Lorimer said steadily. 'But if it comes to the bit, we just have to haul out the boy and take in her accomplices.'

'Will they talk, d'you think?' Mearns asked hopefully. 'Shouldn't we be doing that right now?'

Caroline Flint shook her head. 'That sort will die before they give up one of their own,' she said. 'Trust me, I've come across their type before.'

CHAPTER FORTY-THREE

It was a quiet day in the office, most of the staff preparing for the Christmas night out. Sylvie had been a little surprised when Dominic Fraser, now their senior partner, had said that it would go ahead as planned. *It will take our minds off recent horrible events*, the memo had read but Sylvie reckoned that the deaths of two members of Bryson's staff would be the key subject of conversation in the restaurant tonight. Still, the absence of most of the women, given time off to visit hair salons and suchlike, meant that Sylvie could have a better look in the room that had lain empty since Burns had been killed.

She crept on silent feet, opened the door noiselessly and closed it behind her, a sigh of relief that nobody had seen her.

It was a large room, carpeted in moss green Wilton, the cream walls displaying a selection of Scottish art. Beneath the picture rail the old-fashioned wooden panelling remained, testament to the taste of previous incumbents. Sylvie walked slowly round the room, lifting each painting to see if a safe had been hidden behind one of them, but there was nothing to see but a few sparse cobwebs clinging to their frames. She gave a sigh. Was she being stupid looking here when the police had already combed the place?

She made a second tour of the room, this time tapping the lower panels gently and listening to the sound her knuckles made against the polished wood. Next to a glass-fronted book case full of ledgers that she'd already managed to examine bit by bit over the preceding weeks there was a trolley for tea and coffee. It was empty now, save for a few folded tea cloths, and Sylvie dragged it away from the wall, careful not to let it rattle.

She bent down and rapped the panelling then stopped abruptly. That was a different note, surely? She took a step back and compared the previous sound with this new one. Eyes shining, she crouched down and ran her fingers across the hollow-sounding section.

A gentle push was all it took for the panel to swing open and reveal the space behind. She knelt on the carpet, bending as far as she could, one arm reaching into the secret compartment. Her fingers touched what felt like a pile of folders and she pulled them out, seeing a small cloud of dust rise with them.

Sitting back on her haunches, Sylvie took them onto her lap and flicked through the ring-bound pages.

Yes! A smile lit up her face as she read the names within the documents. Was this what Derek had been going to tell her? And had he confronted these people, only to be brutally killed? With a care borne of much practice, she closed the panel quietly and stacked the files on top of the trolley, covering them with the cotton tea towels.

Her luck held as she opened the office door and peered out. There was nobody in the corridor, so she closed the door behind her and headed for the kitchen. Anybody looking out of their room would not remark on a tea trolley being pushed along, Sylvie reckoned.

Once in the kitchen she pulled the trolley into a corner. There was a roll of black bin liners under the sink. That would do, she thought, ripping one off and emptying the folders inside. She looked around to see if there was anything else that might disguise her find.

Behind the kitchen door someone had hooked a few empty carrier bags by their handles. Sylvie lifted them off and selected a big Christmas bag with the John Lewis logo. That would be perfect, she thought, stuffing the wrapped folders inside and replacing the other bags on the brass coat hook.

'Hello, what's up, Sylvie?'

A voice from the corridor made her start. Fiona, the receptionist, stood, coat slung over her arm, regarding Sylvie with curiosity.

'Shh, present for my boyfriend. He's not supposed to know,' Sylvie laughed, making a face. 'Meeting him after work so I needed to find a big carrier bag to hide it. No one will mind, will they?'

Fiona shook her head. 'Golly, you're leaving it to the last minute,' she remarked. 'Mine were bought and wrapped weeks ago.'

Then, with a wave, the younger woman was gone, no doubt leaving early to prepare for the night out.

Sylvie breathed a long sigh. Her own night out would be

rather different, she guessed, especially when she showed this lot to the detective superintendent.

Helen Street police station loomed out of the dark, streetlights playing on the hard shapes of the building. Somewhere in there Lorimer was waiting, she thought as the taxi pulled into the space beside the staff car park.

In moments Sylvie Maxwell was inside the building and taking the familiar stairs two at a time.

A quick knock then she opened his office door.

'Sir, you have got to see these,' Sylvie said, breathing hard more from anticipation and excitement than from the flights of stairs.

She explained where she had found them, and Lorimer waved her into the seat opposite as she began to unwrap the folders.

Two more days, Mearns had warned and now he had the information they'd needed to make at least one arrest. But not yet, he decided, his stubbled chin resting on one hand. O'Neill was complicit, all right, and there was enough in these documents to show the years of money laundering that he and Burns had been carrying out for various parties in dangerous parts of the Middle East. If they picked up O'Neill too soon, the entire operation might fail. The woman they sought would simply vanish into the night, the way Kohi had described before. Then some other European city would be her target.

Lorimer had already phoned Maggie to apologise, explaining that he had a load of paperwork that couldn't wait till morning. It might take several hours to sift through this lot, write out a report for Flint and Mearns, but he had to have it done for their meeting tomorrow. They were due to gather at Gartcosh at midday and decide once and for all whether they should take action against the Syrians and rescue that poor brainwashed lad down by the riverside.

Tomorrow was the twenty-third of December. One day away from the date on which the terrorist attack was planned. Was it possible to find this Shararah in time? Would the feelers that were spreading out in all directions prove fruitful? The Home Office had been alerted, the security services doing their utmost to track her down. But meantime it was his responsibility to keep the good citizens of Glasgow safe.

It was near midnight by the time Lorimer switched off the light of his office and set out, briefcase in hand. He'd written his report, emailed it to Flint and Mearns. Now it was time to catch a bit of sleep before the next step was taken.

Daniel sat bolt upright, clasping the edge of the duvet to his chin. He could still feel the sensation of the flames licking at his skin, though the dream was already fading. A house, not his own but a strange place full of dark corners where a boy slept on embroidered couches. In his dream it was a candle knocked over that had started the fire and he had shaken the boy to waken him. But the lad had simply opened his eyes and begun to laugh at Daniel.

Then he was trying to run, to escape the sound of fire belching from behind a door, but his feet would not move, no matter how hard he tried. He was fixed to that spot and would be burned to a crisp like . . .

Daniel sat huddled in his bed, the darkness a relief, the memories of his beloved wife and child bringing tears streaming down his cheeks.

The nightmare took various shapes and he would never be sure where he was or what would happen, but it always ended with the thought of his beloved Chipo and Johannes.

'Chipo,' he whispered. Her name meant 'a gift', and so she had been to Daniel. A gift taken cruelly away for ever. He wiped his face with a corner of the bedcover and lay back, afraid to sleep lest the dream returned.

Think of good things, his mother used to tell him when childhood nightmares caused the young Daniel to wake with a cry. Daniel closed his eyes, imagining his mother's voice in his ears, soothing him to sleep. Would he ever hear her voice again? Or was she also lost to him for ever?

CHAPTER FORTY-FOUR

David Mearns sat back and sighed. The morning had been full of officers coming and going, the business of Police Scotland carrying on as if there was no imminent fear of a terrorist attack. He had signed a pile of documents and was about to call for coffee when he leaned down to pick up his briefcase.

For a moment he blinked, wondering where it was. Then he remembered. After work yesterday, the cleaning woman from the letting agency had seen him coming in with the briefcase and he had shoved it into a cupboard in the laundry room downstairs, a secure enough place, he reckoned, away from prying eyes till he could lock it in the safe he'd bought. Then he'd forgotten all about it. But this morning, probably too tired after a restless night punctuated with horrible dreams, Mearns had clean forgotten to pick it up.

He lifted the telephone and pressed a button. 'Kirsten, I'm about to go back home and collect my briefcase. Silly of me, but I'll be back in time for my meeting with Lorimer and Flint,' he told his secretary.

Helena had told him she would be out all day and so there was no point in ringing her at the villa and asking her to bring it in.

Mearns fitted his safety belt and drove as swiftly as the speed limit allowed along the busy streets until he came to a suburb of the city and the tree-lined avenue where he and his daughter currently lived. If all went well, then they could pack up tomorrow and be back home just in time to spend Christmas together. It had been a rare joy to have Helena back in his life again, even if only for a while till her new job began. Then she'd be off, working for yet another multinational, her expertise as an engineer taking her around the world. He was proud of her, of course he was, but that did not diminish the pain at having her so far away. Still, there was the anticipation of a Christmas spent together and he'd already spent a small fortune on gifts that would make him the best dad in Helena's eyes.

When he parked at the kerb outside the villa, David Mearns frowned at the sight of a cream Fiat parked at the side of his rented villa. Surely that was Helena's little runabout on the driveway? He made a face, feeling a bit foolish for having assumed that she would be out. 'Should have called her,' he muttered, annoyed with himself for having made a needless trip back here.

Well, a quick in and out then he'd be back in time to meet Flint and Lorimer.

Mearns leapt out of his car and walked round to the back of the house. The laundry room was off the kitchen and he inserted the back door key, turning it once.

In moments he was bending down and pulling the cupboard door open.

There was nothing there.

Had he picked it up after all, taken it to the office? No, he was certain he had not touched it since coming home late yesterday afternoon.

'Helena? Are you home, darling?' Mearns called out as he strode through the house and made for the staircase that led to their bedrooms.

'Have you seen my briefcase? Helena?'

There was no response and so he climbed the stairs, a puzzled frown on his handsome face.

'Helena . . . ?'

David Mearns stopped short in the doorway of his daughter's room. His laptop was open on her dressing table, the briefcase tossed on the floor.

But it was the sight of what lay on her bed that made his mouth open, words failing to form.

'Helena . . . '

She stood looking at him, green eyes glittering with a malice he had never seen before.

'Shararah,' she hissed. 'My name is Shararah.'

'You . . . ? This . . . ' He pointed to the neat array of explosives tucked into the suicide vest that lay incongruously across his daughter's silken bedspread.

A sick feeling in his stomach made him place a hand across his belly. 'It's *you*?'

She nodded at him, never once taking her eyes from his face.

Mearns took a tentative step, hands outstretched.

'We can do something about this, Helena, I promise. Stop this now and nobody need ever know,' he pleaded.

He made to move towards her, but she dodged as he tried to grasp her arm.

Helena twisted away and then, with a cry that chilled his blood, she lunged at him, one hand clutching a hidden knife.

'No,' he whimpered, staggering backwards as the pain seared his chest. 'Helena ...'

His voice sounded strange to David Mearns' ears, far away as though disappearing into a tunnel.

There was no reply, just the sight of his daughter smiling as he fell, a red mist covering his vision.

Then everything turned black.

CHAPTER FORTY-FIVE

'Where is he?' Caroline Flint paced up and down, shaking her mobile phone irritably. 'Landline is just ringing out. Not even an answering machine on,' she complained. 'And he can't be in his car as his mobile is adapted for hands free, so he'd answer if he got our calls.'

She stopped for a moment and fixed him with a glare. 'I don't like it, Lorimer. Something's wrong, I can feel it.'

'Send an officer over to his house,' Lorimer suggested. 'Maybe his wife's taken unwell?'

'Wife?' Flint stopped for a moment. 'David was widowed a long time ago, Lorimer,' she said. 'Wife died in childbirth. Didn't like to bring it up, knowing your and Maggie's situation,' she admitted.

'And the baby?'

'Poor mite died as well,' Flint sighed. 'Just as well they'd already adopted a little girl. Never thought they could have one of their own till she fell pregnant. Then . . . ' She shrugged. 'What were the chances of that happening?'

Lorimer suddenly thought about another man who had lost both wife and child. Daniel Kohi was meeting the Syrians again today but this time he hoped to be able to track their movements using Kohi's mobile phone.

'What about David? Maybe he's taken ill. Collapsed?'

Flint pulled a face. 'Could be. He's not as young as he used to be. Sudden heart attack, who knows? Pressure of this damned job gets to the best of us,' she growled.

'How far is it to his rented accommodation?'

'Twenty minutes? Fifteen in that souped-up job of yours? What do you think?'

'Come on,' Lorimer urged her. 'Maggie's already been a target. Who knows what might have happened to David.'

Daniel sat in the refugee centre, his eyes flitting between the children playing on the carpet beside the Christmas tree and the glass doors. Qasim and Mohammad were late, and he didn't like it. He had already drunk three mugs of coffee and his nerves were jangling with too much caffeine.

Suddenly they were at the door, beckoning Daniel to rise from his place at the table.

She was there with the two Syrians. Instantly, Daniel had a sense that something was wrong as he saw their faces. The woman was bareheaded today and wore a dark brown coat, its fur collar pulled up and framing her face. Her gloved hands were weighed down with a tan leather briefcase and a rucksack.

'Allow me to help.' Daniel put out his hand to relieve her of what were obviously heavy burdens.

The woman snatched them back and glared at him for a

moment. Then her expression softened. 'Why not,' she said, handing him the briefcase. 'You are our paid help, after all.'

There was something in her sneering tone that Daniel knew only too well, the racist remarks from white Afrikaaners who had occasionally demeaned him in the past. He would not show offence, however.

'Yes, I am here to help, madam,' he said, giving her what he hoped was an obsequious smile.

'Car's along the road,' she snapped. 'Follow us.'

Daniel did as he was told, the two Syrians ignoring him for the moment, and he walked behind the trio as they headed along Byres Road then turned into Ashton Lane. Daniel caught sight of a busy outdoor car park ahead as they turned through a narrow passage and followed the woman towards a small cream car.

So far none of them had pulled at his clothes to see if he was carrying a phone and Daniel put one hand in his pocket to grasp it. Ducking behind a transit van, he was lost to them for the few seconds that it took to press the number.

'Lorimer.'

'One, two, three,' Daniel whispered, their code for the number of suspects that he was accompanying.

'Got it,' Lorimer replied. 'We'll trace you as you go. Taxi?'

'Small cream-coloured Fiat. Can't speak,' he added as he saw the younger Syrian glance back at him.

Daniel slipped the mobile down a side pocket of the brief-case. It would serve to let the police track them now, but it was also safe from discovery should Qasim and Mohammad carry out another body search.

Daniel squeezed into the rear seat next to Mohammad and

placed the briefcase at his feet, hoping that, wherever they were heading, there would be a police presence on their tail.

The traffic held them up at every set of lights as the woman drove along Great Western Road, cursing in English as she glared out of the window. Daniel watched her profile from where he was seated behind Qasim. There was something harsh about her expression today and he sensed that whatever had happened, she was worried.

'Who was that?' Caroline Flint turned to Lorimer as he drove as fast as he dared along the streets towards Mearns' temporary home.

'Friend,' Lorimer said with a sideways smile. 'Nobody you need to know about. Let's just say I reckoned we needed a safe pair of hands.'

'Someone on the outside?'

Lorimer nodded. 'I'm probably breaking every rule in the book but if I'm right, we may just be able to finish this case today and let David Mearns and his daughter home for Christmas.'

A swift call to Helen Street was all it took for things to be put into motion, Kohi's phone now the subject of sudden interest.

The Lexus came to a halt outside a grey stone villa at the end of an avenue of bare-branched trees. 'Car's still here,' he remarked as they walked swiftly to the front door. 'Locked.' Lorimer stepped back and ran around the house, Flint in his wake.

'Back door's open,' he called, pushing it open and hurrying through the kitchen.

'David!' he called then turned to Flint. 'You look down-stairs, Caroline. I'll go up. See if there's any sign of him.'

Upstairs, Lorimer turned to see three white panelled doors along a wood-floored corridor. The first one he pushed open was a bathroom but there was nothing to see.

'David! David! Are you there?' he called then strode along the passage and tried the second door.

It was evidently Mearns's own bedroom, the bed neatly made, his evening clothes still on a hanger behind the door. Lorimer went to close the door again, but something on the bedside table caught his eye and he walked a few paces around the bed instead.

The photograph in its silver frame was of a young woman decked in her graduation robes, a laughing smile on her beautiful face. For a moment Lorimer blinked, unable to believe what he was looking at. For the girl in that pic-ture was exactly how Alicia Milroy and Daniel Kohi had described her: a young Grace Kelly.

'Caroline! Up here!' he shouted, seizing the picture and calling over the balustrade.

The thump of feet then she was at his side.

'Have you found him?' Flint gasped. 'What's this?' she added, as he held the photo frame towards her.

'My God!' she gasped.

Then, her face paling, she looked at him fearfully. 'Where is he? Lorimer, where's David?'

The room at the end of the corridor was where they found him at last, lying beside the bed, the knife still protruding from his chest.

'Oh, dear God, what has she done?' Flint was on her

knees, one hand feeling for a pulse on the man's wrist. Then, turning her head to catch Lorimer's anxious gaze, Caroline Flint shook her head.

'He's gone.' She rose to her feet. 'We need to get someone over here now,' she said, her jaw stiffening with resolve.

Lorimer nodded, reaching for his mobile and stepping back from what was now a crime scene.

But even as he made the necessary call that would bring a team to this place, he drew in a breath, smelling a scent that was at once familiar and deadly.

CHAPTER FORTY-SIX

The woman drew up right outside the door where Qasim had taken him, her lack of concern for parking on the double yellow lines telling Daniel that she was desperate.

She slammed the car door and hurried inside after Qasim had unlocked the premises, Mohammad and Daniel hard on their heels.

Abdul was on his feet when Daniel entered the secondary room, his face wreathed in smiles. The woman bent to take him in her arms and for a brief moment Daniel saw a different side to Shararah. She spoke soft words in Arabic and the lad took a step back, nodding solemnly.

'What's happening?' Daniel whispered, tugging Qasim's sleeve. 'What's she saying to the boy?'

Shararah turned and fixed him with a determined smile.

'Our plans have changed,' she said. 'We will not wait until tomorrow.' She placed a hand on Abdul's shoulder and spoke to him once more in his own tongue.

'It is time,' she said, then bent down to open the rucksack at her feet.

Daniel watched helplessly as she drew out the suicide vest and laid it on the couch. Then, taking Abdul's hand, she uttered some words, gazing heavenwards as if in a trance.

'Allah be praised,' Qasim murmured, then began to lift the boy on top of the couch and take off his tunic.

Daniel felt a shiver down his spine. In moments the lad would be forced into that device and become a weapon for these fanatical people.

He had to stop them even if it meant endangering himself.

'What's that?' Qasim stopped suddenly, the boy's garment in his hands, Abdul holding his arms around his chest, shivering as a cold draught of air blew into the room.

'Police!' Shararah hissed. 'Get him out of here. Quick!' she commanded, pushing the half-naked lad towards Daniel.

Daniel needed no second warning.

Grabbing Abdul by the hand, he hauled him out of the den and ran across the stone-floored space.

Just as they reached the door, it was thrust open and several armed officers sped forwards, pushing him out of the way.

Daniel lifted the boy into his arms and walked on unsteady feet towards the direction of the river, heart thumping.

Abdul had begun to weep, small sobs of anguish that Daniel tried to soothe with hushing sounds, patting the boy on his back. It was raining hard now and the lad was beginning to shiver.

Then, to his relief, Daniel saw a familiar silver car heading towards them and an anxious face straining to see him.

A woman with short hair stepped out of the passenger seat and took the boy from Daniel.

'It's all right,' she said, giving Daniel a curious look. 'I won't ask any names. Lorimer says you are a friend and that's good enough for me.'

Daniel looked along the street as the armed officers trooped back out of the building, the woman and the two Syrians handcuffed and being led away towards a waiting van.

For a moment she turned and looked at him and Daniel Kohi saw not a beautiful woman, but one transformed into a monster, her face a mask of vicious hatred.

Then they were gone, bundled into that police van, an explosives officer carrying the suicide vest gingerly to an area beyond the deserted buildings.

'Will it go off?' Flint asked as she settled the boy into the car and put on his safety belt.

'I don't think so,' Daniel told her. 'She had not had time to set it, I think.'

'Thank God for that,' Flint sighed, wiping the sweat from her brow and sitting beside the still weeping lad.

'I think I will walk home from here,' Daniel told Lorimer. 'Too many questions if I turn up with you.' He grinned.

'Here.' Lorimer pulled out his wallet and thrust a handful of notes into his hand. 'Take a taxi. I think you deserve that at least.'

Lorimer watched as the squad car drove slowly down the drive taking Gerald and Diane O'Neill from the Thorntonhall mansion. It was unlikely that O'Neill would ever return there, he thought, glancing back at their home. A few more hours and they would have been winging their way across the Atlantic, heading towards their holiday home in Florida. But now, thanks to the undercover officer's discovery, Gerald O'Neill would be facing a very long sentence in a place where such extravagances were merely a memory. His involvement with people trafficking and arranging conduits for money to reach the hands of terrorist organisations would see to that, and Lorimer guessed he had been complicit in the murders of at least two people in recent weeks. It would take time to question the woman and her accomplices but at least he now had the satisfaction of seeing them all rounded up at last.

As Daniel inserted the key to his door, a familiar voice called out.

'Daniel, son, you got a wee minute?'

Netta was standing at her door, a huge smile on her face.

'I'm a bit busy right now, Netta, dear,' he began, but the old woman shook her head and came out onto the landing.

'Not too busy to see what I've goat fur ye,' she beamed. 'Come in, right now, son. Ye'll nivver believe this!'

With a sigh of exasperation, Daniel followed her into the warm flat, breathing in the smell of home baking. He was cold and tired, but keen to make contact with the detective superintendent to find out what was happening now that the terrorists had been apprehended. Still, a few minutes with his neighbour would not do any harm.

'Sit yerself down,' Netta said, shaking his arm. 'My goad, yer like a drowned rat, son! Take aff that wet coat and sit by the fire. Now, a wee cuppa tea?'

Daniel sighed. 'It needs to be quick, Netta. I really do have something important to do,' he protested.

Shaking her head, the old lady disappeared into the kitchen then reappeared moments later with a mug of hot tea and a plate of warm scones.

'Get that doon ye, son,' she ordered. 'Now, wait till ah tell ye what came the day!'

In a flash, she held up her mobile phone.

'Ye'll nivver guess who emailed me,' she beamed. 'Gawd knows how ma Christmas card goat there that quick. I did pit a load o' stamps on it, richt enough, but jings! See whit she says, son, go on.'

Daniel took the phone from her hands and stared at the message.

Dear Netta,

I am so happy to hear from you and find that your new neighbour is settling in well. Do send my greetings, won't you? Christmas is a special time for us here at home and this year will be extra special since your card arrived, though not without a lot of sadness. For you know about the ones that are lost to us.

Daniel brushed a hand across his eyes as he felt the tears begin to prick.

I cannot thank you enough for your nice letter. You are a clever lady, Netta Gordon. Perhaps one day we will meet for real and not as pen pals but for now it is enough to send a lot of love with this note.

Here it is hot, not like Scotland, and we are making paper chains for the church hall where there will be a concert on Christmas Eve. Perhaps you can tell your neighbours and family about what we do? Please keep writing to me, my friend.

I send Christian greetings to you and to all the people you hold dear. May our Lord bless you and keep you and our brave lion.

Your friend,
Jeanette Kohi

Daniel let the tears trickle through his fingers.

'Aw, c'mon, son,' Netta whispered. 'You'll have me greetin an' all in a minute,' she said, pulling a tissue from the sleeve of her brown knitted cardigan and blowing her nose noisily.

Daniel looked up at her. 'I can't thank you enough, Netta,' he said softly, reaching out to grasp the old lady's hand. 'That is the best gift anyone could have given me.'

CHAPTER FORTY-SEVEN

'Why did he never tell me?' Sylvie Maxwell shook her head sadly as she and Lorimer sat together in the debriefing room.

'He'd trusted the wrong woman,' Caroline Flint said, before Lorimer had a chance to reply. 'Shararah, as she called herself, was a dangerous sort of female, adept at beguiling men. She had Carter in thrall as well as Burns and, as for her father ...' The deputy chief constable broke off with a sigh. 'He adored her, or at least he adored the person she wanted him to believe in. What a waste,' she murmured. 'Two decent men murdered because of her fanatical desires.'

'What will happen to the boy?' Sylvie asked.

'Social services have placed him in a special psychiatric unit,' Lorimer told her. 'They say he's hardly stopped weeping ever since he was rescued. Poor lad thinks he's going to perish in hell because he failed to carry out that woman's orders.'

'Will he recover?' Sylvie asked.

Lorimer gave a silent shrug. But it was not a throwaway gesture, more a sign of his own inability to grasp the wickedness in filling an innocent lad's mind with such beliefs. Abdul had been groomed for years, it turned out, first by his uncle, Kalil, then by Shararah. It might take some significant length of time to blot out these ingrained ideas of martyrdom and allow the youngster to return to a normal way of life.

'Poor Derek Carter,' Sylvie sighed.

'He'd been suspicious of Burns and the money that he'd seen going through a separate set of accounts. O'Neill has told us that much,' Flint said.

'If only he'd confided in me ...'

'He wasn't to know you were working as an undercover officer. And that shows the degree of care you took in integrating yourself to Bryson's,' Lorimer assured her.

'He did seem to be trying to make up for his earlier mistakes,' Sylvie agreed. 'I know the deaths of those two elderly folk weighed heavily on him.'

'That's why he began to do voluntary work at refugee centres,' Lorimer said. 'The two Syrians got to know him and introduced him to Shararah, or Helena Mearns, as we now know her.'

'She was suspicious of Carter,' Flint added. 'But her way of undermining him was to ingratiate herself into his life to the extent that they were sleeping together. She planted bugs around his house, probably paranoid in case he had given away anything that Burns was keeping hidden.'

Lorimer glanced at the undercover officer. Helena Mearns had a bewitching beauty that Carter must have found difficult to resist. And now the undercover officer was finding it hard to come to terms with the thought that her burgeoning relationship with Carter had probably been doomed from the start.

'She did the same with Vincent Burns,' Flint put in. 'She was perfectly candid in her statement about that.'

'She seduced them both,' Sylvie said quietly.

'But Carter might never have been killed if he hadn't confronted Burns with what he'd found in the accounts you discovered. That was his downfall, thinking he could persuade his boss to turn himself in,' Lorimer told her.

He thought over the recent interrogation when so many details had emerged. Helena Mearns had been brutal in her description of doing away with those men, as if their lives were expendable. All that mattered to her was revenge for her lover's death and the desire to create as much carnage as possible within the city where her father had been posted. He remembered the defiant expression marring that beautiful face as the full facts of the story emerged: how she had gained access to information after identifying the undercover officers then betraying them to the press once their usefulness had ceased. They had never seen her in person, of course, she had boasted to Lorimer, but she knew who they were, and she had gleaned enough to know about their intentions. Helena had heard her father mention Lorimer in several telephone calls and had her spies seek out the senior detective, curious to know about his movements, hungry for information. It was only at the point when David Mearns had begun to lock his laptop away each night that the woman had conceived the plan to break into Lorimer's home.

In a different life, Helena Mearns might have been an asset to the security services instead of one of their targets, her perception and keen mind wasted in the fanatical desires that had ensnared her. Lorimer stifled a sigh, his feelings of outrage against the terrorist tinged with pity.

'So,' Sylvie began, 'who actually murdered Derek?'

'The woman claims it was Burns and so does O'Neill. All the evidence points that way,' Lorimer told her. 'But perhaps we will never know whose hand actually thrust that knife into Carter. All we do know is that Burns was holding it when Daniel Kohi caught sight of him in the lane behind Bryson's and that he and the two Syrians were responsible for dumping the bodies on the Braes.'

'Are you saying it might have been O'Neill or the woman?'

Lorimer shook his head. 'O'Neill has given his wife as an alibi for that particular day, but I still wonder if it was Shararah who killed him.'

'Same knife that she used to kill her father,' Flint added. 'We might get her on both charges yet.'

'Burns had to be put out of the picture, too,' Lorimer said. 'Once he began to show signs of getting cold feet about being involved in an act of terrorism, his fate was sealed.'

Flint shook her head and sighed. 'That woman had absolutely no remorse for killing him. In fact, she seemed to revel in the memory of hitting him on the head and leaving him on the snowy ground.'

'And O'Neill?' Sylvie asked.

'He's looking at a very long time away at Her Majesty's pleasure.' Flint grinned. 'Something tells me that he will not be celebrating Christmas outside prison walls in his lifetime.'

'And you,' Lorimer turned to Sylvie. 'This skiing trip you mentioned, will you pretend to come to grief as planned?'

A small smile played around the undercover officer's mouth as she nodded. 'People in Bryson's will hardly notice my absence after two sensational deaths,' she murmured. 'Sylvie Maxwell will be gone for good, as far as anyone there is concerned.'

Caroline Flint looked at the younger woman appraisingly. 'A new year, new name and new job. But take your time, Detective Sergeant. Enjoy your Christmas.'

CHAPTER FORTY-EIGHT

Christmas Eve in the city was as pretty as Maggie Lorimer had imagined it would be, lights shaped like angels swaying in pastel shades, the smell of cooked food wafting from nearby stalls and a clear sky above them. Best of all, Bill was here too, holding her hand as if he would never let her go. Annett, Matt and the children were over at the German market enjoying their choice of gingerbread hearts and *glühwein* while they waited close by the glass-covered Nativity scene. Hymn sheets had been passed around by the volunteers, the fundraiser for Glasgow City Mission already looking like a success. A young chap wearing a red Santa hat was playing an electric piano, his music drawing the gathering crowds.

'All well?' A voice made them turn and to her delight Maggie saw Daniel coming to their side, an elderly lady clutching his arm.

'This is my friend, Netta Gordon,' he said, introducing the white-haired woman who was looking shyly up at Maggie and Bill.

'Detective Superintendent Lorimer and his wife, Maggie,' Daniel declared proudly.

'Oh, my,' Netta gasped. 'A big shot! Ye nivver telt me yer friend wis top brass, son. Nae wonder ye goat these bad men aff ma back!'

'Pleased to meet you, Mrs Gordon,' Maggie heard Bill say as he bent to take the old lady's hand.

'Jist Netta, son,' she assured him.

'In that case, Netta, please call me Bill,' Lorimer replied.

Then, as the piano played the introduction to the beginning of the carol service, they all gathered closer together and listened as a young boy's voice began the old familiar hymn.

'Once in royal David's city, stood a lowly cattle shed . . .'

And, as the words rang out across the clear and frosty air, Lorimer thought of another David, who would never see Christmas again.

He looked over the heads of the crowds, hundreds of people laughing and having fun, unaware of the dreadful threat that had hovered over this place in recent weeks. They were safe, thanks in part to David Mearns, but also to the man standing by his side, his lusty voice now joining in the second verse of the hymn.

Lorimer felt Maggie's grip on his arm and turned to see her smiling up at him.

'Merry Christmas, darling,' she whispered as the music swelled across the square.

'Merry Christmas,' he replied, putting an arm around her shoulder as he bent to kiss her.

ACKNOWLEDGEMENTS

First thanks must go to my daughter, Suzy, who gave me the idea of refugees and immigrants coming to Glasgow, a birthday gift back in 2019 that grew and grew as soon as she had planted it in my mind. The research for this book took me to Pachedu, a charity in Paisley that assists refugees, and I am indebted to Johannes Gonani and Gregor Smart whose information made all the difference to the character of Daniel. Refuweegee, the charity set up to welcome immigrants to the city, was one of the first places I visited, happily on their open day in Byres Road where the volunteers were willing to talk about their work. By a quirk of fate, the 2019 Edinburgh International Book Festival included three sessions specifically about refugees. Karine Polwart, Val McDermid, Ali Smith and Nayrouz Qarmout were unwitting allies on the day I attended, my notebook full of scrawls as the ideas came thick and fast. Thanks to all of you and especially to Karine, whose haunting 'Maybe There's A Road' lingered with me for a long time. Authors tend to resemble magpies, eager to pick up on the brightest scraps. Reading *Refugee Tales* was a salutary lesson on what dreadful things can happen to refugees, not just on their escape from terror but also once they are here in the UK. Stories of survival made me very humble indeed and grateful to live in a peaceful country like Scotland.

Former DCI Bob Frew of the MIT was kind enough to keep answering my questions about police business. Thanks also to my friend and ex-pupil, former DS Mairi Milne, for giving prompt replies to all my email questions.

I remain grateful to all the officers in Police Scotland from Chief Constable Iain Livingstone down to each uniformed cop who keeps us safe. If we knew even a little of the dangers that might beset us (and from which we are protected 24/7) it would be very hard to sleep at night.

As ever, my imaginary scalpel is guided by my good friend, consultant pathologist Dr Marjorie Turner, and so thank you, Marjorie, for always being so ready to help and check things for Rosie!

Bringing a book to its final destination on bookshelves is a collaborative process and so warm thanks are due to my excellent editor, Rosanna Forte, my dear friend and agent Dr Jenny Brown, Thalia, Steph, Millie, Brionee, Liz and the team at Sphere. It has been wonderful being part of this publishing family for so many years now.

Thanks as always to Donnie who enjoys the peace and quiet when I am upstairs typing and brings me mugs of tea. Thanks, too, for reading the first draft and making helpful notes. Writing this book brought back only good memories of the start of our married life in Zimbabwe, a country that was very different from the one that Daniel experienced.

Alex Gray

Help us make the next generation of readers

We – both author and publisher – hope you enjoyed this book.
We believe that you can become a reader at any time in your life,
but we'd love your help to give the next generation a head start.

Did you know that 9% of children don't have a book of their
own in their home, rising to 12% in disadvantaged families*?
We'd like to try to change that by asking you to consider the role
you could play in helping to build readers of the future.

We'd love you to think of sharing, borrowing, reading, buying or talking
about a book with a child in your life and spreading the love of reading.
We want to make sure the next generation continue to have access
to books, wherever they come from.

And if you would like to consider donating to charities that help
fund literacy projects, find out more at www.literacytrust.org.uk
and www.booktrust.org.uk.

Thank you.

hachette
CHILDREN'S GROUP

little, brown
BOOK GROUP

*As reported by the National Literacy Trust